Praise for

the neighbors are watching

"Debra Ginsberg grabs the reader from the first pages and without letting up delivers a well-written novel full of interesting characters. She proves without a doubt that you can never really know what goes on behind closed doors." —*CHARLESTON POST AND COURIER*

"Ginsberg shows the danger and violence that can enter quiet lives of desperation in the gripping *The Neighbors Are Watching*." —*SOUTH FLORIDA SUN-SENTINEL*

"As you might expect, nothing is as it seems. Everyone has deep, dark secrets." —*NORTH COUNTY TIMES*

"Teeming with secrets . . . dark, funny and sometimes creepy." —*KIRKUS REVIEWS*

"Fans of *Desperate Housewives* will enjoy Ginsberg's engaging . . . mix of domestic drama and psychological suspense . . . Everyone is a suspect here; even seemingly upstanding citizens have closets bulging with skeletons." —*BOOKLIST*

"An immensely interesting novel, *The Neighbors Are Watching* just may cause readers to look more closely out of their own windows." —*BOOKPAGE*

"The characters in Debra Ginsberg's new book have a lot of turmoil below the surface of their cul-de-sac existence." —*SAN DIEGO UNION-TRIBUNE*

"In this explosive, heat-driven melodrama, the mistakes of a misguided teenager establish once again that what goes around, comes around . . . edgy, bracing and inventive, an R-rated treatment of suburbia that combines many of the th me television soap opera, alb rledup.com

"Nobody's secre retive side of suburbia." C MAGAZINE

Also by Debra Ginsberg

The Grift
Blind Submission

Nonfiction

About My Sisters
Raising Blaze
Waiting: The True Confessions of a Waitress

the neighbors

a novel

debra ginsberg

are watching

Broadway Paperbacks

NEW YORK

BROADWAY

Copyright © 2010 by Debra Ginsberg
Reader's Group Guide copyright © 2011

Published in the United States by Broadway Paperbacks, an imprint of the
Crown Publishing Group, a division of Random House, Inc., New York.
www.crownpublishing.com

Broadway Paperbacks and its logo, a letter B bisected on the diagonal,
are trademarks of Random House, Inc.

Originally published in hardcover in slightly different form in the United States by
Crown Publishers, an imprint of the Crown Publishing Group,
a division of Random House, Inc., New York, in 2010.

Library of Congress Cataloging-in-Publication Data
Ginsberg, Debra, 1962–
The neighbors are watching : a novel / Debra Ginsberg. —1st ed.
p.   cm.
1. Pregnant teenagers—Fiction. 2. Birthfathers—Fiction. 3. Suburban life—
California—Fiction. 4. Neighbors—Fiction. 5. Domestic fiction.
6. Psychological fiction. I. Title.
PS3607.I4585N45   2010
813'.6—dc22   2010002095

ISBN 978-0-307-46387-6
eISBN 978-0-307-46388-3

Printed in the United States of America

Design by Lynne Amft

2 4 6 8 10 9 7 5 3 1

First Paperback Edition

For Blaze

the neighbors are watching

prologue

SanDiegoFireBlog.com

Monday, October 22, 2007

Del Mar: Mandatory evacuations listed

Posted @ 6:16 PM

Mandatory evacuations have been ordered for neighborhoods within Del Mar and Carmel Valley. Residents are encouraged to evacuate to Qualcomm Stadium. Residents should call 2-1-1 for all nonemergency calls related to this fire. Residents may also call the City of San Diego Community Access Phone for additional fire information.

91 comments:

Dell said . . .

I'm in Solana Beach. We have been under "advisory" evacuation all afternoon. Now that there's mandatory evacuation in Del Mar, it must mean things are getting worse. That fire is spreading fast.

October 22, 2007 6:41 PM

thinkhard said . . .

Does mandatory mean you must leave? Where do we go?

October 22, 2007 6:42 PM

Dell said . . .

Mandatory means you must leave, advisory is highly recommended. If you can get out, do it. There is no point staying if it is not necessary. That Witch Fire is destroying everything in its path. It's huge.

October 22, 2007 6:43 PM

Laura said . . .

Yes, also wondering what this means for the Fairgrounds evac site—are they going to have to move to Qualcomm too?

October 22, 2007 6:53 PM

Dell said . . .

the del mar fairgrounds are now filled to capacity. i just got the reverse 911 call telling me to be ready to evacuate from solana beach. i believe the evac sites are supposed to be "protected," but i have no idea.

October 22, 2007 6:55 PM

Laura said . . .

Thanks, Dell. I think that makes sense re the fairgrounds—it is surrounded by wetlands.

Good luck to you on the evac . . . be safe.

October 22, 2007 7:00 PM

Dell said . . .

Yes, everyone be safe and god bless!

October 22, 2007 7:10 PM

Tuesday, October 23, 2007

Del Mar evacuation lifted

Posted @ 6:31 PM

The City of Del Mar has lifted all evacuation notices within the city, according to the county's Office of Emergency Services. Residents who evacuated are allowed to return to their homes.

Friday, October 26, 2007

Teen missing in Carmel Valley following evacuation

Posted @ 3:42 PM

A 17 yr. old girl is missing from her Carmel Valley home following this week's evacuation. The family reported Diana Jones missing this morning. Jones failed to return home after the mandatory evacuation on Monday. It is not clear why the family waited until this morning to file the report. Anyone with information is asked to contact the Sheriff's Office at 619-555-4545.

0 comments

Saturday, October 27, 2007

Seeking Information

Posted @ 7:22 PM on Oct 27, 2007
    [Photo]
    Fire and law enforcement officials are seeking help in an investigation into Walter Wayne Simon, 45, who was arrested Oct. 24 for impersonating a firefighter at the Rice fire. Simon was detained in East County driving a Chevy pickup with personalized firefighter license plates. Authorities found fire equipment inside the truck.

Authorities want to know if anyone has seen Simon at the fires or at fire stations. Contact Sheriff's Department.

1 comment:

Anonymous said . . .

Dude looks scary; what a disgrace to the REAL firefighting heroes.

Monday, October 29, 2007

Missing teen was new mother

Posted @ 9:38 AM

Diana Jones, the Carmel Valley teen missing since last week's evacuation of the area, had just given birth, according to a source close to the family. The four-week-old infant is safe with the teen's parents. It is not clear whether Jones and the infant were alone in the house when Jones disappeared. The family is asking anyone with any information or who may have seen Jones to please contact the Sheriff's Office.

4 comments:

Anonymous said . . .

Nobody got hurt in this mess except illegals trying to sneak into this country and they deserve everything they get so this girl's probably fine if she's legal.

October 29, 2007 9:40 AM

Sarasmom said . . .

What a terrible thing to say! What if something happened to her? The parents are probably reading this right now. You should be ashamed of yourself.

October 29, 2007 9:45 AM

Anonymous said . . .

    [comment removed by Administrator]

Anonymous said . . .

    You'll never find her.

October 29, 2007 10:00 AM

july 2007

chapter 1

There was a breeze high up, rustling through the palm trees, but the air below was still and hot. There was no shelter from the bright sun that beat down on her outside the locked front door of the house that belonged, according to its mailbox, to "The Montanas." She could see that some of the other houses on the street had little overhangs on their front doors; a good thing if you didn't want to roast to death while you stood outside in the summer waiting for someone you'd never met to come home.

But this door had no shade, nowhere to rest, and nothing to hide behind. She was tired and overheated. The initial rush of adrenaline she'd felt when she first knocked on the door—not knowing who would answer or how that person would receive her—had worn off, leaving her feeling sweaty and tense. She hated just standing there, her broke-ass suitcase propped up next to her and her worn-out purse on top of it. No way she fit into *this* neighborhood—that much was obvious.

She waited. Five minutes. Maybe ten. Finally, she had to sit. She eased herself down on the burning concrete driveway, folding her thin skirt under her, more out of a need to protect her legs from the heat than a desire for modesty. Her feet were dusty—dirty, really. She needed a shower and some water to drink. Who would have thought it would be hotter here than in Las Vegas? Or maybe it just *felt* hotter because you never sat outside in Vegas in July and cooked yourself like a chicken. The baby kicked hard as if agreeing with her. "Sshh," she whispered, hand to her belly. "You don't have to tell *me*."

The longer she sat, the more nervous she became, and she couldn't understand why. It was a quiet street, peaceful. No dogs barking or lawn mowers running. Just that little whisper of a breeze up high and that tiny hum in the air you could hear when it was superhot, as if things were growing or stretching. Maybe it was *too* quiet here, like there was no human life to make any sound. Like everyone had disappeared or been vaporized and she was the only person left. But no, of course not. For sure there were people behind all those closed doors. It just seemed unnaturally still. Wrong.

She wished she could listen to her iPod—just drown out all this silence—but between packing and fighting with her mother this morning she'd forgotten to charge it. She hadn't even made it through the short flight over here before the battery died. She wondered if you could actually get addicted to an iPod because she was definitely having some kind of withdrawal from hers. Without her music, she barely even knew how to think in a straight line. She pulled herself in, tried to fix on a mental point in space, and came up with how much she hated her mother. That feeling was so strong, so big, it allowed her immediate focus.

How could a woman be so heartless as to kick her own child out of her house?

This was the key question and everything else—the hurt, the anger, the indignity, just built on top of it.

It wasn't bad enough that her mother had pushed her out—*given up on her*—or that her mother was sending her to the home of some asshole white guy who obviously had never even given half a shit that he had a daughter at all. But when her mother had resorted to used-up clichés to defend her actions, that was the worst. Because that made everything—her entire life—meaningless.

It's for your own good, her mother had said.

I'm at my wit's end with you.

You need to learn some responsibility and get your head on straight.

I'm so disappointed in you.

What was her mother most disappointed about, really? That she'd gotten pregnant? Or that she wouldn't have an abortion? She didn't know if she'd ever get an answer to that question, not that she was going to try. It was almost funny how wrong she had been about her mother. You'd think you'd know the person who'd birthed you, wouldn't you? Before telling her mother she was pregnant she'd imagined all kinds of scenarios: She started with the one where her mother cried at first but then took her in her arms and made it all right, the one where her mother shouted and stayed angry but dealt with it, and the one where her mother got disappointed and sad and wanted to discuss "options." But she never would have imagined or predicted her mother's quiet disgust upon hearing the news *or* her explosive rage when she refused to have an abortion.

"How can you even say that?" she'd asked her mother. "How could you even suggest it? What if you'd aborted me? Do you wish you had now?"

"Was I a stupid seventeen-year-old when I had you?" her mother countered. "No. I was a grown-up and fully aware of what I was doing. Not you. You have no idea what it takes to raise a child or what it means to give up yourself for another person."

"So you're sorry you had me? That's what you're saying?"

And it went on like that for a long, long time. Every day she found herself hating her mother a little bit more and that went to the littlest things: her clothes (matching synthetic old-lady-looking tops and pants, ugly white bras bought on sale), her habits (that one cigarette and that one glass of wine every single night), even the way her mouth moved around the food she ate. Every word out of her mouth became a jabbing needle, every freshly disappointed sigh a scrape against her skin. Then it got to where they just didn't talk at all, her mother's disgust getting harder and quieter until it was a thick rock wall between the two of them. It must have been during those silent angry days and nights when her mother hatched this plan to get rid of her and the baby together. Away, shame and disgrace. Though, *come on,* who even cared about this crap anymore? Who paid attention? Were they such celebrities that it made a damn bit of difference if one single mother raised another single mother?

She supposed she could have fought it—refused to go. But by the time school let out she was more than ready to get the hell out. That she should leave—and show up unannounced on this very doorstep—was the only thing she and her mother had agreed on in months.

She held the hate close, burrowed into it, felt its white-hot points stab the backs of her eyes. She would never forgive her mother, no. There was some comfort in that, even though she could feel the tickle of tears starting then oozing down her face. Damn, she hated that too—the crying. *Stop it.* Stop acting like such a girly-girl.

She looked up and out, desperate for distraction, and two things happened at once. The first was the sudden sound of a piano coming from somewhere down the street, behind one of those open windows. She had taken piano lessons herself a long time ago when her mother still cared about *enriching* her, and so she could tell that this performance had nothing to do with a desire to play and everything to do with the command to practice. She recognized the music too, Beethoven's "Moonlight Sonata," which could be the most beautiful piece to listen to, but in this case, sounded like a home invasion. The pianist was technically good, but there was no love in the music. He—it was probably a he, she decided—banged the keys as if he were trying to break the piano. And as the music went on, swirling through the hot summer air, anger and frustration swelled, gaining strength with every note. So much for silence.

At the moment her ears had picked up the sound of the piano, her eyes had caught sight of a woman crouching in front of a bush of purple flowers at the end of the street. It took her a second to realize that the woman was not hiding in the bushes but pruning them with a large pair of scissors so brightly colored that she could see their yellow glow all the way from where she sat. And then, after she'd stared long enough to put all the information together, she realized that the woman (who was wearing what looked like a pink velour tracksuit) was staring at *her*. Her reaction time was slowed by the heat, so it took the baby giving her another hard kick for her to break the stare and look away.

"Sshh," she said again. "Quit it." But by then she was talking to herself as much as the baby. She was so uncomfortable again—this was happening more and more frequently—and she had to pee. If somebody didn't come home soon, that was going to be a big problem because there was only so long she could hold it. She thought about knocking on doors, asking for a bathroom. Hey, welcome to the neighborhood, pregnant girl, come on in and piss in our pot. Sure. Maybe she'd follow the sound of that raging piano. Whoever was playing might be able to understand.

She stood up, looked down the street. Gardening woman stood up too. Wow, there was an ass on her—she could see that even from one, two . . . seven houses down. Gardening woman looked away. A garage door opened across the street. The noise, a creaking hoist, startled her. A woman in spike heels and a very short white skirt opened the trunk of the car inside the garage and leaned in. She could see the outline of the woman's red thong underwear through the too-sheer material of her skirt and the tight muscles in the back of her spray-tanned thighs. The woman straightened, slammed the trunk shut, walked around to the driver's side, and got in. If that bi-atch wasn't a hooker, she played one on TV. No question. The woman peeled out of her garage so fast she was down the street before the garage door finished closing. Exhaust and noise filled the air, and by the time it settled, the pianist had switched tunes. He was on Mozart's "Rondo alla Turca" now, murdering it deader than he had the Beethoven.

Now there was something else in the air too—the faintest whiff of cigarette smoke. She held her breath. Ever since the baby, cigarette smoke made her sick to her stomach, which could be a bit of a problem in Las Vegas, but she hadn't expected to find it here, in San Diego, where apparently you weren't allowed to smoke anywhere. Good thing weed didn't have the same effect. She knew that was weird—weed smoke was still smoke—but it was true. She could be standing in the middle of a weed bonfire and it wouldn't bother her in the slightest. Quite the opposite. In fact, she could really use a nice weed bonfire right about now or even just a goddamned hit. She wondered if the Montanas were weed smokers and if there was a stash somewhere she might raid. She'd have to look around when—or if—she finally got inside. They'd have *something,* even if it wasn't weed. Everybody had something.

The wafting cigarette smoke hit her nostrils again and her stomach gave a slight lurch. She turned her head, looking for the source, and found it halfway down the street. A skinny woman with short black hair stood at the edge of her driveway, leaning against her mailbox, puffing on a smoke like her life depended on it. Maybe she could feel the weight of a stare at her back because she turned, registered, and smiled, waving the cigarette-holding hand as a greeting. As a response, she waved her own hands in front of her face as if to get rid of the smoke, which was rude, but whatever, because it was also rude to stand and smoke on people. Why didn't the woman go do that in her own house where she couldn't pollute other people's air?

She hated people who smoked.

No, she didn't hate people who smoked. She hated her mother. Who smoked one goddamned cigarette—just one—every goddamned day.

Her bladder was totally full now and threatening to burst. She was sweating again and feeling anxious—heart racing. She was seized by something close to panic—maybe it *was* panic—feeling hemmed in suddenly by this street with its garage doors and crazy piano and whores and weird women. The air felt sharp and hot in her nose. Her head pounded. The baby kicked in a flurry like it was trying to get out. Or get away.

I don't want to be here.

Suddenly, it all felt like a huge mistake. If she could . . . If she could she would call her mother this very minute. *Come and get me.* But that bridge had been burned. And she'd been the one who'd torched it. It was then—visions of flaming bridges in her head and her fingers curling around the cell phone in her pocket—that the car drove onto the street and turned into the driveway where she was standing.

So. They were home.

There were a few seconds where nobody did anything. The woman—passenger—and the man—driver—didn't get out of the car, just turned the car off and sat there. They stared at her through the windshield, this stranger in their driveway, and she stared back at them. The cooling engine ticked. Just as it was all starting to feel really, really weird, they both got out simultaneously, slamming their doors behind them.

She could see him now, the white guy she'd never met who was about to get the biggest surprise of his life. For some reason—maybe it was the guilty look in his eyes and the turned-down corner of his mouth—it seemed like he might already know. Like maybe he'd been waiting for this moment.

Not so with the blond, ponytailed tight-ass who had to be his wife. *She* was looking like she wondered what kind of hurricane blew this trash onto her doorstep and what was it going to take to get rid of it. She saw the wife look from her, to her suitcase, to her belly, and to her husband, her blue eyes darting like they had no place to settle, and she had just one thought. *Bitch.* The baby kicked and her bladder screamed with the urge to pee. Damn.

He came up to her, close, and looked right down into her eyes. He was taller than she'd thought he would be. And better looking.

"Hi," he said. "Who are you? Can I help you with something?"

"Are you Joe Montana?" she asked.

"Yes, I am."

And then there was a second where it all threatened to fall apart, where she could taste the tears and fear at the back of her throat, and she had to bite her lip and press her fingernails into her palms just to keep from breaking down and crying. But she pulled it in and got it straight. She cleared her throat once and said, "I'm Diana Jones. I'm your daughter."

chapter 2

Allison lay corpse-still, her back to her husband, unblinking eyes staring at the broken squares of moonlight on the carpet. The window was wide open, but the bedroom felt hot and stifling. The lemon-tinged scent of eucalyptus leaves was heavy in the air, coating her sinuses. Thoughts ran thick and furious inside her head, pulsing through her unmoving body, throbbing between her legs. Two impulses fought for control, both so strong they made her throat constrict. She wanted to kill him—just reach over and choke him until his breath was gone—and she wanted to climb on top of him and screw him senseless. She understood the murderous urge. After what he'd done, who could blame her? But the craving for sex surprised and shamed her. Her cheeks flushed with heat in the dark and she struggled to control her breathing. She didn't want him to feel any movement coming from her side of the bed. She could tell by the light sound of his breathing that he was still awake. Her desire for physical contact was so powerful she knew that if he touched her—just one touch—she'd give in immediately.

He'd done it before. Those nights when they'd had some minor argument and had gone to bed in silence, he'd wait ten, maybe fifteen, minutes and then shift so slightly toward her, his hand moving over to caress the curve of her hip. His fingers would rest there, light, until he felt the tremor of consent under her skin and then he'd roll over, his body falling heavy into hers. It was an agreement they had: He offered and she accepted.

Sometimes, after they'd made love, Allison was sure that their little spats were a form of foreplay. But before, in those few minutes when the space between their bodies was cold and impenetrable, she always felt a sharp bite of fear that he wouldn't reach out—that they'd stay like that forever.

Of course, this time was different. Even he, as thick-skinned as he often was, wouldn't make such a move now, not under these circumstances. The stupid little things they'd found to argue about before had now been made permanently irrelevant. Their entire marriage had twisted into a question mark and nothing would ever be the same or all right again. She thought of that big-bellied girl downstairs and felt acid burning her throat. She didn't know what was worse—the betrayal, the lies, or the secrets. Just the same, she couldn't take the chance that he'd move over, that he'd try to fix it somehow with his body. She'd lie here like this until dawn if she had to.

She couldn't see the clock but knew it was about three in the morning—the blackest, bleakest part of night. On still summer nights like this, when most of the neighbors turned off their air conditioners and opened their windows, you could hear anything you wanted and much of what you didn't—cats yowling, the clink of late-night party wineglasses, and sometimes the menacing rustle of coyotes coming down from the dry hills surrounding the neighborhood. The relentless press of housing development through every empty space over the last ten years had brought those wild dogs ever nearer; a reminder, along with the influx of black crows, of how far civilization was encroaching on the wild.

Now, Allison heard the slow crunch of gravel followed by the sound of a car door opening. No doubt it was coming from one of the many rotating vehicles in Jessalyn's driveway. There'd been a steady stream of late-night visitors to that house since Jessalyn had moved in six months ago, which revealed something about the nature of the callers—all men as far as Allison had been able to tell. Very few of them stayed longer than an hour or two, which revealed something else. The car started promptly, and Allison heard it pulling away.

Allison had spoken to Jessalyn maybe three or four times at most when they were both picking up their mail or pulling into their driveways at the same time. Somehow, even though Allison had tried to keep those encounters as short as possible (something about Jessalyn just repelled Allison), she had still managed to learn that Jessalyn had been on a reality contest show and that she'd lost ("Those shows are all fixed," Jessalyn had told her at the time). She also knew that Jessalyn was "starting over," although she couldn't have been older than twenty-five, was "back in school to get my degree," although Allison had no idea in what, and that she worked in a Del Mar day spa, although she hadn't explained what she did there. Jessalyn's eyes were overly made-up and always glassy—maybe that was what Allison didn't like about her—probably from drugs, which she probably got from Kevin Werner.

Allison could actually hear him now, several houses down, listening to some awful death metal band, the sharp tinny shrieks reaching her ears on wafts of air. She could see him in her mind's eye, pockmarked, surly, and black-clad. The kid was a walking billboard for disaffected youth and just one more reason to hate teenagers. Allison didn't know how anyone managed to teach at the high school level. Her own third graders were bad enough—they already had entitled attitudes and challenged anyone who had the temerity to knock their all-important *self-esteem*. But . . . no, you couldn't blame the kids yet. At that age, it was still the parents. The parents were responsible for all of it. She couldn't understand how Dick and Dorothy Werner maintained their holier-than-thou attitude considering they'd raised that kid, Kevin. Just naming a kid Kevin was asking for trouble. Allison knew from experience that the Kevins in her class were always going to be troublemakers.

Of course, Allison thought, she and Joe had just made it easier for dear Dot to maintain that superior stance forever. Dorothy had been there, kneeling in her star jasmine with her stupid yellow clippers in hand and watching when the girl had shown up. God only knew the conclusions Dorothy had drawn behind that ugly purple visor she always wore. Allison figured Dorothy was already whipping up a cake from a mix that she'd bring over for "you and Joe," but really to find out why there was a pregnant teenager living in their house, information which she could then take back to Dick, who, as the arbiter of decency and American-ness on the block, would probably blow some sort of fuse inside his head. It was already killing him that there were lesbians living on the street and that he was separated from them by only two walls and a eucalyptus tree. Not that she'd heard this directly from Dick. But Dorothy, who had turned passive-aggressiveness into a high art, had dropped enough clues as to his point of view. "Dick's so funny," she'd said once. "He couldn't find our power saw last night so he was going to go next door and ask one of the girls (Dorothy never referred to Sam and Gloria by name—they were always "the girls") if he could borrow theirs. How silly is that? I mean, just because they, you know . . . well, anyway, it doesn't mean they have *tools.* Men are so . . . Right?" And what was really the funniest thing, if you thought about it, was that Dorothy only shared this information with Allison because Dorothy thought of her as a like-minded *friend.*

But Dick and Dorothy weren't Allison's problem. No, her problem was downstairs, nestled under the bright yellow afghan her grandmother had knitted for her before she'd passed away, in the hope that there'd soon be a great-grandchild to celebrate. Allison was glad the woman hadn't lived to see who was sleeping under it now.

It wasn't the girl's fault. Of course it wasn't. Allison knew this intellectually even though there was nothing—*nothing*—appealing about Diana. From the sneering expression on her young face, to her swollen belly, which was proudly exposed and, yes, pierced, Diana was all hostility and bad attitude. The tattooed ankles rounded out the picture nicely.

Diana had a snake on one and an apple on the other and Allison didn't appreciate the biblical references *at all*. And, although the girl's mother was surely to blame for the poor parenting skills that had led to a pregnant, tattooed teenage daughter, Allison couldn't lay fault for her sleepless night there either. No, it was Joe—all Joe. Allison clenched her thighs under the blanket creating a tiny tremor in the fabric. She was desperate for a drink, even though she'd hit the wine pretty hard before going to bed. She just wanted oblivion.

The worst part was that Allison didn't even know how she was supposed to feel. She and Joe had been married *eight years* and in all that time, not even a hint that he had a child somewhere. How could it have been so hidden—so out of her reach? How was it possible that through all the casual intimacies of their life together—shared meals and movies, paying bills, football on Sundays, washing dishes, brushing their teeth, their discussions about their future—there was no whisper, no accidentally dropped words about this girl? It would almost be easier to have woken up and found that *everything* about her life was a lie—that she was part of some grand government experiment, that her memory had been erased, that she was living with space aliens—instead of just this one awful truth. It wouldn't get any better either. Because the girl was here and she was having a baby and Allison had absolutely no idea what role she was meant to play in this sordid little drama. Did Joe really expect her to be a grandma now? The very concept made her entire body stiff with anger. And beneath that anger was a kind of hurt she'd never felt before.

But no, that wasn't true. Of course it wasn't. She *had* felt this way before and then . . . then it had felt so bad Allison couldn't imagine how it was even happening, how she was able to stand it.

Almost over. Another minute. One more minute.

How many minutes in forever? Because that's how long it took.

No, don't. Don't squeeze my hand like that.

There was nothing to hold on to, outside or in, while she was carved and torn.

Just about done now. That's it.

The doctor was wearing a belly pack and the nurse kept her hands far from reach. The noise—that horrible mechanical groan—raging in her ears. Allison wanted to scream, but she had no breath.

Okay. All done now.

It was a mistake, a terrible mistake that couldn't be undone. Joe had been kind and sweet and sorry and they'd talked about it then, talked about how it was the best thing—the *right* thing to do—and that of course it was Allison's choice ultimately. Her choice, of course. But it wasn't, not really. And then, the second it was over, regret, immediate and piercing, opened a wound inside Allison that she didn't know if she could ever close. The only thing she'd felt sure of then was that it would be impossible to experience that kind of pain again. But she'd been wrong about that too. She'd started to tell him this earlier today, but just bringing it up stung like fresh salt in that unclosed wound. Besides, he didn't understand. She didn't know if he ever would.

Joe's breath was coming slow and deep now. His shoulder muscles twitched. He was falling asleep finally. Allison felt her anger spike. He had no right to enjoy the release of unconsciousness while she lay next to him awake and destroyed. She was going to get up, she decided, slide out of bed, go downstairs to the kitchen, and pour herself a big glass of the vodka that had been residing in their freezer for the past three years. She was going to drink it all and too bad if she threw up or had a hangover. She wanted to be drunk into the next day and beyond. As far as she could see, there was no other way to handle this nightmare. At least school was out for the summer. There would have been no way she could have gone to work at this point—drunk *or* sober.

Allison slid one leg to the edge of the bed as if testing the temperature of a bath. She shifted by inches, preparing to roll off and escape, but before she could lift the sheet she felt the warm pressure of Joe's hand on her arm. They both lay suspended for a few seconds—Allison rigid with the bottleneck of her competing emotions and Joe waiting to see what she'd do—and then he leaned in close enough for her to feel the naked skin of his chest against her back.

"Allie?" he said, his voice amplified by the silence of their bedroom. There was so much in it, Allison thought: apology, pleading, an edge of impatience, and warning. She knew this husband of hers so well that she could hear all of these nuances in the way he'd said her name. How then had she missed something so important? He moved his hand to her shoulder and gently rolled her onto her back. Allison didn't resist. He stroked her face and touched his lips to her neck. Allison's legs started shaking as he parted them with his hand, smoothing the skin of her thighs. She didn't help him as he pushed her underwear down below her knees and said nothing as he climbed on top of her. But as he shifted her hips to meet his in exactly the right place, Allison started to cry.

This is the last time. The thought was loud inside her head.

Allison didn't have to wait too long before Joe's heavy breathing turned into satisfied snoring. Her eyes, still sprung open as if by cartoon matchsticks, had stopped leaking tears. No need to worry about waking him now. She pulled her underwear up and slid out of bed. She took a last look at him; his arms sprawled in postcoital surrender as if he'd been shot down where he lay.

In a hurry and unwilling to root around in the dark for a T-shirt or pajama bottoms, Allison grabbed a bathrobe off a hook on the back of their bedroom door. She pulled it tight across her naked breasts and cinched the belt hard.

Never mentioned he had a child. Not once. Not even when she was carrying one herself.

Allison padded barefoot down the beige-carpeted stairs in the dark, making a beeline for the kitchen and the cold oblivion that waited for her in the freezer. She had to stop thinking, had to turn off her brain, if only for a few hours. She visualized the bottle of Absolut Citron and her hand excavating it from behind the bags of frozen vegetables. She didn't turn on the kitchen light. No need. A tumbler sat out on the faux granite counter-top. Perfect. Allison yanked open the freezer handle, bathing herself in a frosty mist of light. She reached and rustled inside, searching. And stopped. There was a noise so faint it took a second for her to realize she'd heard it. Sounded like a sigh. Allison felt cold tension gather between her shoulder blades.

"I couldn't sleep."

Allison jumped back, her throat closing and choking off a scream as she turned her head in the direction of the voice. "Jesus!" Her hands were already shaking. "Jesus, you—you—"

Diana was sitting on a rattan chair in the breakfast nook, barely visible between the pale light of the still-open freezer and the moon coming through the window behind her. Allison could make out the round outline of the white T-shirt stretched impossibly taut over Diana's pregnant belly and the dark tendrils of her curly hair falling down her shoulders.

"I didn't mean to scare you," Diana said. "I thought you saw me when you came in."

"I—" Allison had to catch her breath. She closed the freezer door and flicked on the kitchen light, causing them both to cringe in the sudden glare. "Of course you scared me," Allison said finally. "Why would I have seen you sitting here in the dark?"

Diana drew up her shoulders, her hands moving to her belly as if to protect it, but Allison could see that her eyes sparked with anger. Sulky teenage anger. Because that's what she was—a sulky, pissed-off, pregnant teenager. Allison wanted that drink more than ever.

"I couldn't sleep," Diana said again—more defiant now. "Too much *noise*."

Allison took the tumbler, still clutched so tightly in her hand she was surprised it hadn't shattered, filled it with water straight from the tap, and drank as much of it as she could before the chemical chlorine taste made her gag. Normally, Allison would never even consider drinking San Diego tap water, which was so hard it was almost crunchy, but she didn't care—the watercooler was beyond Diana on the other side of the table and Allison just didn't want to have to maneuver around the girl to get to it.

"It's summer," Allison said. "Everyone has their windows open and the houses are close together. Sometimes it gets a little noisy at night."

"Not that kind of noise," Diana said. "You know where I'm sleeping? It's right below your bedroom." Diana waited a beat for it to sink in. "I can hear everything, you know?" Diana made a sound, some kind of guttural grunt, and Allison felt her breath catch in her throat. "You two were—"

"Stop it!" Allison gripped the side of the sink. Shame spread through her in a thick red flush, heating her thighs, her neck, her face. She was hot now and felt sick—filthy. Whatever happened next—tomorrow, next month, next year—wouldn't matter at all because Allison knew her relationship with this girl would forever be defined by this horrible, horrible moment. God, how she hated Joe. And how she hated this daughter of his.

"I didn't want to come here, you know," Diana said. "This wasn't my idea."

Allison's face was burning and there was a faint ringing in her ears. She couldn't look at Diana. "It's been a long day for *everyone*," Allison said and worked mightily to unclench her jaw. "You should go back to bed. I'm sure you'll be able to sleep now."

Diana got up and walked toward Allison, who turned her head, staring into the eye of the sink's drain. "Hey," Diana said softly, the slightest note of pleading in her voice, but Allison was too angry and embarrassed to answer, and after a second, Diana gave up and walked past her. Allison could smell jasmine in the current of air Diana left in her wake. Allison looked up then to make sure the girl was actually headed to her room. It was funny—almost cruel—how you couldn't tell from behind that she was pregnant at all. The slim tight skin on her café-latte-colored hips and thighs betrayed nothing. Nor did her skinny behind, and Allison got a good long look at *that* because aside from the too-small T-shirt, all Diana was wearing was a little black thong.

Allison waited until she heard the click of the guest bedroom door closing before she reached into the freezer again and turned off the kitchen light.

She took the first drink straight from the bottle.

august 2007

chapter 3

Joe stared at his reflection in the bedroom mirror as he dressed for work, looping his black and yellow–striped tie around itself to form a knot. His hands fiddling with the fabric, Joe observed his face—the Roman nose, rounded chin, wide-set eyes—as if for the first time. The funny thing, he thought, was not that Diana looked like him but that it had taken him weeks to notice the resemblance.

He'd seen it this morning and now it was impossible to *un*-see, like one of those black-and-white pattern-recognition pictures where you see either the vase or two profiles but never both simultaneously. It was during breakfast and the two of them were lifting bagels to their mouths in almost perfect synchronicity. His eyes had just happened to land on Diana instead of being glued to the sports section, which was a safer bet these days than looking at either of the women in his house. In that moment, as he and she were both biting into their chive-cream-cheese-laden "everything" bagels, he saw the curve of her eyebrows, the shape and color of her eyes, and felt as if he were looking at a younger, feminized version of himself. The recognition stunned him, stopping him mid-chew.

"What?" Diana asked, and he realized he was staring. Allison took a long sip from her orange juice (which Joe suspected was spiked with vodka) and banged her glass down on the table loud enough to let him know that she'd seen that look he'd given his daughter—not that she had or ever would use the word *daughter*—and wasn't pleased with it.

"How's your bagel?" he asked Diana, a lame cover but all he could come up with.

Diana rolled her eyes and sighed. "Fine."

"You saw I bought orange juice?" He didn't know why he was continuing the conversation and hated that he felt compelled to.

"Can't drink orange juice. Heartburn."

"And does coffee help your heartburn?" Allison said, pointing to Diana's mug.

"It's *decaf*, okay?"

Then it was the two of them staring daggers at each other until Allison got up from the table with her glass and wandered out to the backyard in the unwashed bathrobe she'd taken to wearing every day, all day. Joe watched Diana's eyes follow her out and saw his own reflection a second time.

Now, tying his tie for the *third* time, Joe's mind wandered back to the day Diana had shown up on his doorstep holding a shabby suitcase and a letter from her mother. He certainly hadn't seen any part of himself in her then, and it wasn't just the color of her skin, even though with his Mediterranean coloring he wasn't much lighter than she was. It was that she was so obviously young and so very pregnant, not at all like someone he'd even know, let alone someone who was related to him. And yet, in that moment, when he turned the wheel, pulled into the driveway, and saw her standing there, he knew exactly who she was.

He and Allison were just coming back from the movies. They'd gone to see *Ratatouille* in an actual theater, rather than waiting for it to come out on DVD like they usually did. He couldn't remember now why they'd chosen that movie, a cartoon of all things, to break from their usual pattern. They'd enjoyed it, though, he remembered that. Allison was smiling. "Do you think it would be possible to make the ratatouille in the movie?" she asked him. "There had to have been a real-life model for it. I want to try it—it looked so delicious." Joe was always happy to sample Allison's culinary experiments. Once in a while, she pulled out something really spectacular, like that heirloom tomato tart with the cornmeal crust, and even her least exotic attempts were pretty good. Joe cooked most of the time—he had always fancied himself a bit of a closet chef—but he loved it when she took over the kitchen. That day in the car, he'd encouraged her to go for the ratatouille, even suggested they shop for the ingredients later in the day, after, he said, winking, "we take a little nap." Allison laughed and put her hand on his knee. There was no need for such a silly euphemism but he used it, like he had before, because Allison thought it was sweet and it always amused her. They laughed, both of them pleased and turned on, the air between them heating up nicely. And then he turned the corner and pulled into the driveway. He couldn't tell exactly when Allison removed her hand from his thigh and the smile from her face, but they were both gone by the time he turned off the engine. There was that one terrible moment of silence between the two of them—the kind that comes between the step outward and the fall off the cliff—and then they were three.

Allison couldn't have known who Diana was at that moment, but she must have sensed it same as he did. Still, he didn't see himself in her then, not even when he looked into her eyes and heard her say she was his daughter. It was the shock, Joe decided. Her showing up like that so suddenly and creating that quiet explosion between him and Allison had prevented him from seeing the resemblance then. Not that he'd tried to deny her. Not then, despite the look of naked dismay on Allison's face, and not now.

Joe had always known that he was Diana's father. He'd made sure of it when she was born, requesting a paternity test and paying for it when it came back positive that he was the father. Yvonne had been extremely pissed off that he'd asked for the test in the first place, but she'd taken it willingly. She was only in her twenties then, but Yvonne already had quite a past with men, and even though they'd been almost attached at the hip for the duration of their brief relationship, you never knew. Certainly no need for a paternity test now, was there? All you had to do was look at the two of them together—and Joe was sure every one of his nosy neighbors had—and you could see that they were father and daughter.

The damn tie still didn't look right and Joe was losing his patience. The restaurant was close, but he was going to be late if he didn't get out the door in the next five minutes. The traffic through Del Mar was an absolute bitch these days, no matter what time of day you were traveling. Allison always helped him with his tie when he got frustrated like this. She knew how to tweak it so that the knot looked sharp. He debated going into the den where she was deep into CNN and whatever drink she was nursing and asking her to help him fix it, but it took only a second to remember that adjusting his tie before he went to work was among the little domestic things Allison didn't do anymore, along with any kind of cooking, cleaning, or sex.

Joe gave up on the tie, folded it, and put it in his jacket pocket. As embarrassing as it would be, he would have to get one of the waitresses to help him with it when he got in since his own wife wouldn't. But he was going to have to do something about Allison, Joe thought, because despite her relative calm, she was spiraling down and she was taking him with her. Exactly what to do, however, was a question whose answer eluded him. And there were more pressing issues to deal with, all of which had to do with Diana: How long was she going to stay, where was she going to have the baby, and what was she going to do with it once it was born? He wished that Allison could bury her anger long enough to help him—and help Diana for that matter—work it out. Allison had married him, hadn't she? Those vows—richer, poorer, et cetera—were supposed to mean something.

It wasn't that he was totally insensitive. Obviously Diana's sudden appearance was more of a shock for Allison than for him. But the reason he'd never told Allison that he'd fathered a child years before he'd even met her wasn't because he wanted to keep it a secret; it was because he had managed to convince *himself* that Diana, Yvonne, and that whole chapter of his life were just done with and gone. And this wasn't purely magical thinking on his part.

He and Yvonne had already broken up by the time she informed him she was pregnant, and he was astounded that she planned to keep the baby even after he told her he wanted nothing to do with it. She threatened and pleaded and then he moved—got out of Los Angeles and came down here to San Diego—and didn't hear anything from her until after the baby was born when some cut-rate lawyer she'd hired sent him a letter demanding child support. After the whole drama with the paternity test, Joe persuaded Yvonne to get rid of the lawyer and promised to send her some money when he could. But he hadn't, nor had he responded to her sporadic letters and the photos of a kid he felt less connection with than his toothbrush. Finally, when Diana must have been about four or five, there was no more communication at all.

He hadn't heard one word from Yvonne for ten years—not a letter, a phone call, or any kind of request for child support. For a couple of years, he'd waited for the other shoe to drop, but there was only silence. He hadn't even known that Yvonne had moved to Las Vegas until Diana told him. By the time he and Allison married, Joe had come to believe that Yvonne had taken responsibility for her own actions—because it was unequivocally *her* decision to get pregnant and have a baby—and was leaving him out of it as he'd asked her to from the minute the second pink line appeared on the pregnancy test.

Joe told Allison all of this the day Diana arrived. After what was surely one of the most awkward family reunions of all time—forget about ratatouille or a "nap," Joe just ordered a pizza for dinner—with the three of them sitting at the dining room table exchanging basic information like when Diana was due and what grade she was in at school, Diana got settled in the guest bedroom, and he and Allison went upstairs to talk.

"I never hid anything from you, Allie," he said. "It was so long over by the time I even met you. I wasn't ever part of her life. Never."

"A child is a big deal, Joe. Not something you omit to tell your wife."

"You have to believe me," he said, "if I thought it would have made any difference . . . and it hasn't made a difference in how I feel about you."

"Of course it makes a difference! It's made all the difference in the world how you feel. If I'd known about her . . . Joe, when I was pregnant . . ." She couldn't finish the sentence and looked away from him. His stomach did a flip then because he didn't want to talk about the abortion again, and he knew that was where Allison was going. He'd never suffered a moment of guilt over the act itself, knowing in his heart that it was the right thing to do, but he knew Allison had. He felt bad about that and sorry that it had caused her pain. But at the same time, he didn't feel responsible for her pain. It had been a joint decision—he was clear on that—and he would have made the same one now even if Allison wouldn't. He understood why she'd bring it up, but he wasn't sure it was fair.

"You know that those two things have nothing to do with each other," he told her quietly.

"That's the problem, Joe, I don't. You should have told me. It would have made a difference."

"Allison, we'd just met. We didn't know . . . We weren't ready."

"We could have been ready," Allison said miserably. "We're married, aren't we?"

"Yes, now," he said. "But that isn't what this is about, is it? I can't undo the past, Allison. This . . . What's happening now is as much a surprise to me as it is to you. I know you're upset and you have a right to be. But let's deal with it together."

"I have to deal with it, don't I?" she said. "It's not like I have a choice."

He'd felt hopeful then, despite the bitterness in her tone. As betrayed as she felt, it still seemed like she was willing to try to work with him. That night, after they'd both been lying there awake for hours absorbing the shock, she'd let him make love to her. His hope turned to relief, Joe remembered, and he was so grateful to her. He took it to mean she could get past it, that she was going to stand by him. It was like having make-up sex before the fight had a chance to get really ugly. But now Joe was starting to think of it as good-bye sex because that was the last time Allison had let him come near her.

They'd talked about Diana again—no way to avoid it, really—but Allison quickly began sealing herself off behind a wall of hurt and indignation. And liquor. She'd gone from a glass of wine at night to full bottles within what seemed like days. Maybe he hadn't noticed her slide because Allison never really seemed to get drunk—just quiet and detached. He didn't want to fight with her, although the silent treatment was probably just as bad, but he was starting to feel sick of feeling sorry. And then too he missed the easiness of their affection, conversation, and companionship. He missed *her*.

Joe gave his dark hair (graying but still thick, thank you very much) a pat in the mirror and grabbed his keys off the dresser. Yvonne's letter was still sitting there—a neatly folded bombshell—and Joe wondered why he hadn't destroyed it or put it away. It wasn't as if he needed to read it again, he'd already committed its brief contents to memory.

> *Dear Joe,*
>
> *You wouldn't have been my choice, then or now. But it's your turn. Until now you've never given either one of us a thing. But Diana has her own mind and will. I have to believe that you'll do the right thing by her. It's pretty clear she's already made some bad choices, but my mother's heart knows her sweetness. She's a good person, Joe. And it's your blood running through her.*
>
> *Yvonne*

She'd always had that way with words, Joe thought, always had that poet's eye. He'd envied that about her. But she was just as headstrong as her daughter had turned out to be. Yvonne wanted a baby and Yvonne got a baby. Joe had just happened to be at the right place at the right time and she'd manipulated him and used him to get what she wanted. He'd had *no* choice in it at all. It made him angry still. A woman's right to choose—it was all you ever heard about. What about a man's right to determine what happened to the rest of his life? That line about doing the right thing killed him. Only a devil would refuse shelter to a pregnant seventeen-year-old who had the papers to prove she was your daughter. And so once again, Joe had found his own choice taken from him. There had to be a way to make Allison understand that.

"Allison?" Joe called out. "I'm leaving." He jogged down the stairs and peered into the kitchen. The back door was open letting hot August dust in through a small tear in the screen. One more thing that needed fixing. The breakfast dishes were still in the sink and the long unwatered cilantro plant on the windowsill shriveled in the late afternoon light. He turned around to see that the guest bedroom door—Diana's room now—was open too. Joe could see clothes scattered on the floor but no Diana. The entire house looked both abandoned and neglected, and Joe felt a surge of angry frustration.

"Allison!"

She was staring at the television in the den, wearing that same dirty bathrobe, bare feet curled under her on the couch, a coffee mug in her hand. She didn't bother to look up when he entered.

"I'm going to work."

"Okay."

"Are you going to get dressed, Allison?"

"What for?"

She looked as neglected as the rest of the house, Joe thought. Her long blond hair was dull and limp and old makeup smudged the rings under her eyes. Her fingernail polish was chipped and her skin had the sunken appearance of dehydration. Joe couldn't recall her ever looking this miserable and he felt a pang of sympathy. Allison had always cared—sometimes too much—about the way she looked, even if she was spending a day at home.

It was important, she always said, because she was a teacher and therefore a role model of sorts. Kids noticed everything—a stray hair, a speck of food on clothing, too-strong perfume—and it affected the way they felt about you. Better to always be at your best. Not now, he thought. Not by a long shot.

"I won't be home late," he said.

"Okay."

"Where's Diana?"

Only then did Allison shift her eyes toward him, fixing him with a look of watery venom. "I don't *know*, Joe. I'm not her *mother*."

Joe's sympathy for her evaporated immediately and it took more will than he thought he possessed not to call her a bitch and tell her to get herself together. "I'll see you later," he said and stomped into the garage letting the door slam behind him. Not that she'd hear it. He doubted she could hear anything except the hum of her own brain. Once again, the need to *do* something about his wife nagged at Joe. Summer was almost over and Allison needed to straighten up and get back to work because he'd be fucked if she thought she was going to parlay this domestic business into time off. He could feel his anger winding up. She'd been indulging herself for too long—and he'd been letting her. It had to stop and he'd have to figure out a way to get through to her.

He was already sweating when he got into his Lexus and punched the garage-door opener fastened on the visor. Still angry, he punched the gas as he reversed out of his driveway. Across the narrow street, another car was also backing out of its garage, and although he hit the brakes as soon as he realized what was going to happen, Joe didn't have enough time to stop before their bumpers struck and the hard plastic of taillights shattered onto the asphalt.

"God*DAMN* it!" Joe smacked the steering wheel hard with the heel of his hand. It was his fault, no question, and now he had to resign himself to being totally late to work. It wasn't as if anyone was keeping score—Joe was general manager—but it threw off his rhythm for the whole night when he came in late and he could never seem to get it back. Joe drove forward a few feet so that he was back in his driveway and got out of his car. He didn't even know who he'd crashed into.

The sexy blond who'd moved in a few months ago but whose name he didn't know had gotten out of her car and was inspecting the damage to the back of her Honda Civic.

"I'm so sorry," Joe said, using his most solicitous please-allow-me-to-offer-you-a-free-dessert tone. "I tried to stop, but . . ."

"It's okay," she said. "It doesn't look that bad."

Joe sighed, taking in the sight of her crushed taillight and bruised bumper. He tried to calculate the odds that she'd just agree to settle it without dragging in the insurance companies and whether he could afford the out-of-pocket expense to fix it. "No," he said, "not too bad, I guess." He extended his hand. "I'm Joe," he said. "Joe Montana."

She smiled at him and shook his hand. "Like the football player?" she said.

"I wish." Relaxing slightly, Joe took her in. Too much makeup and a tan that looked unnaturally deep, but a very pretty face, fantastic breasts peeking out of her sheer top, and great legs totally exposed by her tiny miniskirt.

"Your wife's Allison, right? I'm still getting to know everyone on the street. Guess I missed the last block party. I'm Jessalyn," she said. "Or just Jess."

"It's nice to meet you, Jess. So listen, let me get my insur—"

"You know what, I'm kind of in a hurry right now? I know this sounds bad, but it's not like I don't know where you live—or you don't know where I live. Do you think I could just come over later or maybe—"

"Hey, Joe. I heard the crash. Everything okay out here?"

Reluctantly, Joe shifted his gaze from Jessalyn to see Dick Werner striding over to them, a mayoral look of concern on his face.

"Hey, Dick, how's it going?" Joe had to keep himself from smirking. He couldn't understand how a grown man under the age of seventy would allow himself to be called "Dick." There were so many variations on "Rich-ard" that would work fine—even *Rick,* for god's sake. But that was Dick Werner to a tee, Joe thought, with his side-parted hair, his 1970s porn star mustache, and his Topsiders. He just didn't give a shit about how he ap-peared to anyone else—probably even thought he looked stylish.

"So would that be okay?" Jessalyn said, completely ignoring Dick and giving Joe a little conspiratorial wink—both actions making Joe feel sud-denly manly and cool. "You know, about coming—"

"Sure," Joe said. "Absolutely. I have to get to work also."

"Want me to have a quick look at this for you?" Dick asked Jessalyn. "You could have damage to the—"

"You know what, it's totally fine." Jessalyn brushed him off. "It was totally my fault and we're going to . . . unless your car . . . Is your car okay?" A pretty furrow of concern creased her face and she licked her lips. She was kind of trashy looking, Joe thought, but definitely hot. He wondered how he'd missed noticing her before now. A quick backward glance to his own car told him that she'd taken the brunt of the collision. "No, I mean, yes, I'm fine. And we can—I mean, I can—"

"I'm not going to be back until late," she said. "So why don't I just come over in the morning. That okay?" Joe nodded. She gave him another wink and turned to get back into her car. "Okay, see you then!"

As if to convince them both that the accident had been her fault, Jes-salyn revved her engine and peeled out of the street, leaving Joe and Dick to stare blankly after her.

"Well, *that's* something," Dick said, apropos of nothing, and knelt down to pick up the shards of red plastic. Wanting to leave, but unwilling to let Dick clean up the mess that he'd caused, Joe hurried to scoop up some of the pieces.

"I've got it, Dick, thanks."

"Listen, Joe, since we're here—I was going to come to talk to you anyway—your, uh . . . your . . ." Dick's sallow face flushed. "Her name's Dina, isn't it?"

"Diana?" Joe asked. He stood up, gripping the bits of plastic in his hand. A few yards down, he could see his skinny neighbor Sam leaning against her mailbox, smoking a cigarette and watching them with interest. What the hell, didn't anyone have anything better to do on a Sunday afternoon than eavesdrop?

"Diana, right," Dick said. "Did you know that she's over at my house? She's been over a lot lately, hanging out with Kevin. I didn't know if you knew that."

No, Joe didn't know—having missed that development while trying to keep his marriage together and still earn a living. But what difference could it possibly make to Dick if Diana was spending time with his son, who appeared to be a complete delinquent to everyone but his parents?

"Is that a problem? They're about the same age and Diana's new to the area. It's nice of Kevin to make friends with her." Joe didn't know where Dick was going with his line of inquiry, but he wasn't going to help the man get there. He knew Dick was a right-leaning good ol' boy, but hadn't taken him for an outright racist. He didn't want to think it possible that Diana's color mattered to Dick, but you just couldn't tell with people anymore. Especially not here in this sunny patch of North San Diego County where so many residents were not at all as accepting and easygoing as they'd have you believe.

"Yeah," Dick said, "but, you know, they've been spending a lot of time on the computer together. You know what they—what kids can get up to. I really wanted Kevin to get a job this summer but now it's too late with school starting. And I don't know if . . . Listen, Joe, man-to-man here—"

"Well, it's not like Kevin's going to get her into trouble, is it Dick?" The comment was so unlike him, but Joe's patience had just run out and he had to get away from Dick and the corrosive drama of his home life. In comparison, the hectic dinner shift he was headed into would be paradise. He could see that he'd thrown Dick into an impossible quandary with his statement—there wasn't really a polite response to what he'd just said—and he took advantage of the man's temporary silence by walking over to his car and getting in.

"Sorry, Dick, I've really got to get going. I'm already late."

But instead of saying good-bye and heading back to his own house, Dick followed Joe to his car and leaned in the driver's side window. "I'm just saying, Joe. I thought you'd want to know—you know, where she is."

"Okay, Dick, thanks."

"Is Allison okay?" Dick asked. "Dorothy says she hasn't seen her in church for weeks."

Joe felt his jaw tensing. He'd never been a churchgoer himself and didn't accompany Allison on Sundays, which was probably why it hadn't occurred to him that anyone would have noticed her absence. Of course it would have to be Dick. Who else? Fucking perfect.

"Allison's been under the weather lately," Joe said. "Some kind of bug. Plus she's feeling a little overwhelmed . . . lot of work on the house. . . ."

"Right, of course," Dick said. "It's a lot of work."

"Yes."

"Okay then."

Dick gave the top of Joe's car a tap and finally backed off so that Joe could pull out. It really didn't matter now whether he managed to get to work on time, whether his customers spent a hundred dollars a head tonight, or whether he managed to get through dinner without fielding a single complaint; Joe's night was ruined—unsalvageable. As he rolled to the end of the street, he saw that Sam was still standing at her mailbox, her cigarette burned down to the filter. She waved to him as he went past, smiling at him like she knew something.

chapter 4

Sam was only a quarter way through her bag of carrots when the juicer squealed and jammed to a grinding halt. She reached for the off switch, but her wet hands were too slick and she slipped, dislodging the canister and spilling what little juice she'd already collected.

"Fuck!"

Bright orange liquid flowed everywhere, seeming to expand as it moved across the white-tiled countertop. It would stain permanently no matter how fast she soaked it up or what kind of product she used to clean it.

"Fucking fuck."

She yanked the power cord—something every manual told you not to do—finally bringing the machine to a stop, but the gears had ground against each other too long and she could smell burning plastic. The thing was dead.

"Gloria!" Sam crossed the kitchen to get something to stop the mess from spreading and dripping onto the floor where it could do more damage but froze somewhere in the middle, unsure whether a sponge or paper towels would do a better job. Paralyzed with indecision, she watched as carrot juice seeped ever deeper into the grout. She wanted to cry. These were the kinds of little things that could just kill you, she thought.

A flash of movement outside caught Sam's eye. She looked out the kitchen window into the backyard where she could see Joe Montana's bad-girl prodigal daughter shuffling through the dead eucalyptus leaves on her way to the Werners' house. This had been going on for at least a month, but Sam had never stopped the girl and asked her why she had to maneuver her heavily pregnant self across the backyard to get to the house she could probably reach in less time by going the conventional front way. Sam knew what it meant to be a girl in trouble and it was no skin off her nose, even though it was somewhat ridiculous for a girl in her condition to be creeping through the foliage to go see a boy—because obviously it was Kevin that she was hanging out with and not either one of his asshole parents. Although from what Sam knew of Kevin, he was destined to turn out in the same rotten mold as his bigoted father and his self-loathing, anti-feminist mother.

Sam felt a stab of angry fear in her chest. It was 2007, well into a new *century,* but you'd never know it from the way Dick Werner looked at her and Gloria every time their paths happened to cross—as if they were witches straight out of seventeenth-century Salem. He probably got off on imagining her and Gloria together even while he quietly condemned them. He was just the type. She'd seen it in his piggy little eyes.

Sam watched as Diana ducked behind the Werners' fence and disappeared from view. She had to stifle the urge to run out there and tell her to be careful—to stay away from those people. It wasn't Sam's business after all, even if Diana regularly used her backyard as a connecting artery. The first time it had happened was back in early August on a weekend when neither Sam nor Gloria had their boys. Gloria was upstairs, a cold wet rag to her migraine-plagued forehead, and Sam was sitting outside trying to organize all the boxes of beads, crystals, and semiprecious stones she used for her jewelry. It was way too hot inside and their air conditioning cost upward of fifteen dollars a day to run. There'd been at least the hint of a breeze in the backyard, so Sam poked around in the topaz and turquoise until she was startled to see the very pretty, very pregnant teenager appear before her like some kind of swollen apparition. Sam knew who the girl was, having extracted that much gossip from Dorothy, who'd been more than willing to share it.

"Hey," the girl said. "I'm Diana."

Sam smiled at Diana, a rush of emotions swirling through her. She felt a powerful maternal urge toward the girl, which was only heightened by the fact that she was missing Connor with knifelike intensity. And there was another, much sadder emotion stirred by the girl's appearance. Diana looked so bereft—so lost and frightened in bare feet and an ill-fitting and overly cheerful summer dress—it immediately threw Sam into her own teenage past, almost thirty years ago now, when she'd been in exactly the same situation—young, pregnant, and disgraced.

"My name is Sam," she said simply and bit back the questions—*What are you going to do? Are you going to give up your baby? Because you'll regret it for the rest of your life.*

"Is it okay if I just cut across here? I'm not, like, breaking in or anything." Diana touched her belly, as if that spoke to her credibility.

"Do you want something to drink?" Sam asked her. "Some lemonade or something?"

"It's okay, I'm good," Diana said. She pointed to Sam's jewelry boxes glittering in the sunlight. "Those yours? I mean—what are they for?"

"I make jewelry," Sam said. "Necklaces mostly." Her gaze traveled down to Diana's tattooed ankles. "And some anklets too," she said.

"Cool," Diana said and moved toward the fence. "Well, I'm going to go. Thanks for letting me . . . Thanks."

"Okay," Sam said.

"See ya." And then she was gone. Sam hadn't spoken to her since then, had only seen her slipping across at odd hours of the day and into the evening—a phantom with child. The next time that girl popped around, Sam decided, she was going to make sure she said hello—make sure she gave Diana a little friendly, nonjudgmental advice, because it didn't look as if anyone else was going to.

Sam realized there were tears at the corners of her eyes and she sniffed, jerking herself away from her reverie at the window and grabbing a sponge to mop up the now-congealing carrot juice.

"Gloria!" she called a second time. Again, there was no response, even though Sam knew that wherever she was in their house, Gloria could hear her. Not to mention that Sam's voice carried well enough to be heard through their open windows and out onto the street. But Gloria was in a mood and that meant Sam was going to suffer. Those dark clouds of Gloria's were coming in thicker and more frequently these days and were in direct proportion with Sam's decreasing ability to pull her out of them. But that she had somehow slipped—or been placed—into the role of cajoling cheerleader bothered Sam more every time she found herself trying to head off Gloria's slide into depression. They'd gotten into this thing together with their eyes open, knowing (at least partially) what it would mean.

Not that they had fooled anyone—not then, when they arrived in the neighborhood with their boys or now, after their children had been taken away. Sam remembered the day they moved in, the chaos of toys and boxes and phone calls and pizza. The kids were underfoot the entire day. Those boys were best friends, closer than brothers, and they were thrilled to be living under the same roof. They were so excited about it that they were even looking forward to doing homework together. Sam lined drawers, stacked plates, and sorted utensils. Gloria constructed two twin beds in the boys' room and then made them up with matching blue sheets and pillows. Every five minutes, Connor or Justin would run in with another question or revelation. There was a tree in the backyard perfect for a tree house! Where was the box with Justin's PlayStation? When was the TV going to be hooked up? Connor found a cat in the driveway! Could they go see if there were any other kids to play with on the street? It was exhausting and exhilarating, and, despite the constant anxiety Sam had been feeling since she and Gloria had decided to leave their husbands, she was truly happy that day and allowed herself the possibility that it might just work out.

Of course Dorothy had materialized at their front door that day to welcome them to the neighborhood and offer them a "fresh baked" pumpkin pie that looked like it had come directly from a supermarket shelf. When Sam expressed ironic amazement that people still came over with pies and to borrow cups of sugar and the like, Dorothy looked at her with a curious mix of bafflement and mistrust as if to say that she didn't quite get the joke but that she knew it was at her expense. Sam remembered thinking right then that the nosy, straight arrow Dorothy was going to be a problem. And that was before Dick wandered over in his conservative weekend casuals (god, those slacks were too awful for words) and introduced himself.

"Hello there. Dick Werner."

"Hi. Sam."

"Sam? Like Samantha?"

Was it his tone, Sam wondered now, brimming with condescension and sexism (yes, the sexism was there, even in those five syllables) that kept her from telling him that her full name was Samara? Or was it just a desire to protect even this small part of herself from being exposed?

"No," she told him, "not like Samantha."

In itself, her answer might not have been enough to make an enemy out of a man who actually called himself Dick, but what happened next surely had. Gloria came downstairs and over to the open door where Sam was standing with the Werners. She was wearing tight spandex bike shorts that showed every lush curve and a cropped T-shirt that advertised her flat tan belly. Her hair was still long then—before she had it hacked off into that short brutal cut she wore now—and flowing around her head and shoulders like a rush of gold. Gloria was glorious, even on moving day, without makeup or any artificial enhancements, and in need of a shower. Sam could see the instant leer in Dick's eyes and the jealousy in Dorothy's. Sam had seen this combination so many times; lust and envy greeted Gloria wherever she went, and she could tell the Werners were trying to assess the situation in their own minds. What, their faces asked, was the story with these two women—one of them an absolute stunner—without wedding rings or visible husbands but with two overexcited little boys who clearly belonged to them? If it had just stayed there, with introductions and pie, they might both have come to the same conclusion, that they were recently divorced women who were moving in together to save money. But then Gloria did something that Sam still didn't understand—something that slightly but permanently altered everything. Gloria leaned forward to shake Dick's hand and at the same time, looped her free arm around Sam's shoulders. It wasn't as overt as a hug, nor was there anything sexual in it, but the gesture was proprietary and had an unmistakable intimacy. Even Dick and Dorothy—surprise, disgust, and prurient interest flitting across their American Gothic faces in quick succession—could see that very clearly.

Sam wondered now why she'd never said anything about it to Gloria afterward, why they hadn't even exchanged a knowing look or admission of what she'd done. It was too easy to believe that it hadn't meant anything, that it wasn't a calculated move on Gloria's part, and that the whole exchange was simply a vaguely uncomfortable welcome-to-the-neighborhood interlude. Perhaps that had been the beginning of Gloria's need to push the envelope, to keep driving forward until she got a reaction. Well, she'd gotten one all right. How long had it taken for Gloria's sadistic ex, Frank, to erupt and for their children to become merely visitors in their home? The length of a whisper, Sam thought, and they were gone.

And now Sam was stuck with all the heavy lifting. They were meant to be *each other's* support, she thought. Gloria wasn't the only one who missed her child—Sam was having just as hard a time of it. But Gloria . . . There was something breaking inside her and Sam didn't know how to fix it.

Sam put her hands to her temples and pressed as if that alone could rid her of the tension and pain created by their ex-husbands. Sam knew the hurt she'd caused Noah by leaving him for Gloria went far beyond just the insult to his masculinity, and she was deeply sorry for that. She still cared for him—he was Connor's father, after all, and a good one—and had tried to make things as easy and nonconfrontational as possible. She didn't understand how he could have allowed himself to get so influenced by Frank and join forces with him to take their boys away from their mothers. Sam remembered Shakespeare's line about killing all the lawyers and sighed. Both Noah and Frank were attorneys. What were the chances? And that was the only reason they'd been able to pull off what they had with the boys. Frank's cruel treatment of Gloria since then—well, that was just an added bonus. At least Noah wasn't attempting to poison Connor against his mother the way Frank was with Justin.

Sam put the kettle on for tea and cleaned up the remainder of the carrot juice mess as she waited for the water to boil. They couldn't have hidden their relationship—not really—but they could have been more discreet about it. And by discreet, Sam only meant not rubbing Frank's nose in it, which was what Gloria seemed to want to do.

"I don't want us to sneak around," Gloria said. "That's not who I am. I'm not ashamed of anything."

All well and good, Sam thought, until the phone call from Frank's partner at the firm. God, he'd marshaled half the damned county. Too much money. Too much ego. Sharp tears stung Sam's eyes again when she thought of how horrible it had been to tell the boys that they had to pack up and go back to live with their fathers. Gloria had handled it so well—smiling, joking, making them all Mickey Mouse waffles with whipped cream for dinner with to-hell-with-it abandon. But later, when the kids had gone to bed and after she'd gone upstairs and closed herself in the bathroom, Gloria lost it completely, sobbing like a lost child, as unhappy as Sam had ever seen another human being.

The kettle whistled. Sam put boiling water and a peppermint tea bag into a large clear mug and carried it upstairs.

"Gloria?" she called again. "You okay?"

But of course she wasn't.

Gloria was lying on their bed, the familiar damp washcloth over her eyes and blue foam earplugs in her ears. Well, that explained the lack of response at least. She didn't stir until Sam sat down next to her, making the bed shift.

"Hey."

Gloria removed the earplugs and washcloth. "Headache," she said. Her eyes were red and watery.

"I made you some tea."

"Thanks," Gloria said but made no move to take the mug. Sam set the tea down on the end table and took Gloria's hand, clammy and cool, in hers.

"I was thinking," Sam said, "that maybe we could take the train downtown and go to Extraordinary Desserts? What do you think? It's a beautiful day and it would be a nice ride. Something different. I'll treat."

Sam gave Gloria credit for at least trying to force a smile and didn't take any away when it failed to materialize. Gloria gave her hand a little squeeze.

"I don't think so, Sam. Don't think I'm up for it. Maybe a drink later. Or something."

Suddenly exhausted, Sam lay down on the bed next to Gloria who rolled into her, wrapping her in a full body embrace. They lay like that for a minute, then two. Sam's breathing slowed and her eyes started to close. Then Gloria started crying, softly at first, then increasingly hard until her whole body was shaking.

"Honey," Sam said and stroked Gloria's back with long sweeping passes of her hand.

"It's too hard," Gloria said, her words muffled with tears. "It's not supposed to be this hard."

"I know," Sam said.

september 2007

chapter 5

Dorothy stared at the picked-over remains of a roast chicken that she'd just pulled out of the fridge. Two days ago, it had seemed like a good idea to make chicken salad for the block party, but now she couldn't figure out how she'd even come to that conclusion. Didn't matter if it was the best chicken salad in the world—it would still just be chicken salad. How boring and uninspired could you get? And Dorothy had arranged this block party herself. As the organizer, shouldn't she bring something exciting— something that at least had a little flair? Of course. It was Labor Day and certain kinds of food were expected: burgers, hot dogs, that kind of thing. But Dick was taking care of the burgers and she should really make something special of her own. Something that might even become a signature dish in years to come. It was important that she make something memorable. She wanted to be complimented. She wanted people to go home after the party and say, "Wasn't Dorothy's—fill in the blank—amazing?" Whatever Dorothy made should be good enough for her neighbors to ask her for the recipe. And then, of course, Dorothy would laugh and tell them that there was no recipe, that this—fill in the blank—was something she just threw together.

Yes, that was it. That was it exactly.

Dorothy shoved the chicken back in the fridge and opened the deep drawer beneath the silverware where she kept the stash of cookbooks she used most frequently. There was a larger, more expensive cache of cookbooks in the garage, buried under boxes of Christmas ornaments and Kevin's old baby clothes, but she consulted those only when there was something really big coming up: holiday cakes, for example, or multicourse French dinners for parties. People *expected* you to use cookbooks for those kinds of things. But for the smaller occasions, when it was important that the dishes she cooked *appeared* to be made from her own imagination, Dorothy went to the secret drawer. It probably wasn't necessary to actually hide these cookbooks, but hiding things had long been second nature to Dorothy, as much a part of her as the diamond-shaped mole in the crook of her left arm.

There were neatly folded wads of one-, five-, and ten-dollar bills all over the house, for example. Dorothy knew every individual location, if not the exact amounts. There was one in a rolled pair of socks wedged between two never-used blankets, one in a storage box containing Kevin's old school projects, one behind some plastic San Diego Chargers tumblers on a kitchen shelf, one stuffed inside the hollow metal toilet paper roller. And that wasn't even all of them.

Dorothy also hid documents. She had a secret safety deposit box, the paperwork for which she hid in the box itself, and the key for which she hid in another safety deposit box at a different bank. Because you couldn't be too careful and you just never knew. Which was why Dorothy had also hidden a pack of cigarettes in the kitchen, in an old round tin that had once held caramel-covered popcorn. Dorothy could see it in her mind's eye, the faded red and white image of Santa Claus still visible on its surface. Dorothy didn't smoke (well, *hadn't* smoked for a while anyway), but, again, you never knew when you might really, really need a cigarette and wouldn't have time to go to a store to get one. Of course she would *never* smoke unless she was sure that nobody was watching.

Just as she was finishing that thought—at the moment, in fact, when the concept of being watched entered into her brain—Dorothy felt the chill of a stare at her back and whirled around, her hands clenching at her sides.

That pregnant girl—Diana—was standing in the kitchen doorway, quiet as you please.

"Hi, Mrs. Werner."

Dorothy inhaled slowly. There was nothing to feel guilty about.

"Hello, Diana. Have you come to see Kevin? He's upstairs."

Dorothy didn't know why she felt the need to tell Diana that Kevin was home—or upstairs for that matter. Diana knew where Kevin was all the time; that was why she was here in the first place. Nor had Diana ever once entered the house through the front door, greeted Dorothy before she saw Kevin, or announced her presence in any other way before she sneaked into Kevin's room and the two of them did whatever it was they did for hours on end. But Dorothy felt compelled to adhere to the social ritual just as she had in the past every time one of Kevin's friends had come over to play.

"I was wondering if I could get a glass of water," Diana said. "Would that be okay?"

"Sure," Dorothy said. "Of course."

But neither one of them moved. Diana stood tilted backward slightly to balance her uneven weight with her hands resting on her belly. She was wearing cheap dusty flip-flops and a gauzy sundress that didn't quite hide the outlines of her body underneath it. Her long hair was pulled back into a haphazard ponytail and there were tiny dots of perspiration above her upper lip. She smelled of sweat and white flowers. Dorothy thought that Diana looked particularly young today, but despite that, not at all vulnerable. This confused Dorothy, as did Diana's total lack of shame and her willingness to let—almost force, really—everyone see the state she was in. Dorothy had already been married for years when she became pregnant with Kevin, and even though there was nothing to hide, she'd still been discreet about it. That was the core of it, Dorothy supposed. She just couldn't understand why this girl felt she had nothing to hide. And why was she just standing there, Dorothy wondered. What was she waiting for?

Diana cleared her throat. The vaguest hint of discomfort shadowed her face. "So can I get . . . ? Do you mind if I get that glass of water?"

"Oh," Dorothy said. She realized then that she was standing in the entryway to the kitchen and that in order for Diana to get herself the glass of water she wanted, she'd have to push Dorothy out of the way. Dorothy hadn't even noticed that she'd been hovering like some kind of mountain lioness guarding her territory, but that must surely be the way it looked to Diana.

"I'll get it for you," Dorothy said and opened the cabinet where she kept the glassware. Diana looked relieved. Dorothy filled a glass with water from the faucet and handed it to the girl. "Would you like something to eat? I have some cookies or . . . chicken."

Diana smiled—suddenly and dazzlingly. "Cookies or chicken?" she asked. "Sounds tempting, but no thanks. Do you have any other water, though? This water smells so bleachy. I'm sorry, I just . . . I'm just not used to San Diego water, I guess." She held the glass out to Dorothy, her smile fading but not disappearing entirely, as if they were both in on the same joke. Dorothy wasn't amused. There was something in the gesture that struck Dorothy as not rude, exactly, but presumptuous. As if she were owed something just for being here.

"Sorry," Dorothy said. "All we have is tap." She thought about the gallon of Sparkletts on the top shelf of the fridge and wondered if Diana sensed she was lying. But Diana just stood there impassive, one eyebrow half-raised, and slowly lifted the tumbler to her lips to drink.

"Thanks, Mrs. Werner."

Diana turned, water in hand, and headed back up the stairs to Kevin's bedroom. Dorothy bristled. There was something in Diana's tone that scraped against her nerves. It was uncharitable to feel so hostile toward this girl who clearly had plenty of troubles to deal with, but Dorothy couldn't help herself. There was something about Diana that just made her uneasy. It felt to Dorothy as if Diana had brought an air of bad luck into the neighborhood. And no, Dorothy told herself, that wasn't because Diana was black (well, *half* black, really), or that she was a pregnant teenager, or that she was almost certainly wrecking Joe and Allison's marriage.

That last part was Joe's fault primarily, though Dorothy believed that Diana probably made things much more difficult for Allison than they had to be because, truly, Diana was just not a very endearing person. Really, Allison was the victim in all of this, and you didn't have to be Sherlock Holmes to figure out that Allison was not dealing with it well at all. Allison had only allowed Dorothy in once since Diana had arrived (last month, when Dorothy had taken over one of her famous chocolate cheesecakes in the hope that Allison would unburden herself of what must be a very trying situation—because Dorothy was there to listen and to help), but she could tell that Allison was a mess, all bloodshot and disheveled and unwilling to even grunt out a thank-you before she sent Dorothy back to her own house. She'd been drinking too, pretty heavily by the looks of it, and it was only the middle of the day. Way, way before anything like happy hour. Maybe Allison should have been made of tougher stuff—worse things had happened to people after all—but Dorothy felt bad for her and wished there was a way she could help Allison open up.

The funny thing was that Dorothy had felt she and Allison were really starting to form a bond over the last few months before Diana showed up. Allison had started coming to church, and even though they didn't really talk that much about anything in particular, they'd begun walking to St. William's together on Sundays—it was such an easy, pleasant walk from their street and good exercise to boot—and Dorothy felt they'd developed a sort of camaraderie that went beyond being neighbors. Allison was what in the old days you'd call "a good girl." She had a high moral standard—you could tell just from the way she dressed—conservatively, never showing too much cleavage or leg. This was important for a teacher, even though nobody seemed to pay attention to that fact. Look at all those women having sex with their students who were as young as *thirteen*. Dorothy shuddered just to think about it. Allison was the kind of woman who probably couldn't even wrap her mind around such a concept. Unlike some of their other neighbors. Jessalyn Martin in particular.

Dorothy's thoughts turned dark and silty as her mind formed a picture of Jessalyn's tight skirts, bleached hair, and oversized breasts. Everything about that girl was cheap and nothing about her was real. Which made it even more ironic that Jessalyn's big claim to fame was that she'd been on a reality show. Dorothy couldn't even remember the name of it now, but she did remember Jessalyn's appearance because she had seen every one of the three episodes that Jessalyn had been in. This was not by choice, but because Hank Martin had been so insistent. That was before Jessalyn had moved in, taken over, and packed her father off to Beach Gardens, an assisted-living facility for seniors, even though Hank was in less need of assisted living than his daughter was. He'd been doing fine and loved nothing better than to putter around with dirt and flowers, and had given Dorothy many a gardening tip over the years, like how to get rid of those horrible white flies on her tomato plants with a spray of water and dish soap. Four years ago or so, Hank told Dorothy that his daughter was going to be on television. It was just one of those shows where they put a bunch of people together to see who could argue the loudest and win the money. That was how he put it. You should watch, though, Hank told her. She's very pretty. And smart too. Sure to win.

The show turned out to be an insult to the intelligence of everyone who watched it, including Dorothy, which was why it had barely lasted one season before being canceled. As Dorothy recalled, Jessalyn hadn't actually failed any of the challenges, but had been voted off the show because none of the other contestants could stand her.

Dorothy had been embarrassed for Hank. It was a feeling he must have shared because he never mentioned it to Dorothy again. Nor would she have given it a second thought, but then Jessalyn showed up in all her glory, moved in, and took over. Not that Dorothy wanted to have anything to do with her, but in all the time Jessalyn had been living there, she hadn't been over to say hello even once. Dorothy could only imagine what the house looked like inside now—or what had happened to Hank's cherished garden. But of course, she didn't have to imagine, she'd soon be finding out firsthand. The Neighborhood Watch list needed to be updated, a task that Dick had volunteered for but that Dorothy had been saddled with, and now Dorothy needed to go to each house on the street and get cell phone numbers, license plates, and names of immediate family members.

If she was being honest with herself, Dorothy had to admit that she didn't mind organizing the Neighborhood Watch list as much as she let on. She complained to Dick about it, but there was no real bite in her words. The truth was it made Dorothy feel more secure to know these details about her neighbors. And even though everyone participating got a copy of the list, it was Dorothy who knocked on the doors, who looked inside the houses, and who got to make the final judgment about what she saw there. Mindlessly, Dorothy walked over to the hutch in the breakfast nook just off her kitchen, opened the drawer where they kept all the Neighborhood Watch information, and pulled out the Fuller Court master chart.

Laying it on the table, Dorothy unfolded the chart and smoothed it flat, admiring the clean, color-coded lines she'd drawn to designate the different houses and property boundaries, tracing her finger along the thick upside-down *U* of the street. There they were, the Werners, anchoring Fuller Court, all their information and contacts completed in neat type. Directly across from them were the Suns, a perpetual thorn in Dorothy's side. They were consistently difficult to pin down and get information from. In fact, Dorothy knew almost nothing at all about them and it appeared that they liked it that way.

Mr. Sun left his house, briefcase in hand, every morning at 7:00 AM (Dorothy knew this because her dining room, where she sat with her morning coffee, faced the street and had a direct view of the Suns' driveway) and didn't usually return until 6:00 or 7:00 PM. Their son, who was Kevin's age and who attended Kevin's school but who Kevin didn't hang out with, sometimes came outside in the late afternoon and shot baskets into a hoop installed above their garage. Other than that, Dorothy never saw him and didn't even know his first name ("I don't know," Kevin had told her when she'd asked, "everyone just calls him Sun."). She could, however, hear him practicing piano through open windows on an almost daily basis.

As far as Mrs. Sun went, there were only rare glimpses. Dorothy had caught sight of her only once, when the woman was coming home on foot from a trip to the supermarket, but by the time she had thought of a reasonable excuse to run outside and accidentally-on-purpose run into Mrs. Sun, she'd disappeared inside her house and the opportunity had been missed. Of course, Dorothy had tried just knocking on the door, her Neighborhood Watch list in hand, but had gotten a response only once, when the Sun boy had answered, told Dorothy he'd pass the message along to his mother, and dismissed her. The Suns had been living in that house for over a year, but they might as well have been ghosts for all anyone saw of them. Dorothy understood the need for privacy, but thought that these kinds of extremes indicated that they had something to hide. And if that were the case, the Suns were rank amateurs. The best way to hide things, as Dorothy well knew, was to act as if you had nothing to hide.

Dorothy moved her finger around the bend in her chart, grazing through the Martin house, drifting through the Montanas', and coming to rest at Sam and Gloria's house, which was right next door to hers. Sam and Gloria had two cell phone numbers but only one car listed, Sam's Camry. Gloria's white pickup truck, on which she had plastered a rainbow bumper sticker, was not accounted for. Of all the houses on the street, Sam's was the one Dorothy had the least interest in. Or maybe it wasn't a lack of interest exactly—more like a certain level of repulsion. No, repulsion was too strong a word. She was . . . *repelled*, that was it. Dorothy knew it was well into a new century and she was just as tolerant as the next person. People had a right to live the way they wanted to, et cetera, et cetera. But there was just something *wrong* about those two. Maybe it was the fact that they both had kids, because Dorothy didn't care how many times you read *Heather Has Two Mommies* or *Daddy's Roommate,* it had to be confusing for a child and that just wasn't fair. And obviously *someone* agreed with that notion because Sam's and Gloria's kids didn't live with them, and why wouldn't two small children live with their mothers unless something was very wrong with those mothers? Not that Sam and Gloria ever acted like a couple. No, they *pretended* to be just friends. Dorothy didn't get it. Neither Sam nor Gloria was anything to look at, really. Well, maybe Gloria in a big *athletic* kind of way, but Sam was so skinny and . . .

"Dorothy!"

Dorothy jumped at the sound of Dick's call, instinctively clutching her Neighborhood Watch list, almost crumpling it. Why was he shouting for her? She folded the list and placed it back in its drawer.

"What is it?" she called out, knowing he couldn't hear her over the sound of the television.

"Dorothy!"

Dorothy walked—faster than she wanted to—into the living room. Dick sat in his preferred spot on the couch, eyes on the game, with the remote control in hand and a bowl of chips and can of beer at the ready on the coffee table.

"What is it, Dick?"

He didn't answer her right away—kept his gaze trained on the television as if she wasn't standing there, until a point or a goal or whatever was scored, then shouted, "Yes!" and finally turned to her and said, "Is that girl here again?"

"Yes," Dorothy answered, the simplest response being the easiest in this case.

"What the hell?" he asked her.

"I don't know, Dick." Dorothy wondered—not for the first time—why Dick seemed to have such a needle to Diana. It went beyond her being a knocked-up teenager because his attitude wasn't one of paternal disapproval. It was more like he was *personally* challenged by her—as if she'd done something specifically to anger him, although as far as Dorothy knew, he'd never exchanged more than five words with her.

"What are they doing up there, Dorothy?"

"I don't know. Hanging out. What do kids do?"

Dick raised his eyebrows—slowly, so she'd be sure not to miss his implication.

"You're his mother, Dot. Don't you think you should know?"

"Do you want me to go barging in there and check up on him like he's a baby?"

"Yes. That's exactly what I want you to do."

"I was just about to make . . . you know, for the party . . . you've got the burgers, right? Anyway, I need to get ready for . . . why don't *you* go up there, Dick?"

"Don't be ridiculous," he snapped. "That girl is there. I can't do it. Come on, Dot." He sighed and with reluctance lifted himself from the couch. "Goddamn Joe and his goddamned mess," he muttered. "Is the grill ready?"

"I thought you were going to—"

"Yes, yes, fine, I'm going to." He swept past her, leaving the scent of beer-soaked corn chips in his wake. "Go see what your son is doing, Dorothy."

My son, Dorothy thought. Not *our* son. Not Kevin. Dorothy hated when Dick got into this I'm-disappointed-in-everything mood because it made him particularly irritable and difficult to please. Her head had started a slow throb and she could tell it was only the beginning of what would become a major headache. It was going to be chicken salad after all, she thought. Too bad, but she no longer had the time or energy to get creative. Maybe she'd put pickles in it to spice it up. Or some of those olives from Barron's.

She thought about the olives—the red color of the label, the difficulty she always had opening the jar—as she headed up the stairs to Kevin's room. When did children reach the point when they no longer needed to be watched over, she wondered. She stood in the upstairs hallway, at Kevin's closed door, listening. She heard giggling and then a muffled, "Kevin, stop," and then more laughing. Dorothy's head pounded with every beat of her heart. She knocked and waited. Heard whispering, more laughing, the sound of being ignored. She knocked again.

"Kevin?"

This was ridiculous. She turned the door handle and found it locked. When had Kevin managed to put a lock on his bedroom door?

"Kevin!" Dorothy heard the slight note of hysteria in her voice and cleared her throat. The headache raged in full force. She was going to have to attend to it. "Open the door, Kevin."

The door opened suddenly, sucking the air out of the hallway, and Dorothy found herself facing a smiling Diana.

"What's up, Mrs. Werner? Sorry we didn't hear you."

Dorothy could feel Dick's hostility to this girl creeping into her own skin. What must it be like for Allison to have to live with her every day? No wonder she was drinking.

"Don't you need to go home?" Dorothy asked. "I mean, isn't there—"

"Jesus, Mom!" Kevin's voice boomed from behind the door. It was a man's voice—deeper than Dick's. When had that happened? Kevin yanked the door open all the way and sidled up next to Diana. His face was flushed and angry.

"That's so fucking rude," he growled.

"Kevin!"

"What? God, Mom, forget it! I can't even believe you just said that to her!"

"It's okay, I can go," Diana said, unmoving, every bit of body language implying she was staying right where she was.

"No, you don't need to go anywhere," Kevin said. "*You* need to go." He stabbed his finger in Dorothy's direction and then slammed the door shut. Dorothy heard the click of the new lock, which, of course, she was going to have to remove as soon as Kevin left his room. She thought about knocking again, about apologizing, about threatening, even, for a second, about getting Dick and making a huge scene that they'd all live to regret. But in the end Dorothy did none of these things. She opted instead to go to her bedroom, shutting the door behind her, and then to the bathroom with that door shut and locked too, and then to the linen closet inside the bathroom, to the very back, behind the hand towels and never-used washcloths, to a box of tampons, inside the box, between the supers and the light days, to a bottle, and inside the bottle to some pills. Dorothy opened the bottle, took a pill, swallowed it, and chased it with water from the bathroom sink. She breathed in and out exactly six times. And then she took another pill.

It was, after all, a very bad headache.

labor day, 2007

At 3:00 PM, Fuller Court was drowsy. Two crows swooped, cawing halfheartedly, and a skinny gray cat slunk through the hedges looking for trouble. A sprinkler hissed then sputtered out. Faint cheers from a televised baseball game rose and fell from one open window, strident piano chords came through another. It was warm enough for the beach, but nobody on the block had gone. The beach was full of tourists having their last hurrah before they had to go home to their cold dark places. *Let them have it,* the locals thought. *Come tomorrow, the coastline is ours again.*

At 4:30 PM, the neighborhood stirred to life bit by bit, a chick emerging from its shell. Dick Werner rolled his new state-of-the-art grill to the end of his driveway and busied himself with charcoal and butane. Dorothy was right behind him with a folding picnic table and its red-checked plastic covering. It took her another three trips to bring out the cooler, bags of ice, and twelve-packs of beer.

"Let's hope somebody else brings some this time," Dick told her as she tucked the cans into the ice. "Last year we supplied the whole neighborhood. Nobody brought even a single can of their own beer. Remember that? You put it on the flyer, right?"

"Sure did," Dorothy said, crouching down to get better leverage. "BYOB, just like I did last year and the year before. We'll see, I guess."

"Where's Kevin?" Dick asked. "I could use some help with these patties."

"Let me just get the chicken salad and the buns," Dorothy said, "and then I'll come help you."

"Just get Kevin," Dick said. "You're doing more than enough. Hand me one of those beers, will you?"

At 5:15 PM, the smell and smoke of grilled burgers was thick in the air and seeping through screens, as clear a signal as church bells. Garage doors opened and people drifted out onto the street carrying plastic containers.

Dorothy had changed her clothes and was now wearing a pair of generously cut beige cropped pants and a fitted light blue button-down shirt. She'd put some lipstick on too, a neutral not-quite-pink shade that didn't make her fair skin look washed out. She stacked paper plates and napkins on the table and loaded plastic forks into an oversized cup. She'd ladled the chicken salad on top of lettuce leaves to give it a bit of color and put it in a nice red bowl next to a loaf of white bread in case anyone wanted to make their own sandwiches.

Dick attended to his burgers with great care. He'd made his own barbecue sauce this year—a combination of ketchup, Worcestershire sauce, and mustard—and was basting each burger liberally. He'd donned his "Don't Mess with the Chef" apron, but not before he managed to spatter his green polo shirt with grease.

The first people out were Sam and Gloria, who walked close together—almost touching—toward Dorothy's table. Dorothy smiled and waved, even though they were only a few feet away. Sam was wearing a festive skirt, long, full, and decorated with bright yellow and orange geometric patterns that contrasted nicely with the turquoise necklace and bracelet she'd designed and created. The skirt and jewelry were set off by a plain white T-shirt, which was simple but of good quality and which flattered Sam's olive skin and slim figure.

Gloria wasn't as dressed up as Sam but had traded her usual yoga pants for a pair of painted-on jeans and a purple halter top. Her short gold hair was still damp from the shower. Sunlight bounced off the large silver hoops in her ears and her breasts swayed slightly against the thin fabric of her top. Dick turned his head as she passed him, his eyes quickly taking a full inventory of her hips and thighs.

"That looks good," Sam said, pointing at Dorothy's chicken salad.

"Please try some," Dorothy said. "I made it with these special olives I got down at . . . you know, that store. . . . I'm totally drawing a blank right now! But help yourself."

"I made a fruit salad," Sam said. "It's kind of my take on ambrosia, but without all the things that are bad for you."

Dorothy tipped her head, smiling politely. "Oh?"

Dick scraped the grill. Flames rose up and he slapped on another patty.

"Don't worry, Dick, we also brought beer," Gloria said and put the two six-packs of Dos Equis she'd been carrying on the table. "*Good* beer," she said.

Dick turned to her, grinning.

"Great," he said. "Burgers are just about there. Time to grab some buns." His eyes flickered quickly to her ass and then back up to his grill.

Gloria rolled her eyes and Sam reached out with her hand, grabbed hold of Gloria's arm, and squeezed lightly. Gloria understood and patted Sam on the back. *Don't worry about it, I'm fine.*

"Okay if I just leave it here for now?" Sam said, placing her fruit salad on the table.

"Sure, of course," Dorothy said, brightness lifting her words. "Oh, look, there's Joe!" She smiled, quickly rubbing a finger across her teeth in case there was any smeared lipstick there.

. . .

At 6:00 PM, Kevin joined his father at the grill. He held a bag of corn chips and dipped into it frequently, chewing as he spoke.

"Need help, Dad?"

"I needed help an hour ago, Kevin. Not much to do now, is there?"

Kevin shrugged and looked over at Diana who was standing off to the side, giggling. Kevin smiled at her, sharing the joke.

"What's she laughing about?" Dick said. "What's so funny?"

"You know, Dad, whatever."

Dick looked at the girl, watched her laugh harder, her hands resting on top of her swollen belly. "Is she going to eat something?" Dick asked Kevin.

Diana waved away a puff of grill smoke that had blown in her direction. "I don't eat the flesh of animals," she said, "but thanks anyway." She started laughing afresh and Kevin joined in.

"Oh, for god's sake," Dick said, turning away from both of them, his lips compressed into a thin line.

Kevin offered his chips to Diana and she took the whole bag. "Now these . . ." she said. The two of them drifted away from the grill, across the street where Sun was bouncing a basketball in his driveway.

"Hey," Diana said by way of greeting.

"Hey." Sun checked her from the corner of his eye, his face flushing. He could see her legs and breasts through her thin dress. Her navel had popped out from the pressure of the baby, making a tiny bump in the fabric.

"What's up?" Kevin said.

"Nothing."

Diana handed the chips back to Kevin and slapped the basketball from Sun's hand. She bounced it on the driveway, awkwardly at first, but then easier, thunking it hard. "Can I have a try?"

"You sure?" Sun laughed a little. She was standing right next to him now, smelling of sweat and weed and flowery perfume. Diana bounced the ball three times, then lifted it, pointed, and shot. It hit the rim and bounded back to them. Kevin caught it, leaning over and spilling corn chips on Sun's driveway.

"Let me try again," she said. Perspiration shone on her upper lip.

"Maybe you shouldn't," Sun said.

The door of Sun's house opened and Mrs. Sun appeared in the doorway, shaking her head. She barked out a command to Sun in Chinese and he answered her in the same language, his tone deferential. She shut the door.

"Dude, what's up with your mom?" Kevin giggled.

"I gotta go," Sun said and took back his ball. "Not bad for a girl," he called over his shoulder to Diana before he disappeared inside his house.

It was 6:30 PM and the neighbors thronged on their street, eating and drinking. There was still plenty of light—the sun wouldn't set until just after seven. It was warm and didn't feel like fall was anywhere near. Joe stood in front of Sam and Gloria's house, drinking a beer and talking to Jessalyn, who was holding a paper plate of Sam's fruit salad but making no move to eat it.

"Is Allison going to come out for a bit?" Jessalyn said. "It's pretty nice outside right now."

"Maybe," Joe said, taking a long pull from the bottle, "but she's not feeling well so I don't know."

"That's too bad." Jessalyn smiled, her teeth shining. She was wearing white shorts and a tiny black top made out of synthetic fabric. Her skin was perfectly tan and glowing from the minuscule flecks of glitter in her body lotion.

"Well, at least *you* get to enjoy it," she said, tucking a stray wisp of hair behind her ear. "You don't have to work tonight?"

"Nice thing about being the boss," Joe answered, "is once in a while you get to set your own schedule."

"Do they do pretty well there at Luna Piena?" Jessalyn asked. "The servers, I mean."

"Why?" Joe smiled wide. "You looking for a job?"

"Well, you never know." She laughed, high and sparkling.

"You should come by sometime," he said. "Sit at the bar and check it out. I'll take care of you. Least I can do after slamming into your car like that."

"Oh," she said, "that would be *great*."

At 7:30 PM, Dorothy placed the empty beer containers in a large garbage bag and started cleaning up. It was just about dark and the party was winding down. Her chicken salad remained virtually untouched and would now have to be thrown away. Bottles and cans clinked against one another as she settled them in the bag.

"Well, people certainly brought their own this year," she told Dick, who was busy cleaning his grill before rolling it back behind the house.

"They did," he said. "Can't complain about that."

"Your burgers seemed to be a hit," she said.

"I think so," he said and gave her a grin. "Not bad, that sauce."

Dorothy patted him on the shoulder. "Not bad at all."

It was 9:00 PM and Fuller Court was quiet. Light made glowing squares of drawn windows and a faint breeze shifted dying eucalyptus leaves off the trees. In the honeysuckle behind Sam and Gloria's house there was a disturbance—the sound of small branches crackling underfoot. Diana slipped home alone, the faint light of a last quarter moon at her back.

chapter 6

It was 11:00 AM and warm. Allison couldn't sleep. Her back ached from spending too many hours prone and the sheets felt grainy. Over the summer, it had been easier to avoid getting out of bed. Some days she'd even managed to hibernate there until close to dusk. Some nights she went to bed at eight o'clock and slept twelve hours without stirring. Other times she roamed the house at night, drinking and muttering, like a cut-rate version of Lady Macbeth, moving from couch to kitchen, clinking ice cubes and staring at the flickering light of the muted television, marking the difference between late night and wee hours by which shows were on.

But as soon as Labor Day came and went, it was as if a switch had been flipped inside her and she was awake as soon as the sunlight began seeping between the slats of the tightly drawn blinds. She fought consciousness with all the tools at her disposal, one of which was a brand-new Ambien prescription, but they were all weak against the force of her circadian rhythms. After a decade of teaching, her body knew when summer was over and it was time to go back to work. But so far her body had refused to accept her brain's memo that for her school was still out, work was off, and the best plan of action was to remain suspended in unconsciousness until further notice.

She turned her pillow over and moved to Joe's considerably cooler side of the bed. He'd left for work early—at eight or nine. Allison's sense of time had become sketchy. She didn't even know whether Joe was working mostly days or nights anymore. Once upon a time they'd tried to synchronize their schedules so that they could spend as much time together as possible. Now Allison suspected he was putting in extra hours at the restaurant just to get out of the house. Because he *was* putting in extra hours, he'd made sure to point that out to her. Since she was taking a leave of absence from school, he said, it was necessary for him to be as diligent as possible at his own job. This didn't make a blind bit of difference because Joe was on salary, but he thought—or at least he *said*—that being there more "might lead to more opportunities."

As she shut her eyes against the slanting light in the room, it occurred to Allison how strange it was that she and Joe still slept in the same bed every night. It wasn't that she had asked or even hinted that he should sleep elsewhere, nor had she moved to another room, but she couldn't understand how he could get into bed next to her every night without any sign of discomfort. There might as well have been a glacier between the two of them for all the cold distance in their relationship, yet Joe never seemed bothered by it—at least not enough to lose any sleep—and Allison resented his lack of insomnia.

Allison had read plenty of women's magazines and novels and knew well the story of a wife who realizes one day that the husband she thought she knew was a stranger to her. Allison thought it might actually be easier if Joe *was* like a stranger to her, but he was more familiar to her now than ever. Diana's sudden appearance in their lives had changed everything *except* Joe.

Joe's stoicism—or at least his ability to carry on as if everything was just fine—was something Allison had always admired. They'd had a slab leak a few years ago; they'd come downstairs to find the carpet soaked through with water from a leaking pipe laid beneath the house in California's famously shifting earth. Allison's first response was to become slightly hysterical over the cost to fix it and the damage to the floor and carpet, but

Joe was completely calm and methodical, even joking at one point about what else they might find buried under the house.

There had also been the time, not long after they had married, when Allison's mother's health deteriorated rapidly for no apparent reason. Joe had been wonderful then, Allison remembered, encouraging her to keep taking care of her own self in order to better help her mother. He was unwaveringly supportive and showed her the importance of continuing to eat, sleep, and work regularly—of not letting the main problem cause other problems. In the end, her mother's health improved in the same mysterious way it had declined, but Allison was sure that without Joe's support—without his get-on-with-it approach—she would have crumpled under the strain. But now, she *was* falling apart, and watching Joe continue to eat, work, and sleep as usual grated on her precisely because he *could*. She wondered if this was simply because he didn't have the emotional capacity to truly understand what she was going through. Maybe he never had.

Whenever they'd had disagreements or, more accurately, whenever there was something bothering Allison about their relationship, Joe's approach was almost always the same. First he asked her if she wanted to talk about it—always hoping that she'd say no because that would enable him to skip the next step, which was to actually attempt a full discussion. Allison knew that Joe disliked this kind of conversation; it was too confrontational for him, and, as he so often told her, he got enough of that at work, having to settle disputes between waiters or pacify customers. So sometimes Allison gave him a pass on the "talk" and just ceded the argument. But when she did press him, Joe had a limited tolerance. There was only so far he could go before he shut down and left them both in silence. Inevitably, though, Joe moved to his final phase, which was to avoid words altogether and go straight to sex. And that, thought Allison, always worked. At least it had until now.

For the first couple of weeks after Diana's arrival, Joe had leaned over to her in bed and pawed at her like a starving bear. At first she said nothing, just lay there unresponsive in the dark until he sighed, gave up, and went to sleep. It wasn't that she was disgusted by him. In fact, Allison believed that no matter what happened she would never find Joe physically repulsive. But there was now a searing shame in the sexual act for Allison—and that was not even counting the deeply disturbing comment Diana had made about listening to the two of them on that awful night—and it left no room for desire even if she had been willing to allow desire in. There was more. Sex and grief had become inextricably tangled for Allison now and there was no undoing it. But Joe couldn't or wouldn't sense this, so he kept trying; he kept trying to make it right with his body, kept trying to get them to be one flesh. Finally, after several such attempts, Allison just came out with it. One of his hands was on her breast, squeezing it like a fruit, and the other was probing between her legs with all the subtlety of a gynecological exam.

"Stop it, Joe."

He'd frozen in shock, his hands still where they lay, and Allison realized that in all the years they'd been together—edging in on a decade—she'd never once said no. He got it then, Allison remembered. After a moment, he moved his hands from her body and turned away from her. Allison didn't lie there much longer before getting up and going downstairs for a drink.

Since then, Joe had just carried on as usual, and there was nothing strange about that at all. No, Allison would not wake up and find herself married to a stranger. She wished she would. At least then they'd both have an excuse for what had happened to their marriage. But then Joe needed no excuse. He had no emotional torment to keep him from eating, sleeping, or working as he always did—which is why he came to their bed every night and slept like a baby.

Baby.

The very word gave Allison pain. She tried to push the images down, deep into the swamp of her feelings, but they wouldn't stay there. They never did anymore. Instead she tried to piece it out, to separate the elements of her misery and look at each one to better understand why their sum was causing her such pain.

She and Joe had been dating for six months when she got pregnant—a shock for both of them, though not as unpleasant for Allison as it was for Joe. She told nobody, not even her own mother. Allison still regretted that and didn't understand why she'd isolated herself in that way. Joe had been calm, but very clear. They didn't know each other well enough, Allison was so young and just beginning her career, he wasn't ready to be a father and didn't think he could give enough of anything to a child. He didn't want it. Unequivocally. No. But ultimately, he told her, it would be her decision. He couldn't force her to do anything. The next thing he should have said but never did was that he would support her no matter what. But Joe told her he couldn't guarantee anything beyond his legal obligations. "I'm just not ready," he said. "And I don't think you are either."

Allison believed him. So she agreed that, yes, it was the best thing. She arranged it herself. Joe paid and waited outside for her. He took her home afterward and tucked her into bed, lying next to her on top of the blankets and holding her hand. "I'm so sorry," he said. And again she believed him. Three months later he asked her to marry him. Before this moment she'd never thought of that proposal as a reward.

Allison had never made her peace with that decision; it was impossible when she was the one who was ultimately responsible for making it. That was a big part of the reason that she never brought it up with Joe, why she never asked him—when he said yes they would have a baby one day when they were ready because there was plenty of time, why not then? Why weren't we ready then? Now, when she wanted to scream it at him her voice was strangled inside her.

At least there was one part of this mess—Diana and her pregnancy, with all its in-your-face evidence of betrayal and babies—that would soon be over, Allison thought. Diana would deliver, some couple would get the infant they couldn't create on their own, and then Joe's daughter would go home to the mother who'd banished her. Perhaps then Allison would even be able to think about puzzling together the exploded pieces of her life and her marriage to see if anything could be made whole again.

Allison felt a stab of pure hatred for Diana's mother, and not because the woman had sent her own daughter to live with strangers at a time when she most needed a mother to guide her. What twisted Allison's gut was deeper than that. She was angry at this woman she had never met for giving birth to Diana in the first place. Why had she and not Allison been allowed to have Joe's baby? Why had that woman been allowed to make a different decision?

Allison kicked off the sheets and sat up. The temperature in the room seemed to have gone up by at least ten degrees in the last ten minutes. It was going to be another hot, dry day; that much was clear. It hadn't rained for months. The air was parched. It had never bothered her before. She'd always loved the sunshine—been a complete hog for it—and this city had always obliged. But now rain—slashing, driving sheets of it—was all she wanted.

It was one of those rare rainy days, Allison now remembered, when she'd met Joe. She was attending some ridiculous singles mixer—a hideously awkward event that she'd allowed her mother to talk her into. Her mother, in some ways a complete throwback, thought that her daughter was in danger of becoming a permanent spinster because Allison was still single at the overripened age of twenty-four. Allison wasn't even dating at the time; she was too focused on teaching her new class of third graders and pacifying their overanxious, demanding parents. But her mother was so insistent ("Oh, just give it a try, Allison; it isn't normal to sit at home night after night. Soon you'll be getting a cat, then two cats, and you know where that goes. What's the worst thing that can happen: You'll have some fun for a change?") that Allison gave in just so that she could say she'd done it and get her mother to back off.

The group she joined arranged a Sunday brunch gathering of about twenty singles at a local restaurant, and, despite her better judgment, Allison put on a blue wraparound dress and matching sensibly heeled shoes and headed out.

The storm was unexpected and the rain was biblical in its intensity, hurling sheets of water at Allison's windshield as she drove into Del Mar to the Italian restaurant she'd never eaten in before. She'd almost turned around and gone home at least three times, once even going as far as to exit the freeway only to loop back once more. But Allison always finished what she started. It was both a saving grace and a tragic flaw.

By the time she'd parked and walked up to the restaurant, her clothing was plastered to her body with rain. The place was steamy and smelled of wet wool and smoke from the wood-burning ovens. It was also loud; a cacophony of clinking plates, silverware, orders, and conversation that seemed to grow with every step she took toward the long banquet table filled with people who looked at least as uncomfortable as she felt. Despite the rain, everyone else was there already, and Allison had to take the last seat at the end of the table bordering the drafty hall that led to the bathroom.

The man sitting next to her had at least ten years on her as well as an emptied beer bottle and a rapidly dwindling mimosa in front of him. He wouldn't have been bad looking, Allison thought, if not for the spider veins that were already beginning on his face and the paunch he couldn't quite conceal under his casual blazer.

"So what do *you* do?" he asked her, draining his mimosa.

"I'm a teacher," Allison told him, hearing the primness in her voice.

"Yeah? Great," he said and swiveled his head, searching for a server to bring him another drink. "What grade?"

"Third."

"Nice." He waved his hand, trying to get somebody's attention. Nobody was that desperate for a mimosa, Allison thought at the time, no matter how unlubricated the social situation. "You teach around here?"

"In Carlsbad," Allison said. "Fairly close." But he wasn't listening to anything she said; he was too intent on finding someone to bring him another drink. His need infected Allison, making her tense and anxious. She too began scanning the busy restaurant for a waiter who could help them. "This sucks," the man said. "I don't know why they wanted to do this here. You can't get service to save your life in this place."

"It seems that way," Allison said mostly for her own benefit. And at that moment she decided she'd had enough. There was plenty to tell her mother about, including her dangerous drive in the pouring rain and her miserable alcoholic tablemate, and plenty of ammunition to make her mother feel guilty for even suggesting this debacle. She looked up, planning her exit, when she saw Joe for the first time, striding over to her end of the table, and Allison decided to stay put.

Much later, Joe told her that he'd been trying to keep his eye on the table because any party that large needed overseeing, but that he'd been so swamped with the rain, which made all the outdoor seating impossible, he hadn't gotten a chance to attend to them. And then he saw her and dropped everything. ("Literally," Joe said later. "I dropped the silverware and napkins I was holding and rushed over to you.")

What Allison remembered most vividly was the sense of relief she felt as Joe approached her. He was wearing a beautifully tailored blue suit, crisp white shirt, and a bright yellow tie that somehow managed to be both cheerful and stylish. He was broad-shouldered and olive-skinned (*manly,* Allison remembered thinking) and surrounded by an air of capability, as if he'd be able to resolve any problem no matter how large—or trivial. "How are you doing?" he'd asked, a question that could have been aimed at anyone at the table but was clearly intended for her. "What can I do for you?"

"You can get me another one of these to start," the man next to Allison answered, holding his empty champagne glass aloft. "I don't think we have a waiter here. I've been trying to get a drink for quite a while now. I know it's busy, but—"

"Of course, sir, right away," Joe said. His tone was conciliatory but not obsequious in any way. Smooth, Allison thought. "And for you, *signorina?* Have you had a chance to look at the menu? Perhaps I could make a suggestion?" His eyes were dark and twinkling, complicit. Allison felt he understood her predicament perfectly. She didn't belong with this party, his smiling confident expression told her, but he was very glad she had come.

"You looked so pretty," he told her the night they made love for the first time, "and so pissed off. I could tell you didn't belong in that ridiculous group."

"So you liked that I was mad?" she said, smiling.

"Well, that combined with your wet clothes. I could see every curve. It was very hot. You were the best thing the rain ever brought into that place."

Rain, Allison thought again. How she wished it would rain like that again.

But there was no hope of rain today and no chance of sleep until later. Reluctantly—almost resentfully—she pulled on a T-shirt and an old pair of yoga pants, twisted her hair into a loose ponytail, and opened her bedroom door. She was already in the hall, on the way to the bathroom to brush her teeth, when she heard the voices downstairs and stopped dead, suddenly terrified to see anyone other than the two people she lived with and couldn't avoid.

She could identify Diana's voice, usually husky and defiant, but now raised in girlish excitement. She was actually *giggling*. The other voice was familiar, but it took Allison a second to identify it as belonging to their neighbor Sam. Allison couldn't imagine what possible ruse Sam had found to come over to her house. At the best of times, there was little the two of them had in common. But Allison could hear her exclaiming and laughing along with Diana. Allison's underarms prickled with perspiration and her neck felt stiff.

Sam was probably here on some kind of fact-finding mission, just like every other busybody on this cul-de-sac. Well, Allison corrected herself, maybe not everyone. It was mostly Dorothy and Dick. But hadn't Jessalyn Martin come by at some point? Allison was hazy, but she was sure she'd heard Joe talking to her at the door. It was coming back to her now in wispy bits of memory, Joe saying something about hitting Jessalyn's car and having to exchange insurance information and Allison not being interested enough in that piece of news to bother registering it.

But it was Dorothy's snooping that concerned Allison. Those early days she'd come around with a seemingly endless supply of horrible instant cakes and offers of "help." Allison couldn't even pretend to be polite. It was so inappropriate to bring food in the first place, as if there'd been a death in the house and the Montanas were in need of pie and casseroles to sustain them. It was one thing, Allison thought, to walk to church with Dorothy on Sundays and chatter about inconsequential trivia like PTA troublemakers or the difficulty of growing wisteria, but they weren't *girlfriends* by any stretch. There was no way Allison would ever tell Dorothy—prissy, judgmental Dorothy—anything remotely private. Like, for example, how her husband had neglected to mention he had a child. A mixed-race child, at that. Dick was such a racist. Allison could easily imagine the conversations the Werners had been having since Diana started spending every day with Kevin and was sure that most of them ended with some kind of epithet. It didn't matter that Kevin was almost definitely taking drugs—maybe even dealing them—in Dick Werner's mind Diana would be the bad influence; Allison was sure of it. And who knew what went on in Dorothy's head? How was it possible for a woman to be so detached from what was going on inside her own house? Allison's throat constricted. She was no better than Dorothy. She'd been as blindsided by Diana's existence as anyone else on their street.

Allison heard a yelp of surprise coming from Diana followed by a chuckle from Sam. She needed to go downstairs, to investigate and head off this ill-timed visit, but she couldn't seem to move from her spot in the hall. She leaned against the wall, her forehead pressed against the cool plaster. She was glad Diana was spending all her time with Kevin, and she didn't care at all that Diana, young and pregnant as she was, might be smoking weed, popping pills, or screwing Kevin's teenage brains out. The truth was she was glad that someone else had to bear her burden. Let Dick and Dorothy worry about it—about both of them. Neither Kevin nor Diana were Allison's responsibility and she'd had no part in their making. There was a bitter burn inside Allison's chest. Heartburn in the most literal sense. Her own child would have been eight years old now, in third grade, maybe even in her own class. She pictured herself at the whiteboard at school, turning to look at her students and finding her own child in the front row. She—because Allison had always thought it would be a girl—would be blond and wear a white headband and shirts with Peter Pan collars. Allison stared at the internal image until her eyes burned with tears and she wanted to die. Then, having tortured herself enough to justify a very large, very cold drink—lemonade with vodka, she was thinking—Allison finally stood up straight and walked downstairs.

Making her way across the landing, Allison cursed the layout of her house, which forced her to walk through the dining room to get to the kitchen. Because the dining room was where Sam sat with Diana, the two of them looking for all the world like best girlfriends (no, Allison amended, not girlfriends, like *mother and daughter*), laughing and cooing over some fabric swatches spread out over the table. But no, that was wrong too, Allison thought as she got closer and the two of them raised their heads at the same time, sensing her presence. They weren't looking at fabric swatches at all. Those were baby clothes spread out on Allison's polished-oak dining room table. Little fluffy onesies in powder blue and lemon yellow, tiny moccasins, a miniature V-neck sweater in hunter green.

Allison opened her mouth to say something, but no words came. For a single spinning moment Allison wondered if she'd had some kind of stroke and been rendered mute. Diana looked at her accusingly, the corners of her full lips turning down and her eyes flashing sparks of antipathy. But Sam smiled.

"Hi, Allison. How are you doing?"

"How am I doing," Allison repeated thickly. She pointed at the table. "Are those baby clothes?"

Why were there baby clothes in her house?

Sam's smile faded, although she seemed to be making an effort to keep it plastered on her face.

"These? Yes, these are—well they *were* Connor's. They're all so cute and—I had so much fun shopping for them—he grew out of them so fast I don't think—there are a few things here he never even wore!"

"You brought those over here?" Allison asked stupidly.

"Um . . ." Sam shot a quick worried glance at Diana, who shrugged lazily, and then turned back to Allison with something like fear, or maybe worry, in her eyes. "Yes, Allison, I thought, since they're in such great shape—I mean they're hardly used at all—I thought maybe Diana could use them for . . . They're hardly used, Allison."

"Diana didn't tell you?" Allison asked. She tried to force lightness into her tone, but there was cold fear curling up at the base of her spine.

"Tell me what?"

"Diana, why don't you fill Sam in?"

But Diana said nothing. Her hands moved to her belly and her eyes threw flames at Allison. Sam's hands fluttered above a bright red Christmas suit, as if she was unsure whether to grab it or push it away.

"She's not keeping the baby," Allison said. "She's giving it up for adoption."

chapter 7

Sam stood at the kitchen cabinet where she and Gloria kept all their teas, debating what to offer Diana. There were so many here, she thought: medicinal-strength ginger tea and loose Darjeeling, mango-flavored and spicy, decaffeinated, extra strength, Irish Breakfast, white, green, jasmine, and oolong in boxes, bags, and sachets. They'd managed to accumulate quite a collection, so much in fact that it didn't all fit next to Gloria's assortment of Brazilian and Guatemalan shade-grown, fair-trade coffees. Sam didn't drink coffee at all, finding it emotionally exhausting to make sure that coffee met all the qualifications for sustainability and political correctness. She and Gloria had once been able to laugh about that kind of thing back when their kids were little and sweet and laughs were easier to come by. It was, Sam thought now, what had drawn them together in the first place.

She remembered the day they'd run into each other on the way down to school to pick up their boys from after-school care. They'd both been early and both had the same thought, which was to leave the boys a little longer and go get coffee at the Starbucks near the school. Sam ordered a chai latte and Gloria some huge, sweet coffee drink laden with whipped cream. Gloria insisted on paying, Sam remembered, in that smiling, pushy, but weirdly self-conscious way she had.

"Honey," Gloria had said, flicking a tan wrist heavy with gold bracelets, "you have no idea how much money I have access to. Let me spend some of it, please!"

"Really?" Sam said, inspecting her cup. "You should give some of it to the rain forest or the whales or something." When Gloria smiled a light turned on behind her eyes and her entire face became bright. Sam saw that transformation for the first time at Starbucks that day.

"You think so?" Gloria asked. "I give a lot, believe me. Wherever I can. Whenever my husband lets me. And to whatever needs saving. By the way, I think the whales are cool now, you know? They got saved already. You need to update your causes."

Then Sam herself had to smile. She'd known Gloria for almost a year at that point—since their boys had started kindergarten together—but this was the first time they'd had a conversation that didn't have to do with bouncy houses, who was bringing cupcakes for open house, or how to keep dog hair off the sofa. Sam found herself surprised by Gloria, whom she'd just assumed was another pretty, pampered, and self-absorbed suburban mommy, albeit one who always had a clever quip at the ready. But as soon as they started talking, Sam saw a woman much like herself: intelligent and devoted to her child but frustrated in her marriage and guilty about trading her independence for the comfort of a big house, a maid, and all the local organic produce she could eat.

"At least I don't have a nanny," Gloria said, "or I'd be a complete cliché. Besides, my mother would kill me. She'd never recover from such an insult."

"Do you have a pool boy, though?" Sam asked. "That's the real test, isn't it?"

Gloria raised a professionally and beautifully shaped eyebrow. "I have a pool," she said. "And there's an old guy who comes around once a week and drags a net through it. Does that count?" When Sam laughed, Gloria added, "That's Frank I'm talking about—my husband. He's the old guy who cleans my pool." The last sentence came out slowly, Gloria's voice lingering on the vowels, enunciating the consonants as if she were reading a line of poetry. There was sadness in it too, Sam felt, and maybe the slightest tinge of desperation.

That might have been the moment, Sam thought now, when she fell in love with Gloria. But it would be a long time before she—or Gloria—realized it. And by the time they did it was too late to stop the train wreck that had already been set in motion. Sam wondered what might have happened if she'd been her usual reserved self that day, if she hadn't allowed herself to sink into the warmth of that lovely afternoon with Gloria, the two of them staying much longer than they'd planned and then having to rush in the near dark to pick up Connor and Justin—their two little boys who were the last children left in the after-school day care class. What might have happened if their boys hadn't been standing there, their small backpacks at their feet and their shoes untied, identical looks of angry betrayal on their dirty faces?

"We're so sorry," they told the scowling girl who'd been forced to stay late. "We completely lost track of time." They'd exchanged a guilty look—Sam could still see it now—the first of many they would share. Would it have made a difference if Sam had recognized it then? Would she have been able to see all the loss? Because it was all gone—the houses, the pools, the maids. Frank and then Noah had taken everything. Even their children. Their precious, angry boys.

Sam blinked away the tears that had formed in her eyes and slammed the door of the tea cabinet. Tea was a stupid idea—it was way too hot. She'd make lemonade instead. She had some simple syrup in the fridge and there was a whole bag of lemons in the fruit bowl just waiting to be used. *When life gives you lemons,* Sam thought. "Great," she added out loud, "now I've turned into Pollyanna."

"Who's Pollyanna?"

Sam startled and turned. Diana was standing in the middle of the kitchen as if she'd just been beamed in. She was wearing an extra-large gray T-shirt, the collar gaping at her neck, stretchy black shorts, and dusty rubber flip-flops.

"Oh, hi!"

"Hey . . . Did I scare you? I'm sorry. I came in through the back door. . . . It was open. Is that okay? I'm sorry."

"Honey, don't worry," Sam said, "it's fine. Come sit down. I was just going to make you some lemonade. Do you like lemonade?" Sam laughed. "Do you *want* lemonade?"

"Sure," Diana said. "Thanks. Are you going to make it fresh?"

"That was the plan," Sam said.

"Cool." Diana smiled, showing off her lovely, straight white teeth. Sam wondered if she'd had braces or was just lucky. She was such a pretty girl with that smooth clear skin and long, thick, gorgeously curling hair cascading down her back. Her face was a little puffy now though, this late in her pregnancy, and when Sam glanced down she could see that Diana's ankles were swollen too, the skin stretching around her tattoos. Sam flushed with sudden concern and anger. Was anyone taking care of this girl?

"Come sit down," she said again, gesturing to the little round table and chairs they kept in the kitchen. "How are you doing, hon? Are you feeling okay?"

Diana's hands went instinctively to her huge belly, which Sam noticed was much lower than it had been the last time she'd seen Diana. *Any minute now,* Sam thought. She remembered the feeling vividly; how when you got toward the end, there was no space left anywhere—in your body or your mind—for anything but the formless life that had taken over your own. Heaviness and waiting, that was all.

"I'm all right," Diana said, pulling out a chair and sitting down much more gracefully than Sam would have thought possible. "Just, you know . . ." She patted her belly. "It's so big," she said. "I never would have thought it could get so big." Diana was still smiling, but Sam could see the strain around her eyes and in the dark half moons below them. She probably wasn't sleeping much. Sleeping was hard in the ninth month; there was just no way of getting comfortable. She pulled a few lemons out of the fruit bowl and started slicing.

"You must be due soon, right?"

"In one week exactly," Diana said. "But they say first babies come late, don't they?"

"Not always," Sam said. The first lemon was practically dry. It took all Sam's strength just to wring out a couple of tablespoons of juice. She picked up a second and tried again. "What does your doctor say?" When Diana didn't answer, Sam looked up sharply, stopping midsqueeze. "You do have a doctor, don't you?"

"I'm going . . ." Diana smoothed the big T-shirt over the beach-ball lump in her lap. "We checked out the hospital and everything," she said. "But I don't really have a regular doctor. Something about the insurance. It's my mom's coverage and over here—"

"But surely—" Sam stopped herself before she could say anything else. She didn't know how far she could go with Diana and she didn't want to push. It wasn't her business really, no matter how drawn she felt to this girl and her baby. And Allison was such a loose cannon lately, Sam didn't want to piss her off. As for Joe, Sam simply couldn't understand why he hadn't shown more backbone. She didn't know him well, it was true, but she'd always gotten the sense from him that he was a little more open, a little more *decent* than most of the people in this neighborhood. She was disappointed by his lack of caring or connection. All you had to do was look at Diana—Joe was there in every curve and angle of her face. How was it possible for him to ignore that? But then, Sam remembered, she'd been wrong about Noah too. If someone—*anyone*—had told her how nasty and vindictive he'd become after she moved in with Gloria, Sam would have laughed in disbelief. Maybe it was just that she knew nothing about men. For all of their carrying on about how they were essentially simple beings and it was women who were complicated, men were way more screwed up and emotionally convoluted than women.

"I mean," Sam said, taking care with her words, "you've had an exam recently? Even if—"

"It's fine," Diana interrupted.

"Okay," Sam said, although she suspected nothing was okay and was becoming desperate to try to remedy that situation. She was on the fourth lemon now and had barely a half a glass of juice. Well, that was going to have to be enough. She took the simple syrup out of the fridge and measured out a quarter cup, combined it with a half liter of Pellegrino, and stirred in the lemon juice. "I think," she said, "I even have a sprig of mint around here somewhere."

"So who's Pollyanna?" Diana asked as Sam rummaged through the crisper looking for the mint. "You were saying something about Pollyanna when I came in."

"Right, Pollyanna," Sam said, pulling out the wilted mint and searching for a usable sprig. "Poor Pollyanna got kind of a bad rap. It was a kid's book, written probably a hundred years ago about a girl—an orphan, I think—who plays this game where she finds the good in everything. She's an eternal optimist, even when bad things happen. She's always looking on the bright side even when she has an accident and becomes paralyzed."

"That would be seriously annoying," Diana said.

"Exactly," Sam said, tearing a mint leaf and stirring it into the glass of lemonade, "which is why *Pollyanna* has become a term for someone who's foolishly or blindly optimistic with no good reason." She handed the glass to Diana. "Here you go."

"So you were calling yourself Pollyanna?"

"Right before you came in, I was thinking . . ." Sam trailed off, remembering exactly what she'd been thinking about and seeing, once more, Gloria's face as it had been that long-ago day, all lit up from inside. "I was thinking about making you something to drink and I remembered that phrase 'when life gives you lemons, make lemonade,' which is probably one of the most Pollyannaish expressions there is."

"So what kind of lemons do you have in your life?" Diana asked. She took a long swig from the glass. "This is so good. Thanks."

"Well, everyone has lemons," Sam said, smiling, glad Diana looked relaxed, and happy she was enjoying the lemonade. Diana took another long sip and put the glass on the table. She wanted to say something, Sam could tell, but the words weren't coming easily. Sam waited and Diana rubbed at the condensation on the glass. The silence between them was weighted but not uncomfortable.

"I'm sorry I didn't tell you about the adoption before. You know, when you came over with the baby clothes. I should have said something. It was really nice of you to bring them over. They're really cute."

"Oh, honey, don't worry about that," Sam said and reached out to cover Diana's hand with her own. "It's totally fine. You didn't have to tell me anything. I should have asked. I mean, no, not asked, but—"

"I just didn't know Allison was going to be such a complete bitch about it," Diana said sharply. "She can't wait, you know. She's counting the fucking seconds until I'm gone."

"I'm sure that isn't true," Sam said and almost gagged at the insincerity of her words. Diana, frowning, could hear it too. Sam didn't want to lie to this girl or offer her useless nostrums. She needed someone she could trust, someone she could feel safe sharing her feelings with. "Okay," Sam said, "I'll agree with you that, from what I've seen, Allison doesn't seem to be managing things all that well."

Diana snorted. "You got *that* right."

"But," Sam continued, "maybe that's because she doesn't know what to do or say. She isn't a bad person. She teaches third grade. You know that, right? My son was in her class a couple of years ago. She was great with him—with all the kids."

"So what?" Diana spat. "My mother's a teacher too. It doesn't mean anything if you're great with other people's kids if you can't handle your own."

"I'm just saying, maybe Allison's confused and it's not coming out the right way."

"She's a bitch," Diana said. "She has been since the day I got here. I get that she's pissed off she never knew her husband had a kid, but it's not my fault Joe didn't tell her about me, is it?"

"No," Sam said, "but it's probably more complicated than that."

"You know," Diana said, shifting in her chair, "everyone always says that when old—" Diana caught herself and smiled quickly. "I mean, when *older* people behave badly. If you're, like, under twenty-five and you act like an asshole, it's because you're an asshole. If you're older than that, it's *complicated.*"

Sam had to laugh. There was more than a little truth to what Diana was saying, although her classification of anyone over the age of twenty-five as "older" made her feel ancient. "Okay, I'll give you that," she said. "But, even though it really isn't my place to say, I'd guess that there's a story behind Allison's actions—or, her feelings, I should say—that started being written long before you came along. It's just a pity. . . ."

"What?" Diana said. "What's a pity?"

"It's a pity that she can't talk to you about it."

"You mean it's a pity she can't act like a grown-up?"

"I didn't say that, Diana." Sam sighed. She'd said something so similar to Gloria just the other night when the two of them were having yet another argument. *Why can't you just grow up?* Sam couldn't believe she'd even said it. It was the first time she'd ever referenced the ten-year age difference between herself and Gloria. Before now, it hadn't made a difference, but these days that decade felt more like an entire generation.

"What I'm trying to say," Sam said, "is that it's difficult for some people to communicate how they're feeling. Like Allison. But it's a pity she can't get around that because you could probably really use someone on your side right now." Sam pursed her lips as if to keep back the words she was about to say. She shouldn't ask and she would probably regret it, but she was powerless to stop herself. "Diana, can I ask you . . . ? The adoption—was that your idea? I mean, have you been able to talk about it with anyone? Your mom?"

Diana turned her head so that Sam wouldn't see the tears welling in her eyes. "I'm done talking to my mother," she told Sam. "My mother kicked me out. I hate her." She swallowed hard and Sam could see her struggling mightily to keep from crying. Sam felt Diana's pain inside her own heart—so sharply she could feel her eyes sting and water. Because as much as she wanted to reach Diana, it was herself she wanted to help, to go back all those years ago to when she was the same frightened, angry girl about to make a decision she would regret for the rest of her life and stop her.

"She doesn't give a shit what happens to me," Diana said. "Why else would she let me come here?" She said "here" as if it were the bottom rung of a stepladder to hell.

"Maybe she felt you'd be protected here," Sam said, wondering why Diana used the phrase *let me come* instead of *sent me.*

"Protected from *what?*"

"From gossip?" Sam began and then realized she was in over her head. "The kids at school? Sometimes kids your age can be pretty cruel."

Diana gave Sam a look of genuine puzzlement. As she should, Sam thought, because who cared if a teenage girl came to school pregnant anymore? It was no longer the scarlet letter it had been for Sam. Now, when your abstinence-only education led to you getting knocked up you were actually lauded for "choosing life," even if the life you were sacrificing in the process was your own.

"No, that's not it," Diana said. "School would have been fine. And my mother never tried to protect me from shit. She just didn't want to be *embarrassed* by me. She didn't want to be reminded of the same mistake *she* made." Diana's tears fell, finally, big drops rolling down both cheeks. "Like I could have helped it. It wasn't my choice to be born. And this wasn't my choice either." She was weeping openly now, sobbing and hiccupping.

"What wasn't your choice, honey?" Sam asked very softly.

"N-noth . . ." Diana took a breath and wiped her cheeks with her hands. "Nothing," she said.

"You mean the adoption? You didn't choose the adoption?"

Diana shook her head, her long dark curls trailing across her shoulders. "It's the best thing to do to give her up," Diana said.

"Her?" Sam's throat tightened.

"It's a girl. I had an ultrasound and they told me. She's . . . It'll be better for her if I give her up." There was no conviction in her words at all, and Sam worried again that Diana was being pushed into a corner by the confused adults in her life who couldn't possibly understand. . . . There was Allison with no kids of her own and Joe who obviously hadn't wanted the one he'd made. The odds were not stacked in Diana's favor.

"Are you sure about that?" Sam said and again wondered if she was going too far. "I mean, are you sure you want to do that?"

Diana nodded.

"What about . . . Have you spoken with the . . . the father? I mean, sometimes there's a legal obligation to—"

"Forget it," Diana said, her voice suddenly hard and guarded. "He's got nothing to do with it." She took a long drink from her forgotten glass of lemonade, draining it. Sam wondered what the story was. A bad breakup? Some asshole kid who'd dumped her as soon as she told him she was pregnant? Or someone older—someone married? Or just a poor, sweet boy who loved her and didn't know what to do? But no, that was Sam's particular cross to bear. Because it wasn't just her own baby she'd given up, it was *his* too.

"It might seem that way now," Sam said, "but he might—"

"No," Diana said. "He won't."

"How can you be so sure?"

"Because he doesn't know."

"Maybe you should tell him."

"I can't."

"Why not?"

"I don't even know his name."

Sam tried to keep her face passive, but Diana saw it—that flicker of distaste—and seized on it. "You think I'm a whore, huh? So does my mother."

"No, no, not at all," Sam said. "I was your age once, you know," she added. "Hard as that might seem to believe. I'm not judging you."

"Yeah, you are," Diana said, drawing herself up and in, shielding herself behind toughness. "But whatever. You're probably right anyway. It was my fault. I should have known better."

The word *fault* triggered a rush of anger and recrimination in Sam. So much of her life, it seemed, had been about who was at fault and who should be punished. "What was your fault?" she said.

"I shouldn't even have gone to that party," Diana said.

"What party?" Sam asked.

"Just . . . it was a bunch of UNLV people. Like, sophomores and juniors, I think. My friend Sasha was supposed to meet me there and of course she never showed up. She's such a flake. I was the only high school kid there. I should have left. But I didn't. And I shouldn't have had anything to drink. But I did. My bad. All of it."

"So you—"

"I remember dancing with him. I told him I was eighteen, but I don't know if he believed that. I don't think he did. I remember he said my eyes were like dark suns. I thought that was so cool, you know? And then . . . I can't remember anything after that. I woke up in somebody's bedroom and I was . . . I could tell he . . ." Diana's face flushed. Her hands were fists in her lap. "Everyone was gone. It was the middle of the night. I had to find my jeans on the floor. It smelled so bad in there. And I left." She opened her hands, splaying them out on the table. "He didn't even take my shirt off," she said.

"Diana, that's—"

"My fault," Diana said, leveling a stare at Sam. "I told you."

"No," Sam said, "it's not your fault at all. You have to believe that.

Diana, that's—" Sam couldn't say it. The word was lodged like a bone in her throat. "Did you tell your mother about this?"

"I told you, my mother thinks I'm a slut. It wouldn't matter what I said, her mind was already made up. I wasn't supposed to be there anyway. That *is* my fault."

"But you have to tell someone, Diana."

"Why?" Diana said. "It's all done and finished and here we are."

"But—"

"Hey, it's all cool," Diana said, flicking some hair off her shoulders. "And I'm fine. It's all worked out." She pulled the T-shirt tighter over her belly. "One more week and then we'll . . . and then it'll be over." She leaned on the table and pulled herself up. "Hey, do you know what time it is?" she asked Sam. "I'm supposed to meet someone." Her demeanor had taken an abrupt turn. She squared her shoulders and hardened her mouth. The tears were gone and her eyes were dry and slightly suspicious. There was no overt hostility, but Diana's body language was eloquent in commanding that she be left alone. She was back to being the tough chick with an attitude Sam had met first; before she'd encountered the soft, frightened girl who'd been sitting opposite her only moments ago. Sam knew this was a defense mechanism, albeit a highly convincing one. It was difficult to tell who the real Diana was or if there even was a real Diana yet. She was so young; there hadn't been time for her to formulate what kind of person she would become. This steely exterior was a way of coping and now that Sam knew the circumstances of Diana's pregnancy, she wondered if there were other, more destructive ways she'd found to deal with everything that was happening to her. If she had to take a guess, Sam would put Kevin Werner (who was certainly the "someone" Diana was meeting) uppermost on that list.

"It's around noon," Sam said. "Who are you meeting?" Diana gave her head a little angry shake and Sam realized her mistake. "I mean," Sam said, "do you need a ride? I'm happy to take you wherever you need to go."

"Really?" Diana was laughing. "Why would you want to do that?"

"I'm flexible," Sam said. "It's one of the advantages of working at home. And I don't mind at all."

Diana pushed some stray hair out of her eyes and gave Sam a quizzical look. Then she shrugged as if she'd come to some sort of internal decision and said, "Thanks, but I'm just going next door."

"Kevin?"

"You got a problem with that too?" Diana's tone contained more frustration than anger, but Sam knew to tread carefully.

"Isn't he in school?" Sam asked and quickly cursed herself. What a stupid question.

"He gets out early today. I'm going over to help him with his homework." Diana winked, a bizarrely inappropriate gesture. "I forgot to tell you, I'm also a straight-A student in addition to being a slut. At least I was."

"So," Sam said, "there are people who have a problem with you helping him study?" They were playing some kind of verbal chess, all their words masking what they were really trying to tell each other, and Sam was rapidly losing her way.

"I'm pretty sure Kevin's parents think I'm a bad influence on their son," Diana snorted. "As if."

"What do you mean, 'as if'?" Sam said.

"I don't know if you know them very well," Diana said, "but those people are totally out of touch with reality. I'm, like, the least of their problems."

"Really?"

"Come on," Diana said. "No offense, but people around here are seriously fucked up. I mean, I've only been here since July and it's really obvious to me all the shit that's going on in this neighborhood. And I'm not even paying that much attention. As far as I can see people around here are a bunch of losers. But you all think you've got it going on. Well, maybe not you. Again, no offense."

"None taken," Sam said. "But what do you mean? What's going on?"

But Diana wasn't listening. She'd put her hands on her belly and was paying rapt attention to what was going on inside it. "She's moving around a lot today," Diana said. "It's like she can't wait to get out. I don't blame her. I don't want to be inside me either."

"Diana . . ."

"I gotta go. Thanks for the lemonade."

"Diana, you know you're welcome over here anytime. And if you want to talk about anything at all, you can. I understand what you're going through, I really do."

"Yeah, I know," Diana said, heading out of the kitchen, "you were young once." Sam followed her into the living room, a sense of helplessness growing with each step Diana took closer to the back door. But then Diana stopped and Sam saw her looking at a framed photograph on the wall. It was one of Sam's favorites, a candid snap she'd taken of Gloria a couple of years before when the two of them had taken their boys to the zoo. Gloria's hair was still long then, flowing down her back, glinting in the sunlight, and she'd raised a hand to clear it out of her eyes. Gloria was laughing. Happy.

"That's your girl, right?" Diana asked, pointing at the picture.

Sam felt her entire body go cold and the blood drain from her face. Was Diana talking about the baby Sam had given away? How could she have known about that?

"I'm sorry," Diana said. "Are you one of those . . . I mean, do you not like to be called *girl*?" Sam was still too stunned to talk. Her tongue felt thick. "This picture—it's your woman, right? I don't know her name. She's really pretty, but I like her better with long hair."

Sam had to swallow twice to get enough moisture in her throat to answer. "Gloria," she said finally. "You meant Gloria."

"Yeah, Gloria, whatever," Diana said and paused at the threshold of the door, one foot already outside. Those dusty, ragged flip-flops wouldn't last another week, Sam thought. "Listen, I don't care, okay?" Diana said at last. "I'm not like these other people. It's not, like, a big deal that you're with her. Girls get with other girls all the time, everyone knows that. I mean, it's cool that you're doing what you want to do. I don't know why it's such a big deal."

"Who?" Sam managed to say. "Who thinks it's a big deal?"

"You know," Diana said. "People."

"And what do people say?" Sam asked, but it was too late for an answer. Diana had slipped out as effortlessly as she'd come in and was already gliding across Sam's backyard on her way to the very people she'd just been talking about. "Diana!" she called out. The girl turned, almost in slow motion, her hair and body swaying. The sunlight hit her shoulders, giving her a golden glow. Sam was struck again by how very young and vulnerable she seemed.

"Come over anytime, okay?" Sam called out to her. "I mean that."

Diana smiled and gave Sam a quick nod. And then she was gone.

chapter 8

Joe hadn't intended it to happen. But then, who would have? Nobody planned these things.

He lay on his side, one arm growing numb under the weight of his own torso and one circled around her rib cage. His face was pressed into the soft flesh of her breast and his eyes were closed. Her skin smelled of sex and peach-scented lotion. His heart was still thumping; vibrating through his body with every beat, but his breath came slow and even. He was deep inside himself, in that place of senseless satisfaction, holding on for as long as he could before the rest of it—words, guilt, the reassembling of the future—came crashing in. He nestled into the feeling, savoring it, and watched as a series of stop-action still frames of the immediate past played out in delicious succession behind his closed lids.

The first was Jessalyn beckoning, her short red skirt in high contrast with the white bedding and the tan of her thighs. She moved her hand in a half wave—a come-hither motion that had a snake charmer's pull. There was the turned-up corner of her lacquered mouth, the same color as her skirt. Not a smile exactly but not a sneer. A little Mona Lisa twist for his pleasure.

Then the first full physical contact; their two bodies crushed together

hard in that wave of need. The clothes shed somehow. Her fingers on but-
tons and zippers. Her hands everywhere. It was Jessalyn who had stripped
them both bare. Joe hadn't done anything himself. They were clothed, then
naked. It was effortless and so fast he could barely remember it happening.
Joe's brain moved on to the next frame: the curve of her hip, the give of her
body as he pressed himself into it, and her warm breath in his ear. The
picture scrambled and sleep tugged at him, pulling him into sated blackness. Joe felt himself giving way. And then Jessalyn moved, her leg peeling
away from his and creating a cold spot where their bodies had been joined.
He felt the tension in her body now—she was ready to get up, change the
venue—and just like that Joe was wide awake and returned unceremoni-
ously to his senses. The contours of the room—soft and dreamlike only
moments before—came into sharp hard focus as Joe cleared his throat and
raised himself. Jessalyn smiled at him, and something about the smile
caught Joe by unpleasant surprise. It took him a second to identify what it
was that was troubling him.

The smile was . . . *polite*.

It was the kind of smile a person gave you when you stood on line
together at Starbucks or caught each other's eyes on a train, an acknowledgment of the other's existence and a gesture of wordless, if bland, goodwill.
It was not the sort of smile one received or gave after fierce, sweaty, illicit
sex. Joe felt the slightest tremor at the base of his spine. He looked away,
blinked hard, and turned back to her. Now there was no smile, just a look
of *wantonness* and something else in her expression that Joe took for satisfaction. She licked her smudged lips and smoothed the hair out of her
eyes.

"Hey," she said. "You okay?"

It struck Joe as an odd question, but it didn't worry him. Not like the
shadow of that strange smile. She was holding herself still as if she was
waiting for some kind of signal from him that she could get up, or get
dressed, or maybe . . . maybe she wanted more. He ran his hand up the
length of her thigh, stopping just short of the professionally waxed *V* be-

tween her legs and letting his fingers linger there. If only he could stay there, he thought. Just *there*. Forever.

"I'm great," he said. "I mean, really great."

"Good," she said and grabbed his hand, lacing her fingers into his and then, miraculously, guiding those fingers home. "For a minute there you looked kind of worried." She was talking, Joe thought, talking and rubbing and now making little *mmm* noises of satisfaction. He was acting in his own porno and this was the part, he thought, where the couple did it again. He lunged, his mouth hungry, but she laughed.

"Baby," she said. "You think we have time?"

Joe didn't know if it was because she used the term *baby*, which nobody had ever called him before and which rang loud and wrong in his ear, but something about her words stopped him.

"No," he said. "And we shouldn't. I mean . . ."

"I know," she said and instantly the look of desire on her face changed to one of concern. *Polite* concern. Joe thought again about how he hadn't planned any of this, but now he wondered if perhaps Jessalyn had. He remembered the moment he'd gotten out of his car that Sunday afternoon after he'd backed into her as she was coming out of her driveway. Had she known it then? Had she seen the two of them here on her tangled sheets on another hot Sunday afternoon no more than a few weeks later? Had *he*?

No, he hadn't. Not even when he'd gone over to see her with his insurance information soon after their fender bender. Nor when he'd chatted her up at the block party. It hadn't occurred to him then that there would ever be more than anything between the two of them other than flirting (had it?). Even later, when he'd dropped by again to give her the rest of the insurance documentation, it hadn't been for anything more than a bit of company—a bit of attention—just a reason to get away from the crushing female oppression in his own house. And how could he be blamed for that? Because there was nothing Joe could do or say or *be* to either his wife or his daughter that would remove him from the rank of perpetual asshole, and it had been that way from the moment Diana had arrived.

He ran his hands through his hair and moved to the edge of the bed. He was light-headed—almost dizzy. And then the guilt hit hard and suddenly. He could see Allison in his mind's eye, her face aging with submerged anger, her eyes filled with constant accusation. Her progression from quiet hurt to silent scorn had been so quick. He'd tried talking to her, tried leaving her alone. He'd tried being angry—the best defense being a good offense—but that hadn't worked either. He'd even floated the idea of going to see a marriage counselor, although the very thought of it gave him indigestion. But Allison had shut him down there too. "What would be the point?" she'd asked him. "Why should we share our dirty laundry with someone else?"

"What is it about our laundry that's so dirty, Allison?" he'd asked. "Can you even tell me?"

"I think you know the answer to that question, Joe."

"I'd like to hear your version. That's why I'm asking."

Allison didn't bother to answer that one in words. She lifted the glass to her lips and that was response enough. At least she'd laid off the booze a little the last couple of weeks, saving her slide into drunkenness until after 5:00 PM. He supposed there was some small mercy in that. And at least she was a quiet drunk. Of course, it didn't make up for the fact that she'd taken a leave from work for no good reason. Exactly the wrong time, Joe thought, to be taking time off, because they needed that second income. It was her way, Joe supposed, of making sure that neither Diana nor her baby stayed with them one second longer than necessary. Of course, he'd just let Allison do it, let her put in for a leave from teaching with hardly an argument. She'd counted on that, Joe realized, sure that he'd be too guilty to protest. Well, now he was.

"You want a beer or something?" Jessalyn was standing over him in her bra and skirt, sliding her feet into her high-heeled mules. How had she managed to get dressed that quickly? Joe had the sudden paranoid thought that Allison had set this whole thing up. When was the last time she'd gone out on a Sunday? Certainly not since Diana had been living with them.

But today of all days she was dressed before noon, relatively sober, and headed out "shopping," not to return until "dinnertime." He hadn't thought about it too much then, except maybe to allow himself the faintest glimmer of hope that she was going to pull herself together, but now he wondered if it was to purposely leave him alone so that he'd go over to Jessalyn's house as soon as Diana lugged herself over to the Werners' (as regular an event as the sunrise). And that was exactly what he had done. And maybe Allison was back already and waiting for him to come home coated with the unmistakable smell of sex, which could penetrate even the strongest of vodka fumes so that she could pound the final nail into the coffin that housed their dead marriage.

But no, that was ridiculous. He hadn't been here that long and he would have heard Allison's car if she'd come home. It wasn't as if the house were that far away. He was overreacting. But it was also the beginning of what Joe knew would turn into the long slow burn of panicky guilt.

"I'm okay, thanks," he said, finally pulling himself up and picking up his clothes, which were not in a pile on the floor as he would have thought, but semifolded and draped over the arm of the white overstuffed chair in Jessalyn's bedroom. "I should probably get home."

"You sure?" She smiled, brilliant and sweet, and rubbed his back a little as he stepped into his shorts. She was stunning, Joe thought, and not nearly as dumb or flighty as she made herself out to be. She grazed his lips with hers—not really a kiss, but more than enough to get him aroused all over again. "Seems like you could use it," she said.

"I probably could," Joe said. *Because it takes balls to fool around with a woman who lives on your own street,* he added silently. *Definitely enough to make a person thirsty.* "I'm going to go, Jessalyn," he said.

"Hey," she said, running her hand up his arm and squeezing his shoulder, "call me Jess, would you? Jessalyn feels so formal, you know?"

"Okay."

Jessalyn gave out a little sigh. She looked confused or undecided. Joe couldn't tell which and he suspected she didn't know either. It was another slightly off expression to match the polite smile as if she felt the need to display the appropriate emotion at the appropriate time. He couldn't shake the feeling that everything about her was just a little bit staged or manufactured as if there was always a camera rolling to catch her reactions. But maybe he was just too old. At forty-eight he had missed growing up in a reality-show culture where people were always the stars of their own shows and every stupid thought and action was considered worthy of an audience. Jessalyn—only in her twenties—had even been on one of those shows. For a second it made the age gap between them seem like a canyon. But then Joe decided it actually made her more endearing. That don't-know-any-better narcissism gave her a weird kind of innocence and he found it very appealing.

"Look, Joe," she said, "I don't know what this is, but . . ." She sighed again—a little puff of air between them. "I know you're not the kind of guy who just . . ."

"We don't have to talk about this," he said, and then laughed in spite of himself. "At least, not yet."

"I just wanted you to know that I'm okay with, you know, whatever you want to do."

"What do you mean, Jess?"

"I mean, you lead, Joe. You've got . . . I know what you've got, is what I'm saying."

She was looking at him not politely now, but with real understanding and sympathy. He hadn't noticed before now just how blue her eyes were. Or how lovely. And then he thought he could fall in love with this girl if he let himself. It wasn't an unpleasant notion. Joe knew he was on a precipice. He had a glimpse—fleeting but unmistakable—of what was in store: furtive meetings, jealousies, a great deal of sex, whispered endearments, maybe even love. If Joe did nothing, if he just let it happen, it would become a runaway train and he would be powerless to do anything but just let it run right over him.

"Thank you, Jess," he said. "I mean it."

"You're okay, then?"

"Of course I'm okay."

She took his hand and led him out of the bedroom, down the hall, and to the top of the stairs. It occurred to him for the first time that Jessalyn's bedroom—or at least the room they'd just been in—was not the master bedroom. All the houses on the street had the same basic floor plan, Joe knew, and when she'd taken him upstairs earlier he'd had a disconcerting moment when he felt as if he was heading to the bedroom in his own house. All of that had vanished the minute she'd pulled him past the master bedroom and into the smaller one at the end of the hall. But now he wondered why she hadn't used the larger room.

"Do you have an office here?" he asked her. "I didn't think you worked at home."

Jessalyn bristled. "I don't," she said quickly. "Or, I guess, sometimes I do have f-friends come over for, you know, like . . . facials? Or, um, waxings?" She turned to him, her face flushed. "I'm not really supposed to do that at home," she said. "Well, I mean, I am, I have a license and everything, but I'm not supposed to use the products. . . . I'm an aesthetician. I told you that, right? Anyway, why do you ask?"

"I just . . . no reason. I was just wondering about . . . the other bedroom. It's bigger, isn't it?"

Jessalyn's blue eyes grew icy and hard, and for a moment she looked much older than she was. "I know what people say about me on this street, Joe. I'm not an idiot."

"What?" Joe was genuinely baffled. *Now* what had he done? "I never said you were an idiot, Jess."

She looked away from him. He could see the muscles of her jaw working, the long fair line of her neck, the soft blond hair caught behind her ear. "I'm sorry," she said. "Of course you didn't." She kissed him. "Go ahead," she said. "I just have to visit the . . . restroom. I'll be down in a minute."

"No problem," Joe said. "I have to get back. I'll just let myself out, okay?"

"Okay, Joe." She stood there for a moment, her head tilted slightly to one side, and then turned around and disappeared into the bathroom.

Joe's paranoia returned in a sweaty rush. Now he *had* to get out of her house and back to his own as quickly and as invisibly as possible. He checked his clothing for stray strands of blond hair, brushing imaginary evidence off his shoulders. His hands needed washing. Everything needed washing. He jogged down the stairs, his to-do list for the rest of the day crystallizing into one item: a hot shower. So intent was he on closing the distance between himself and his own bathroom that he kept his head down as he shut her front door and strode back to his house. He didn't look up in fact until it was almost too late to avoid plowing into Diana, who was standing—a pregnant stone statue—in the middle of their driveway.

Joe felt every second of his life compressed into the look that passed between them. Every mistake he'd ever made—every small wrong he'd ever committed—was reflected in the dark glass of her eyes. Perspiration crawled down his back.

He couldn't look away from her and he couldn't speak.

"I need a ride to the hospital," she said. "I think I'm in labor."

october 2007

chapter 9

Dorothy sat with her right leg over her left and her hands in her lap. But then, worried that this pose might look too casual and not anxious or pained enough, she uncrossed her legs and rested her hands on her knees. She furrowed her brow and squinted against the fluorescent light in the waiting room. And then, for good measure, she rubbed her eyes, her temples, and the back of her neck. She stole a glance to see if either of the girls at the reception desk was watching her, but one was busy with the headset blinking at her ear and the other was talking to an elderly woman about the best time to schedule a flu shot.

Dorothy wondered how long she would have to wait. This had been a sick call, not a regularly scheduled visit, and sometimes the wait times varied depending on where you were in the queue or how sick you were. But Dorothy was sure that she'd managed to convey an impressive constellation of symptoms when she'd called reception earlier. She'd fallen, she explained, and had twisted something in her back. And when she'd landed, she thought she'd heard a kind of pop. It was silly; she never should have been on the ladder in the first place because she'd been having dizzy spells from her sinuses, which had also been flaring up. It had really hurt her at the time, but she hadn't done anything about it, hoping it would just go away.

But now she was having terrible back pain and headaches as well. Also, she was having trouble sleeping, probably from the pain. Anyway, she thought it best if she came to see Dr. Smithfield at this point: Did the doctor have any openings today? The receptionist told Dorothy that Dr. Smithfield was on vacation, but that Dr. Fakoor had an opening at 3:00 PM if Dorothy wanted to come in then. If it had been any other time, any other circumstance, Dorothy would have waited rather than see a doctor with a name like Fakoor. But these were extraordinary circumstances and Dorothy was forced to go outside her comfort zone. She thanked the receptionist and took the appointment without even asking if Dr. Fakoor was male or female.

There were only three other people in the waiting room, a man and two women, and none of them seemed visibly ill. Dorothy tried to observe them without making eye contact but it was difficult. Nobody, it seemed, was interested in reading magazines today. She just wanted to get through this as quickly as possible, obtain a prescription or hopefully two, and get home undetected. Not that home would offer any peace—home was the reason she was here today, after all—but at least it offered familiarity. Dorothy's things were at home: her casserole dishes, her gardening tools, her photo albums—items she could look at and touch and reassure herself that the external structure of her life was still firmly in place. It felt strange to even think it, but these days Dorothy had greater faith in such inanimate objects than in people. Objects—things like dishwashers, cars, and televisions that one counted on to get one through the day—sometimes didn't work correctly and sometimes they just broke, but they never disappointed you or, worse, betrayed your trust in who they were. And in this case she was thinking about Kevin, a person who had emerged from her own body and yet might as well have come directly from Mars for all he acknowledged that and for all she knew him.

But Dorothy had known him once. She was sure of that.

Kevin had been a very sensitive baby, sweet but never completely happy. The littlest things could make him cry. It began when he was an infant when merely substituting squash for bananas was enough to set him off weeping like his small world was coming to an end. Later, if he couldn't find the right piece for a puzzle or figure out how to keep his toy trains on their tracks, his eyes would fill with frustrated tears and he'd start bawling. He never hurled his toys, Dorothy remembered, or threw tantrums in an attempt to destroy the things that were causing him grief, but he was constantly—bitterly—disappointed when they did. When he started school, friends were difficult for him too. The loyalty he expected from his fellow kindergartners involved allegiance to him above all else..Kevin expected his friends to sit with him at lunchtime and play the games that he wanted to play during recess. He directed all the activities during playdates, creating his own rules and giving specific directions as to how his toys were to be handled. Games were also a problem, especially at school. "Kevin gets very upset if he doesn't win," Dorothy heard from more than one teacher. "Perhaps you could practice some of these games at home so he can improve those social skills."

"But who doesn't want to win?" That was always Dick's response when Dorothy told him (because most often, Dorothy attended those parent-teacher conferences alone). "If he didn't want to win, he'd be a quitter or a pussy. I'd be more concerned if he *didn't* get upset." Dick's biggest fear, of course, was that Kevin would turn out to be a pussy. He didn't buy into Dorothy's theory that Kevin was just a little too sensitive and would grow out of it. Sensitive equaled queer and Dick wouldn't have any part of that.

Response and comfort fell to Dorothy, and for a long time, Kevin did come to her with his woes. The two of them forged a sort of alliance and an unspoken understanding about when it was all right to cry (in front of Dorothy if the two of them were alone) and when it wasn't (in front of Dick, ever).

Dorothy couldn't remember exactly when Kevin had stopped reacting to his hurts by turning on the waterworks, but she knew it was later than even she would have liked. Then there came a point when he stopped talking to her at all. He must have been about twelve or thirteen, Dorothy guessed, when all he did when he came home from school was head straight to his room. And that, Dorothy realized, was where he had been until now.

Dick hadn't made much of an effort to disguise his disappointment with how Kevin was turning out. When Kevin was born, Dick had so hoped his son would play a sport—any sport—and become a champion. Dick tried everything from soccer to Pee Wee football but nothing took. Kevin hated all of it and never kept that a secret. When Dick insisted that he give it more time, Kevin made sure that he got injured every time he played. After a broken collarbone and ankle, a dislocated shoulder, and two concussions, it was evident that it was time to ease off or risk Kevin doing permanent damage to his body. Dorothy didn't think Dick ever really forgave Kevin for that, although he'd never admit it. Still, it might not have been so bad if Kevin had shown an aptitude for anything. But he had never been a scholar and sometime around middle school his grades went from mediocre to bad. Dorothy hadn't seen a report card for a while, but she suspected that he was barely passing his classes. He didn't even show an interest in driving. That might have been the last straw for Dick, Dorothy thought. Aside from sports, driving, preferably fast cars, was probably Dick's main indicator of maleness. What red-blooded man or boy didn't want to get behind the wheel and floor it as soon as he was able?

At least Kevin was attracted to girls—Dick managed to ascertain that much from his limited heart-to-heart talks with his son. And when it seemed Kevin, who had remained girlfriend-less for his entire adolescence so far, was lacking interest in that area, Dorothy had done her duty by both her husband and her son and told Dick about the random bits of strictly heterosexual pornography that she turned up in Kevin's room from time to time. She found it revolting, of course, but knew it was important that he had it. And so she never said anything about it to Kevin and only faintly protested to Dick—just enough so that he'd feel reassured.

Well, no worry about that now, was there? Kevin had certainly convinced them both of his attraction to girls. It was why Dorothy was sitting
in the waiting room right now, prepared to try to convince some Arab doctor that she needed something for the pain. Because suddenly, out of the
clear blue sky and with such a wealth of others to choose from, her oversen-
sitive, underachieving son had managed to fall helplessly in love (or whatever he was confusing with love) with an uppity pregnant girl who had no
business even being in the neighborhood in the first place. What's more,
that girl had managed to persuade her son to take on a baby that he wasn't
even responsible for. And all of this at *seventeen*.

Dorothy remembered thinking that Diana had blown in on an ill
wind, creating a general feeling of uneasiness for everyone. It couldn't have
been more than a month ago that Diana stood in her kitchen with that
disrespectful look on her face and those nasty tattoos on her legs. Dorothy
had just assumed she was an unpleasant but temporary distraction for
Kevin that would disappear as soon as she had that baby and went back to
where she came from. Now vague unpleasantness would be a welcome relief. Dorothy wished she could go back to that moment in her kitchen
when she had a chance to change the future, when she could have gotten
rid of that girl before it was too late. She wasn't sure exactly what she would
have said or done, but she was resourceful. People never gave Dorothy the
credit she was due as far as that went. If people knew . . .

Well, at any rate, she would have found a way to make sure that girl
never set foot in their house again. Doing so would have been a blessing for
everyone, *including* Joe and Allison. Kevin would have been furious, of
course, but what boy his age wasn't furious at his parents? He would have
gotten over it in time anyway and they all could have gone on with their
lives. Instead there was this dreadful mess and Dorothy's family—Dorothy
herself—was in the center of it. No, that wasn't exactly right. There was a
baby at the center of it. A baby who was born innocent and who deserved
a chance at a decent life, but also a baby who was not Dorothy's and who

was certainly, certainly not Kevin's. Out of everything that happened in the last few weeks, Kevin's sudden grab at fatherhood was perhaps the most surprising to Dorothy. What had that girl done to him or *for* him to render him quite so senseless?

But Dorothy already knew the answer to that question: It was the same thing Diana had done to get herself pregnant in the first place.

Disgusting. It was all so disgusting.

A nurse wearing lavender scrubs and staring at a clipboard appeared from the hallway. "Sarah Johnson?" she said, without looking up. The nurse's voice sliced through Dorothy. Why was she speaking so loudly? There were only four of them sitting here—was there really a need to broadcast the first and last name? Dorothy hoped this wasn't the same nurse who would be calling her in. She couldn't stand to hear her full name called out like that, even if it wasn't the name she was born with. The nurse and patient disappeared into the hallway and Dorothy searched for a place to rest her gaze. She didn't want to be caught looking at anyone, but she didn't want to seem as if she was staring into space either.

Sometimes it was so difficult just to sit somewhere. Dorothy's head was starting to throb but she didn't mind—her description of the pain would be that much more authentic. And if Dick found out that she'd come here today (and there was no reason he should, because Dorothy was paying for this visit in cash and no record of it would show up on insurance statements), she'd have a legitimate reason. Not that Dick would be likely to pay attention to such a thing now that he had so much else to be upset about. Dorothy shut her eyes for a moment as if that would block out the memory that came rushing to her now.

They were eating dinner. Dorothy had made shepherd's pie, one of Dick's favorites. She usually waited until the temperature dipped to make this dish, but it seemed it was never going to cool off this year—they were already into October and it still felt like the middle of summer. So instead of her usual baked green bean side dish, Dorothy prepared a cold salad to go with the pie, iceberg lettuce and tomatoes tossed with a little ranch dressing. They were enjoying their meal with a nice chardonnay Dorothy had picked up on sale at Vons. They rarely had wine with dinner, and Dorothy wondered now if she'd had some kind of sixth sense about that night without even knowing it because she'd also taken special care with the table, setting it with the good china and using cloth napkins instead of paper. Her efforts did seem to have a positive effect. Dick was in a relatively good mood and for a change they were having a pleasant conversation that didn't have anything to do with money or Kevin or what needed to be done around the house. Dick asked her if she'd done something different with the shepherd's pie because it tasted better than usual and Dorothy, pleased that he'd noticed, told him that she'd used a little of the chardonnay in the pan when she cooked the meat. Then he asked her if she'd noticed that FOR SALE sign hanging off the Suns' mailbox, and Dorothy said she had and that she'd been wondering about it. Dick said that they'd never get rid of it for what they paid—not in this market.

"You should go over there," Dick said. "See what they're asking."

"I can't just knock on the door and ask them how much they want for their house, Dick."

"Why not?"

Dorothy hesitated, trying to think of why, in fact, she didn't feel she could go across the street and ask Mrs. Sun about the price of her house, and in that moment Dick's attention shifted abruptly—back to the one thing that constantly chafed at him, that perpetual rock in his shoe.

"Where's Kevin?" he asked.

Dorothy considered lying. She could have told Dick that he was at a friend's house or had gone to a movie. She might even have gotten away with telling him that Kevin was in his room. He might not have checked, might not have cared that Kevin wasn't eating dinner with them, especially because Kevin had been skipping a good percentage of meals at the table anyway. But she wasn't fast enough, either for a lie or the truth.

"Is he over at Joe's with that girl? Goddamn it, Dorothy."

"I don't know if he's over there, Dick."

"Well, where the hell else would he be? Goddamn *Joe's* never there. The man can't control his house at all so he just takes off. When's the last time you saw him around here taking care of his business?"

"I don't know. Joe does work unusual hours at the restaurant so he's not here in the evening. I do know that."

"Bullshit. He's hiding or running away and leaving other people to clean up his mess. And Kevin has to be right there in the middle of it." He paused, his mouth twitching around a thought. "Hasn't she had that baby yet?"

"You know she had the baby, Dick. Last week."

"And how would I know that, Dorothy?"

"Because I told you. We had that conversation."

Dick had put down his fork and knife by then and pushed his plate forward. There were beads of ranch dressing caught in the hairs of his mustache and Dorothy wondered why he hadn't noticed, hadn't wiped his face. Usually he was so fastidious about that kind of thing. The tension gathered fast then, making the air around the table thick and heavy like the still before a tornado or the painless pressure before the onslaught of a migraine.

"Maybe you could refresh my memory," he said, "because I don't seem to have any recollection of that conversation."

"She had a girl," Dorothy said, and stopped. What other information could he need beyond that?

"And?"

"And nothing. She had the baby and now she's—*they* are home."

"But they aren't *home,* Dorothy. They're still here. Why are they still here?"

"I don't know why you think I'd know, Dick. It's not like I talk to Allison anymore."

But, of course, Dorothy did know. She knew that somewhere between the onset of Diana's labor and her release from the hospital, it had all gone wrong. Instead of turning the baby over to the family who had meant to adopt her, Diana had done a complete about-face and brought the baby back to Fuller Court. And Dorothy suspected that her own son had something to do with that decision.

Dick stood up, knocking into the table. Their wineglasses shivered with the impact and the silverware rattled on their plates. Dorothy lunged, anticipating the sound of broken glass, but nothing fell.

"It's enough, Dorothy," he said. "We should have put a stop to this already. Look what happens when you let things go. Give an inch and they'll take a mile, isn't that right?"

"What do you mean, Dick?" Dorothy had started feeling queasy, anxiety churning her stomach. Dick was on the verge of a full-blown rant, his anger and frustration with his own life turning outward to find fault with everything in the world at large. He'd never been the most open man, but she'd always accepted his strong beliefs, even taken them for a sign of inner strength. More and more lately, though, that strength seemed like aggression and utter inflexibility. There had once been a time when she'd been able to soften him, to present another point of view without challenging him, but she'd lost that skill set and the will to relearn it.

"This used to be a decent neighborhood," he said, his voice rising. "People around here used to have some *values,* Dorothy. It wasn't that long ago that people didn't even advertise living together if they weren't married. You know, I remember that and I'm not even that old. Now you can do any perverted thing you want way out in the open without any fear. You know why, Dorothy? Because the goddamn liberals are running everything. Everyone's got to have their goddamn *civil rights.* But what about mine? What about my right to raise my own kid in an unpolluted atmosphere—"

"Dick, I don't think—"

"No, you don't, Dorothy, and that's part of the problem. If you hadn't been so soft on him all the time—"

"You're his father!"

"That's right. I'm his goddamned father and I'm putting an end to this now. I'm going over there."

"Dick, wait."

"Why?"

"What are you going to do?"

"He needs to get his ass back home. I'm going to go get him."

Dorothy wondered now if it would have made a difference if she hadn't followed Dick to the Montanas' house, if the outcome might have been better had she not been there to witness it, or if it might have gotten even worse if she'd decided to stay there at her dining room table, staring at the remains of their ruined dinner. In the end, it probably didn't matter because it wasn't as if her presence had made much of an impact to begin with.

Dick had at least a two-minute lead on her because she'd stopped to get her keys, make sure the back door was shut, and lock the front door behind her. By the time she'd done all of that, he was a good way down the street. Outside it was warm and dry. The tall eucalyptus and palms were outlined against the sky, swaying very slightly. The air had a tang of wood smoke and lemony tree bark, and it was so still that she could hear Dick clear his throat as he passed Sam and Gloria's house on his way to the Montanas. The only other sound was the regular thunk of a basketball as it hit the backboard because the Sun boy was outside too, practicing his shots in the gathering dark. He looked at her briefly as she passed by and stopped for a moment.

"Hi, Mrs. Werner."

"Oh, hi . . ." Dorothy fumbled. She didn't know his name and couldn't just call him by his last name. "Hi," she said again and quickened her pace.

Joe and Allison's door was unlocked when she got there and Dick was already inside. Dorothy fought an onslaught of sensory information the moment she crossed the foyer into the dining room, a path identical to the one in her own house. The first thing to hit her was that newborn smell of diapers, milk, and birth suddenly so familiar to Dorothy despite the many years since she'd had her own child. Then there was the mess, a mad jumble of clothes and empty packages, half-filled coffee cups, and unopened mail. It looked as if the floor hadn't seen a mop in months, and Dorothy didn't even want to think how long it had been since anyone had dusted the place. There was an aura of chaos and neglect in the house that seemed somehow intentional. The people in the room seemed messy too—all standing at odd angles to one another, waving their arms, their faces in disarray. There was Allison, her hair stringy and dirty like Dorothy had never seen it before, wearing old sweatpants and a stained T-shirt without—and Dorothy couldn't believe she was seeing this—*a bra*. Joe, who was in fact here in his own house and not working, was standing very close to Dick, his face flushed and angry. Behind all of them, on the edge of the darkened living room, stood Diana clutching a pink bundle to her chest and Kevin right there next to her. Dorothy wondered why she couldn't hear the baby making any noise. But then, as if someone had unmuted the sound in the room, noise came rushing in and Dorothy had to struggle to separate it all and put it in some kind of order.

Joe was barking something at Dick, and Dick was responding in kind. Allison had raised her voice as well, something about this being her house and people needing to leave. The baby was crying—a thin, high-pitched wail winding itself around everything else. Finally, as Dorothy stood there like a holograph projected into a room full of people, the words she was hearing began making sense.

"What difference should it make to you, Dick?" Joe was shouting. "How the hell does it affect your life in any way?"

"When you let that girl run around with no supervision—and I don't care how you were raised, Joe, but that's not the way it works in my house!"

"Are you fucking kidding me?" Joe raised his hands, palms up, a bitter smile twisting his face. "You want to talk about a lack of supervision? Do you know what your own kid is into, Dick? If anything—"

"If you're going to yell, could you do it somewhere else?" Allison interjected. "This is my house, after all."

"—I should be the one who's pissed off."

"What's that supposed to mean?"

"My God, you can't be serious. You don't know how heavily your own kid's into drugs? Look at him!"

"What the hell are you talking about, Joe?"

"You should leave, Dick," Allison said loudly but without anger.

"Do you know she was high when I took her to the hospital?" Joe gestured angrily toward Diana. "She reeked of pot smoke. I had to make her go change her clothes. And who was she with? *Your fucking kid!*"

"Hey, everybody shut up!" That was Kevin. He'd stepped forward from the dark edges of the living room and positioned himself at the foot of the staircase in a neat, almost military triangulation with everyone else in the room. "You all need to hear something."

"Kevin—" Dick warned.

"No, listen to me," Kevin said. Dorothy noticed for the first time how tall her son had become. Of course she'd known his height, but she hadn't realized what it meant in relation to other people. He had both his father and Joe by several inches. But standing there, preparing to deliver his announcement, he seemed smaller and slighter than both men. His face was splotchy and dotted with acne. He looked like what he was—a boy. Dorothy wanted to say something that would soothe him, make him stop whatever he was going to say, but at that moment she had no body, no mouth, and no words.

"Diana . . ." Kevin began again. He looked over at her, still standing in the shadows, swaying back and forth with that squalling baby. "Me and Diana have been together for a while now," he said. "She's a beautiful person and we love each other. We want to be together and we're going to get married."

"Oh Jesus, Kevin, don't be ridiculous," Allison said. Dorothy's eyes widened. She didn't know what surprised her more, the alcohol she could hear in Allison's voice or her casual blasphemy.

"No, this is real." There was something in his voice that worried Dorothy although she couldn't identify it. It sounded like a buzz or a hum, some kind of weird vibration distorting his words ever so slightly. She thought about what Joe had said about drugs and felt panic clutch at her throat. "This baby needs a father and I am going to be one for her."

"Kevin, shut up," Dick said. Dorothy thought she'd never heard him sound quite so disgusted.

"The baby doesn't need *you* for a father, Kevin—it needs two parents to give it a good home, which is where it should be right now. This was your brilliant idea, right? To keep the baby?" Allison choked on a laugh.

"Allison, please. . . ." Joe sounded very tired, but still angry. Dorothy almost felt sorry for him.

"No, Joe. This is the reason she backed off the adoption. This, right here." She gestured toward Kevin.

"I don't think so," Kevin said, staring at Allison. "She never wanted to give her baby away—that was *your* idea. She told me about it so don't try to pretend you don't know what I'm talking about."

"You don't know anything about anything," Allison said.

"Don't you talk to him that way," Dick interjected. "As far as I can see, you have no right to judge anybody."

"Listen to me," Joe said, inching closer to Dick, "I'm going to tell you one more time—"

"Go home, Kevin," Dick commanded. "Now."

Kevin rolled his eyes. "What are you gonna do, Dad? You can't make me do anything. I'm almost eighteen."

"This is a private family matter," Dick said through clenched teeth, "and while you are living in my house, eating my food—"

"Have you even heard anything I've said?" Kevin said. Dorothy could hear the beginning of that childhood wail in his voice now. He looked over at Diana, who was standing still at the edge of the room. By some miracle the baby had stopped crying. But Diana had started. Dorothy could see the shine of silent tears on her face. "We're going to be together," Kevin said, "and there's nothing any of you can do to stop us or take the baby away."

"Kevin, I said NOW!"

"Mom?" Kevin looked over at Dorothy, an expression of naked pleading on his face. She hadn't even thought he knew she was there. "You want to say something about this?"

Dorothy looked at all the eyes turned on her and wanted to shrink away into nothing. What did Kevin imagine that she could say or do to help him, or anyone? She was surprised by the flash of anger that hit her then. Kevin had received so much more nurturing than she had—so much more parenting. He'd been provided with everything, had wanted for nothing, and yet he couldn't stop taking. This time he was asking too much.

"You need to listen to your father, Kevin. Go home."

The room seemed to contract then, Dorothy remembered, and everything got much brighter—almost painfully so. The baby started up again, that knifelike newborn scream, and Allison shouted at Diana that she needed to feed it. Dick threatened that if Joe didn't keep Diana away from his son he would make sure that the authorities were contacted. Joe became very quiet and threatened to do the same if Dick didn't leave his house at that very moment. But it was Kevin who left, striding out the front door, without so much as slamming it closed for punctuation. Then Allison walked over and opened it wide. "Go," she said. "This is over."

Wishful thinking, thought Dorothy, because that night was only the beginning.

. . .

"Dorothy Werner?"

Dorothy jumped, clutching at her purse, a tiny grunt of fear escaping from her throat. She'd forgotten where she was. The nurse in lavender scrubs was back, still looking at her clipboard. Dorothy sprang from her seat.

"I'm here," she said, making sure her name wasn't called a second time.

october 21, 2007

Sunday dawned clear and warm. The forecast called for heat and anxiety. Before noon, exactly as predicted, the Santa Ana winds began blowing hard across San Diego, raising red-flag warnings all the way to the coast. Visibility was sharp and bright with twinkling dust; the air buzzed with electricity and crackling nerves. Then again, this time of year always made Southern Californians apprehensive. The Santa Anas, those arid devil winds, drew every bit of moisture from skin, lips, and hair and set allergies raging. People cursed, felt like crap, and made dark jokes about "earthquake weather." Psychics did a booming business, reading cards for nervous patrons wanting a glimpse into a better future, and chiropractors adjusted more backs than they had all summer.

Prescriptions for antidepressants increased as soon as the wind starting whipping through the canyons, due, some theorized, to positively charged CO_2 ions produced by the Santa Anas that literally altered brain chemistry and threw serotonin levels out of whack. The local news stations advised staying hydrated. Just make sure to get enough water, the sentiment went, and you'll do fine. But despite all these precautions and incantations, the unease persisted. Because what everyone really meant when they talked about the wind and the weather was fire. Fire had its own season in this part of California; a season that was becoming longer and more treacherous every year. By the time the wicked wind cut across the Mojave and rushed toward the Pacific, the entire county had become particularly flammable. The local newspaper used words like *scary* and *danger* to describe the outlook for the hot, parched week ahead.

Campers in Harris Ranch, just north of the Mexican border, paid heed and tended their illegal campfire carefully, making sure to extinguish the embers they left behind. But those hot bits of char were lovingly caressed back to life by the fire-loving Santa Ana wind. As San Diegans sat down for their Indian summer brunches in kitchens, on patios, and in outdoor cafés, the dead campfire became a major conflagration, burning north, burning west, incinerating everything in its path.

The wind continued on its dash from east to west, racing across the Anza-Borrego, picking up pollen and tiny particles of desert debris, which it showered on Julian, a quaint town known for its homemade pies and homegrown artists, and its western neighbor Ramona, a rustic enclave with an overworked fire department. Residents sniffed the air, shook their heads, and checked the conditions of their garden hoses. Between those two towns and slightly to the north was the community of Witch Creek, home to a small but growing vineyard and acres of chaparral dryer than bleached bones.

By noon, the temperature was well into the eighties and Witch Creek was a box of angry matchsticks. The wind tossed brush and trees and slapped at power lines. Excited currents sizzled, arcing in temperatures hotter than the surface of the sun.

The wind was the only witness to the inevitable first spark and hungry flame. Within minutes the new fire had gorged itself on tinder and exploded. The blaze expanded, stoked with ready fuel, scorching the air at sixty miles per hour. The billowing white smoke of burning brush fanned westward, signaling the fire's advance. By early afternoon, it was a monster named the Witch Fire and it was headed into the heart of Ramona. Photo albums were gathered, pets marshaled, and cars loaded with items that couldn't be replaced. By late afternoon, the smoke was a hundred-mile cloak over the landscape, swirling in doorways and blowing soot through open windows. And by dinnertime, ash was raining into the ocean.

chapter 10

Allison was anxious. She held the remote control in one hand and a cup of coffee in the other, alternating sips and flips. One channel to the next, all were covering the fires. On-the-scene reporters gestured to shelters and fire trucks, smoke blowing through their hair, the sound of wind in their microphones. In the studios, the anchors seemed to have made a pact to dress for disaster. The men had taken off their jackets and loosened their ties. The women wore yesterday's makeup and pulled back their hair. "We'll be here all day," they said, "bringing you this story as it develops."

There were fires every year. This time of fall there was always at least a hint of smoke in the air. And four years ago—"almost to the day," as the newscasters kept repeating—there was the Cedar Fire, an inferno that had qualified several counties as major disaster areas. Allison remembered the pall of smoke. School was closed for an entire week owing to the unbreathable air. Allison had been edgy then, but calm. There were evacuations happening everywhere, some only a few miles to the south, and so Allison made sure that all the important documents were in a fireproof box and ready to go. She might have mobilized more, but Joe was completely unconcerned. Wildfires never made it all the way to the ocean, he told her. His biggest worry was that business at the restaurant was taking a dive because everyone was in a panic. So, although she couldn't avoid paying attention to it, the Cedar Fire hadn't caused Allison that much anxiety.

But this was different.

The wind had started yesterday, whipping up dust and swirling leaves. Sometime in the afternoon, she noticed that the entire house smelled like an ashtray and that there was black soot accumulating in the doorsills. She closed the windows, but the smell remained and the air inside was thick and heavy. Still, that was nothing compared to what happened after sundown. The wind . . . Allison had never heard anything like it. Palm trees smacking the house, howling gusts finding every available corner to scream through. She couldn't remember ever being so frightened by wind. She'd grown up with it, after all. The Santa Anas were a fact of life—an excuse to buy expensive moisturizer and an annual topic of conversation.

Can you believe how dry it is? It's so hot too. Do you remember it being this hot? Sure is pretty out, though, isn't it?

But those winds had never felt like this before—wrathful and insane. Last night she'd paced around downstairs at first, trying to watch television. Then Diana appeared in the living room with the baby and proceeded to feed her on the couch. Allison tried not to look when Diana pulled down the straps of her dress and began struggling with her breasts and blankets, but it was impossible to ignore the baby's frustrated cries. She turned her head and saw Diana, half naked and wild-haired, moving the baby from one side of her body to the other. The baby's arms flailed, tiny fists shaking.

"I can't do this," Diana said. There were tears shining on her face. Allison held back the words that sprang to her mouth. What did this girl expect? She could have been back in school by now, all of this behind her. It was impossible to feel sorry for her. It didn't matter that she was so young—she'd had no trouble making her own decisions and ignoring the advice of everyone around her. Now she had to live with the consequences.

"She doesn't want to nurse," Diana said, a note of pleading in her voice. "I don't know what's wrong with her."

"Maybe she doesn't want the breast," Allison said. "Or maybe you're not making enough milk. I've heard that happens sometimes when—"

"When *what?*" Diana snapped. "Why don't you just say it?"

Allison waited a beat and then two. The baby cried louder, the shrieks piercing Allison's brain. "Just give her a bottle," Allison said. "She needs to be fed."

Diana looked at Allison with a mixture of anger and helplessness. She shifted the baby, wiped her eyes with her free hand, and pulled her dress back up. "Okay," she said. "Okay." She got up off the couch, dragging and dropping a pink receiving blanket on the floor, and walked over to Allison. "Can you please . . ." she began and thrust the baby toward Allison, "Can you *please* hold her for a minute? I'm going to get her a bottle."

Allison bristled, her back stiffening, but somehow her arms reached out. Diana placed the small, struggling weight there and ran to the kitchen. Allison clutched the baby, trying to contain her small limbs. The baby worked her tiny red mouth, her chest heaving from the effort of all that crying. Allison repositioned her, her hand under the baby's sweaty head, and held her close. For a moment everything stopped—the wailing, the wind, and her own breathing. But there was no peace in the silence. All Allison could think was that this was not her baby, not her life, and not what she had asked for. By the time Diana returned with a small bottle of milk, the baby was squirming again and Allison was desperate for a drink or for sleep or for anything that would turn off her brain. She handed the baby back to Diana without a word and practically ran upstairs to her own bedroom.

At two in the morning, she was still awake and listening to the wind rage. And Joe, who'd been gone all night, was still missing in action. He'd said he'd be working late, something about supervising inventory. At least she thought that's what he'd said when he'd left sometime in the afternoon.

Lying in the dark, she struggled to recall his exact words, wishing that she'd paid better attention. Something about him had been off. As the picture formed in her mind, she remembered thinking that it was his clothes—more casual than his usual work attire. He wasn't wearing a jacket and tie as he always did when he worked dinners. He was wearing slacks and a short-sleeved rayon shirt. It was an outfit just this side of lounge lizard. He'd said something about it too. . . . That was when the explanation about inventory came in, she recalled. It was odd, because Allison hadn't said a word about how he looked. She was already distracted by the wind and the threat of fire it was bringing. But something about the vaguely sleazy overall impression he left her with set off some faint alarm in her brain.

Allison put her cup down on the coffee table and switched the channel. Evacuations were being called for. East County was burning. A reverse 911 system was in place. People were being called and told to get out now.

What time had she fallen asleep last night?

It had to have been close to dawn and she couldn't have been out for more than a few hours. She'd woken up perspiring and disoriented. She couldn't remember now whether or not she'd dreamed that Joe had come home. He wasn't sleeping next to her, but his side of the bed was rumpled as if he'd been in it. It was light outside, but hard to tell what time it was. She rolled over and looked at the clock. It was 9:00 AM. She got out of bed, went downstairs, and put on a pot of coffee. The view from the kitchen window was frightening. The air was orange and thick with smoky grit. Leaves and palm fronds everywhere. She looked in the garage. Joe's car was gone. Diana's door was closed. Quiet.

The news was showing aerial shots of the fire consuming everything in its path. There were two fires, they said, and both had names. The Witch Fire was the one heading straight toward them, jumping freeways and roaring into canyons.

Maybe Joe was having an affair.

Allison took the thought out and looked at it for a moment, wondering how she felt about it. It wasn't as if, over the years they'd been married, she hadn't speculated. He had plenty of opportunity at work between cute little waitresses and lusty patrons. Allison had spent some time at the Luna Piena bar and she knew what went on. Joe flirted, an occupational necessity, and got plenty of response. And he'd met *her* at the restaurant, after all. There had been times when it had crossed her mind, when she thought about how easy it would be to give in to the right amount of coaxing, which, face it, didn't need to be much at all for almost any man. But either she was stupid or just not a jealous enough person because Allison never seriously entertained the idea that Joe was seeing someone else.

No, it wasn't stupidity, it was trust. Until July, they'd had a happy marriage. Not too happy, not falsely happy, and not unrealistically happy either. And because of that, theirs was a more solid marriage than most, Allison thought. But there was something else as well. Joe was a dozen years older than Allison. He'd lived a whole adult life full of women and affairs when he met her. He knew who he was and hadn't been stuck in a marriage that he'd grown out of or been ditched by a wife who stopped loving him at some point. He'd waited. And when he met Allison he was ready and he knew what he wanted. He was honest about telling her when he found a woman attractive and she never minded. So, no, she never really worried about him wandering. She trusted him.

Had trusted him.

But obviously there was plenty about Joe and the women in his past that Allison hadn't known—or bothered to find out. Why not an affair now then? Allison still didn't know how she felt about this. It was as if her capacity for emotion related to Joe had been surgically removed or at least delayed until Diana left. Joe had promised Allison that would happen. She was still waiting—her entire life on hold—but he had told her to be patient. Now that they were embroiled in this nastiness with the Werners, they'd moved a fraction of an inch closer in purpose. *United* was way too strong a word, but at least they were both in agreement about their distaste for the Werners and their desire to put an end to the ugly situation they'd been caught in. And ending it required Diana leaving for good. Allison hadn't thought much beyond that single point, but she knew that it would involve deciding whether or not she and Joe still had a salvageable marriage.

Allison turned the channel. A list of school closures appeared on the screen. She was momentarily relieved that it didn't seem very long, but relief quickly turned to panic when she realized that there were too many closures to show at once. The screen blinked and scrolled, showing more names. Everything was closed, including the school where she taught, which was literally down the street. Allison hit the remote again. A newscaster was explaining the difference between voluntary and mandatory evacuations. It didn't bode well, Allison thought, if people didn't understand either one of those concepts. To help drive the point home, the news anchor displayed a list of communities in the path of the Witch Fire where voluntary evacuations were suggested and which would, if the weather continued as predicted, likely be subject to mandatory evacuations later in the day. It didn't take very long for Allison to notice that her own neighborhood was on the list. So Joe was wrong. It seemed that this time, fire was determined to burn its way right into the ocean.

Allison set the remote down next to her coffee cup and walked over to the foyer where she kept her cell phone. There were no messages from Joe, but then there was no reason for him to have called her cell phone. He would have called the house phone if he'd wanted to tell her anything, like where he was. She hit the speed dial number for his phone and listened to it ring. When his voice mail picked up, she was unprepared.

"Joe . . ." she began and hesitated. What did she want to tell him? To come home? To take control of *something?* Allison waited too long and lost the connection. Well, she thought, he'd have to figure it out.

There was a scrape and rattle at the front door. She opened it without thinking and allowed a strong gust of wind to blow ashy bougainvillea leaves into her foyer. A large palm frond had broken off the tree next to their house and blown into their door. Allison didn't bother to move it. She stepped over it and peered down the street. Aside from the ugly debris scattered everywhere and the apocalyptic color of the air, Fuller Court looked much the same as it did every Monday morning after its residents had left for work and school; quiet and unremarkable. Allison didn't see any signs of panic or even any signs of life. She stepped back, kicking the frond out of her way, and was about to close the door behind her when she saw something so odd it made her stop. She stood in the doorway, her gaze fixed.

Dick Werner had appeared as if from nowhere and was standing in the middle of the street. He was wearing a T-shirt and sweatpants and holding something in his hand—Allison couldn't tell exactly what it was from this distance. She squinted, tried to make it out. Something rubbery and dark. It was a flip-flop, Allison realized suddenly. Just one. She raised her eyes to Dick's face. He was turned toward her house. He was staring right at her. Allison jumped, slammed the door shut, and slid the dead bolt that they almost never used. Her heart was thumping overtime. What the hell was he doing out there? Allison shook her head as if to clear it. Her heart slowed. She slid back the dead bolt and opened the door again, just a crack, which, if this were a movie, was exactly the wrong thing to be doing. In the movies, that false sense of security was always followed by carnage. But of course it wasn't a movie, despite the drama her life had become, and Allison saw nothing. In the minute she'd had the door closed, he'd vanished. Well, not vanished, Allison thought, just gone back into his house.

"Stupid," she said out loud. She coughed and closed the door a second time. The air was becoming too thick to breathe. In the living room, the television was still blaring. In the few moments she'd spent peering at Dick Werner, the anchors seemed to have spun themselves into full catastrophe mode, their voices sharp with alarm. Allison didn't know if it was the fear she heard in their controlled voices, the smoke-filled air, or just the bitterness of the coffee on her tongue, but something inside her tipped. She'd had enough.

She didn't bother to turn the television off or place her coffee cup in the sink. She went upstairs, moving faster than she had in months, and into her bedroom. She changed into a pair of jeans and a loose cotton sweater and forced her too-long hair into a ponytail. She grabbed her purse, her prescriptions, and the slim wad of emergency cash she kept stashed in her dresser drawer and ran downstairs. Allison snatched her keys, hanging on a hook next to the front door, and picked up her cell phone. She dialed Joe once more and waited impatiently for his voice mail to pick up.

"Joe," she said, hearing the breathlessness in her voice and trying her best to quell it, "I'm leaving. I'm not staying here and waiting to go up in flames. You decide what you want to do." She paused. "Or take," she said. "You decide what to take because I don't have anything."

Allison clicked off and threw the phone into her purse. She was almost out—almost gone—and then she remembered. She walked over to Diana's closed door and put her hand up as if to knock and held it there, hesitating. "Diana?" she said. No response. She tried again. "Diana? I'm leaving, okay?" Nothing. They must both be out cold, she thought. She'd heard the baby crying late, late into the night. Well, she wasn't going to risk waking up either one of them. Joe would be coming home soon. Joe could deal with it. For once. She turned, keys in hand, and walked fast to the garage. She made sure to lock the door behind her.

You couldn't be too careful.

chapter 11

When his phone rang, flashing Allison's number for the second time, Joe was sitting in his unmoving car on Del Mar Heights Road at the end of a line doubled back behind a gas station. He could have answered it—his hands were quite free—but he just let it ring until it stopped. Saturated and speechless with guilt, he couldn't even think about talking to Allison. It was a problem. Joe had never had an affair before and he didn't know what he was doing or how he was supposed to act. It was one thing to lapse once, but he'd moved into an entirely different place with Jessalyn and the territory was wholly unfamiliar. Joe heard the chirping tone alerting him that Allison had left another message. He picked up his phone and held it. But no, he wasn't even going to listen to the messages. He simply wasn't ready. He'd listen to it, he decided, after he filled up the tank and was on his way home.

Joe turned on the car radio and shifted through his presets until he found a station that actually seemed to be broadcasting live. All the talk was about fire and how it was shaping up to be the worst in San Diego history. The fires were being fanned by the Santa Anas and were spreading west at an uncontrollable pace. No containment in sight. Evacuations on a massive scale. Beautiful homes in danger or already destroyed. Joe had experienced California fire season often enough not to go into an immediate state of alarm, but this one sounded particularly bad. Now they were saying that the fires—there were at least two and maybe more—had been burning for twenty-four hours.

Joe had missed a good portion of those hours holed up with Jessalyn; the world condensed into the small hot space created by their bodies. Outside, the landscape had been going up in flames. Good thing he wasn't a religious man, Joe thought, because if he were, this conflagration—a direct punishment for his sins—would surely have driven him to some sort of ill-advised confession. He didn't know what he was going to tell Allison, but confession wasn't part of it. He knew that much at least, even if Jessalyn seemed to have some doubt.

"I don't know if you're cut out for this, Joe," she'd said last night. She was sitting on the bed, naked. She'd been waiting for him. He'd just gotten there and was strangely anxious, hesitant.

"What makes you say that?" he'd asked her. She shrugged. "I'm here," she said, "and you're there. Maybe you don't really want to do this."

"Let's not talk about it," Joe said, pulling off his shirt. And they hadn't.

Joe wondered if she'd left the hotel yet and tried to figure out what he would do if by some quirk of timing they pulled into their driveways at the same time. The thought made him sweaty and anxious. Maybe Jessalyn was right after all.

By the time he could even pull up close enough to see that only two pumps were actually operational, Joe had been sitting in the gas line for forty-five minutes. The scene was like something out of one of those low-budget disaster movies, everyone scrambling before the onslaught of tsunami, meteor, or alien attack. People were frazzled and yelling at one another. There was a worst-case scenario every-man-for-himself feeling of panic in the smoky air. Joe saw a woman in sweatpants and a tank top exiting the gas station's convenience store burdened under the weight of several liters of bottled water, a giant-sized slushy, and an oversized bag of potato chips. Food of the apocalypse, he thought. More of the same followed;

people getting out of their cars and heading into the convenience store, coming out with bad coffee, water, candy bars, mini powdered donuts, soft drinks . . . and diapers. Joe didn't know that places like these sold diapers. But of course he'd never paid attention to that kind of thing before. He'd never had to.

The diapers forced Joe to think about Diana and the baby. A bitter mixture of remorse and resentment rose up in his chest, burning his throat. He still wasn't entirely sure whether Diana knew about him and Jessalyn. He couldn't forget the judgmental look she'd given him that day on the driveway when she'd gone into labor, as if she knew where he'd been and what he'd been doing and was prepared to use it against him. She could have, Joe thought, she'd had plenty of opportunities over the last few weeks. But there was a bit of quid pro quo as well, as far as that went. Before they left for the hospital, he told her to brush her teeth and change her clothes. "You stink of pot smoke," he told her. "Probably not a great idea to show up at the hospital like that."

"I wasn't smoking it," she said. "I was *in the room with it* is all."

"Right," he told her, "of course."

He'd given her a pass then and hadn't pressed it. From her perspective that had to count for something. Not that he expected any big gifts next time Father's Day rolled around.

Joe rubbed his eyes, which were stinging from all the smoke in the air. He felt like he'd tried to do right by Diana, he really did. It wasn't her fault that Yvonne hadn't bothered to tell her about her own father until this most inappropriate time and then sent her off to him when she was at her most vulnerable. He understood all of that. And although he never would have raised her the way Yvonne had—had she put *any* limits on Diana at all?—he knew that this too was not Diana's doing, and he had tried to steer her in the right direction, had tried to . . . well, *be a father* to her wasn't quite right. It was too late for him to be a real father to her, and Diana was already predisposed to dislike him, but he had tried to be paternal at least. He had tried to get to know her—as difficult as that was considering the circumstances and Allison's unyielding resistance—but she'd gravitated right away to that hopeless Kevin and there wasn't anything he could have done to pry her away from him once she'd made up her mind that she was in love with him. What idiocy. It was exactly those kinds of bad choices that had gotten her knocked up in the first place. Well, that and poor parenting.

Joe felt bitterness rising in his throat again. He opened the glove compartment and rooted around for an antacid. No luck, though he could have sworn he'd left a roll of Tums in there only last week. Par for the course, Joe thought, because it seemed the world at large was conspiring to make him feel as bad as possible, literally and figuratively. Sure, some of it had to do with his chickens coming home to roost, but *in general* he didn't deserve the kind of consistently shitty hand fate was dealing him these days.

Take this bullshit with the Werners for a start. Goddamn Dick was so deluded he actually thought Diana was a bad influence on *Kevin*. The man had gone as far as to threaten a restraining order. Against Diana! And of course the real problem was that Dick was a frustrated blowhard with a fat-assed wife who probably never gave him any satisfaction (assuming of course Dick's dick even worked), and then all of a sudden his reject druggie son starts getting cozy with a beautiful girl who also happened to be African American. That's what really set Dick off. Joe knew it and Dick knew Joe knew it. This wasn't about two stupid kids thinking they loved each other; it was about Dick's racism. That Dick was an equal opportunity bigot didn't make it any better. Joe cringed when he remembered the misogynistic comments Dick had dropped from time to time about Sam and Gloria. Really mean-spirited, childish stuff. And now that Dick's Church Lady wife had gotten involved, who knew what kind of venom the Werners were spewing all over town. They couldn't make trouble for *him*—it was almost impossible to impugn the reputation of a restaurant manager—but they could make things difficult for Allison. She worked at an elementary school and those overprotective, self-righteous, litigious parents were just looking for an excuse to get angry about something.

And there was that vague threat Dick had made about calling Child Protective Services, although on what grounds Joe couldn't imagine. Still, a visit from CPS was the last thing any one of them needed. And if there was one thing Joe had learned in his life, it was that you could never underestimate the power of bigotry and stupidity.

And then there was the baby herself. Zoë. Joe had to admit that he liked the name—somehow it suited the tiny little thing. He also wondered about how close that name was to his own and if that had factored into Diana's decision. He hadn't been happy at first that she'd named the baby at all because that meant she was going to keep it—that she'd never been serious about the adoption. Then again, Joe hadn't expected the sharp twinge of emotion he'd felt when he looked at the baby for the first time either.

They were in the hospital. Joe had checked Diana in and stayed in the waiting room while she was in labor. She'd told him he could go—that she'd call him when she needed a ride home—but Joe saw that for the fake bravado it was and told her of course he was going to stay. He happened to be off work that day anyway and she should have someone there. She hadn't called her mother. And Kevin was nowhere to be seen, fortunately. He identified himself to the nurse as Diana's father and was very relieved when nobody asked him to stay in the delivery room. He called Allison, who still wasn't home, and left a message telling her what was going on. It hadn't taken as long as he'd thought. He'd heard all kinds of horror stories of labor going on for days and nights, but a few hours after they'd checked in, during which time Joe read several magazines cover to cover and watched an entire news cycle on the waiting room television, a big square-bodied nurse came out to tell Joe that Diana had delivered a girl and that both mother and baby were fine. Then the nurse smiled and added, "Your daughter's a pretty tough cookie, you know that? Not one complaint out of her the whole time. She did a great job. You should tell her." Joe couldn't tell if the comment was a compliment or a reproach. She told Joe that Diana and the baby were being moved to another floor and he could go see them both in a few minutes. "Congratulations, Grandpa," she said. Joe gave her a quizzical look. Diana and the baby weren't supposed to be together. Even he knew a new mother shouldn't bond with a baby she meant to give up for adoption. That's when he realized there wasn't going to be an adoption—and that maybe Diana had known that all along.

He still hadn't decided what he was going to say to her when he went downstairs to her room or even what his attitude should be. It was going to complicate things if she insisted on keeping the baby, but one way or another she had to go home. They all knew that baby or no, Diana wasn't going to be happy living with him and Allison, even if Allison would allow such a thing to happen. That part of the plan was rock solid and Diana knew it. As far as he could tell she'd barely spoken to her mother since she'd arrived—if at all. But they were going to have to patch it up—especially if Diana was planning to keep the baby. That was what he was thinking when he walked into the room, and what went out of his head almost immediately after he saw Diana, exhausted and limp in her bed, holding on to the tiny swaddled bundle as if someone would rip it from her at any moment.

"Are you okay?" he asked her. Diana nodded, too tired to speak. Joe pulled a chair up next to the bed. "The nurse said you did great," he offered. Diana didn't smile. There were dark circles under her eyes and her face seemed drained of blood. She turned a little in the bed so that she could tip the bundle toward Joe.

"This is Zoë," she said, peeling back the edge of the receiving blanket. Joe looked at the miniature red mouth and curly lashed eyes shut tight against a bright new world. You could see the shape of the nose already, he thought, the nose all three of them shared. He had the same shock of recognition as when he'd first seen himself in Diana—the obviousness of kin.

He felt a strong protective urge—a need to shelter both of them—and a not entirely comfortable tenderness toward this little brand-new being. "Her name means *life*," Diana said. The word stirred a strange mix of emotions in Joe, and he felt his throat tightening. He wondered how different all of their lives would have been if he had made a different choice all those years ago. If he'd stayed with Yvonne—even married her. But he still believed, even now looking at this child—these children—that none of it had been his choice to make. And once again a woman was making a choice that would decide his own fate without him having any say in it at all. So he'd made the one choice that was irrevocably his and had plunged into a full-scale affair with Jessalyn. And this, Joe thought, was how it had come to be four weeks later and still nothing had been resolved with Diana, Zoë, or Allison.

Although the thought of it increased the acid in his gorge, Joe realized he was going to have to schedule a family discussion. They were all going to have to sit down and talk about the Werners, Kevin, Yvonne, and getting Diana back home. And then, after that, he was going to have to have a real conversation with Allison about their marriage. Where Jessalyn fit into all of this he didn't know. He was just so tired of feeling bad about everything. At least with Jessalyn he had a chance to feel good, if only for a few moments.

Joe inched closer to the pump. He could see now that small flecks of ash were collecting on his windshield. All at once the frenzy penetrated his skin. He felt a clutch of panic in his gut. They'd never been evacuated this far west, but it looked as if this time it was actually going to happen. Joe started thinking about what he needed to take out of the house and where they were all going to go if an evacuation was called for. Allison had always taken care of emergency plans before. He didn't even know where she kept the lockbox with all their important documents. He picked up his phone again. Had it already happened? Is that why she'd called? He pressed 1 and waited impatiently for the voice mail cues to finish. The first message was very weird—just his name and then nothing but the distant sound of the television in the background before she hung up. The second message made Joe both angry and fearful. Allison sounded like she'd lost her mind. Where the hell did she think she was going? She hadn't even mentioned Diana or Zoë. Clearly, she was just leaving them there to fend for themselves. Joe was sick to death of her bullshit. Why had he let her get away with it all this time? And now they were in the middle of a crisis and he was going to have to deal with it all himself. He wouldn't even have the luxury of bitching her out when he got home. Frantic to get out of this line and back to his house, Joe attempted to squeeze out of his space without getting his gas, but he was forced to wait. When he made it to the pump at last, his hands were shaking so badly he spilled gas all over them.

He was sweating and coughing by the time he finally pulled onto Fuller Court. The street looked awful, full of downed branches and leaves blowing around. It was going to be hell to clean up when this was all over. The sun was unable to break through the smoke, but it was hot and everything was suffused with a burnt orange glow. There were no signs of life on the street and that was, in its way, even more troubling than the scene at the gas station. Joe pulled into the garage and closed it behind him before he got out of his car.

The goddamn door from the garage into the house was locked and Joe spent several futile minutes trying to find the right key on his chain, which also held all the keys to the restaurant. He pounded on the door but nobody answered. Of course not. Frustrated to the point of mindlessness, Joe grabbed the closest thing he could find to a battering ram, a long-abandoned baseball bat, and ran it into the door at full speed until he splintered the cheap thing and it swung open. He'd successfully broken into his own house.

He could smell smoke and burnt coffee and could tell, without even going upstairs, that he was the only person in the house. Allison's phone and keys were gone. Diana's door was open and her room was empty so obviously she'd taken Zoë and abandoned the house as well. Joe looked behind him at the broken door and felt embarrassed. He'd done something to his shoulder with that stupid macho gesture and now it throbbed with pain. He pulled out his phone and dialed Allison's number. It went straight to voice mail.

"You'd better call me, Allison," he said into the phone. He didn't add "or else," but he hoped it was obvious enough from his tone. Then he dialed Diana's cell phone, but it too went straight to voice mail. "Diana, it's Joe. Call me when you get this." He clicked off and stood there for a moment, suddenly overwhelmed by the complexity and weight of both his immediate and long-term situations. He needed a break.

He dialed his phone again. It rang only once before she picked up.

"Hey, Joe," she said.

"Hey," he answered. "Where are you?"

"I'm still here."

"Good," he said. "I'm coming back."

chapter 12

"I don't care how hysterical they are on the news," Dick said. He was sitting at the dining room table, staring intently at his laptop. "I don't see any reason to leave my house and go running around looking for some overpriced hotel room—even if we could find one at this point—and throw away a whole lot of money for nothing."

"But they're saying we're in a mandatory evacuation zone," Dorothy said. She stood in front of the television, watching as it cut back and forth across the county. There were too many images—it was all starting to blur into one big ball of flame. There were so many different fires in San Diego that the news couldn't even begin to cover those burning in Los Angeles County, one of which was busy consuming some gazillion-dollar mansions in Malibu. Even the major networks and CNN were covering the story and had crews all over the place.

Dorothy was nervous and had been since yesterday evening when it had become too smoky to leave a window open for even a moment without everything getting covered with soot. But the fires still seemed far away, removed enough as to be unreal. She wondered if it would take seeing actual flames for her to feel a sense of real danger and decided that maybe she'd gotten so used to seeing catastrophes on a small television screen that they all seemed manageable and contained. All you had to do was turn off the television and everything stopped. Dorothy didn't have any real-world experience with natural disasters; that was the problem.

But she knew very well what mandatory evacuation meant and she didn't care if it was just a precaution. Mandatory meant officials were involved—maybe in person—and the very last thing Dorothy would allow was to get involved in any way with officials or police. She didn't understand why Dick wanted to dig in his heels all of a sudden because it wasn't as if he was the world's most devoted homeowner. He mowed the backyard reluctantly, took no interest in gardening or landscaping, and cared nothing about interior design. Dick left all the details to Dorothy. However she wanted to decorate was fine with him as long as it was cheap. That was really at the heart of it, she thought. Dick was never going to be *that guy* who burned to death while trying to protect his house—he just wanted to save a few bucks.

"Dick," she said again, "mandatory evacuation means you have to leave. It's not optional."

"Don't be ridiculous," he said. "Since when are you buying into all that crap? I'm looking at this blog right now that they've set up about the fires. Nobody out here is panicking. Anyway, Dorothy, do you want to go sleep at Qualcomm Stadium? Because that's the only place where you can get a room right now."

"Why don't we call a few hotels?" Dorothy asked. "I can call if you want."

"Go ahead," Dick said, "you won't find anything."

Dorothy hesitated, thinking of another option. "We could go stay with your brother," she said.

"In *Arizona?*" From her spot in front of the television, Dorothy couldn't see Dick's face, but she could picture his expression anyway— disbelief crossed with irritation. "What's gotten into you, Dot?"

"I just think we should go if they're telling us to go."

"I'm not going anywhere," Dick said, a harsh edge creeping into his voice. He cleared his throat. "That fire has to come all the way down the fifty-six and jump across all kinds of freeway before it gets here. It's not going to happen. They're not going to let it."

"Dick . . ."

"Where's Kevin?" Dick asked, shifting abruptly to the one topic guaranteed to get Dorothy off her quest to evacuate. "I haven't seen him since . . . for hours."

Instinctively, Dorothy turned her head toward the top of the staircase as if Kevin would appear on it at any second.

"Well?" The air around Dorothy seemed to get hotter and less oxygenated. "Dorothy?"

Dorothy focused on the flickering orange and yellow flames on the television. "He went out with his friends," she said. "School's going to be closed tomorrow—probably until next Monday. They're . . . you know how kids are. They're taking advantage. Like the snow days we—" Dorothy inhaled sharply, realizing her slip a split second too late. She felt the nerves and muscles in her neck and shoulders contract into a painful spasm.

"What friends?" Dick had missed it. She squeezed her eyes shut in relief.

"You know," she said, trying to keep the tremor out of her voice, "those guys he's in . . . uh, Spanish class with . . . Jason, I think, and, um, Mike."

"Spanish?" Dick was incredulous. "Since when does he take Spanish?"

"Since it's a requirement to graduate." Dick didn't answer that one so Dorothy shifted her position so that she could see his face. He'd found something on the computer that had captured his attention and bent his head toward the screen. She saw the bluish light reflecting off his reading glasses and his lips a thin line of concentration half-buried under his mustache as he started typing.

He seemed to have bought her story completely. She was glad, but also surprisingly annoyed at his total lack of perceptiveness. She hadn't done a very good job of lying and that was maybe accidentally-on-purpose she thought now, because certainly she was capable of much greater deceptions. It was a sort of test to see if he—what? Cared? Was paying attention to anything other than his own wants and needs? Dorothy didn't know and didn't really understand why she would want to test him in the first place. It wasn't as if she could afford to risk another scene. They'd already called way too much attention to themselves as it was, getting all tangled up with the Montanas and Dick with his threats of legal action that she'd only barely managed to talk him out of. It was ridiculous anyway, insisting that Kevin and Diana remain apart—almost guaranteed to turn them into Romeo and Juliet and make them want to be together even more. Let them spend as much time together as they wanted, Dorothy thought, and they'd get sick of each other in no time. Kevin, a father! He couldn't even keep his own room clean. And if that stupid, stupid girl was going to insist on keeping that baby she'd get tired of having some carless, penniless, totally dependent teenage boy hanging around her neck real quick.

But no, Dick *had* to get all macho about it and that only made it forbidden fruit, which, as Dorothy knew intimately, was the most tempting and sweetest of all.

She'd tried to tell Dick all of this, but she guessed she hadn't been clear enough. Or, Dorothy thought now, maybe Dick just hadn't listened to her. He was completely unreasonable about that girl, his intense dislike of her totally out of proportion. Although Dorothy was certainly no fan of Diana's, she couldn't muster up the kind of extreme emotion Dick seemed to feel. Dorothy didn't understand it and it made her vaguely uneasy. As for Kevin, he was probably with Diana at this very moment. Although she didn't see how they were managing any secret trysts. Joe and Allison had been just as clear as Dick about not wanting Kevin and Diana to see each other, so Kevin would have to be sneaking into their house and hiding out because there was no way they were hanging out anywhere else with that baby.

On the other hand, maybe he wasn't with her at all. It had been hours since she'd seen him last, heading for the front door. She'd called to him from the living room where she'd been following the news updates on the fires.

"Kevin, wait a minute."

"What?" He stood with his hand on the doorknob, so anxious to be gone that he didn't even turn to look at her. He was wearing a grubby white T-shirt with a rash of what looked like pinholes at the hem, ultrabaggy jeans that slid halfway down his backside showing the green-striped top of his boxer shorts, and a maroon baseball cap pulled down over his eyes. Not for the first time she wondered when he had become this angry inarticulate person and how she had managed to miss the transformation.

"Where are you going?"

"Out."

"Out *where?*"

"Just out."

"Kevin . . ."

"I'm meeting a friend, okay? A guy I know from school. We're gonna see a *movie,* okay? Now you know."

"You know, everything's being evacuated, Kevin. The theater might not even be open. We might have to leave. And are you going to walk over there? Because the air's really bad."

"That's the last fucking thing I'm worried about," he said and made his exit before she could chastise him for his terrible language, slamming the door behind him.

Would it have made a difference if she'd run after him? If she'd watched to see where he was headed? Would he have talked to her then?

Dorothy's neck tensed up again. She could feel a headache crouching at the bottom of her skull, ready to burst out. She needed relief. Instantly, her mind's eye focused on that spot buried deep in the bathroom where she knew she could find it. She'd been getting so many bad headaches lately and that doctor hadn't given her nearly as many pills as she needed and no refill either, and so she was running dangerously low. She was going to have to be careful and conserve or else . . . Dorothy clamped down hard on the thought that had started to wind its way into her brain. No, she told herself. No, no, no.

"Dick," she said, "I'm going upstairs to put a few things together. In case we need to leave. I just think it's a good idea to be prepared."

"Okay," he said without looking up. He was deep into whatever he was reading on the computer and she could tell he hadn't heard a word she'd said.

Dorothy headed to her special place in the bathroom, fished out a pill, and swallowed it without water. She was about to put the bottle back when it occurred to her that she really might need to pack some essentials in case she could change Dick's mind and get him to leave. She should keep some pills handy. She opened the bottle and poured a few into her hand. Of course, if they did leave, she'd have to find Kevin as well. He probably wouldn't answer his cell phone, but she'd send him a text message—she knew he looked at those—and find out where to pick him up. In fact, she thought, she should probably do that now. It was getting late. Dorothy slid her hand inside her top and emptied the pills into her bra, trying to visualize where she'd left her cell phone. She was halfway back down the stairs and headed to the living room when she stopped herself short—her hand involuntarily moving to her heart. She'd put the pills in her bra. Without even thinking about it. It had been more than twenty years since she'd done that. Dorothy bit the inside of her lip. Something was happening, she thought. Something bad. As if on cue, the doorbell rang at that very moment and her blood jumped with the surge of adrenaline.

"Dorothy!" Dick called. "Can you get that?"

Dorothy wanted to shout down that she couldn't, that she was busy, but nothing came out of her mouth. The bell sounded again.

"Dorothy!"

Finally, she moved. Down the stairs and over to the front door. Dick, still seated at the table with his head in the computer, didn't even look at her as she walked by him. With great reluctance, she unlocked their front door and pulled it open. Sam stood under the awning, one arm reaching out to ring the doorbell a third time and the other holding a bundled-up baby close to her chest. Dorothy's eyes widened in surprise.

"Sam?"

"Hi, Dorothy. Can I come in please? I don't want the baby to breathe in this air."

"Sure, of course."

Sam walked in and Dorothy closed the door behind her. Dorothy could hear the baby now, muffled little noises coming from under layers of blankets. Sam's eyebrows were drawn together in worry and her whole body seemed tense and rigid. "I'm glad you're still here," Sam said. "I thought maybe you'd be gone already. You are evacuating, right?"

"Well, we—" Dorothy began, but suddenly Dick was next to her and interrupting.

"What's going on?" he said.

Sam gave Dick as cutting a look as Dorothy had ever seen, yet the words that came out of her mouth were polite, even beseeching. "I'm sorry to drop in like this," she said. "I would have called, but I can't seem to find my Watch list and I figured you're so close."

"Whose baby is that?" Dorothy asked, although she already knew.

"It's Diana's baby. Zoë." She wrapped both arms around the baby and started rocking. "That's why I came over. I'm wondering if you know where Diana is. She left the baby—"

"Why would we know where she is?" Dick barked.

"I know she's . . . She's friends with Kevin, isn't she? I just thought maybe she was here. With Kevin."

"Kevin's not even home."

"Well, do you know where he *is?*" Sam asked. She held her ground, her tone strong, her expression stony. She wasn't intimidated by Dick in the least, Dorothy thought, feeling a passing twinge of envy. "Maybe Diana is with him. I need to find her. We have to evacuate and if I can't find her, I'm going to have to take the baby with me. There's nobody home at the Montanas. I think they've left. I don't know where they are." Sam frowned. "I'm just trying to do the right thing here, Dick." Dorothy shifted her gaze from Sam to Dick. His face looked folded up, closed and angry.

"So do you know where he is?" Sam asked. "Please."

"He's not here," Dick said again.

"Are you sure?"

Dick flushed. "Are you saying you don't believe me?"

"No," Sam said calmly, "I'm just asking if you're sure."

Dick turned abruptly and almost ran up the stairs. A few seconds later she could hear him rattling Kevin's door.

"I don't understand why you have the baby," Dorothy said. "Did Diana leave her with you? Are you babysitting?"

"No," Sam said. "That's why I came over here. I went over there hours ago—to Joe and Allison's. I wanted to see if they needed any help." Sam paused for a second, her jaw working. "I wanted to see if *Diana* needed any help. But when I got there—"

"Kevin's asleep in his room," Dick said, coming down the stairs, "so I guess he is here after all." He walked over to Dorothy and stood next to her, placing one hand on her shoulder. She looked at him—studied his face—and realized he was telling the truth. "But he's *by himself.* Sorry Sam, can't help you. That girl isn't here."

Dorothy's brain scrambled for an explanation. How could she have missed Kevin coming in? She was sure—

"This isn't right," Sam said. She was getting agitated, nervous. "When I went over there, nobody answered the door, but I could hear the baby crying. She was screaming. So I got concerned and went around the back. The back door was open so I figured somebody must be home, but the place was empty except for her." Sam patted the baby. "She was all alone, screaming her head off. So I took her over to my house. Just until . . ." Sam looked at them, pleading. "I left a note," she said. "But that was hours ago. Nobody's come home."

"I don't know what to tell you," Dick said, shrugging. "The way those people run their lives is none of our business." Dorothy noted the "our" and the disgust with which he delivered his statement.

"Would you mind asking Kevin?" Sam asked. "Maybe he knows where she is."

"He doesn't know anything," Dick said. "He's finally figured out how to leave well enough alone and I'm not going to get him involved all over again."

Sam turned to Dorothy, her eyes flashing accusation. *I can't,* Dorothy wanted to tell her. *I'm sorry but I can't.* "Do you have Joe or Allison's cell phone numbers?" Sam asked. "I could try those."

As Dorothy went to the kitchen to extract her master copy of the Neighborhood Watch list, she heard Sam asking Dick again to please ask Kevin when he woke up if he knew where Diana had gone and to please call her if he found anything out. Then Dorothy lost the train of their conversation for a minute and when she came back out, Sam was explaining to Dick that she had packed up her car with a few things and was going to find a place to stay until the evacuation orders were lifted. "You have my cell phone number," Sam said. "Please call me. I have to take the baby with me. I can't leave her."

"Here you go," Dorothy said, handing Sam the phone numbers she'd copied. "I'm sure it's just a misunderstanding. They'll probably be home any minute now."

Sam looked at Dorothy with an expression that suggested she thought Dorothy was a hopelessly lost cause. "Are you going to leave?" she asked. "You know we're under mandatory evacuation here, right?"

"Thanks," Dick said, "but you don't need to worry about us too. Looks like you've got your hands pretty full."

"Wow. I sure do," Sam said, sarcasm making her words sound sharp and pointed. "And thank you for all your help, Dick. I'll let myself out."

Dorothy's head had started to throb in earnest and her throat felt tight and dry. "Dick," she said, after she'd locked the door behind Sam, "I really think we should go. I'm going to call some hotels."

"Suit yourself. I'm getting a beer," Dick said and headed to the kitchen.

Dorothy went into the living room, overwhelmed by a weariness so crushing she could barely propel herself to the couch. If she could just sit for a moment and relax, she thought, she would be fine. Just a minute was all she needed. Dorothy slumped onto the couch, her head turned toward the television. Just one second, she thought. Just one.

The doorbell was ringing again. Dorothy sat up, disoriented. Her mouth was parched and her head felt like it weighed a hundred pounds. How long had she been out? It couldn't have been long because Dick was still sitting at the table—no, getting up to go to the door now—and the news looked exactly the same. She heard Dick open the door.

"Good evening, Officers, what can I do for you?"

Dorothy's heart seized in her chest and she froze on the couch. Blood rushed in her ears so loudly she couldn't make out what Dick was saying. She remembered the pills she'd put in her bra and thought about shoveling all of them into her mouth. She was terrified, couldn't breathe. She had to get up, get *out*. She eyed the back door, tried to figure how long it would take her to get there and how she would open the sliding glass door without making any noise. Her heart was pounding, shaking her whole body.

The front door slammed shut. Dick appeared in the living room, holding a can of beer in his hand. "That was the police," he said. Dorothy could only manage a nod. "They're going around telling people to leave." Dorothy tried to speak, but all that came out was a strangled hiccup. "What's the matter with you, Dot?"

"Please, Dick," she said and heard her voice tremble. "Can we please go now?"

"Dorothy . . ."

And then Dorothy did something that she hadn't done for years, maybe even decades—she started crying, big heaving sobs. "Please," she wept, "please."

"*Okay,* Dorothy, okay. Jesus." Dick looked at her with a mixture of concern and puzzlement. "Why don't you call . . . No, why don't you just get some stuff together and let's just go then, okay? I'll go wake up Kevin and get him going. Okay, Dot?"

Dorothy nodded again and wiped her eyes with the sleeve of her top. Her scalp prickled as if she were being stuck by a thousand tiny needles. "Okay," she said, shuddering. Dick went upstairs and Dorothy lifted herself from the couch. It took a second for her to understand the confusing mix of physical sensations she felt—cold, damp, sticky—and then she looked down at the dark stain on the couch and put her hand to her pants. She'd wet herself.

The first thing to do was go to the laundry room where there was surely a clean pair of sweatpants in the dryer. Then she would worry about the couch. Dorothy's cheeks burned, though whether with fever or shame she couldn't tell. But there was no time to figure it out. Dorothy almost wept with relief when she saw the pair of sweatpants sitting on top of the dryer waiting for her. Jumbled thoughts raced through her head. She was trying to untangle them, trying to think through surging adrenaline.

But now Dick was yelling down at her—a sharp edge of sheer panic in his voice that she'd never heard before.

"Dorothy, call 911! *He's not breathing!* CALL 911!"

He's not breathing.

Dorothy ran for the phone.

chapter 13

Sam wiped her kitchen windowsill hard but it made no difference because the glass itself was filthy and coated with a thick layer of grit. And it wasn't just the windows; everything was dirty. It felt as if she'd been trying to clean up forever instead of a mere three days. It was a losing battle. Evidence of the fires was everywhere. Soot had covered every surface, collected in every doorway, blown down every road, and been tracked into every house. And that was the least of it. The entire county was traumatized in one way or another. Thousands of people were now homeless or had lost their businesses. A few lost souls had died. And one . . . One had just disappeared.

Goddamn it, she thought. *Where was Diana? Where had she gone?*

Sam looked over to her kitchen table where tiny Zoë lay in the Moses baby basket that Sam herself had supplied. She was still asleep, but Sam's maternal instinct told her that she would soon be awake and needing the bottle that was warming in a bowl of hot water. She peered into the basket, adjusting the thick pink blanket slightly. Such a pretty baby, Sam thought, and then, there it was again—that peculiar mixture of anxiety, joy, and possessiveness she felt with Zoë now. It had started the moment she'd taken her from Joe's house—*rescued* her—and deepened over the course of that night. She knew she was forming a dangerously strong attachment to Zoë, but she felt powerless to stop it. And it wasn't just because this baby was unusually helpless or unusually lovely, there was something special about this little one.

Sam looked at her miniature features: the perfect bow mouth, tiny nose that you could see even now was going to be exactly like Diana's, dark curly eyelashes and dimpled cheeks the exact color of a late summer peach. Zoë had none of the reddened, wrinkled, alarmed look of most newborns, who often seemed startled and not entirely happy about being thrust into the world. Instead she appeared peaceful, at least in sleep, and . . . was *resigned* the right word? Sam thought she was probably projecting too much onto this brand-new person, but still that was the impression she got.

At first, Sam just assumed she was so drawn to Zoë because she reminded Sam of her own lost daughter. There had to be some of that in it, but it was only part of the whole. Zoë made Sam want to reach outside of herself and help someone else, or contribute to the greater good. Sam couldn't quite verbalize it, even to herself, but it was something along those lines. She also felt the need to shield Zoë, knowing the turmoil into which she'd been born. And now, with Diana missing . . .

Sam's heart contracted at the thought of where Diana might be or what could have happened to her. Joe was still saying he was sure she'd run away, but Sam suspected that was his guilt speaking. He'd waited too long, it was as simple as that.

It had felt so wrong at first—taking the baby with them when she and Gloria evacuated on Monday night. What if Diana had just gone to let off a little steam somewhere (*very* bad idea, but she was a teenager and not, Sam now realized, a particularly mature one) and came back to find her baby missing? What if she thought the baby had been kidnapped? Sam couldn't imagine how panicked Diana would be, but in the end Sam didn't feel there was anything else she could have done. The whole day and night was so strange and ominous, from the moment she'd walked up to the house and heard the baby crying right through the time when she, Gloria, and Zoë piled into what had to be the last motel room available in the only part of the county that wasn't on fire. There was something so wrong about it all. As flighty as she could be, Sam couldn't believe Diana would leave her baby alone in the house. Nor could she imagine Allison doing that. She'd been sure Diana was with Kevin. And maybe she had been. Maybe she was there and Dick just didn't . . . But no, she knew now that wasn't possible. Still, Dick and Dorothy both seemed really odd and tetchy that night. What the hell went on in that house? Sam couldn't begin to guess.

She hadn't been able to reach Joe until late Tuesday, when they were all allowed to return home. Sam told him what had happened and he just kept saying, "I'm sorry," over and over. No explanations, no offers of information. That was when Sam realized that he didn't know where Diana was either. She'd volunteered to keep Zoë for another night, since he was utterly unprepared to take care of a baby of any age, let alone a newborn. But by Wednesday, when she went over to his house again, he was still alone and he still hadn't contacted the police.

"Would it be okay if you kept her tonight too, Sam?" he asked. "It's just . . . I really have to work. I was going to ask Je— um, I know someone who could probably watch her, but you're really good with her and . . ."

"No, Joe, of course I don't mind, but you have to find Diana. I don't understand why—"

"I really appreciate you doing this, Sam," he said. "I know it's an incredible imposition and you've done so much already."

He was on his way to work, hair slicked back, collar up, and wafting cologne. He'd obviously just showered and shaved, but his shirt was already stained with dark circles of perspiration. He seemed to have become grayer at the temples, but Sam thought she could have been imagining that. His face was pinched and thin and it was clear from the puffiness around his eyes that he hadn't been sleeping much.

"I said I'm happy to do it, Joe. I offered, remember? But Joe, when are you going to—"

"It's just that I have to work," he continued as if she'd said nothing at all, "and Allison—" He caught himself, but it was too late.

"Allison what?"

A flush darkened Joe's face. "Allison has decided to stay with her mother for a while. In L.A. It's a bad time, but . . ." His tone was calm, but he bit his lip, a small gesture of the frustration he must have been feeling. "She's been having kind of a hard time with things lately. It hasn't been easy for her, all this with Diana. But I . . . I'm pretty sure she'll be home soon and then I'm sure she'll be able to help with the baby." But, Sam noted, Joe didn't even pretend to sound as if he believed this. "Anyway, Diana will be back by then." He looked at Sam pleadingly then, as if he could will her into buying into whatever fantasy he had constructed.

"Joe," she'd told him, "this is serious. You need to talk to the police. What are you waiting for?"

"I know where she is, Sam," he'd said. "She's with that degenerate Kevin Werner. I don't know where Dick and Dorothy are—it's all been such a mess with these fires—but as soon as I find them—"

"Have you spoken to her, Joe? Because if you haven't—"

"Come on," he said, "there's nowhere else she could be."

"I told you, I went over there Monday night. She wasn't there."

"Are you totally sure about that?"

"Joe . . ."

"Okay," he'd said, his hands raised in a gesture of surrender. "If she isn't back by tomorrow morning . . . Look, I know she's with him, Sam. With *them*. Goddamn Dick."

Sam had let it go then, although she didn't know why—then or now. Perhaps she too wanted to believe that Diana had run off with Kevin. Because even that pathetic scenario was preferable to some of the alternatives. Perhaps part of it was simply sympathy for Joe. He was trying very hard to keep it together, but he was cracking badly under the sudden pressures of his life. Sam doubted he'd ever had to deal with anything even as remotely troubling in his entire life as what he was going through now. Part of her felt he deserved it because he'd brought every bit of his current suffering upon himself. But her more compassionate side recognized that he was flailing and in way over his head.

Or maybe, and Sam didn't even want to admit this to herself, she just wanted to keep Zoë a little longer.

So she'd collected diapers, blankets, and bottles from Diana's room—all the while depressed to find that Diana had accumulated so little in the way of baby clothes and toys and all the small things that people gave you when you had a new baby. Maybe, she'd thought as she bundled all the items together, Diana really had just resorted to her most immature teenage self and taken off with Kevin. Then again, maybe she'd just run away. Diana could have been suffering from postpartum depression and just flipped out. Sam had been turning these theories over in her head endlessly since Monday afternoon when she'd discovered Zoë screaming her head off all alone in that house, but they still didn't sit any easier or make any more sense. Unless she'd been completely off base about Diana, the girl was just upset and confused about her life; anyone in her position would be. And it was clear how much she loved Zoë. To Sam, Diana was many things— determined, frightened, naive, and willful to name just a few—but never depressed and never desperate.

Still, as late as Wednesday, Sam was willing to believe that she was wrong about that too. One never really knew what went on inside the hearts of other people, even those hearts you thought you knew as well as your own. But on Thursday (dear god, Sam thought, was that only *yesterday?*) the Werners came home and the landscape shifted once again.

She hadn't gotten the full story because Joe had been terse at best. He'd come to pick up Zoë late in the afternoon looking anxious and jittery. She and Gloria had been arguing. Sam couldn't even remember now over what. It was some small thing—whose turn it was to unload the dishwasher or something like that—that had blown up into a fight about something else entirely. The air was charged with tension and anger when Gloria let Joe in, but he didn't seem to notice and launched immediately into his speech.

"Well, she's not with Kevin," he said. "At least not right now. That stupid kid is in the hospital. They wouldn't tell me anything, but it's obvious he overdosed on something."

"Who's in the hospital, Joe?"

"Kevin," Joe said. "But you know what really amazes me? That even now, that asshole has the gall to try to pin this on Diana."

"Where is Diana, Joe?" Sam asked, but she could tell that the only thing Joe knew for sure was that what remained of his world was about to fall apart. "I don't know," he said. "But Dick knows, I'm sure of it. And that kid of his knows too. He wouldn't even tell me what hospital Kevin's in."

"Joe, I really think it's time—" Sam began, but Joe cut her off.

"I know, Sam. I know what you think. I'm going to do it. Right now." He took Zoë from Sam then and gathered up all her things. Sam thought about protesting and offering to keep the baby while Joe went to talk to the police, but was stopped by some odd sense of propriety. Zoë *was* his granddaughter after all, and Sam had no claim to her. That was a mistake, she now realized. Joe had taken Zoë, but he had not gone to the police as he'd said he was going to. Sam didn't know what he'd done with the rest of his day yesterday, but this morning he was back at her door with Zoë, asking if she could lend a hand once more.

"What did the police say?" Sam asked.

"I'm going over there now," he answered. Sam was stunned into silence, but Joe filled it quickly. "Look, I was sure she'd be home by now," he said. "I'll be back to get the baby after I get done over there."

Like it was laundry he had to pick up or something, Sam thought. But he'd been gone for hours already. Sam didn't know whether to consider that a bad sign or an even worse one.

Zoë was stirring. She turned her head, her little hands jerking up and her mouth opening, forming a cry. Sam reached into the basket and lifted her out before she could get out a full yell. You weren't supposed to do that, she thought. There were all these "baby whisperers" around now who said that it spoiled babies if you soothed them right away. You were supposed to let them cry. Ridiculous, Sam thought. This baby needed comforting in spades. She adjusted Zoë in her arms and then rocked her for a minute to see if she'd go back to sleep or if she was genuinely hungry. The baby gurgled, flirting with the idea of a solid cry, then hiccupped, then demanded to be fed. Sam sat at the kitchen table—the same spot where she'd served Diana lemonade not even two months ago—and gave Zoë her bottle. Ten years since she'd rocked and fed her own baby, she thought, and it still came so easily. She drifted, narcotized by the small warm weight in her lap and the baby's sweet smell. It was easy to forget everything else when you were holding a baby—feeding an infant was such an elemental, focused task. Her thoughts, woolly and meandering, began to unravel. And so when Gloria walked into the kitchen in old sweatpants and a torn white T-shirt, she was surprised. It took a few seconds for her to remember that Gloria was home because the community college where she worked was closed for the entire week.

Gloria pulled a bottle of some designer water out of the fridge and drank it in big noisy gulps. She looked over at Sam, then down at the baby. Not for the first time these last few months, Sam could not read Gloria's expression. She had the impression that Gloria was removing herself by inches and in doing so becoming blurrier and blurrier. Soon, Sam thought, she wouldn't be able to see Gloria at all.

"What are we into here?" Gloria asked finally.

"What do you mean?" Sam shifted the baby in her arms, gripping her a little tighter. Something in Gloria's tone made her tense. She could feel her stomach muscles tighten.

"The baby." She gestured to Zoë. "Are we keeping her?" Gloria smiled to soften the question, an indication to Sam that she was being sarcastic, but there was no mirth or the slightest bit of warmth in it.

"Come on, Glo," Sam said, and then stopped herself, wondering why she was using this pet name for Gloria and why there was the sound of pleading in her voice. She could feel herself catering to Gloria's mood again, and it annoyed her. All at once she found herself resentful and irritated at always having to be the patient one, the understanding one. "It's not a problem to take care of her for a little bit," she said, her voice hardening. "It's the least we can do. It's the least *I* can do."

"Because I'm the bitch, right? That's what you're saying?" She still had that cheerless grimace on her face. For the first time, Sam noticed the beginnings of crow's feet at Gloria's eyes.

"No, of course that's not what I'm saying. Why do you have to be so difficult? This poor baby. . . . What a way to start a life. Who knows where Diana is? It's just about having some compassion, you know?"

"I get it," Gloria said. "I have a kid, remember?" For a moment Gloria just let that hang in the air between them. Sam compressed her lips, holding it in, repressing all the things she could say if she wanted to start another one of their energy-sucking arguments. Gloria finished her water and put the bottle down on the kitchen countertop. She ran her hand over her hair, still getting used to it being so short. Gloria had worn her hair long her entire life—it had been a point of pride with her. Sam felt a physical pang thinking of that beautiful curling hair. She was a stunning woman, Gloria was. It would take more than a bad haircut to spoil her, but that shorn look didn't suit her. And it certainly didn't suit Sam.

"Look, Sam," she said, "I don't want to get into it again, okay? I don't want to fight. I just want to know . . . I want to know why you had to get so involved with all of this? I mean, it's not like we don't have enough to deal with ourselves, is it?"

"It's not about us," Sam said. "It's about helping someone else, isn't it? Why are you so worried about my getting involved, anyway? Can you explain that to me?"

But Gloria didn't answer. She shuffled over to the table and pulled up a chair next to Sam. She pulled back a corner of Zoë's blanket and leaned

in to look. Her nearness disrupted the protective bubble that Sam had created around herself and Zoë, and she shifted in her seat. She could smell
the faint whiff of yesterday's beer on Gloria, and it worried her. How many
had there been? Sam had gone to bed exhausted at ten and left Gloria
watching television and nursing a can of Coors that she'd been working on
all evening. Obviously there had been quite a few more. And then Gloria
moved her hand, turning it so that she could stroke Zoë's cheek with her
finger, and Sam saw the tattoo for the first time.

It was small, less than an inch long, and very dark on the fair skin of
Gloria's wrist. Sam thought it was a snake at first, curled and ready to strike,
but then realized that it was a letter. She was hit with a rush of emotion so
intense it brought the prickle of tears to her eyes. *S* as in Sam.

"When did you get *that?*" she asked.

Gloria pulled back her arm reflexively as if Sam had caught her at
something criminal and lowered her eyes. But she didn't get up—didn't
leave. Sam looked at the half-turned face, the graceful curve of her cheek-
bone, and the slight tremble of her lips and was thrown back in time. The
sudden memory unfolded in front of her as clearly as if it were playing on
a screen. There was no sound with the picture, just as silent as it had been
that hot summer afternoon. They were reclined on the chaises around Gloria's swimming pool. The boys were playing together somewhere inside the
vast walls of her house. The sun was bright on the water and hot on the
skin. Gloria's eyes were shaded with sunglasses. They'd been talking about
coyotes and how Gloria could hear them howling at night in the hills
around her house. Sam had made a joke about how they were both living
in the Wild West. They'd fallen into a stupefied speechlessness—tension
growing in the hot air between them. Gloria lifted her shades, her green
eyes searching, questioning Sam's. The answer was there—sudden but
somehow inevitable.

Their chairs were very close together, yet Gloria still had to lean over
for Sam to hear her whisper, "How long have you known?" Perspiration
shone in the hollow of Gloria's throat. Her long lashes cast thin shadows

under her eyes. Sam moved toward her so slightly, the hesitation there, knowing it was one of those moments that could never be undone or forgotten, but Gloria closed the small distance. Their lips met for the first time, soft and warm, tasting of sugar and suntan lotion. Sam fell, irretrievably lost in the kiss somewhere between the beginning and the end.

They could have stayed like that, Sam thought. They could have turned into a cliché of male fantasy, sneaking steamy afternoons in each other's marital beds while their children played video games in another room. They could have gone on indefinitely—shopping together, best friends with benefits forever. They could have justified it—it wasn't cheating because it wasn't with another man. It could have been the best of all worlds: money, husbands, houses, and sex. Nobody to judge them. No fights and bitterness and poisonous insults that made their children cry. "You could have had everything," Gloria's husband had told her. "What would it have cost you to keep it to yourself?"

Because it wasn't enough for her, Sam thought. Sam never questioned Gloria's devotion to Justin or even, in the early days, to Frank. Nor did Sam ever doubt the intensity of Gloria's feelings for her. It was never a game for Gloria, never an experiment. But Gloria's need was vast and had the gravitational pull of a collapsing sun. She gave of herself, but she took much more, Sam thought. There was something she wanted in exchange for her love now, some form of payment for her pain. But, Sam realized, it was possible that nothing she could give would ever be enough for Gloria.

As if she could hear the thoughts inside Sam's head, Gloria leaned over the baby and kissed Sam hard on the mouth. "I did it for you," she said. It took Sam a second to realize she was talking about the tattoo.

"How?" Sam asked. "How did you do it for me?"

"I want you to get one too," Gloria said, deftly avoiding the question with another demand. Sam lifted Zoë, who had consumed half the formula in her bottle, and started rubbing her back. "They had some nice *G*s there. You can do a lot with a *G,* you know? I never realized."

"I'm not going to get a tattoo, Gloria."

"Why not?"

"Because I'm not seventeen. I didn't know we had to exchange blood oaths now."

"You could loosen up a little, Sam. It wouldn't hurt you."

Sam sighed and Zoë burped. Sam turned her around and offered her the rest of her bottle. Gloria pushed her chair backward, making it scrape against the floor. The sound startled Zoë, who let out a milky yelp. "Gloria, we need—"

"To talk," Gloria interrupted. "I know." She reached up to her head again, her hand searching again for the hair that wasn't there. "It hasn't been easy to get to you lately, Sam. I want to talk, I do. But you've been obsessed with this baby. You don't even know how much."

"It's only been a couple of days, Gloria."

"Yeah, but do you see yourself? You've gotten all Connor's things out of storage. All his blankets and his baby clothes—and that basket. It's like you're settling in or something, I don't know. And you've had her almost nonstop this whole week. What is it about her, Sam?"

"I can't do this, Gloria. Not now."

"I want to get married," Gloria said suddenly. "And I want us to have a baby. Of our own."

Sam started laughing, unable to stop herself even though she knew it would probably aggravate Gloria who seemed for all the world to be totally serious.

"This is the problem right here," Gloria said. "You can't even listen to what I have to say. Is this funny to you?"

"I just can't believe what you're saying. In one breath you tell me I'm obsessed with this baby and I'm getting too attached to her and then you stand there and tell me you want us to have a baby. And get married! To *whom*, Gloria? And how?"

"Okay, okay, not *married* married. But you know what I mean, Sam, don't pretend you don't. I want us to have some kind of ceremony. I want us to be *real*. And yes, I think we should have a baby."

"And that, of course, ensures that we will stay completely low profile," Sam said. "Wasn't the idea not to make Frank and Noah angrier than they already are?"

"What can that asshole do to make my life worse?"

"Plenty," Sam said.

"Can he make me not Justin's mother? I have a right to live with and be with anyone I want."

"Gloria, listen—"

"No, Sam, *you* listen. It's time we stood up for who we are and what we believe in."

So there it was, Sam thought, the place where Gloria's need had led her. She realized, with a bitterness she didn't know she was capable of, that what Gloria meant by "real" was the same as so many misguided heterosexual couples in trouble—let's get married and have a baby because that will solve everything. Trying to turn it into a political statement as Gloria wanted to do wouldn't make it any more successful.

Sam looked down at the baby. Despite their not-quiet voices, Zoë had fallen asleep again, the nipple still in her mouth. She lifted her carefully and placed her gently in the basket. Sam's lower back hurt and her arms were stiff from holding Zoë. Getting old, she thought. That thing about forty being the new thirty was utter bullshit. The forties were killing her. And there was Gloria, ten years behind her, unaware, and not even looking ahead. She had no idea, Sam thought, of how badly your own body could betray you. Never mind individual people—or society in general. The decade between them had never loomed as large as it did now. For a terrifying moment, Sam felt as if she could be Gloria's mother.

"I love you," she told Gloria. "I don't need to stand up for anything else."

Gloria's face clouded. "Does that mean you won't get a tattoo or that you don't want to marry me?"

Sam tucked the blanket around Zoë. In the end, what was more important than this little innocent? Once more, she felt a cold twinge of fear for Diana. It didn't matter whether the girl had run away or been taken, the danger was the same and it was this baby who would suffer the most. It was ridiculous to stand there talking about tattoos while Diana, a teenage mother with an infant, was missing, and the only person who might know her whereabouts was in the hospital coming off an overdose of something he'd probably found in his mother's medicine cabinet, and nobody seemed particularly alarmed about any of this. Sam turned to Gloria, who was waiting for an answer to her last question, ready to tell her all of this, wanting her to somehow understand without Sam having to explain every little detail, but she didn't have a chance to let out a single syllable because just as she opened her mouth to speak the doorbell rang, followed by hard knocking, as if the person on the other side couldn't take any kind of chance of going unheard. Zoë woke up and immediately started wailing.

"Goddamn," Gloria said, hustling to the front door, and then, "Okay, okay! I'm coming!"

Sam picked up the baby once more and rocked her as she followed behind Gloria, but this time Zoë refused to be pacified and her crying escalated into screams. Gloria was standing at the door, one arm out and resting on the jamb as if she were barring entrance to Joe, who was on the other side.

"Joe?" Sam said. "Do you want to come in?"

Gloria looked back at Sam with an impatient expression and let her arm down so that Joe could cross the threshold. He looked like crap: wan and drawn and those bags under his eyes were darker and puffier than when she'd last seen him. His shirt was wrinkled and the collar was askew as if he'd been pulling it away from his neck repeatedly. Sam didn't know him well enough to be able to tell whether the hard set and deepening lines of his face indicated anger, sorrow, anxiety, or some combination of all three.

"Thanks for taking care of the baby, Sam. I'll take her home now." He looked over at Gloria, who was posed in some kind of warrior stance with her legs straight and slightly spread and her arms folded across her chest. "You too, Gloria," he added. "Thanks."

"What happened, Joe?" Sam asked. "What did the police say?"

"They have . . ." For a moment he looked as if he was going to break down, his face on the verge of crumbling, but then he drew it all back together, put the pieces where they belonged. "They've taken the information. I've filed a missing persons report. They're going to . . . it's been a few days since anyone's . . . since I've seen her, so she might be . . ." He paused for a moment, gathering himself, taking a breath. Zoë was still crying. Sam couldn't quiet her no matter which direction she moved. Joe raised his eyebrows a little as if to ask her why.

"Look, I'm really sorry," he said. "I know this is above and beyond the neighbor's call of duty—"

"But?" Gloria said. She walked over to Sam, put an arm around her as if to protect her.

"They want to ask you some questions," Joe said. "The police. The detectives on this . . . this case. You found the baby, Sam, and they want to know . . . Well, they want to ask you some questions. I'm sorry."

"When?" Gloria said.

Joe started to answer, but Sam stopped him. "It doesn't matter when," she said and shot a pleading glance at Gloria. "Of course we'll *both* help in any way we can." She walked over to Joe and patted him on the shoulder with her free hand.

"We'll find her," she said. "Don't worry. We'll find her."

chapter 14

Jessalyn looked at the little basket and the baby sleeping within it and felt something close to panic. This is what happened, she thought, when you let them in close—when you allowed them to see you unwaxed or without makeup, or told them what you really thought or felt, even if only for a moment when they probably weren't listening anyway. It was her fault, she admitted it. She hadn't laid down any ground rules with Joe. It was almost the opposite, in fact. She'd left the details up to him: where they would meet, how often, and what they would do when they got together. And she'd made the critical mistake of *telling* him all this—telling him she wasn't going to put any pressure on him, that they would take it exactly as he wanted to.

What the hell had she been thinking?

She liked Joe. She liked him so much that she thought it could even head into a kind of love. Whatever love was. Jessalyn had been in love once before and it was an experience that she never wanted to repeat. It was, she thought, like having the flu in combination with the worst hangover you'd ever experienced. Again, probably her fault for falling for someone named *Hunter*—not his real name but one he had chosen to advance his going-nowhere acting career. He was probably the best-looking man Jessalyn had ever met and he wasn't just a dumb blond—he had a brain and he was funny. She'd met him on that ridiculous reality show that had done nothing to improve her life or career in any way, especially considering that it was canceled so quickly. It was funny, Jessalyn thought, so many of those stupid plastic bitches who went on those shows—there were so many of them it was impossible to keep track—acted badly. They drank too much, they cursed like sailors, and they fucked half the contestants on the show *on and off camera* and still, after all that, they got guest-hosting spots on other shows or book deals or at least some kind of tabloid celebrity that lasted long enough to bank a little cash. But no, there was none of that for her.

She had fallen hard for Hunter on the show, and he was interested enough in her that it pissed off the five other jealous bitches on the set who then got her voted out in a big hurry and made her look like a worthless slut in the process. Most of the situations on that set had been staged, written, and tailored, but group female jealousy—that shit just wrote itself. Jessalyn had been left with nothing except her feelings for Hunter. And those feelings made her feel sick: trembling, feverish, nauseated, and dizzy. It was so bad that even after he kicked her to the curb, she continued to chase him down, to follow him, park outside his house, go through all the pathetic stalker motions she'd sworn she'd never stoop to.

That was love and Jessalyn didn't ever want to go through it again. But Joe . . . Joe was something else. Affection? She couldn't figure out what the attraction was. He wasn't the best-looking guy in the world, although he was definitely all right—and a big cut above almost all of her regular dates. He wasn't very wealthy either. There wasn't anything outstanding or particularly special about him. He was really just a regular *Joe.* He was married too, which wasn't necessarily a disadvantage. *Married* meant he was guilty, and when they got guilty they were usually nicer all around, trying to make up for something even while they were doing it. Married also meant passion without obligation. But he was a neighbor and that made him a little too close for her comfort. And maybe that was why they had drifted into this place in their relationship—because at this point it *was* a relationship—where he could drop this baby on her and ask her to take care of it.

Because there was no other reason she could think of why he would think that it was an okay thing to do.

He'd said it was only for a few hours, while he went to work, and that he'd be back before she knew it and if the baby woke up, all she needed to do was give her a bottle—and maybe change her diaper—and she'd be fine. He didn't ask, he begged. And when she looked at him then, so stressed out by what was going on in his life, she felt sorry for him, and the words that were on the edge of her lips, about how she didn't feel comfortable taking care of a baby so young because she didn't really have the experience and that maybe he should consider getting a sitter who knew what she was doing, stayed unspoken in her mouth. And maybe there was a little more to it than that as well. She felt real warmth for this man with his domestic dramas and respectful manner. That was it, she now realized, the reason why she felt the stirrings of something that could be more than affection. He seemed to respect her. He was hot for her, sure, that was how it all got started in the first place, but underneath all of that there was a kind of innocent courtesy toward her. She remembered when they were getting dressed and ready to leave the hotel a few days ago, and he had, for no other reason than just to be chivalrous, slipped her shoes onto her feet while she was sitting on the bed buttoning her shirt. Prince Charming did that kind of thing. And Jessalyn was a sucker for all things Prince Charming.

But now here she was with a baby in a basket on her bed and no idea what she would do if the baby woke up and started crying. It was supposed to just come naturally to you if you were a woman. Somehow you were just expected to know what to do with a baby, but Jessalyn had serious doubts about her own maternal capabilities. She had never felt the call to motherhood—never felt a biological or emotional need to reproduce, to create a miniature version of herself. If the time ever came, and Jessalyn assumed that it would, she would have a baby for a man. But for herself, no, Jessalyn did not want a baby. Ever. Of all her secrets, this was the one she guarded the most carefully. There was no bigger sin for a woman—no clearer sign of her lack of normality—than to remain childless by choice, and not because you had some kind of high-powered career (that in and of itself was never a good enough excuse) but because you didn't really like babies or because you didn't think you'd know what to do with a baby if you had one. She glanced over at the infant she'd been entrusted with. Sure, she seemed like she was down for the count, but how long would it be before she woke up and started crying? Then what?

Jessalyn leaned in for a closer look. Well, she *was* very cute at least. Hard to believe you could have a mouth that little, and those tiny eyelashes were adorable. And that smooth tight skin. Jessalyn sighed. You spent the whole rest of your life trying to re-create the skin you had as a baby. Was there ever a moment as a girl when you were happy with the way you looked? If there was, Jessalyn couldn't remember it. There was constantly something too big, not big enough, too loose, too ugly, too soft, too hard, too fat, too fat, too fat. . . . That was always at the core of it, she thought, that permanent worry about looking too fat. It would never end. And soon she'd have to add other procedures to the boob job she'd already had. Botox, collagen, tummy tuck . . . they were probably all in her future.

All this maintenance was expensive. And after a certain point it just stopped working. There was nothing worse than that sucked-out, dried-up, perpetually surprised look of women who had had too much plastic surgery, and it was not the future that Jessalyn wanted for herself. Not that there was much of a future in what she was doing now, even though she really didn't mind it. The sex wasn't all bad and her guys were handpicked: easygoing and not particularly demanding. As far as she was concerned, it was an even exchange. She was willing, they were willing, and everybody got what they wanted. There was never any negotiation. There were *expectations* of generosity, gifts, appreciation. . . . It was all totally on the up and up and more honest than probably half the wives in this neighborhood who gave their husbands annual blow jobs for birthdays or when they wanted jewelry. And it was okay to talk about that too—totally socially acceptable to talk about screwing one's *husband* for money. Jessalyn had heard those conversations herself. Yet those same people wouldn't hesitate to condemn her lifestyle (if they knew anything about it) in the harshest possible terms, as if she were some kind of animal. In the end Jessalyn and the trophy wife up on her hill were the same breed but for one key difference. The wives had security. Jessalyn could count on none of that. She was dependent on her own talent, looks, and the shifting goodwill of the men she dated. There was no way of telling how long any of that would last. Her current situation was fine—even comfortable—but, no, it was not where she wanted to end up.

But, she thought looking down at the baby, neither was this. A love affair was one thing, but a baby—a grandchild, no less—well, that was something else. Jessalyn wasn't about to let herself fall into the role of babysitter or stepmom or whatever position it was Joe wanted to give her. She wondered if he was trying to turn her into Allison, who, she'd just found out, had totally walked out on him. He hadn't given Jessalyn any explanation for that, except to tell her that it had nothing to do with the two of them; he was sure that Allison didn't know anything about their affair. Jessalyn wasn't so sure, but she kept that information to herself. Still, even if Allison did know about them, it probably wasn't the main reason she'd taken off. Joe had told Jessalyn a little about Diana and how she had come to be staying with them. It didn't take a genius to figure out that this whole scenario didn't sit well with Allison, who was a prissy bitch to begin with from what Jessalyn could see. Diana running off and leaving her baby for the two of them to take care of was probably the last straw.

Jessalyn sighed. She hadn't wanted to get caught up in this particular family drama at all, but she supposed it was impossible to avoid it—dirty laundry was the emotional price you paid to be involved romantically with another person. In fact, Jessalyn thought wryly, if you wanted romance without drama, you had to pay cash. But Joe did seem pretty anxious about Diana, and Jessalyn felt bad about that. When he'd brought the baby over, he'd told her about how he'd spent the afternoon with the cops, reporting her as missing, and how, at first, he'd gotten the feeling that they thought he was trying to unload his own parental responsibilities onto them by sending them after a kid who was just playing possum. It took him a while to convince them he wasn't just another rich guy trying to use the police to discipline his spoiled child, he said, and by the end of it he'd become really worried about Diana. Jessalyn had tried to reassure him that Diana was likely fine and just acting out. She'd probably run off before, Jessalyn told him, and this was her way of making a grab for attention. Joe didn't seem convinced, but he guessed it was true, he told her; he didn't really know Diana that well, and even though he couldn't see the point of running away from a place you'd already run away *to,* he wasn't an expert on teenagers.

"They're more adult than most adults these days," Jessalyn told him then. "They know exactly what they're doing."

"I don't think so," he said. "You know that Werner kid, Kevin?"

Jessalyn rolled her eyes, thinking about that fat-assed Dorothy with her mom jeans and her leering husband. "What about him?"

"Diana's been hanging out with him since she got here. He's a bad seed and I just hope she hasn't gotten involved in any kind of drug thing with him. He's in the hospital. At least that's what Dick Werner says. I think he OD'd on something."

"Well, that's not a total surprise," Jessalyn said. "All the kids around here are into that shit. If they aren't taking them, they're selling them."

"What? How do you know that?"

Jessalyn wanted to kick herself. It was entirely unnecessary for Joe to know how she'd come into that particular piece of information, especially since he seemed so completely naive about what was going on in his own neighborhood. In her haste to reassure him, she'd revealed too much, and there was little time to dial it all back. So Jessalyn gave him what she liked to think of as "the look," an expression that promised a good time but only if the questioning stopped immediately. It had taken her years to perfect that look with its bedroom eyes, tilted chin, and pouting lips, but it was worth the effort—her own form of instant hypnosis.

"Joe," she said, giving his face a quick but meaningful caress, "it'll all be fine. You'll see."

He'd left it there, not willing to press for more details and needing to go to work, for which he was already late. Plus, he was so relieved that she'd agreed to watch the baby that he was practically stammering with gratitude.

Jessalyn backed out of her bedroom quietly, as if turning around would wake the baby. She left the door open but didn't know if she'd be able to hear any crying from downstairs. She decided she'd just have to keep coming upstairs to check and make sure, which seemed like a ridiculous plan, but that was what you got for leaving your baby with someone like her. As she wandered into her living room, idly turning on the television and flipping through the channels on mute, she thought about Diana and felt a twinge of annoyance for this girl whom she didn't even know. Why had she decided to have the baby in the first place? Did she want to be like one of those celebrity teen moms? Why didn't these girls realize that nothing was like it seemed on TV? Jessalyn was less than ten years removed from her own high school graduation, but it seemed like things had gone backward by at least fifty. None of the girls she knew who'd gotten pregnant in high school weighed any options other than which clinic would provide the easiest and least expensive abortion. It wasn't smarter or more honorable to have a baby and then not be able to deal with it afterward, which was obviously what had happened to Diana. Unless the girl really *was* in trouble. But Jessalyn didn't want to think about that.

There was nothing worth watching on television. Since her own dismal experience, Jessalyn had a hard time watching any kind of reality show without gagging, but these days reality shows were all you could find. She was about to settle for a lame cooking show on the Food Network when she heard her doorbell ring and froze, her hand gripping the remote control like it was a gun. She wasn't expecting a date, her night was free, and none of her very small circle of friends would drop by unannounced. An unexpected visitor could only mean trouble or bad news and for that reason Jessalyn wanted to ignore it—pretend she'd never heard it in the first place. But all her lights were on and it was obvious she was home. Her visitor would know that, whoever it was. She took a step toward the door and stopped again, half-amazed by her own indecision. But when the bell sounded a second time, she realized that it was probably Joe and that thankfully, he'd come back earlier than he'd said. She ran a hand through her hair, tousling it a little, and strutted over to the door.

The man she knew only as Spence (first name or last she had no idea and had never asked) stood in her doorway holding a bottle of Veuve Clicquot in one hand and a small silver box in the other. He was wearing suit pants and a dress shirt unbuttoned at the neck. His round forehead was shiny with perspiration and his eyes were very dark. His face was pale, but his neck looked flushed. She opened her mouth to speak, but he was prepared and got the words out first.

"I know, I know," he said, grinning. "But I need to celebrate. It was a big day for me today. A *big* day. And nobody I know can appreciate that more than you."

"I . . ." It had never happened before, Jessalyn realized. Not one of them had ever just shown up. There were rules. There were levels of fantasy to maintain. She hadn't prepared for this, didn't know what to say, and was angry at herself because of it.

"If it's not convenient, just say the word," he said. Jessalyn could see that he was looking over her shoulder into the house, his eyes scanning for signs of another man. If he could get away with it, Jessalyn thought, he'd probably be sniffing the air. "I know this is *unexpected,* but"—he waved the bottle of bubbly in the air—"I took a chance. What do you say, Jessie? Are you up for a little company—because I know *I* am."

Jessalyn smiled and made a show of licking her lips. She was playing for time, the wheels in her brain turning too slowly. Spence was changing the parameters of their relationship and it was going to have to be discussed and sorted out. But she couldn't talk to him about it now—he was in no frame of mind to have one of those conversations. He was obviously high.

Something speedy—coke or meth. She could practically hear the crackle of his brain and crease of his cheeks as he stretched them with that frantic grin. The Widow might mellow him out, though. It was lucky that she happened to be wearing low-rise workout pants and a cropped T-shirt and hadn't taken a shower since the morning. Spence had a thing about the gym and felt about activewear the way most men felt about lingerie. He liked athleticism—and the taste of sweat. And it was also fortunate that there was nobody else around so that part of the fantasy stayed intact, which was probably a big relief for him even if he did know he was taking a chance of ruining everything with this impromptu visit. So there was that. There was also need—for both of them. And just like that, the decision was made.

"Well," she said, "I just had a workout. I was going to jump in the shower, but I could wait for . . ."

"About an hour?" he asked, one foot already crossing the threshold.

"I could wait for an hour," she said, and stood aside to let him in.

Wrong, Jessalyn thought. Something was wrong and she should have known it as soon as she saw him at the door. She was sitting in mud-flap girl pose, her knees drawn up and her head tilted backward. There was a line of cocaine on her left breast and a pool of champagne on her crotch. Spence was bent over her like a dog, alternately snorting and lapping. She could feel anger or tension buzzing off him, something barely controlled—not like him. She should have known. He didn't want any small talk—no time for a civilized drink out of crystal flutes in the living room—just straight upstairs to the big room and the big bed.

"I brought you a little present," he said, and placed the small silver box on the nightstand. Her eyes followed his hand, watching the box land, taking note of its exact placement, and when she turned back to him he was already unbuttoning his pants. "Not the bed," he said. "The floor."

"So," she said, "what's your big news?" But it was useless. She was sticking to a script that had been changed without her knowledge or approval and he was having none of it.

Now here they were—the drugs a new twist, but one that she hadn't had the nerve to forbid. There was something wrong with him and she should have known better. Her eyes found the clock and calculated the twenty-six minutes left in what she already knew was going to be the longest hour of her life. He was grunting. "Lay down," he barked. He poured the remainder of the bottle over her. This wasn't the way it was supposed to be, she thought as he loomed over her. His eyes, black from their dilated pupils, were forming a plan, and Jessalyn knew—knew now with no doubt—that it was about to go badly wrong.

"What the fuck is that?" He jerked his head up, reddening—those expensive hair plugs of his standing out in sharp relief against the shine of his head.

"Wha—" Jessalyn started, but then she too heard it outside the buzz of her own head. The baby. In her bedroom the baby she'd completely forgotten about had woken up and was screaming her little head off.

"Is that a fucking *baby?* What the *fuck?*"

"I . . ." Jessalyn sat up. Champagne rolled sparkling and sticky to the floor. "Shit. I'm sorry, I forgot."

"What?"

"It's the neighbor's baby. I—I'm babysitting."

"What the fuck?" he repeated. He stood up. The baby's wails grew louder. Jessalyn couldn't decide whether she should go pacify the baby or stay there and pacify Spence.

"I wasn't expecting you tonight," Jessalyn said.

"You could have told me there was a baby here," he said. "Before you let me in."

Jessalyn stood up, and they stared at each other for a moment. She tried so hard not to, but Jessalyn flicked her gaze downward, just long enough to see that Spence was done in and long enough for him to see her do it. "Are you going to do something about that crying?" he said.

"I could . . ." Jessalyn was lost—completely unable to figure out what was the right thing to do. "I could go and close the door," she said. "It'll just take a second. She'll quiet down."

As she was looking at it, Jessalyn knew she would remember the expression on his face until the day she died. It was a toxic mix of disgust and contempt shaded by loathing, both for her and for himself, the likes of which she had never seen. Never, never before this moment had Jessalyn felt as naked or as ashamed.

"Fuck that," he said and picked up his pants from the floor. He looked over at the silver box and then back to her. "Keep it," his mouth said, but what Jessalyn heard was *Whore,* as loud as if he'd screamed it in her ear.

He was gone less than five minutes later and she knew he would never be back. Jessalyn put on a thick white terry-cloth robe and went into her bedroom. She picked up the baby and held her to her padded shoulder. "Okay," she said, "okay now." She rubbed the baby's back, so small and sweaty, and smoothed the back of her head. "Okay, shh, baby, okay." Jessalyn rocked from side to side, patting, rubbing, soothing. In a minute she got quieter, still crying but no longer hysterical, small sounds of need coming from deep inside her baby chest.

"I'm sorry," Jessalyn said. "I'm so sorry."

chapter 15

Dorothy hid under the eaves, her back pressed hard against the stucco wall, and drew deeply from her first cigarette in too many years to count. It was very stale, but that didn't matter at all. She blew out a cloud, watched the breeze waft it over her star jasmine, and inhaled another. No coughing, no awkwardness holding it between her fingers. Smoking, like so many other relinquished bad habits, was like riding a bicycle. It didn't matter how long it had been, you never forgot how. She held the cigarette to her lips again. She hadn't realized how much she'd missed this bad old friend until now. For a minute all she had to do was focus on inhaling, exhaling, and feeling the nicotine rush inside her skull. It didn't stop the thoughts from jamming her brain, but it made them, however briefly, a little more tolerable. At the very least, it gave her something to do and a reason to stand still as she pondered what was surely coming next.

Dorothy had never believed in karma, either as a serious philosophy or a light half-joking explanation for unpleasantness or bad luck. She believed, instead, that it was possible to nullify the past with the present. In her opinion everything had an expiration date and that included actions and events. In other words, if a tree fell in the woods thirty years ago and there was nobody around now who had heard it, then it had never fallen in the first place. It had been imperative for Dorothy to hold fast to this line of thinking in order to form the days, months, and years of her life into her own reality. But that thick layer of protection she'd constructed over time had suddenly thinned into nothing. What went around had indeed come around.

But not all of it.

Dorothy inhaled the last of her cigarette and carefully crushed it out in a small glass ramekin she'd brought outside for this express purpose. The rest of it—maybe even the worst of it—was still on the way. Although, she thought, what had happened with Kevin was already bad enough for this and several other lifetimes.

Dick was with Kevin now. The two of them were investigating an alternative school in which Kevin could finish his senior year and graduate high school. Dorothy had not been invited on this outing. The excuse Dick gave for excluding her was that he needed "man time" alone with his son, but Dorothy knew the real reason was that he blamed her for everything and thought that by shutting her out of this particular decision he could make it all right. Ultimately of course he would have to ask Dorothy what she thought and would have to bring her along for any kind of meeting because Dorothy alone had gone to see teachers, counselors, and principals throughout Kevin's school years. Dick would have no idea what to do or say—especially when he had to explain why Kevin needed a new school to begin with. Because Dick still didn't believe that Kevin had a *substance abuse problem,* even though Kevin had admitted to taking drugs. It was, Dick believed, someone else's fault: society, Dorothy, even that girl. Especially that girl. As if Kevin were completely lacking in any kind of free will. And as if another school, another location, or another mother would make a difference.

But Dick's attitude, including his resentment at her failure as a mother, didn't hurt Dorothy nearly as much as the blame she heaped on herself. To not have noticed—or maybe to have willfully ignored—that Kevin had a drug problem was both inexplicable and unforgivable. How much longer would he have lived if Dick hadn't gone into his room at that moment and tried to wake him up? And what if she hadn't insisted that they leave, thus prompting him to go up there in the first place? Dorothy could barely even ask herself those questions, let alone speculate on their answers. Although she'd been almost catatonic with shock and fear at the hospital, she managed to gather that it had been a close call. She couldn't get the image out of her mind—it flashed in front of her all day and woke her up at night—of her son lying there on his bed, one arm fallen to the floor, his skin so pale, and Dick leaning over him, desperately trying to breathe life into him to keep him alive until the paramedics arrived. She hated to admit it to herself even now, but at that terrible moment as she stood frozen in the doorway watching Dick sweat and work on his son, gasping the command "Breathe!" as if Kevin could hear him, Dorothy was sure that they'd lost him. She sensed the weight of excruciating grief descending on her and knew that she wouldn't be able to bear it. She gave up. And for that moment of faithless surrender Dorothy's guilt was the sharpest and most painful. Because even after the paramedics arrived and raced Kevin to the hospital, even after she and Dick stumbled into the brightness of the emergency room and allowed the doctors to take over, she still didn't believe her son would survive. When a doctor came to tell them that Kevin was okay, Dorothy was surprised. It seemed like a cheat—the last one she would ever be able to get away with.

What was so strange, although of course *not* surprising, was that in those minutes and hours she and Dick were closer to each other—more intimate and truly *married*—than they'd ever been before. There wasn't much talking between the two of them. They stood outside the trauma room, their own separate fears intersecting and blending. At one point Dick took her hand in his and held it. She couldn't remember the last time he'd done that, if he ever had. She remembered little else of the physical details of those hours, but she could still feel the pressure of his fingers around hers and how cold his hand felt. They were, for once, in complete harmony with each other—on the same wavelength, you might say, although that wave was the size of a tsunami. It reminded her of the day

Kevin was born in that very hospital. She'd been dozing with Kevin in his little Isolette next to her. When she woke, Dick had appeared in the room. He was sitting on the chair next to her bed, holding the tiny bundle that was their son and staring at him with a look of complete joy on his face. There was pride there too, Dorothy remembered, and hope. Then Dick looked up and his eyes met hers with such thankfulness and love that Dorothy almost cried. Until that moment outside the trauma room, Dorothy had never felt as joined to her husband.

But that closeness didn't last. It couldn't.

As soon as they learned that Kevin was going to survive, but before they knew exactly what had happened to him, Dorothy could feel something inside Dick turn stony and cold. He kept it all together, jaw muscles clenched, as the doctor described how Kevin had overdosed on narcotics and that he'd seen this kind of thing before in kids Kevin's age and asked them again what if any prescription medications they might have in the house that Kevin could have gotten hold of. Dick managed to answer the questions, and, Dorothy now thought, he must have filled out all the paperwork at the hospital and dealt with the insurance, but she had no memory of any of that. But afterward, so soon afterward, he began to look at Dorothy with accusation.

"How is it possible you didn't know about this?" he asked.

"How would I have been able to tell?" she asked.

"Because he's your son," Dick spat. "You're supposed to know."

"But you didn't see anything either."

"I'm not his mother, Dorothy! I'm not home with him every day. I work, remember?"

"Dick, if I'd had any idea, don't you think I would have said something to you?"

"I don't know, Dorothy, would you have?"

And it went on like that. Pretty soon, though, Dick started assigning the blame for Kevin's problems to whomever he could think of, including random degenerates who sold drugs to Kevin (he didn't know who these might be, but he suspected they were spoiled rich kids from Kevin's school who had too much time and money on their hands) and various "bad influences" that included everyone from Diana to Dorothy herself.

"I thought he was out," Dorothy repeated over and over again. "I saw him leave. I didn't even know he was at home until you went up there."

Of course, Dick hadn't seen that there was anything wrong with Kevin then either. Dorothy didn't mention that, but she knew Dick was thinking about it. Still, it didn't matter who had done what at those moments, because as soon as the immediate crisis was over, the long, grueling calamity began.

Dick had restrained himself while Kevin was in the hospital, barely saying anything to his son other than, "We'll work this all out once you're out of here," but Dorothy knew, as she was sure Kevin did too, that Dick was storing all of his anger for their private homecoming. And although Kevin could hardly look at her while he was in the hospital, the few flashes of stark fear she'd seen on his face were enough to convince her that he was dreading his release.

Dorothy took a second cigarette from her ancient pack and lit it. She was going to have to figure out how to dispose of these butts once she'd finished. It was such a minor concern, yet Dorothy fretted inwardly, anxious to hide this evidence of her transgression. She wouldn't be able to stand up to an interrogation about it—not even one as soft as the one Dick had ultimately given Kevin. Well, maybe *soft* wasn't exactly the right word. It was more . . . *suggestive.* It was obvious how Dick wanted Kevin to answer. And even after all Kevin had been through, he was able to pick up on that and oblige.

"First of all, what was it, Kevin? What were you taking?" Dick had stood, hands on his hips, stiffly squared off against his completely defenseless son, and Dorothy remembered thinking that her husband would make a really crappy cop.

It was another one of those times when Dorothy was in the room physically yet strangely absent from it at the same time. She'd felt like that before—the last time was when they'd had that dreadful confrontation with Joe and Allison—as if she were a moving image who could see and hear but had no voice or substance.

"Oxy," Kevin said. Dorothy could see that it wasn't worth it to him to lie. It was going to come out anyway.

"Oxy? What's that?"

Kevin sighed as if he could hardly stand to explain such things to his hopelessly out-of-it father, but he managed to get out a brief description of OxyContin: prescription painkillers in pill form. Dick looked baffled.

"Where do you get such a thing?" he asked, and Kevin shrugged. "Around," he answered.

"What does that mean, 'around'?"

"You know," Kevin said. "People have it."

"Other kids have it?"

"Yeah."

"Your friends?"

"Yeah."

"Which friends?"

"You don't know them, Dad."

"So, what, you decided to try it once? Is that what happened?"

That was the turning point, Dorothy thought, the moment where Kevin understood fully what his father wanted to hear and gave it to him.

It was only the first time, Kevin told Dick; no, okay, the second time he had tried it, and he didn't know how strong it was. It was a mistake and he shouldn't have done it, and yes, he knew it was stupid, but it wasn't as if he had a *problem* or anything. Everybody did it. Everybody.

He looked down at his hands almost the entire time he delivered this unimpressive little speech the likes of which had been given to parents since the beginning of time. Dorothy didn't believe him—not because she didn't want to but because she couldn't. Now that the blinders had been removed, it was easy to recognize the signs of dependence in Kevin. How far or deep it went Dorothy didn't know, but when Kevin lifted his head she could see a familiar hurt in his light blue eyes. How had it gotten there, she wondered. Was it handed down in the blood? Had she . . . had she passed it to him inside her womb? Guilt rose in her throat, bitter and sharp. Her heart ached for him, but she was too far removed, too buried, too hidden away to say it. To say anything.

And so Dick carried on with his questioning, periodically interrupting himself to interject something about how Kevin would have to be disciplined because he couldn't expect, after scaring his parents out of their minds ("You almost *died,* Kevin, do you understand that?") with his own selfishness and stupidity because he certainly hadn't been raised that way, to be let off scot-free. There were going to be changes made, big changes. And the first thing was to take him out of that damn school where he was hanging out with all these *friends* who were giving him those pills, whatever they were called.

"Right," Kevin said at one point. "It's definitely the school's fault."

Even Kevin knew how ridiculous that was, Dorothy thought.

"You think you're so smart?" Dick asked. "You want to blame someone else? Me, maybe? Or your mother? Because the two of us have denied you so much? Because you've had such a goddamned tough life?"

But it was Dick who was blaming everyone else.

"Sending me to another school's not going to change anything."

"What's that mean? That you're going to do this again? Is that what you're saying, Kevin?"

"No, Dad, I told you. . . . I told you. . . ."

Dick drew himself up then as Kevin sank farther into the couch. He needed a haircut, Dorothy thought, and some sun. He was so pale, so defeated.

"There's one more thing," Dick said, "and you better be very careful how you answer me now, Kevin. I'm only going to warn you once." He paused dramatically and Dorothy thought she could see Kevin shiver.

"What has that girl got to do with this? Tell me, Kevin, and don't even *think* about lying to me."

Kevin looked up at his father, a tiny spark of defiance lighting his eyes. "What *girl*, Dad?"

"That—" Dick caught himself and cleared his throat. "That girl down the street. The girl with the baby. You *know* what girl I'm talking about, Kevin."

"Diana," Kevin said. Dorothy could hear the emotion strangled in the back of his throat. "Her name's Diana."

"Well?" Dick asked. "What did she have to do with all of this? Is she the one you got those pills from? Is she?"

Kevin shook his head. "Of course not," he said. "She was—" He clamped his lips abruptly. "No," he repeated. "And I don't know why you would even ask that."

"You don't know why? Are you kidding me?" Dick clapped his hands together for punctuation. "Everything's gone downhill around here since that girl arrived. Everything. So I don't see why you'd be surprised that I ask a question like that. I'm going to ask you again, Kevin, is that who you got the pills from?"

"No."

"Then *who?*"

For the briefest moment, Dorothy saw Kevin's eyes flick toward the front window as if he was worried someone was watching them and then come back to Dick. "I don't know," he said. "Just some . . . people. Some kids at school. I don't even know if they go to school there. I couldn't even tell you their names."

"Kevin, do you know where she is?" Dorothy heard her own voice echoing in her ears.

"Where who is?"

"Diana. Where is she?"

"What do you mean, where is she?" Kevin said. He couldn't look at her or Dick. He picked at a hole in his jeans and kept his eyes fixed downward.

"She's missing. Or hiding. Or ran away," Dick said harshly. "They're looking for her. They've been looking for her and they're going to ask you if you know where she is. So do you know anything? You'd better tell us if you do."

But Kevin knew nothing, at least nothing that he shared with them, and Dorothy believed that he was truly in the dark about Diana's whereabouts. Exactly when he had seen her last was not as clear. Kevin said he hadn't seen her for a long time, although he couldn't be specific about when exactly.

"I don't know," he kept saying. "Sometime, I don't know."

"Well?" Dick pressed on. "*Tell us,* Kevin. I—we know you've seen her."

Kevin admitted it then—owned up that he and Diana had spent time together even after the edict that they remain apart. But they hadn't seen each other for a while. And they weren't together anymore anyway, Kevin added, so Dick didn't have to worry himself about it any longer.

"Why not?" Dorothy asked, surprising herself with the question. "Why aren't you together anymore? What happened?"

Dick and Kevin both turned to her, looking perplexed. "What's it matter?" Kevin said, and in his tone, Dorothy heard everything. For whatever reason, Diana had split up with him and he was heartbroken.

"I don't know," Dorothy said, "but maybe it has something to do with why she's not here anymore. Or where she went."

"What's the big deal?" Kevin snorted. "She probably just went home."

"But why would she leave the baby, Kevin? Do you know anything about that?" Dorothy hadn't realized how much she'd hoped that Kevin would have an explanation for this until he looked at her, shock and misery plain on his face.

"She left the baby?" Kevin's voice was small and strained.

"Give it a rest, Dorothy," Dick barked. "He said he doesn't know."

And then Dorothy knew that things were going to get much worse. Because if Kevin didn't know where Diana had gone, Joe certainly didn't.

And if Joe didn't, the police were going to get even more involved than they already had. And if the police became involved, they were going to want to talk to everyone.

Dorothy drew deeply from her cigarette, which had finally succeeded in making her feel dizzy and nauseated. Kevin probably knew more than he was saying, but he didn't know enough.

Where had she gone?

Maybe it wasn't as easy now, heaven only knew, with cell phones and the Internet, everything traceable to the point where you almost had a computer chip implanted in your skin, but if a person wanted to disappear—just wanted to escape the mess she'd made and start over from scratch, everything fresh and new—it could still be done. Yes, Dorothy believed it could. Diana wouldn't have gone back to her mother. No, she'd never see her mother again nor any of these people she'd left behind. That would all have to go, as well as her name, the clothes she wore, the way she spoke, the personal history she had once claimed. Those tattoos, Dorothy thought, remembering the snake around one of Diana's ankles and the apple on the other. Those tattoos would have to go as well. It wouldn't be difficult. You could do that now. The internal marks were harder to erase, but even those could be covered. Dorothy knew all about that.

But there was the baby. . . . That was a sacrifice so big it gave Dorothy pause.

How could she have left her baby behind?

At that moment, just as Dorothy's mind formed the question, she heard rustling leaves on Sam's side of the fence and then what sounded like footsteps. Instinctively, Dorothy crushed what remained of her cigarette in the ramekin and waved the lingering smoke away with her hands.

"Dorothy? I didn't know you smoked."

She could just turn away, Dorothy thought. Just take her dead cigarettes and go inside, pretending she hadn't heard anything or seen Sam peering through an opening in the fence slats looking for conversation. But for once Dorothy was too tired to even move. She could feel the adrenaline surging, signaling fight or flight, but both her body and mind were unresponsive to the call. Her hands were trembling. She stepped out from under the eaves, her legs feeling leaden.

"I don't smoke," she said. She could just make out Sam's face in the narrow opening, but she saw the edges of her smile. For sure Dick didn't know about this gap in the fence or he would have made sure to close it long ago.

"I know," Sam said conspiratorially. "I don't smoke either."

"No, really," Dorothy said. "I just . . . I just found this pack. It's very old." She took another step closer to the fence. "And I thought . . ."

"Yeah," Sam said. There was another rustle as Sam stepped backward into the pile of leaves collected on her side of the fence. Dorothy thought she was going to back up all the way and retreat into her house, but she didn't. "Dorothy . . . Listen, I wanted to ask you . . ."

Dorothy froze again, trying to figure out how she felt about this encounter, trying to imagine what question Sam could possibly have for her.

"Is Kevin okay?" Sam asked. "I mean, I know it's not my business, Dorothy, but . . . I'm a mom too."

Dorothy felt dizzy again. Little dots of light danced in front of her. There was a bit of a breeze and for that she was very thankful, even though it was still so warm. It was never going to cool down this year. At this rate they'd all be celebrating Christmas on the beach like it was the Fourth of July. She tried to steady herself, but it seemed like the earth beneath her was shifting. Was it an earthquake or was everything else just cracking apart? Something was happening, she thought. Something. Her head started pounding. She was so low on her medication, but she had to take a pill. It was only going to get worse.

"Dorothy?"

"Kevin?" she asked. What to say? Kevin wasn't okay. Nothing was okay, really, and there was no easy way of packaging that in a short sentence. "Kevin's home," she said. "I mean, he's not home at this very moment, he's out with Dick. They're both out right now. But he was . . . he was in the hospital. He's home now. I mean, not . . . Sorry, I said that already."

"Dorothy, would you mind if I came over for a minute? Would that be okay?"

"Um . . ." Dorothy tried to think of a reason to say no and couldn't come up with one.

"Just hold on," Sam said. "I'm coming right over. Just stay there, okay?"

"Why?" Dorothy asked. "I mean, do you want some coffee or something? Should I make some coffee? I think I have some cake. . . ."

But Sam had already disappeared from her place at the fence, leaving Dorothy talking to the leaves. Dorothy clenched and unclenched her fingers. The pain in her head was increasing, sharp points pressing into her skull. She looked down at what she was wearing: an old pair of high-waisted jeans with a bleach stain at the left hem and a tired gray T-shirt that was fraying at the sleeves. She really wasn't prepared for company. And then she thought she should probably go inside and make sure that the kitchen was clean because suddenly she couldn't remember if she had done the breakfast dishes yet, although she must have because that was when she got the idea to dig into her old can and pull out these stale cigarettes. But before she could turn and walk back into her house, she saw the oddest thing: Sam appeared at the back of her yard, clambering across her star jasmine and holding a baby—yes, a baby, all bundled up in a fluffy white blanket. She walked right up to Dorothy, her eyes looking concerned but also kind.

"Sam," Dorothy said, "I do have a front door."

Sam laughed; the sound full of genuine amusement and, Dorothy thought, relief. She reached out with her free hand and clasped Dorothy's shoulder. "I'm sorry, Dorothy, I know. I just . . . You seemed a little strange for a minute there. I am sorry."

Dorothy didn't move Sam's hand off her shoulder. It felt warm and comforting somehow. She gestured toward the baby. "Is that—"

The smile faded quickly from Sam's face. "Diana's baby," she said. "I've been taking care of her while Joe . . . It's been kind of hard for him with Allison gone and . . . everything." Sam shifted the baby from her shoulder to the crook of her arm and Dorothy looked in at her sleeping face.

"So little," Dorothy said, reaching out, despite herself, to stroke the small plump cheek and then stopping just in time when she smelled the residue of stale smoke on her own hand.

"And she hardly cries at all," Sam said without missing a beat. "She's so easy." She rocked back and forth a little. Sam was pretty, Dorothy thought. A little on the thin side, but it suited her. She'd never really noticed that before and she wondered why.

"Have the police talked to Kevin yet, Dorothy?"

"The police?"

"About Diana? Have they? Joe waited so long. The posters are up, but I don't even think people look at those."

"Posters?"

"I'm really getting worried about her, Dorothy. This isn't right. I mean, I don't think she just took off."

For a moment, Dorothy couldn't breathe. It was as if all the air had been sucked out of her lungs and they couldn't reexpand. She felt as if she were standing on the edge of the Earth with one foot dangling off, about to fall and plunge into space. She opened her mouth and took in a big gulping breath, feeling the oxygen flood her brain. There were, she thought, two very distinct ways of leaping off the edge. It took only a second to decide which one to take.

"Do you want to come inside?" she asked Sam.

november 2007

Joe was already on the freeway headed south toward the airport when he realized that he'd forgotten to move the stack of "Missing" posters off the passenger seat. He hadn't wanted that to be the first thing Yvonne saw when she got into the car. Leaving one hand on the steering wheel he grabbed the papers and attempted to move them to the backseat. But they weren't banded together and slid out of his grasp as he reached backward and they fell, splaying out on the floor behind the seat. Perfect, he thought, he'd managed to make it even worse. Now it looked like he was so heartless he couldn't even be bothered to keep these posters—themselves an indictment of his failure to take care of Diana—in an orderly, respectful pile. He hoped he'd have enough time to stop and deal with them before Yvonne made her way off the plane.

He saw that one of the posters had gotten caught between the seat and the gear shift. He pulled it free, folded it, and slipped it into the glove compartment but not without once again seeing the incredible sadness in the cheaply reproduced photo of Diana. He wished he'd had a better one to offer, but who would have thought he'd need a current photo for the purposes of identification? They weren't the kind of family that snapped endless shots of one another in every conceivable pose. In the short time Diana had been with them, nobody had felt either familial or particularly photogenic. Had Diana not decided she needed some photos of Zoë, there might not have been one of her either. She'd asked to borrow his digital camera, Joe recalled, only a couple of weeks ago—it was right before the fire, he'd told the police when he'd given them the photo—so she could take pictures of the baby. She'd snapped a few of Zoë and then he'd taken the camera from her and taken a few of them together and one close-up of Diana. She was looking away from the camera, down at Zoë in her arms, not smiling. It was soft and sad and slightly blurred. Diana didn't like it and told him to delete the photo, but he kept it anyway. He could never have anticipated that it would end up being the most recent photograph anyone had of her.

Joe felt the toxic combination of guilt, fear, and helplessness churning his stomach into a too-familiar sickness. It was disgraceful, really, that he had only those few photographs of Diana and Zoë to show for the time she'd been living with him. He didn't know how he'd manage to explain that to Yvonne either, when he saw her. What parent—no matter how late he'd come to the game—didn't take pictures of his own daughter for the mantel? The truth of the matter was that neither he nor Yvonne was going to win any parenting awards, but Diana hadn't disappeared from Yvonne's house; she'd gone missing on *his* watch. That was a critical difference.

Worse still, and what made Joe feel like a complete asshole, was that he hadn't formed a strong enough attachment to Diana to even miss her now. Well no, that wasn't quite right. Her absence filled him with dread, but it wasn't as if he missed seeing her every morning at breakfast or every evening at dinner. They just hadn't had enough time or normalcy to develop those routines. Of course he was worried about where she was and what might have happened to her and all kinds of grim scenarios had been going through his head every day and night since she'd been gone. He wasn't an idiot; he knew that even the best case (that she'd run away) had the potential for a bad outcome, and he couldn't even bring himself to imagine the worst case. But despite this fear, he wasn't grief stricken or terrified or moved to any kind of extreme action just so that he could be *doing something.* Joe knew that these were the kinds of responses that parents of missing children had and he didn't feel any of them.

He wished—more than he had ever wished for anything in his entire life—that none of this had ever happened. But he wasn't emotionally devastated. And for this, guilt gnawed at his guts. Because while he couldn't be faulted for not knowing Diana before she'd arrived at his door that hot July day, he was entirely responsible for not getting closer to her afterward. He didn't know if they could have created such a deep father-daughter bond in that period, but he regretted now that he hadn't tried harder. Maybe if they'd developed more of a relationship she wouldn't have run off. And maybe if he'd gotten to know her better, he would be able to understand *why* she'd run off. *If* she'd run off.

Joe knew he respected Diana's innate toughness and admired what he'd thought was a quick intellect, but there were way too many open questions about her essential nature and personality that he didn't have answers to because there just hadn't been time. If she'd grown up with him—even near him—Joe would have known how he felt about Diana. It wouldn't have even mattered whether or not he liked her because he was her parent and he would have loved her.

But Joe hadn't had a chance to learn to like her *or* love her. Not really and not the way he should. And that, of course, was the real problem. Because that kind of uncertainty showed. And maybe it even looked like guilt. He could see it in the faces of the cops when he'd gone to report her missing and then in the attitudes of the detectives, Garcia and Williams, who were assigned to the case. He felt it from Sam when she cared for the baby, which, he admitted, was probably more often than she should considering she wasn't an actual relative. *Why did you wait so long? Why don't you know where she is? Isn't she your daughter?* That they couldn't possibly understand the situation didn't matter. Because how could he be expected to explain it in the first place?

And then there was Yvonne. Whatever subtle accusation he'd felt insinuated by the police or Sam or anyone else who was privy to his personal nightmare was nothing compared to the level of reproach he'd felt coming from Yvonne when he'd finally gotten her on the phone. That call too had been delayed longer than it should have. Although the rational part of him knew it was unlikely, a much bigger part wanted to believe that Diana had just gone home to her mother, and he clung to that belief in the hours and days after the evacuation. Of course he should have called Yvonne right away, he knew that. But . . .

They hadn't spoken to each other since Diana had arrived. They'd exchanged some very brief messages *through* Diana, mostly having to do with health insurance, but hadn't actually heard each other's voices. Although Diana hadn't gone into details, it was obvious that her relationship with her mother was at some kind of low point. Joe didn't know—and could hardly be expected to know—whether Diana had more than the usual teenage anger and hostility toward her mother, but she did seem, especially as her foolish romance with Kevin had gained traction, particularly hostile and bitter about Yvonne. She'd even said at one point, although Joe couldn't remember now when it was, that she hated her mother and never wanted to live with her again. He'd taken it for what he assumed it was—typical mother/daughter stuff rooted in whatever psychologists were touting as the latest reason for friction between parents and children—but he'd wondered if there was something else going on between them that went deeper than that. He just didn't see what could be gained by talking to Yvonne about any of it, though, so he hadn't tried to contact her on his own until . . . well, until he had to.

And even then he couldn't get her on the phone at first. He left a message—halting and weird even to his own ears—giving no details but telling her that she should call him as soon as possible. He waited longer than he thought he'd have to for a call back from her, although he assumed—and Yvonne later confirmed—that she'd tried Diana's phone first, thinking that she and Joe had gotten into some kind of argument, but got no response. By the time they finally spoke, both of them were edgy and anxious.

It was funny, Joe thought, the things you remembered and those you forgot. It was close on twenty years since he'd seen or spoken to Yvonne, yet her voice, with its low intonations and lilting cadences, brought him right back to the last day they'd spent together. He answered the phone and she said, "Hello, Joe," and he was back there in that small hot Los Angeles garden apartment they'd shared briefly—the one with the drunken feuding neighbors and the barking dogs—her breath in his ear, whispering and imploring, always wanting something more from him than he was able to give. He remembered it instantly, viscerally, that terrible fight they'd had, both of them screaming ugly things that could never be taken back, then both of them crying, both of them cursing, then kissing and crazy, angry, exquisite sex, and then nothing more to say. But as clear as that was, at the same time he couldn't remember any specifics about the way she looked other than that she was always stylish, chic, and beautiful. He had an image, of course, glowing and dreamlike from its long storage in his memory, but it was vague—more shape and curve than detail. He couldn't recall, for example, precisely what color her eyes were. He thought he remembered that they were a kind of burnt amber color, but he couldn't be sure. He remembered vividly the soft feel of her skin beneath his hands but not how she wore her hair, or any of the exact sentences they had exchanged that last day.

"Yvonne," he said, and then there was a long, sweaty pause full of uncertainty and deep-packed regret.

"I got your message," she said finally. "And I'm guessing that you want Diana to come home?" She cleared her throat and when she spoke again her voice was harder and edged with anger. "Is that right?"

"She's not there?" Joe asked. "Diana hasn't come home? I was hoping she might be there. With you."

There was another pause and this time Joe could feel tension and fear grow and crackle between them. "What's going on, Joe?" she said at last. "Where's my daughter?"

He told her, choosing his words as carefully as he could, about the fires (surely she'd heard about how a half-million people were evacuated from San Diego County?), the confusion afterward, everyone scattered in various places and hotels very hard to come by, and then, when they all came back home after the evacuation orders were lifted . . . He thought Diana was with one of the neighbors. But when he found out that the baby was with another neighbor . . .

He stopped and started many times, his voice and story sounding progressively more strained, but Yvonne didn't interrupt him. It was as if she wanted to pay attention to all the information he was giving so that she could put it together, draw from it, figure out what had happened.

When he finally sputtered out, Yvonne asked him if they'd had an argument. Asked if Joe had told Diana to leave. He heard the accusation in her voice and almost said something about how that was more *her* style because that was how Diana ended up with him in the first place, but he held it back. He was amazed that she could make him angry so quickly like that—it was the kind of conditioned response that Yvonne had always been so good at getting out of him. He told her that there hadn't been any kind of argument that would have led to Diana running away (he skipped the whole part about telling her not to see Kevin because technically that wasn't an argument), and he had most certainly not insisted or even asked that she leave. The plan was *ultimately* for Diana to go home, but they hadn't even discussed that yet. Yvonne asked him if he was sure about that and Joe said he was.

"Well, then why would she leave, Joe?" Yvonne asked.

"Don't you think you have a better answer to that question than I do?" Joe answered. And that was when Yvonne unleashed the resentment she'd been holding on to for seventeen years. How she'd never asked him for anything, how she'd struggled all these years to raise his daughter, how he never showed any interest at all in his own flesh and blood, how many nights she'd lain awake wondering how that could be so, and now, now this. Joe mostly listened and let her go on. There was no point, he thought, in challenging her.

In the end, the conversation went on so long that Joe's cell phone was hot and out of bars by the time he hung up. Yvonne had gone from calm to angry to controlled and then finally to a contained sort of panic. She and Joe had agreed on a coordinated plan: She would talk to all of Diana's friends in Las Vegas in case she had called any of them or, with any luck, had gone to stay with one of them, and Joe would talk to the police, the neighbors, anyone who Diana might have confided in.

"She's a headstrong girl," Yvonne said. "I've never been able to tell her anything about anything. But she isn't stupid. She's never been stupid."

Joe didn't know what to add to that, so he just agreed that he didn't think Diana was stupid at all. And then he said, "I'm sure she's okay," but he didn't sound convincing, even to himself, and he was sure that Yvonne heard him wavering as well. They made a plan to speak again the next day—or sooner if either one of them discovered anything—and take it from there.

It wasn't until they disconnected that Joe realized they'd only barely mentioned Zoë and that Allison hadn't come up at all. She had to know he was married, he thought. Certainly, Diana had said something to her about Allison. But no, it was as if everyone else in their lives—including their own grandchild—had disappeared for the length of that awful conversation, leaving just the two of them, their mutual history, and the missing child they'd created together.

Traffic slowed, as it always did, at the split between the 805 and 5 freeways going south. As Joe crawled through the bottleneck, he tried to remember whose idea it had been for him to pick up Yvonne at the airport, why she wasn't renting a car, and why he'd invited her to stay at his house. It was a ridiculous plan, and when Allison came home (and she was going to *have* to come home eventually, if only to talk to the damn police and pick up her stuff) things were really going to get insane. But he hadn't really been in a position to say no or even to suggest an alternate plan. Any way you looked at this scenario, he was the bad guy.

Diana hadn't turned up anywhere Yvonne could find in Las Vegas. She told him that none of Diana's friends knew where she was or had even heard from her, in most cases, since she'd left for San Diego. On the other hand, Yvonne said, it wasn't a very big list. Diana really had only one good friend, Sasha, and they'd had some kind of falling out recently. Joe was no closer to finding Diana either, although he'd gone into a sort of overdrive after he spoke to Yvonne the first time. That was when Yvonne said she was going to come out as soon as she could gather some things together and get the time off. She needed to be there, she said, and yes, of course you do, Joe said. Of course. And now here he was, the sunlight sparkling off Mission Bay to his right, the airport only minutes away, and the reality of Yvonne—in his increasingly surreal life—finally sinking in.

Joe had always thought he possessed a deep, instinctive understanding of women—ironic, considering the shambles all his relationships were in now. He'd grown up with two sisters, who were close to him in both age and temperament and from whom he'd gleaned much about how women truly felt about themselves and about men, especially when they'd all been in high school at the same time. Then his sisters freely shared with Joe what they thought "worked" and what didn't when it came to guys, what they liked to hear and what they liked to talk about. He watched them struggle too with body image—both of them regularly dieting and despairing over the shapes they'd been born with. Ultimately, he'd decided that women were simply nicer than men, although capable of being just as shallow when it came to judging the opposite sex on looks and image. Both of his sisters lived in Washington State now and he'd drifted into a much more distant relationship with them, but until recently Joe felt what he'd learned from them was still just as relevant as it had been when they were kids. It had helped him so many times at work, dealing with waitresses and female patrons alike. All the girls on staff liked him because he was sensitive to their needs, he complimented them but never hit on them, always knew where to draw the line. You could ask anyone at Luna Piena—they'd all tell you Joe was a stand-up guy.

But now, faced with his missing daughter, the imminent arrival of his ex, and his angry, disturbed wife, Joe had to admit that he knew far less about what women thought or felt than he'd believed. And then there was Jessalyn. It was she who had convinced him that what little he did know was complete bullshit. There was nothing about her that followed a straight line, from the first encounter they'd had to the most recent—when he'd come to pick up Zoë after asking her to watch the baby for a few hours while he worked.

Sure, maybe it was a little presumptuous of him to ask such a thing considering the status of their relationship, but it was only because he was desperate and didn't want to leave the baby with Sam *again*. And she could have said no; it wasn't as if he just dropped Zoë off, *expecting* her to help. Besides, after the two nights they'd spent together in that little bed-and-breakfast, Joe believed that they'd developed a level of intimacy that went beyond a garden-variety affair. He felt indescribably bad about those nights now, of course, because somewhere in between them Diana had gone missing and Allison had abandoned him, but he couldn't bring himself to regret them. Not yet. And he'd gotten the distinct feeling from Jessalyn that she'd felt the same way. Nothing had been decided, and they hadn't even discussed where their relationship was headed or even if they *had* a relationship, but it didn't seem like they needed to. Between lovemaking sessions that were alternately deeply passionate and exhaustingly athletic, they had talked—no, he had talked and she had mostly listened—about incidentals, the little parts of life that you only discussed with someone you were just getting to know when it was just the two of you, alone. Things like what music you listened to and what kinds of crazy requests people made when they went out to eat in a restaurant or how long it took you to complete a Sudoku puzzle. He was touched and impressed by how intently she'd listened to him, how she'd paid attention and seemed genuinely interested. If she wasn't, it was one of the best acts in the world—which in itself was a testament to her interest in him.

Even later, after that lovely bubble had burst, and he'd had to tell her about how both Diana and Allison were gone, she seemed sympathetic, in tune with him somehow. And she hadn't objected to watching Zoë, at least not that he could tell. But when he'd returned to pick up the baby, she seemed to have transformed into an entirely different person: cold, rattled, even a little hostile toward him.

"This was a really bad idea, Joe," she'd said. "I don't know why you thought it wouldn't be, even though it's my fault for saying yes." She was holding the baby, rocking her back and forth a little frantically, even though Zoë was asleep.

"Did something happen?" Joe asked. "Is she okay?"

"Of course she's *okay*," Jessalyn snapped at him. "But I'm not a nanny or . . . or a *wife*. That's not who I am." Joe noticed then that she looked wrung out and somehow wrong. She was wearing a bathrobe, her hair hanging loose and limp, and her makeup was smudged, showing the dark circles under her eyes. "I don't do babies, Joe. Okay?"

"I'm sorry," Joe said, wishing he knew what was really bothering her, "I just thought—"

"No, *I'm* sorry," she said, going through a lightning-quick change of emotion and becoming suddenly contrite. "I shouldn't have barked at you and she's fine—the baby's fine, I just don't think we . . . this . . ." She ran a hand through her hair, which looked like it was sticking together in clumps, and sighed. "I think maybe we should just cool it for a minute, you know? There's so much going on and maybe . . . I don't know, Joe."

Like an idiot, he asked, "What do you mean by 'cool it'?" and immediately regretted the words, more so when he saw how hard her face got after she heard them.

"I can't," she said. "I just can't do this. I think you should go now."

As he gathered up Zoë and walked across the street to his deserted house, Joe thought about that phrase, *I think you should go now,* and how rarely it was used in real life. You heard it all the time in movies, but real people just didn't speak like that. And in any case, it was never followed by absolute silence and a man slinking off with a baby. He hadn't spoken to Jessalyn since then, although it hadn't been that long. He'd noticed that she'd made herself pretty scarce, and he wasn't sure how he felt about that yet. What he did know was that she wasn't who he'd thought she was. And the immediate corollary to that realization was that he wasn't even sure who he'd thought she was in the first place. All of which led him right back to the fact that he had completely lost his ability (if he had ever had it) to understand or deal with the women in his life. At least Zoë was too small yet to speak or else he was sure she'd be reading him the riot act too.

He was surprised by how much affection he felt for her, but Joe was by no means comfortable with Zoë. He had zero experience with infants, although over the last few weeks he had at least become acquainted with this one, and he was afraid that every time he handled her he was doing something wrong. The nights that he'd been alone with her had been some of the most difficult he'd ever experienced. Sam had been very decent about showing him the basics of feeding and changing, and in truth she had taken care of Zoë more than he had if you added up all the hours. But despite all of Sam's help he felt his abilities were entirely inadequate. It wasn't that he didn't feel for the little thing, because he found himself increasingly attached to her. She spent what seemed like a lot of time crying, but Sam told him that as infants went, Zoë was one of the calmest she'd ever seen. And there was a biological connection, something that Joe would have scoffed at only a few months ago, but now believed existed on a fundamental level. That tie was powerful and elemental and it bonded him to Zoë in a way he would never have anticipated. He wondered if he would have felt the same way with Diana if he'd known her as an infant. Even though he never doubted that Diana was his daughter, meeting her at seventeen—fully formed and carrying her own child—made a huge difference in how he felt about that relationship. It was the helplessness and total innocence of babies, he supposed, that appealed to you on a deep cellular level and compelled you to take care of them, protect them, and raise them so that your DNA could carry on into future generations. But as much as he was bonding with his granddaughter, Joe felt overwhelmed and unprepared to cope with her needs.

After claiming that Allison's mother had been burned out of her home, he had asked for and received a few emergency days off from work. It was a total lie, of course, but he didn't think it was necessary for corporate headquarters—or, for that matter, his staff—to know the details of his spinning-out-of-control life. He hoped against hope that by the time those days ran out Diana would come back, Yvonne could go home, Allison would return, and that they could all dial their lives back to where they were a few short months ago. Joe sighed. He could feel the muscle above his left eye twitching. He hadn't told Allison that Yvonne was going to be staying at their house. He had barely spoken to Allison since the fires. But still.

Joe opened his window to let some air into the suddenly stifling car. A gust of smoky wind blew over him. The whole county still smelled like a barbecue gone wrong, he thought. It was going to take forever to get that charred odor out of the air. He was taking the Sassafras exit now, just minutes away from the airport, which was located squarely in the middle of the city. Overhead, planes flew so low over the freeway you could almost see the passengers inside.

It was a forty-five-minute flight from Las Vegas to San Diego, so casual that people flew it in their pajamas and flip-flops. Joe wondered if Yvonne had ever made this flight before and what she was thinking at this very moment. He snaked through the brief traffic jam at the airport entrance and headed to the Southwest Airlines terminal, slowed, and searched for Yvonne in the clumps of people waiting with their bags resting against their legs. He felt a small rush of panic when he realized that he might not recognize her. He felt hot, sweaty, and gritty. His T-shirt was sticking to his back. This was the most cursed fall ever—a season of heat and fire that felt as if it was never going to end. He swept the entrances once more and found nobody who could possibly be Yvonne. He advanced farther, still nothing. There was no place to stop so Joe moved up, preparing to make another loop around the terminal. But just as he was about to merge and disappear into traffic he saw her—completely different and yet somehow matching his memory exactly—and he swerved right so that he could pull up to the curb.

It took Yvonne a little longer to find him in the thick line of cars picking up and dropping off passengers outside the terminal, so he had a chance to study her a little, make all the internal adjustments he needed, and then compose his face so that he appeared casual and neutral when she finally saw him. The first thing Joe noticed was that she had gained a little weight around her hips and thighs, but not enough for anyone to classify her as overweight. She had been very slender—if not skinny—when he knew her, and now she just looked a little more solid. Her hair was pulled back from her face in a tight twist at the back of her head, which emphasized her high cheekbones but also gave her a severe, almost angry look. He could see the weight of seventeen years in her expression and behind her eyes, even from this distance. There was disappointment there and maybe discontent and worry in the turned-down corners of her mouth. But her skin and her features still looked youthful. You wouldn't know she was over forty, he thought. Not at all. What surprised him—and it even surprised him that he would notice such a thing—was what she was wearing. Or at least how she was wearing it. She was dressed like a dowdy schoolmarm, a conservative matron much older than she was. He didn't know which was least attractive—the old-lady brown polyester pants, the cream and tan mix-and-match chiffon blouse with the ruffle at the neck, or the sensible shoes. They all made him think of Geritol and mothballs. The worst thing was that she looked so *dated* and so absolutely opposite the stylish woman he'd known. It was so strange to him that he almost believed the clothes she wore now were a costume for her—some part she was playing in a reality show of someone else's life.

He was pondering the reasons for this transformation in Yvonne when she finally spied his car, then him, and caught his gaze with her own. There was the briefest look of startled surprise in her eyes, then a deeper recognition, then finally a small, tight smile as she wheeled her bag over to the car. Joe popped the trunk and got out of the driver's seat, coming around to meet her, put her bag away, and open the passenger door for her. There was a moment of excruciating awkwardness as they met on the passenger side of the car; neither one of them knew whether to embrace, shake hands, or even touch at all. A warm wind whipped between them carrying the smell of jet fuel with it.

"Hi, Joe," she said.

"Hello, Yvonne," he said and gave her a clumsy half embrace with one arm as he reached for her bag with the other. "Let me get this for you. I'll put it in the trunk."

"Thanks."

Joe loaded her suitcase—a flower-patterned cloth affair that made him as sad as the rest of her attire—into the trunk, realizing as he did that he had forgotten to tidy up the posters in the back of the car. He ushered her into the passenger seat, positioning his body so that she wouldn't be able to see them, and felt like a moron when she had to sidle past him to get in. Finally, he got back in behind the wheel, pulled away from the curb, and merged with the traffic heading out. The inside of the car was full of the smell of gardenia, not mothballs, but also not a scent he'd associated with her. It wasn't unpleasant, but it made him vaguely uneasy.

"It's hot," she said. "It's like Vegas here."

"It's been really bad," he said. "It just hasn't let up." He felt himself sweating again as he flicked quick glances in her direction. He wondered if she'd seen the posters. She couldn't have or surely they would have skipped the weather altogether, their seventeen-year estrangement notwithstanding.

"You look good, Joe."

"So do you," he said quickly. He smiled and looked over at her, longer this time, and realized that it was true. Aside from the clothes, she was still beautiful in that way that had hypnotized him so long ago. And now in her face he also saw Diana for the first time, and it pierced him sharply and unexpectedly. His eyes stung and watered, and for a horrified second he thought he might be crying. He blinked and quickly shifted his gaze back to the road.

They drove in hot, fraught silence for several minutes. Biting the inside of his lip, Joe stared straight ahead as he navigated back onto the freeway. The traffic was lighter heading north than it had been on the way down. He considered pointing out landmarks along the way, but stopped himself when he realized it would make him sound like a half-assed tour guide. Then he thought about asking Yvonne if she was hungry and wanted to stop somewhere for lunch, even though it was well into the afternoon, but the words and how to phrase them got tangled up in his brain. Something about her physical proximity after all this time was frying his neural circuits. Memories of their time together kept sliding through his mind unbidden: little flashing images of the night they met (at a party when he bummed a cigarette from her), a romantic but interrupted picnic dinner they had on the beach that washed away in a sudden high tide, watching her sleep in the gray light of early morning. These intimate pictures were strange and uncomfortable because at the same time the woman sitting next to him was a stranger.

They were approaching La Jolla when he finally turned to look at her again. He cleared his throat, about to tell her that they'd be home in a few minutes, but the words died in his throat. Yvonne was weeping. Her cheeks were wet and shiny with tears and her mouth trembled with held-back sobs. Her hands were clenched in her lap. Instinctively, he turned his head away as if he had been caught intruding on a moment of private grief, but then looked back at her again, searching for words—any words—that would soothe her. She met his glance, her eyes, the burnt amber color that he had remembered, full of water and sorrow.

"Yvonne . . ."

"Where is she, Joe? Where is my girl?"

"I don't . . . I wish I knew."

"Why don't you know? You have to know. *Somebody* has to know!"

"We're going to find her, Yvonne."

She wiped her eyes with a quick stroke of her hand and gave him a look so intense he almost recoiled. But he couldn't read what was in it, couldn't tell if it was hatred or fear or anger or all of those things. Or none of them. She drew a long shuddering breath and he watched as she composed herself, erasing the anguish from her face.

"You'd better tell me everything," she said.

chapter 17

Kevin wanted to die.

He lay on his bed with a pillow over his head to block out the light and Kanye blasting through his headphones to block out everything else. He was listening to "Stronger," a song about overcoming obstacles. But Kevin wasn't buying that message.

Better to die than try to overcome. Really die—like blackness, never-wake-up die. Finished and over. He didn't think he was scared. He tried to imagine what it would be like and couldn't. He knew it wasn't going to be a tunnel and a white light and angels greeting him on the other side. He knew that because he'd come this close. Maybe he even had died for a minute or two. That's what his father had said, but Kevin knew he was trying to be as dramatic as possible to get Kevin to understand the fucking *gravity* of his *actions*. Either way, he'd been right there at the doorway to eternity, just hadn't gone through it. And he didn't remember anything about getting to that doorway except feeling so fucked up that it seemed like the walls were dissolving. Then there was just nothing until he woke up. The worst wake-up ever. He hadn't really tried to kill himself—that wasn't the point—but his very first thought when he came out of that nowhere state was disappointment that he hadn't succeeded in doing it. What kind of loser couldn't even get an overdose right? Exactly. Which made him think that if he actually *tried* to do it he might fuck it up even worse. If only just wishing you were dead was enough to kill you. But then, Kevin guessed, the world would probably be full of dead people. Because as far as he could tell, nobody on Earth was having a particularly good time.

Barring death, Kevin wanted desperately to get high. That he couldn't—that he was being watched and monitored like he was under house arrest or something compounded his misery to the point that it almost hurt. No, it *did* hurt. He could feel the pain spreading through his rib cage and all the way to his heart. Unless that was still the bruising caused by his father's aggressive attempt at CPR. The asshole probably *tried* to break his ribs.

"You owe me your life *twice*," he had told Kevin when they'd gotten home from the hospital. "I *gave* you life and then I *saved* your life. I don't think you understand that."

Kevin didn't think it was possible to despise his father more than he had that night at the Montanas' when the man had ordered him home like he was a little boy on the playground, disrespecting him down to his bones. But when he'd said that about Kevin owing him double for the very breath he took, Kevin felt his hate grow, gaining the force and gravity of a black hole, sucking in all the other feelings he might ever have had for his father and destroying them completely.

He wished the man weren't his biological father so that he'd have a valid excuse for loathing him this much. If only his mother had had an affair and he was the secret result. He didn't look much like his dad, so it was possible. On the other hand, he didn't look much like his mother either, except that their eyes were the same color blue and they both sunburned easily. But that could apply to anyone, really. And his mother wasn't the type to have an affair—she lived in fear of his father as it was. She'd never have the kind of guts it took to pull off something like an affair and pass off someone else's baby as his. Still, it was a fantasy Kevin spun regularly, the kind of thing that he'd actually consider a gift from his mother if only she would offer it. But no. He was stuck with the fucking son of a bitch.

His mother had really screwed up on that one.

But Kevin didn't hate his mother for that. He didn't hate her, period. And if he really thought about it, he wasn't even truly angry at her. What he couldn't believe was how she refused to stand up for him with his father. He didn't know what to call the feeling this gave him, but it was worse than anger or hate, and he couldn't do anything to get rid of it. He wished his mother would realize what an asshole his father really was and just leave him. He treated her so badly—why couldn't she see that? She just rolled over every time his father barked at her to do something or made fun of her in some little way that she didn't seem to get or care about. The worst thing, though, and what had been happening ever since Kevin could remember, was that she never, *never* had his back even when she *knew* he was in the right. A long time ago, he had been able to talk to his mother about what was going on in his life and she seemed to listen to him. She even seemed to understand how he felt about things and more often than not she took his side. But then when it came time to defend him to his dad, she always just folded up and disappeared. He could never figure out why because when she disagreed with his father about other things—and yes, they were little things like when to do yard work and what to have for dinner—she didn't have a problem saying so. But when his father and he were involved, she just seemed to go blank, turn off inside, and not come back until everything was all smoothed over. It was such a betrayal.

He'd never been able to tell anyone about this because he thought it made him sound like such a baby—until Diana. She had her own theories. "You know your mom's totally wasted, right?" she said one day after talking to his mother in the kitchen.

"What are you talking about?" he said, half-laughing because Diana was always throwing crazy shit out there like that.

"I'm serious," Diana said. "I don't know what it is, but she's on something. Don't you know? More importantly, where can we get some?"

"No way," he said. Diana smiled and shrugged like whatever he wanted to believe was fine with her. But now he was thinking maybe she was on to something because maybe that disconnected blankness of his mother's had some kind of chemical explanation. And if there was one thing Diana knew about, it was being wasted. She knew about every prescription drug there was and she had plenty of stories about getting trashed on almost all of them. She was an expert—made his own experiences look like kindergarten shit. Diana really, really loved to get high and she talked about it all the time. But she was pretty good about resisting before Zoë came. She was trying . . . and she wasn't doing any of the really strong shit while she was pregnant, just a little weed and not really anything else. At least never with him. He wouldn't have let her anyway. That's what nobody seemed to understand—he'd done his best to protect Diana. She'd been through so much shit in her life, she really needed somebody. How did that make *him* a bad influence on *her?* He was a *good* influence before Zoë came. But after Zoë . . . He didn't know.

Diana had been getting so weird. She told him she loved him. But he never had the courage to ask her *how* she loved him—as a boyfriend, a brother, or just a friend. Okay, not a brother. Diana acted a lot of different ways, but not like a sister. Sisters and brothers didn't do what they'd done. Or what she'd let him do. But friends did. Friends with benefits. That was always what he was afraid they were. But it felt so good to have her close, to have her there. To talk to her. He never wanted to ruin it. He would have given her anything, would have done anything to keep it just like that forever.

Kevin rolled over and instinctively reached for his cell phone to call her. And then he remembered. His father had cut off his cell phone. And Diana was gone. The pain in his chest got sharper. He wanted to talk to her so badly. He *needed* to talk to her. He remembered what she said and it hurt all over again. *Don't call me for a while. It's better if we don't hang out right now.*

He pressed his knuckles into his closed eyes, but he couldn't get rid of the pictures in his brain. He was kissing her for the first time again, over and over. He couldn't stop remembering and it was killing him. She never asked him if he'd been with another girl before her. She knew and she didn't care.

"It's fine," she said. "It's all fine. Better like this."

He didn't know what he was doing, but it didn't matter. She was so beautiful. He was never going to be with a girl as beautiful as Diana ever again. He knew this with a kind of dead certainty, and it made him want to punch a hole in the wall. If only he had the energy or the will.

It was his idea that he and Diana should get married. He knew it sounded stupid and ridiculous—why would she want to raise her baby with a loser like him?—but she didn't say no, at least not at first. Diana didn't really have a plan for what to do when Zoë was born. All she knew was that she didn't want to "give her away like a puppy I don't have room for in my house." But at the same time, she never really prepared herself to be a mother. Not that Kevin knew what getting prepared meant, but it involved more than just waiting around until you gave birth. Because that's what it seemed like she was doing. Maybe it was because she was trying to convince the Montanas that she was planning to give the baby up for adoption. Diana said Joe and Allison were insisting on adoption, and they would probably kick her out of the house if she told them that she wanted to keep the baby, so she had to keep pretending. But then Diana changed the story and said it was really Allison who was pressuring her to give the baby up for adoption. She said Allison was the world's biggest bitch and would probably kill her *and* the baby if she thought she could get away with it. "No, seriously," Diana told Kevin when he laughed at this (sometimes it was hard to know when Diana was kidding or when she wanted to amuse you with what she was saying), "she's evil. You should see the way she looks at me when she thinks nobody's looking."

Diana could be very convincing when she wanted to be. Kevin had known Allison since elementary school (he still thought of her as *Mrs. Montana* most of the time) and couldn't imagine her as the evil stepmother that Diana made her out to be, but who knew what went on in people's houses when there was nobody else around to watch what they were doing? And you only had to look inside his own house—at his own fucked-up family—to know that was true. So he believed Diana when she said Allison was out to get her and Joe didn't really care what happened to her. And he believed her when she said she could never go home because her own mother was worse than Joe, Allison, Kevin's father, and any other shitty parent you wanted to throw in all wrapped into one. Her mother was so cold she kicked her pregnant daughter out of her house. What kind of mother did a thing like that? Kevin didn't know if his own father could even be that cold—he couldn't imagine it, but that didn't mean it wasn't possible. He did know a thing or two about what it felt like to have a parent who didn't like you or want you around. Nobody could force Diana to give up her baby, he was pretty sure of that, but it didn't mean they couldn't make her life totally miserable. And that was where *he* came in. It wasn't so crazy to think that they could be together, was it? He could get a job somewhere, couldn't he?

But then Zoë was born and everything changed with Diana. It didn't happen all at the same time, but from the minute she got the first labor pains he could see something turn in her. They were here—right here on his bed—when it happened. It was a Sunday afternoon and they were alone in the house. She was leaning into him, heavy on his chest, his arms around her, his hands on her belly, feeling the baby roll around and kick his fingers. Then he felt her take in a quick breath like you did when you felt a sharp pain. Her belly was hard as a rock.

"What?" he said. "What is it?"

"Nothing," she said after a minute. "Nothing." She relaxed a little, asked him for a hit of weed. He was going to ask her if she thought that was the best thing to be doing, but he thought better of it and just gave her some. There was a damp spot on his T-shirt where she'd been leaning against him and he could see that her face was shiny with sweat.

"It's so fucking hot," she said. "Don't you have AC?"

"My dad doesn't let my mom turn it on ever," he said. "He says it's too expensive. He says it never gets so hot that you need AC, you can just open a window."

"Well open the fucking window then."

"It's open."

She laughed a little and then leaned over, taking another one of those breaths, this time with a little groan.

"Is it the baby?" he said.

She waited until it passed and then she looked up at him through the long curls that fell across her face. That's when he saw it—she was different. Scared and trying not to show it—retreating inside herself. "I think I have to go," she said.

"I'm going to come with you."

"No!"

"Why not?"

"You can't, Kevin, you just can't, okay?"

"Let me come with you. Let me help you."

"Trust me on this, okay? You don't want to come with me." She put her hands on her belly and looked down. "I'm going to go . . . go get my . . . I'm going to get Joe," she said. And then she just left him there. He didn't follow her. He should have. He felt bad about that. He sat looking out his bedroom window after she left. He could see a good way up the street and he sat there and waited. Pretty soon, though not as soon as he would have thought, he saw the two of them—Joe and Diana—heading out to the hospital. Right after that he saw Sun come out and start tossing baskets. So he went outside like he was going somewhere and pretended that he'd just happened to notice Sun out there and had decided to go say hey. Sun saw him, gave him the questioning look, and Kevin nodded. Sun passed him the ball. Kevin took a shot and missed.

"Nobody's home," Kevin said. "So you can come over."

"Okay," Sun said. "You need anything extra?"

"The usual," Kevin said, trying to look as if he didn't care and wasn't desperate.

"Is Diana over?" Sun asked and tipped his head toward Kevin's house.

"Nah, she's . . ." But Kevin stopped himself. He didn't want to tell Sun where Diana had gone or what she was doing. ". . . not there," he finished.

It was hours later—the middle of the night—he was fucked up, passed out for who knows how long, when he heard his phone go off. Diana had sent him a text message.

its a girl. zoe. we're good. c u soon.

He didn't see Diana again for days. Maybe it was a week, he wasn't sure. He went to school and came home. He sent her text messages. Sometimes she answered, sometimes she didn't. And then one day she sent him a text telling him to come over. He snuck around the back and then went in through her bedroom window—good thing it was on the ground floor—to avoid being seen by anyone. It was a mess. And it was so weird to see her all skinny without her big belly. She looked tired, like she'd been awake for days, and she was all jittery. He knew what she wanted—she didn't even have to ask—and he gave it to her.

It was funny, he thought now, that they had never talked about Zoë's daddy. It was the one thing that Diana never volunteered and he never felt comfortable asking her about it even though they talked about everything else. Kevin didn't know if the dude was a boyfriend, just some guy she met, or somebody else's boyfriend. Or husband. Shit like that happened all the time. He knew that girl Lori in last year's English class who slept with one of her father's friends (disgusting) and then got pregnant. Everyone was talking about it. The gossip got so bad Lori had to transfer out of school at the end of the year. He didn't want to believe that Diana had done something like that, but he didn't know. And maybe he didn't want to ask because he was afraid she would say she was in love with the guy and going back to be with him. All he knew was that if Zoë was his baby, he'd step up and be a man about it. Sometimes, he fantasized that Zoë *was* his—it wasn't that hard to do. You couldn't really tell what she was going to look like yet, she was too small, but Kevin had checked her little mouth and chin and he thought they looked a little like his. Enough like his. He wondered if Zoë's father even knew she existed. Maybe Diana hadn't even told him.

He should have asked her. Why hadn't he?

But after Zoë was born it got harder to talk to Diana about anything. She was sometimes frazzled and sometimes just stared off into space like she was in a trance. Having Zoë seemed to have really freaked her out. That's when he offered to marry her.

He felt really stupid about that now. Because even though she seemed to go along with it for a minute, he didn't think she was ever really into it or ever meant to try to be with him. She was just treading water. And he was pretty sure she'd gone back to taking pills or whatever so that she could even herself out. He didn't blame her, really. Diana's life was fucked up even if she did love Zoë. No wonder she'd run away. Well, *if* she'd run away. But he couldn't believe that anything had happened to her. Diana could take care of herself pretty well, he was sure of that. He reached for his phone again without thinking only to find it gone once more.

"FUCK!" The music was up so loud he couldn't even hear the sound of his own voice. He turned it up even louder, so loud it wasn't music anymore, just screaming vibrations in his head. But it didn't help. Nothing fucking helped anymore.

Kevin didn't know where Diana had gone, but he wasn't that surprised that she hadn't taken Zoë with her. Not really. Kevin thought Diana always knew that it was going to be hard for her to take care of Zoë properly. He thought that was what bothered her more than anything. And now he couldn't help her at all, even if he wanted to. He couldn't call her, even if he was going to ignore her plea for him to leave her alone. And she couldn't call him because his fucking father had cut off his fucking phone.

But then he thought, *fuck her anyway.* Bitch.

Kevin's eyes felt hot and there was a pain in his forehead. He was crying. He was fucking *crying.* God, he didn't *deserve* to live. He pulled his earbuds out of his ear and threw them, iPod still attached, off the edge of his bed. Then he got up off the bed, walked to his window, and looked through the blinds at Sun's basketball hoop across the street. Their window was open and he could hear Sun whaling away on the piano. He didn't get why Sun kept practicing even though he hated the fucking piano so much. He'd asked about it once and Sun had said, "My mom gets on me to do it," but that never seemed like enough of a reason to Kevin. He hadn't been able to get over to Sun's for fucking months, it felt like. Too many people watching his every move. Well, fuck it, he was over this shit—he was going over there right now, even though Sun didn't like it when he just came to the door. Too bad. Sun had a product and he was so looking to buy.

There were footsteps outside his door (which both his parents had told him to keep open, but fuck that, he wasn't an animal) and then the sound of the knob rattling. Kevin turned his head.

"Mom, wh—" But it wasn't his mother, it was their neighbor Sam from next door. It was so weird to see her standing in his bedroom that Kevin was rendered speechless. His first thought was that she must be in the wrong house. But then he looked at her face and his second thought was that something was very wrong.

"Hi, Kevin," she said. "Your mom asked me to come up and get you. There are a couple of detectives downstairs."

Kevin just stared at her, his brain having real difficulty putting all the pieces together.

"They want to talk to you," Sam said.

Kevin felt the pain in his chest turn cold and heavy. "Why?"

"They want to talk to you about Diana."

chapter 18

Sam stood in front of the nearly empty refrigerator and felt the surprise of unwelcome tears welling in her eyes. She couldn't tell exactly what had caused them—the barren crisper or that she'd just realized that Thanksgiving, usually her favorite holiday, was around the corner and was likely going to be one of the worst days in a long, bad year. *Annus horribilis.* Wasn't that what the queen of England had called it when all her princes broke up with their wives and her castle burned? Sam thought about castles burning and heard the strains of Neil Young in her head. What was the title of that song?

"Don't Let It Bring You Down."

Yet faced with the prospect of celebrating Thanksgiving without Connor, Sam couldn't help but feel immensely brought down. She could have fought Noah about this—she was supposed to have Connor for the holidays—because he'd reneged on his part of the agreement by scheduling a surprise trip to Hawaii for Thanksgiving, but ultimately all that would do was upset Connor, who quite obviously favored a trip to the islands rather than a sad, strained dinner with his mother. Not to mention Gloria, who would likely cause Connor even more discomfort now that he and Justin were no longer friends. This detail, that Connor had lost a friend who had been like a brother to him since preschool, bothered Sam as much as anything else that had happened since she and Noah had separated. It wasn't a big deal, Noah had assured her, kids changed loyalties regularly and the two of them were just expanding their friendships with others, and it wasn't as if they'd had a falling out or anything and Connor didn't seem at all upset over it. But Sam didn't believe any of this. She believed, rather, that Frank had completely poisoned Justin against Connor if not outright banned Connor from his house, and maybe Noah had "encouraged" Connor to find other friends as well. No doubt Frank and Noah had gotten together on the visitation schedule so that now the boys visited their mothers on alternate days or weekends so there was almost no overlap. Not that either boy spent much time with them anyway. She thought about how happy those boys had been with each other—how they had shared everything—and her heart broke.

Even though she'd had so much time to get used to it, Sam still couldn't believe how vindictive Frank had become. The man was a bigger bitch than either she or Gloria could ever be. That his wounded male ego was more important than the emotional well-being of his own son was worse still. And the biggest irony of all was that while Frank claimed he was protecting Justin from "bad values" and "immorality," that was exactly what he was exposing Justin to with his own behavior.

Sam hadn't even discussed Thanksgiving with Gloria yet and didn't know what flavor of torture Frank had in mind for them. Gloria had been uncharacteristically close-mouthed about her conversations with Frank lately, so Sam was in the dark about what either one of them might be plotting. This period of silence had come hard on the heels of Gloria's admission that Frank was trying a new tack—attempting to persuade Gloria to dump Sam and come back to him. He'd thought about it long and hard, Gloria told Sam, quoting her ex, and had decided that he would take her back. Under certain conditions, of course. Sam had been astounded.

"You're kidding, right?" she'd asked Gloria. "Even *he* couldn't be that big of an asshole."

Gloria shrugged and lifted her hands in a what-can-you-do gesture.

"Maybe he really, really misses me," she said. "Maybe he knows he'll never get over me. Maybe he still loves me."

"What the hell, Gloria? Are you serious?"

"I'm just saying . . ."

"Are you considering it?" Sam scoffed. "You're going to have to change your look. You know how Frank likes it."

"Don't be that way."

"I'm sorry, I just can't believe that after all—"

"You don't understand how hard this is for me, Sam."

"I *don't?*"

But Gloria just shook her head and walked out of the room, leaving Sam on the verge of her own frustrated tears. Since then, there hadn't been one word of discussion about Frank or Noah. And last weekend, Gloria had spent her visitation with Justin everywhere but at the house. Sam didn't even know where they had gone and Gloria didn't want to talk about it. Sam wasn't particularly disappointed that she no longer had to spend hours talking about what they were going to do about Frank's latest attempt to make their lives hell, but Gloria's new silence was more worrisome to Sam than her previous histrionics had been. At the very least, they'd been of some support to each other in the past, no matter how contentious their arguments had sometimes become. But now it almost seemed as if Gloria was hiding something from her. Sam needed to talk to Gloria about the plan for Thanksgiving. For the first time it occurred to her that maybe Gloria wasn't even planning to spend the holiday with her.

Sam's eyes blurred and she realized she was still staring into the open fridge at several mostly empty jars, two cans of cheap beer, a wrinkled to-mato, and a cucumber that had seen better days. She closed the fridge door before it could depress her any further. The food in the house—or rather the lack of it—was an accurate reflection of what was going on with her and Gloria. Over the past few weeks, Sam had been eating steadily less and limiting herself to things like carrots and olives. Limiting what and how much she ate was a way of feeling control over something in her life. It was childish, un-self-realized behavior, but it gave her a twisted kind of comfort. Gloria had gone in another direction: eating take-out almost exclusively and not decent take-out, either. She came home regularly with greasy bags of French fries and burgers, pizza, and fried chicken. The old Gloria was a harsh critic of women who fed their kids at McDonald's even once a month and wouldn't consider touching the stuff herself, which she said couldn't even be categorized as real food. There was the vanity aspect too. Gloria was very proud of her luscious body and clear skin and worked hard to keep them both that way. Fast food never fit into that equation. The new Gloria, though, the aggressive Gloria of tattoos, chopped hair, and beer—*that* Gloria seemed to love fatty, meaty, fried anything. And it was starting to show. It was as if Gloria was sabotaging herself, Sam thought. Well, they were both sabotaging themselves, just going about it from opposite directions.

Sam took in a deep breath and exhaled slowly. It was so difficult not to just give up. Although it felt as if she and Gloria were constantly starting over, Sam had to keep trying. And it wasn't as if they had it that bad. Look at Dorothy, for god's sake. What a nightmare *she* was living. Or Joe. And that poor little baby. No, she and Gloria were actually doing well in comparison. It was all a question of effort, wasn't it?

"Gloria!" she called upstairs. And waited. And waited some more. One more time. "Gloria!" *Please don't make me beg,* she thought. *Please, Gloria.*

Finally, she heard it. "What?" The question was muffled. Sam didn't respond right away, letting Gloria come closer.

"What is it, Sam?"

Sam stepped out of the kitchen just so Gloria could see her from where she stood at the top of the stairs. She was wearing tight torn jeans, a white T-shirt, and a black head scarf. Her face was damp, freshly scrubbed. She looked so young, Sam thought. Like a teenager.

"Let's have dinner," Sam said.

"Okay," Gloria said, nonplussed.

"I mean, let's *make* dinner. And eat it. When's the last time we did that? It's been a while."

"So this is a joint effort?" Gloria asked.

Sam massaged her temples to alleviate the tension that had suddenly gathered there. "I'm trying really hard, Gloria," she said. "Can you meet me halfway?"

Gloria let out a noise. Sam couldn't tell if it was a loud sigh or a grunt of dissatisfaction, but she came down the stairs and literally met Sam halfway between the staircase and the kitchen. The scent of apricot face wash wafted over to Sam.

"Okay," Gloria said, "dinner. You have my attention."

"I was thinking something with vegetables," Sam said.

"What do we have?"

"Not much."

Gloria put her hands on her hips and tilted her head. Sam could see her vacillating between anger and amusement. Finally, she conceded and gave a little laugh. "Fine," she said, "let's go look at what there is and start there, okay?"

Gloria followed Sam into the kitchen and they started rummaging around in separate cabinets. The memory of their moving-in day flashed through Sam's mind. All the things they'd stocked their pantry with—juice boxes for the boys, lots of fresh fruit, so many different kinds of cereal because they all ate cereal and every one of them had his or her own unique demands: with nuts, without sugar, plain flakes, whole grain oatmeal. . . . It hadn't been that long ago, Sam thought, but she felt like she'd aged a lifetime since then.

"We have pasta," Gloria said, hauling out various packets from the back of the pantry. "There's some penne here and . . . shells. We can mix them together."

"Okay. I have olives."

"There's a can of tomatoes back here too. Are you thinking about puttanesca? What about capers?"

"Um . . ." Sam opened the fridge again and leaned in, shuffling through old jars and ketchup bottles, finally finding a tiny jar that contained enough capers to count, which meant not enough for any kind of sauce. "Not really," she said, holding it out.

Gloria tipped her head to the side, considering. "We could make it work," she said. "As long as there are red pepper flakes."

"Always."

"Well then. . . ."

Sam and Gloria began gathering utensils and ingredients, sidling past each other as they moved around their small kitchen. Sam decided the tomato wasn't too old to be chopped and sauced but was unsure whether the cucumber would hold up even if she salted and dressed it properly. Gloria grabbed a sauté pan and olive oil. Sam handed her the onion she'd discovered hiding on the back of the refrigerator shelf.

"Why do they call it *puttanesca?*" Gloria asked suddenly. "I mean, why *whore* pasta? One assumes *virgin* pasta would be more appealing than whore pasta, right?"

"Um," Sam said, "is it because of the chili flakes, maybe? Whores are spicy? Hot?"

"And there's *pasta al diavolo*," Gloria continued, "which is the devil's pasta. But there's no God pasta or Jesus pasta. I wonder how Jesus pasta would go over? What do you think?"

Sam checked Gloria's expression. She looked amused but also like a naughty child who thought she was getting away with something. It was that Catholic upbringing, Sam thought. Even though Gloria had long ago rejected religious observance, the old fear of hell and damnation was still deeply embedded on some unconscious level. Sam, who had been raised by nonobservant Jewish parents who cherry-picked various rituals that suited them, knew that she could never truly understand how Gloria's hardwired sense of sin affected her. They had talked about this before, Sam always pressing Gloria to examine how she really felt about God and her religion, but Gloria had always laughed Sam off. It didn't mean anything, Gloria said, and she was long over all of that. Over the nuns and the restrictions and the sins—venal and mortal alike. But Sam found that hard to believe.

She knew a thing or two about repression and how it could fester beneath the surface. Gloria had married young—had gone almost directly from her parents' house to Frank's—and had followed all the rules along the way, until they met, of course. Sam wondered if Gloria's actions now were just part of some long-held-back rebellion. But she didn't say anything about that. She couldn't. Instead, she smiled and avoided the question of Jesus pasta altogether.

Gloria chopped the onion expertly into a small dice, rubbing the tears from her eyes with the back of her hand. "Have you seen—" Gloria stopped, sniffed, moved over to the faucet, and held her hands under cold running water.

"Seen what?"

"Allison," Gloria said. "She's back. I figured you'd seen her."

"I did—I mean, I know she's come back."

"And?" Gloria questioned. Sam couldn't figure out from her tone whether Gloria was just hungry for gossip or pressing for something else.

"And . . . nothing, really. I haven't talked to her. I talked to Joe. And Yvonne. But I haven't talked to Allison. Who knows what's going on in *her* head."

"Yvonne? You mean the—you mean Diana's mother? You talked to her? When was that?"

Sam hesitated. She didn't want to try to relay the contents of her conversations with Yvonne to Gloria. No, that wasn't entirely accurate. It was more a case of not knowing *how* to explain those conversations. It bothered her to think that Gloria wouldn't be able to grasp the emotional subtext, but that was exactly how she felt. And Sam liked Yvonne. Gloria wouldn't understand that. "You know, when she got here. Joe introduced us and I talked to her a little bit. I told you that, remember?"

"No," Gloria said. "No, I don't."

"She's in a bad way," Sam said, ignoring the cold edge that had crept into Gloria's voice. "I can't imagine what she's going through."

"Maybe she should have thought about that when she kicked her pregnant daughter out of the house."

"It's not like that, Glo," Sam said, using the nickname to soften her admonishment. So her instincts had been right, after all. Gloria didn't understand. "It's so much more complicated than that."

"It can't be that complicated," Gloria scoffed. "She was a pregnant teenager and her mother sent her packing. Nothing to figure out there. There's right and there's wrong. A kid is a kid and a parent is a parent. That's all."

Sam shook her head. "That isn't all of it, Gloria. You don't choose your kids. Or your parents."

"What does that mean?"

"It means if you're lucky you get a kid you get along with—a kid you *like*. Because they all come in with their own personalities. You always love them, but you don't always like them. And as for parents . . ."

"Your parents didn't send you away, Sam. And in those days—"

"Yvonne didn't kick Diana out of the house," Sam said. "That's not what happened." She hadn't wanted to tell Gloria even this much, and now Sam understood why she was hesitating. She'd been wrong about Diana—that realization coming as soon as she sat down with Yvonne. Little Zoë was between them, cooing in her basket, and Yvonne played with the fraying edge of her shirtsleeve as she described her fraught relationship with her daughter. The pregnancy was only the most recent in a string of acting-out behaviors that had progressively more serious consequences. Yvonne knew she'd smoked pot, but suspected other drugs too. There was a series of bad boyfriends—older, college guys with all the worst intentions. There were the tattoos—not so bad in and of themselves, but representative of the direction she was headed. . . . And perhaps worst of all there was the anger.

"I suppose she told you what a terrible mother I am," Yvonne had said, her eyes filling with tears, her mouth set in frustration. "That I kicked her out because she got pregnant? It was all her decision to come here—all of it. You know, I would have done anything for that girl—anything to make her feel right, but she was always so furious at me."

Sam had listened, thinking all the while how quickly she'd bought into Diana's story and how automatic her condemnation of Yvonne had been. It didn't make her dislike Diana, who was still, after all, just a girl, but it did make her doubt herself and this was something she just didn't want to share with Gloria.

"Well," Gloria was saying, "what did happen then?"

Sam minced the garlic more carefully than usual, afraid to look up and show Gloria the warring emotions on her face. "Like I said, it's complicated. I don't think any of us have the right to judge each other as mothers."

Gloria scraped her knife against the cutting board and said, "Really? Because I'm not so sure about that. Me and you, Sam? We're the good ones. Yvonne? Not looking so good to me, sorry. And as for Dorothy Werner . . ."

Sam measured out some olive oil for the sauté pan. She hadn't said anything to Gloria about the long, unlikely conversation she'd had with Dorothy or what had been exposed, but Gloria obviously knew they'd been talking. She thought about Dorothy—about the huge well of pain that woman had revealed to her—and she felt a gathering tension and ache at the back of her head. She hadn't left Gloria out of that particular loop because she was worried that Gloria would judge her for befriending a woman who'd previously shown both of them, at best, a sort of passive-aggressive hostility or because she thought Gloria wouldn't get it. When she thought about it carefully, Sam realized the reason she was holding back—or, really, holding out—was that she actually felt protective of Dorothy. Sam didn't understand where this feeling had come from or why she felt the need to protect Dorothy from Gloria of all people. It didn't make sense. And yet when she remembered that afternoon at the Werners'—so peculiar it had taken on a tinge of unreality—she sensed again the depth of Dorothy's anguish and how much it seemed to cost her to speak at all. It was as if some force had pulled the words from her despite her efforts to keep them inside. It was possible, Sam thought, that she just didn't trust Gloria with what Dorothy had told her. And maybe the same was true of her new friendship with Yvonne as well. The shock of that realization hit Sam like a rush of cold water. It was wrong to feel this way about Gloria, the person she loved and was completely committed to. Maybe it was her fault that they'd become so distant from each other. Maybe Sam just didn't know how to share.

"Don't you think, Sam?"

"Think what?"

"That Dorothy Werner is a freak of nature."

"That's going a bit far, isn't it?"

"Is it? Well, you should know. You're pretty hot and heavy with all the neighbors lately, aren't you?"

"I'm just trying to help out," Sam said quickly. "With the baby and everything. That poor little thing."

"You're missing her, aren't you? She got you all babied up."

Sam shrugged. "I guess I am," she said.

"It's funny; I never would have expected that you'd go all Earth Mother, Sam. What happened to that snappy sarcastic mama I used to know? Now you're all about solving the world's problems and shit."

"Not exactly the *world*," Sam mumbled. She put a big pot of water up to boil and started cutting up the cucumber.

"What's going on with the investigation?" Gloria asked, suddenly serious. "Have they found anything at all?"

"Not that I know of," Sam said. "Unless something's come up recently that Joe hasn't told me. It's like she just vanished. They haven't found anything—not her cell phone, no credit card records, and Joe says they don't even have any halfway credible leads from the usual crazies who call in on these kinds of cases. If she's hiding out somewhere she's doing a hell of a job." Sam closed her eyes for a second, sending up a silent prayer for Diana. She thought about what Dorothy had told her—about how, if you really needed to, you could just start all over. It was possible, Sam thought, that Diana had just slipped away and was, at this very moment, reinventing herself somewhere, but even Sam's most optimistic self saw that possibility as highly unrealistic. She didn't want to give in to the cold dread she felt pressing into her consciousness, but it was getting very difficult to stop it from taking over.

"Of course, the longer she's out there . . ." Sam started and faltered, searching for the right words. "The longer she's gone, the harder it is to find her. That's just the way it is with these . . . things. We've had the posters up for a while now. They did a news spot on it too—you didn't see that, but I did, it was just a quick thing. I'm hoping they can do a longer story. I asked Joe about it, but he hasn't—we haven't talked about it. He's kind of got his hands full right now. I should just call myself, tell them the full story. . . ."

"Why, do you know something Joe doesn't?"

"No, I just meant, you know, the human interest side of the story. She isn't just a teenager, she's a new mom, a teenage mom."

"Maybe," Gloria said pointedly, "but Diana doesn't really fit the profile of this neighborhood, does she? That might make a difference in how much coverage you could get."

Sam gave Gloria a long look, trying to decide whether or not she wanted to know what she really meant by that last comment. "We don't fit the profile either, Gloria. As far as that goes."

"I'm just saying," Gloria added, "that she's not exactly all sweetness and purity, is she? And then there's the whole drug thing."

"What do you mean?" Sam said.

"Kevin. He OD'd, didn't he? They were together all the time."

"Yes," Sam said, "but he said she never took any drugs with him. That's what he told the police."

"When did he tell the police that? And how do you know?"

Sam thought again about Dorothy and how now would be the time to tell Gloria about what they'd talked about—how Dorothy had literally broken down and cried in her own kitchen while Sam sat there helplessly, rocking Zoë back and forth, and how days later, Dorothy had come back looking for Sam, calling over the fence for Sam to come help her, please, please help her—but the story was so complicated and intricate and involved so much emotion. And there was Gloria standing there waiting for an answer, and Sam just couldn't do it. Later, she told herself. There will be plenty of time for it later.

"I was over there the other day," Sam said, "and the detectives were there talking to Kevin."

Gloria's eyes widened slightly. Sam could almost see the questions flitting across her face like so many clouds. "And so what did he say?" she said after a beat.

"Well, it's pretty obvious that he was using drugs himself," Sam said, "so he didn't bother trying to deny that, but he swore up and down that Diana never did any and that he never gave her any."

"Did they believe him?" Gloria studied Sam for a moment. "Did *you?*"

"I don't know," Sam said, remembering Kevin's pale tortured face and the look of hopelessness in his eyes. Sam had never found Kevin particularly appealing, but her heart had ached for him then. He flushed, he stammered, he got angry, but he stuck to his story that he didn't know where Diana was or even where she might have gone, and he was insistent that she loved her baby and didn't do any drugs because that would hurt Zoë. There was no doubting the depth of his emotion, Sam thought, but it was impossible to tell whether or not he was telling the truth.

"It's so much worse now than when we—when I was in school," Gloria was saying. "So many more drugs and they're all prescription. Everyone thinks these are such nice kids. I think some of them probably even trade their own prescriptions with their parents. The moms are all buzzed on Ritalin and the kids are fucked up on painkillers. Although I'll bet the only thing Kevin found in *Dick's* medicine cabinet was a whole lot of Viagra. Don't you think?"

"I don't know," Sam said again. She thought about Dorothy. Heroin,

Dorothy had told her. That was her addiction. She hadn't even started off slow—hadn't progressed from something like pot or pills. She had a boyfriend and he had a habit and then so did she.

"Did they ask him where he got the drugs?" Gloria said. "Surely they wanted to know."

"He was pretty hazy on that," Sam said. "Told them about friends of friends, didn't know their names, that kind of thing. They have to understand that, though. Nobody wants to narc anyone out. It's the first rule, isn't it?"

"They ought to look at that Asian kid across the street," Gloria said, turning the heat on under the sauté pan. There were three burners going now and the kitchen was starting to warm considerably.

Sam opened the can of tomatoes, put them in a pot, and then on the stove to heat. "The piano kid? What do you mean they should look at him?"

Gloria shrugged, pushing the browning garlic around in the pan. "That kid's the hook-up around here. I don't know where he gets it or how he does it, but he's got it." She reached for the chopped onion and scraped it into the pan. It hit with a hiss and sizzle, sending tiny droplets of hot oil spraying out. Gloria lowered the flame on the burner.

"How do you know that, Gloria?"

"You know," Gloria said, "you hear things. You see things."

"But what—"

"You just don't pay that much attention, Sam. You think you do, but you don't."

"What does *that* mean?" Something about the air in the room had changed—it was staticky and electrified as if the molecules were vibrating. Sam could feel herself being drawn into the undertow of an argument; she dug her heels in, unwilling to get washed away. She stood up straighter, feeling off center and somehow crooked. "Are you saying that I haven't been paying attention to *you*, Gloria? Because if that's how you feel, just tell me." But Gloria remained silent, moving her wooden spoon in the pan until the onions became glassy and then, abruptly, turning off the heat. "Gloria? Is it Zoë? Are you upset that I've been spending so much time with the baby?"

Gloria sighed and looked up, her eyes searching Sam's face. For what, Sam didn't know. "No, Sam. I'm not jealous of Zoë."

"Because you're right about my getting attached to her. These last couple of weeks . . ." Tears pushed at the backs of her eyes. She turned her head so that Gloria couldn't see. The last thing she wanted now was to descend into weepiness because she wasn't sure that if the waterworks started there would be any turning them off. Still, she was tired—bone weary—of having to explain, of being the strong one in this relationship, of shouldering all the guilt for everything that had happened with Noah and Frank, and of being cast as the villain in this movie. She wanted to be petulant, to throw a fit, to throw *something,* and just be able to get away with it. She felt a sharp tang of longing for Zoë, that soft baby smell and sleepy warmth. Then it was gone, leaving a dark streak of resentment in its place.

"It's almost Thanksgiving," Sam said, her voice sounding ragged and harsh. "What are we going to do?"

"I need to spend Thanksgiving with Justin," Gloria said sharply. Her tone was off, Sam thought. It was almost as if she'd been expecting this question and had the answer all prepared and ready to go.

"Noah's taking Connor to Hawaii," Sam said.

"You told me that."

"Did I? Sorry, I forgot."

"I thought you were going to try to talk him out of it."

"What, and risk having Connor hate me for ruining his vacation? Noah's promised him snorkeling and surfing and who knows what else. Probably money. He's probably promised him a fucking offshore bank account."

"I'm sorry about that, Sam, I really am. It's a prick move."

Sam's eyes filled again, but this time she just let the tears fall. The pasta water was about to boil. She tipped the warmed, spiced tomatoes into the saucepan and mixed them with the garlic and onion, turned the heat on low. "Is Frank going to let Justin be with you on Thanksgiving?" Sam said. "You haven't told me anything about what's going on with the holidays. I'm dreading Christmas. I don't even know what that's going to be like." She wiped her wet cheek with the back of her hand. "I was thinking I could do something really special and different. It's been such a crap year; it would be great to just blow it out with something spectacular."

"You mean cook here? At this house?"

"Well, where else, Gloria?"

"I have to be with Justin, Sam. I'm his mother."

"I know. So is Justin coming here or what?"

"Frank . . ." Gloria put her hand to her head—that nervous habit again, smoothing hair that wasn't there. "I'm going to Frank's for Thanksgiving. It's the only way I can see Justin."

"Jesus, Gloria."

"Don't, Sam. Just don't."

"You're going to leave me—on Thanksgiving—and go eat dinner at Frank's house?"

"It's not about you; it's about Justin."

"It isn't about Justin. It's about Frank." Sam emptied the boxes of pasta into the boiling water and stirred. The sauce smelled delicious. In eight minutes it would be perfect. But Sam had completely lost her appetite. "It's about Frank and what Frank wants and about how bad he can make you feel. *That's* what it's about."

"Let's not do this now, okay, Sam? Let's just call it off at least until after dinner. Okay?"

Sam said nothing—she let the silence speak for her. A minute ticked by. Sam felt the craving for a cigarette—something she'd only thought about intermittently since she'd given them up weeks ago—descend on her like a falling anvil.

"We need Parmesan," Gloria said after a moment.

"I don't know what to tell you about that," Sam said. "We don't have any."

Gloria hovered for a moment, fidgeting, and then came to some sort of decision. "I'm just going to run out and pick some up," she said and moved toward the hallway where they kept their keys on a giant hook.

"But dinner's ready, Gloria."

"I'll be back in five minutes. Seven, tops. You can time me. I need cheese, Sam. I can't have puttanesca without it. You want to come with me? We can do a drive-by. I'll keep the engine running, and you can dash in and out."

"Can't leave it like this, it'll get ruined," Sam said. "Okay, go. But please hurry, Gloria, I don't want to eat it cold." *Or at all now,* she thought.

"Five minutes," Gloria said, her voice disappearing into the garage. Sam heard the garage door creak open and Gloria peel out in her truck. She waited for the sound of the door sliding shut but didn't hear it. Gloria had left it open to save time for when she came back in. It was true; if the check-out lines were moving, it wouldn't take her more than a few minutes to get to the grocery store and back. Its proximity to the shopping center was one of the reasons they'd chosen this neighborhood. Sam stirred the pasta again. The penne needed longer in the water than the shells so as a result neither would be perfectly cooked. The penne would be too under-cooked if the shells were just right. So it was going to be slightly mushy shells and perfect penne, Sam decided.

The house was suddenly quiet without Gloria in it, which struck Sam as odd because they hadn't exactly been filling it with noise lately. It was her presence, Sam thought. Gloria's mere presence had a sound of its own. Sam stirred the sauce again and then the pasta. She banged the spoon against the pot and wondered if she had a secret stash of cigarettes she'd forgotten about somewhere in the house. In her mind she traveled through the hall-way and into the linen closet, through her shoe boxes and into coat pockets and empty purses. Rainy day cigarettes—every ex-smoker had some, but in her imagining Sam came up blank. She hadn't saved any cigarettes because she hadn't cared enough to worry about wanting one. She'd finished her last pack and thrown it out. End of story. Until this minute quitting had seemed very easy.

Sam glanced at the clock above the oven. Five minutes and Gloria wasn't back yet. Well, five minutes was probably unrealistic anyway. But if she wasn't back in ten, Sam was going to be pissed. She took out silverware, plates, and napkins and put them on the table. Should have told her to get something to drink, Sam thought, and wondered whether or not to call Gloria and tell her to pick something up. But she was probably out of the check-out line already and on the way home. So it was going to be water for her and probably that nasty beer for Gloria. She spooned out a shell and a piece of penne from the boiling water, blew on them, and popped first one, then the other into her mouth, burning her tongue despite the precaution. The shells were done. One more minute on the penne.

The stinging on Sam's tongue was a physical manifestation of her regret. She wished she could reel in the last ten minutes of her conversation with Gloria and take back all those burning words. It was the right time to talk, but not about babies and not about Frank. Better to have a nice, relaxed dinner and just talk about nothing until they both warmed up. It wasn't a tough thing to figure out, but neither one of them had been very good about communicating. It was too easy to fall into resentment and silence and avoid doing the work that was required in any relationship, especially this relationship. They were both guilty of it. What they needed was more sensitivity for each other. It wasn't easy for anyone. Once more, Sam saw the image in her mind's eye of Dorothy weeping over her store-bought crumb cake.

She'd never told anyone, so many years now—more than thirty, though it hardly seemed possible—about that other life she'd had. She was a girl, just a girl, fallen in with a bad crowd and a bad boy to go with it. He had a motorcycle, Dorothy said. Have you ever been with a boy on a motorcycle? It's not something you forget. Do you remember what it was like back then? Dorothy asked Sam. In the seventies we all wanted to be Charlie's Angels. That hair, those bikinis. Everybody beautiful and having fun. We had a pool—a swimming pool—because it was so hot in the summer. The adults hung around with drinks. You know, you had cocktails at the pool in those days. . . .

Although she didn't know where Dorothy was going with any of it, Sam let her ramble on without interrupting. Dorothy's eyes were turned inward to her long-buried memories, watching a scene she hadn't allowed herself to see for three decades and relating what she found there in a breathless rush. She hadn't known any better, Dorothy went on, and she hadn't given it any thought. She was bad, of a weak character. It was so quick from that first little taste. Almost no time at all before she couldn't live without it. They say it's a gene, that addiction runs in families. Well, her parents had been huge drinkers and maybe that was it right there. But she had never been interested in alcohol, no. Even now, even now . . .

"I had to run away," Dorothy whispered. "I had to."

"But Dorothy," Sam had said then, "you were just a kid and it happens all the time. You weren't hurting anyone but yourself. You could have gotten help."

Dorothy had closed her eyes then, and Sam saw that the lids were red and rough from crying. "No," she said. And then, "Please, Sam, please don't—"

"No, I won't say anything to anyone, Dorothy, of course not. I promise you."

It felt so awkward, Sam recalled now, to reach over to Dorothy and touch her. She was holding Zoë in one arm and had to lean across the table to find Dorothy's hands, which were both clenched in front of her, so that she could cover them with her own. Dorothy's hands were cold and trembling. She didn't give any indication that she felt Sam's hand, didn't move closer or pull back. Sam couldn't help thinking how strange it was that she was trying to comfort someone who wouldn't have even invited her in only a few weeks before. It was stranger still that she was able to feel not pity or

even sympathy, but empathy for Dorothy. As she felt Dorothy's skin under
her own palm, Sam experienced a moment of true compassion and connection with the woman sitting across from her. The secret that Dorothy
had revealed shed some light on her personality and perhaps explained why
she seemed so buttoned up, but it didn't change who she was. Sam doubted
that she and Dorothy would ever read the same books, enjoy the same
movies, or ever have one of those girls' nights out that women seemed
compelled to go on, no matter what dark skeletons either one of them
pulled from their respective closets. And that Dorothy had been a junkie in
her wild, misspent youth didn't make the fact that she had grown up and
married Dick Werner any easier to understand—or tolerate. It wasn't that
Dorothy underwent some sort of transformation in Sam's eyes when she
opened up those floodgates and let loose, but Sam felt her pain as acutely
as if it had been her own. Maybe, Sam thought, that was because it *was* her
pain too. The whole world was in pain and Sam felt it swirling around
them, enveloping them—their connectedness a ribbon of sweetness in the
sorrow.

It had helped Dorothy to talk to Sam, a slight release of the pressure
that had been building for thirty years. Dorothy told Sam that she had
never told anyone a single word of the story she had just shared and Sam
believed her. Even then, stripped bare and eyes watering, Sam could see the
tautness still inside Dorothy—a tension that was threatening to break her.
Telling Sam, who couldn't figure whether she had just been in the right
place at the right time for the confession or if Dorothy just sensed that she
could trust her, had alleviated some of Dorothy's stress. But when Sam left
later that afternoon, she could tell that Dorothy was deeply troubled and
perhaps even more paranoid than before. In the days since then Sam felt
Dorothy's silent despair like a vortex pulling at her from next door.

Sam heard splashing and the hiss of steam. She looked at the stove and
saw that the pasta water was boiling over. She'd drifted and let it go too
long. She turned the stove off and drained the pasta. Without even sam-
pling she could see that the shells were way overdone and that the penne

was right on the edge. It couldn't have been more than a couple of minutes, what the hell? And where was Gloria? Sam looked at the clock again. Gloria had been gone over ten minutes and Sam was annoyed despite her resolve to put aside all of her complaints until after dinner. She poured a small amount of olive oil on the pasta and transferred it back to the pot, putting the lid on. The sauce was past ready so she turned the heat off there as well. She sat down at the table and folded her hands. *I'm not going to get angry. I'm not.*

After another five minutes spent staring at the brown weave of the place mat in front of her, Sam reluctantly picked up her cell phone and dialed. So she was a nagging bitch, but it had been more than fifteen minutes and Gloria had promised, damn it. But before she could hit the send button, Sam snapped the phone shut and laid it down. She waited another minute and another after that. The air in the kitchen had cooled off, but the aroma of the tomato sauce hung like a scented cloud in the middle of the room. Sam picked up her phone a second time, hesitated again, and then dialed Gloria's full phone number rather than the speed dial digit she'd been assigned, so as to take more time. It rang and rang—Sam lost count of how many times, so surprised was she that Gloria didn't pick it up, even just to say, "Can't talk, Sam, on my way." Finally, it just went to voice mail and Sam heard Gloria's curt voice instructing her to "speak after the beep and make it good." Sam clicked her phone shut before the tone ended. There was no message. *That* was the message. Sam poured herself a glass of water and forced herself to drink it very slowly.

After another ten minutes, Sam was seized with that familiar mother's panic—*what if she got into an accident and is lying dead in the street?*—the irrational fears of death and destruction that couldn't be palliated with logic or reason. But no, she would have heard sirens. Or something. Maybe she stopped to talk to somebody at the store, Sam thought. Which would be fucking inconsiderate, but a better option than sprawled headless and bloody on the windshield of her car. Sam dialed Gloria again and again it went to voice mail. This time, Sam almost beat the tone when she said,

"Gloria, what the *fuck?* You said five minutes and it's been a half hour. You could at least call me."

There was nothing for it now, Sam thought as she hung up. Dinner was ruined.

After fifteen more minutes, Sam got up and closed the garage door that Gloria had left open. It was dark, and she felt exposed with the door open like that—a big empty space just asking for trouble. She went to the fridge and took out one of Gloria's beers and popped the top, took a long drink, and fought the urge throw it back up.

It was only after another hour and the second beer, almost two hours since Gloria had gone out, that Sam threw the food away. She dumped the pasta in the sink and tossed the sauce in after it, turning on the garbage disposal and listening to the growl and grind of mechanical mastication. It was impossible to name the emotion coursing through her blood, pounding at her head, making her throat tight and sore. It was beyond anger or frustration or even sadness. Sam was somewhere in the middle of ashamed and humiliated and she was not nearly drunk enough.

Ninety minutes later, after several pony glasses of a bad cut-rate port she'd found at the back of the highest cabinet in the kitchen, Sam stumbled out of the kitchen into the darkness of the living room and fell onto the couch. Fuck the dirty pots and pans and sink. Fuck everything because she was never going to eat another fucking thing ever again anyway. Feeling stifled, Sam opened the sliding glass back door to get a little air and almost fell through the screen door in the process. Her stomach lurched. A puff of wind blew in, bringing with it the sound of a baby crying. It must be Zoë, Sam thought, and started to weep, big fat splashing tears that seemed to have no end. She fell down on the couch and cried until she passed out.

Hours later, in the blackest part of night, Sam's nausea woke her up and she raced to the bathroom just in time to hurl the contents of her stomach into the toilet. But in all the time she spent throwing up—and it was much longer than she ever remembered doing when she was in high school and college and drinking to excess—Sam didn't even consider how sick she felt or how miserable she was going to be if it ever decided to be morning again. What she thought, over and over again, was that the old saw was really true, it really happened and wasn't just a saying. People really went out for a pack of cigarettes and never came back. It was almost funny.

Gloria came home at 5:01 AM. Sam knew this because she opened her eyes and looked into the red glow of their bedside clock as Gloria ascended the stairs. Sam was under the covers and shivering a little, her back to the bedroom door when Gloria came in and stood at the edge of the bed for a long time unmoving. Sam could hear her breathing. Then, very quietly, Gloria sat down on the bed. Sam shut her eyes tightly and didn't move. She could smell alcohol fumes radiating off Gloria despite those that were surely coming from her own pores. She'd had more than a few, had Gloria. Sam didn't want whatever was coming next, but she couldn't stop it.

Gloria reached over, put her hand on Sam's hip. "Sam?" She could sense that Sam was awake. She knew. Sam didn't answer. The hand stayed there, a light pressure through the blanket and sheets, for several minutes— so long that Sam thought Gloria had passed out sitting up. But then she leaned over and lay down, spooning Sam's body with her own. Gloria brought her arm around, held Sam tightly, pushed her face into Sam's hair. She breathed in and out, in and out.

"Sam."

"What are we going to do, Gloria?" Sam asked without turning around, without moving a single muscle in her body. "Please, just tell me."

Gloria breathed in and out, her body warm and firm against Sam's. "I'm sorry, Sam," she said. "I'm so sorry."

She's sorry, Sam thought, and wished she knew for whom.

chapter 19

Allison took the freshly baked crescent rolls out of the oven and set them on a cooling rack. They smelled delicious even though they had come out of a cardboard tube and were loaded with preservatives. She felt vaguely guilty about serving something so artificial, but she wasn't trying to fool anyone and nobody was going to believe that she'd stood in her kitchen and prepared perfectly shaped, risen, and browned dinner rolls anyway. She'd bought cookies as well and good-quality coffee for the occasion. She put the rolls on a serving platter and the cookies on a plate and took both into the dining room where she'd already laid the table with a serviceable but attractive yellow tablecloth, napkins, and small paper plates. She needed to put cups out—paper or ceramic?—spoons, creamer, and sugar. Suddenly the rolls and cookies looked lost and half-finished on the table, as if something central was missing. Still, food was really beside the point. It wasn't a party. Far from it. But Allison didn't know how to classify what it *was*, either. There weren't any truly accurate names for this kind of gathering.

Was it a neighborhood meeting?

Close enough.

Back in the kitchen Allison checked the clock and decided it was time to turn on the coffee. She then put water in the kettle and turned the burner on. It was going to have to be decaffeinated tea for her. She was already feeling jittery flips in her stomach and didn't want to take the chance of being kept awake and buzzed later. Sleep was elusive and hard-won for Allison these days—a punishment perhaps for the months she'd spent in bed—and she had to be careful not to tip herself into insomnia. She still had sleeping pills, of course, a few different kinds in sample packs the doctor had given her, but they were all becoming ineffective and Allison was scared that she'd end up taking too many. She wasn't stupid—she knew how easy it was to build up a tolerance and then just go overboard. She didn't want to die—just sleep.

Truth be told, she also wanted a drink. The craving was so strong it made her eyes water, but satisfying it was completely out of the question. Allison was straining, exerting willpower she didn't know she possessed to avoid any and all alcohol. Although she was succeeding in overcoming the urge, it was only by a hair.

Allison had spent more than three months in a booze-soaked haze and in the last three sober weeks she had relived every minute of them. One would have thought that some of that extended lost weekend would be gone, washed away or drowned in all the wine and vodka she'd consumed, but no. Blackouts were terrible things and people always lived to regret them, but in a way they were merciful, Allison thought. Given the choice, she would have turned July through October into one long black hole that she could never again see into. It would have been an indescribable relief. But if anything Allison was experiencing a reverse blackout. The long days and endless trailing nights of those months stretched out for Allison like a badly painted canvas. Without the dulling benefit of a single drink since that horrible day when the county had gone up in flames, Allison had been forced to look at and remember every detail. It was torturous but also necessary. In playing back the film of her life since the summer Allison realized that she'd become—in a matter of minutes it seemed—a spiteful drunk whom everyone hated and, let's face it, *blamed*. It was funny, she thought, how quickly you could go from being the injured party to being the perpetrator.

Still, the instant sobriety she had tumbled into had shown Allison that from the day of Diana's arrival onward, she had only made life more difficult for herself. It was impossible to generate sympathy when you were so obviously drunk off your ass. At all hours of the day. Every day of the week. It was too late to undo any of that now and useless to fixate or wallow in shame over her actions. But she could manage the here and now and reshape the twisted opinions of her that people now had. All of this required not drinking. And not drinking required Allison to fake a level of equanimity that she did not have. But she believed in the "fake it until you make it" philosophy, which was exactly what she was doing and why she was hosting this nonparty to begin with. It was why she'd come home in the first place.

When she got to her mother's house in Pasadena late that Monday afternoon of the fires, Allison fully expected to stay there indefinitely. It had been a brutal drive, hot and gritty, the freeway jam-packed and choked with smoke blowing in from every direction. The tension and growing panic of all the drivers combined to create a giant hovering cloud of impending disaster. The usually two-hour trip took Allison four and a half hours, and her already-fried nerves were completely shorted out by the time she got there. To make matters worse, she was technically still drunk from the night before despite the coffee she'd consumed that morning. It was nothing short of a divine piece of luck that she hadn't been stopped by the CHP at any point on that harrowing drive because she probably couldn't have passed a field sobriety test. Not to mention that she'd left her house looking like a cross between a bag lady and a mental patient on a weekend pass. Not sexy, not together, but an accurate representation of what she was at that point—a mad housewife. The cops would have seen that instantly.

She'd called her mother from the road and had anticipated that she would be greeted with instant and unreserved love, support, and a safe haven when she got there, but that was not at all what she got when she knocked hard against her mother's cheerful yellow door.

"What's going on, Allie?" her mother said, first thing. "What is all of this about?"

"I have nowhere else to go, Mom." It was meant to sound plaintive, but even Allison could tell it was just coming off as surly.

"Where's Joe?" was the next question, one that Allison was never able to answer to her mother's satisfaction. She had always believed that her mother was unequivocally on her side and would defend her to the death if necessary, so it was an unpleasant shock when her mother seemed to take the opposite approach when Allison showed up at her house.

"What is this really about?" her mother asked. "It's been months since that girl came to live with you, and you haven't moved beyond the fact that he didn't tell you he had a daughter. It's self-indulgent, Allie. Move on or move out."

"I can't believe you aren't behind me on this."

"But I *am*. You're feeling so sorry for yourself you can't even see how much behind you I am." And then she dealt an even worse blow. "I love you, but I can't let you stay here forever, Allie."

"How long is forever, Mom?"

Allison retired to the pink and sea foam green bedroom in which she'd spent much of her childhood, lay on the same bed where she'd dreamed of so many happy endings, and pressed her fingers into her eyes to keep from seeing all the ugly images that kept playing behind her closed lids. It was a long, bad night—the first in more than she could count without a drink to dull the edges—and made somehow inexplicably worse by the fact that Joe had left only one message on her cell phone. She didn't want to talk to him—she'd left him, after all, and was debating making that a permanent state. He'd lied to her, betrayed her, and was possibly cheating on her. And yet. Lying there in the dark, hungry and hollow in every way, Allison felt bereft and completely alone.

Why wouldn't he call? She was his *wife*.

The calls came later, of course—angry and increasingly desperate messages piling up on her phone. *Where is Diana? What happened between the two of you? Why did you leave the baby by herself? Diana is missing. When are you coming home? Diana is missing and the police need to talk to you. What is going on, Allison? Call me. Allison, you have to call me.*

But those messages didn't change Allison's mind, nor did the terse conversations she had with Joe when she finally called him back. She might not have come home—she might have tried to persuade her mother to let her stay—at least through the holidays. What changed her mind—what compelled Allison to get into her car and go home—was the message from Joe telling her that Yvonne had come to stay at their house.

Allison startled at the sound of the kettle. She turned off the gas and in the absence of whistling heard Zoë crying in what Allison now perversely thought of as Diana's bedroom. When Diana had actually been living here and up through the moment that Yvonne had left a week ago, Allison had thought of it only as the guest bedroom. Allison waited a moment to see if Joe was going to go check on the baby but realized he was probably upstairs and out of earshot, so she quickly washed and dried her hands at the kitchen sink and hurried into the bedroom.

The room was dark but for the tiny glow of a fairy princess nightlight near Zoë's little basket, which was sitting on Diana's made-up bed. Allison couldn't call it Yvonne's bed even though she'd been its most recent inhabitant. While she had been staying at the house, Yvonne had gotten up with Zoë, but now that she'd gone back to Las Vegas (temporarily, Allison reminded herself), Allison and Joe had moved the crib upstairs into their bedroom and had been taking turns getting up and feeding her. For Allison, this was perhaps the strangest twist in a life that hadn't seemed her own since that hot July day when she'd come home to find Diana standing in her driveway. That she and Joe were even sharing the same bed was peculiar enough, but that they were jointly caring for Zoë—that they were capable of it—was still stunning to her.

Allison wasn't sure how it had happened. But somehow they'd fallen into a pattern of preparing formula, stacking diapers, and wordlessly alternating shifts. They hadn't had any kind of discussion about it and Joe hadn't even asked her if she was willing. He'd just assumed she wasn't. But when Zoë started crying the first night after Yvonne left, Allison went over to her and picked her up. She still didn't know why she'd done it because there had been no thought in it at all—it was just movement and . . . instinct. The thing was, Zoë wasn't a difficult newborn. She woke when she had to, did what she needed, and promptly went back to sleep. Even Joe could handle that. And, Allison had to concede, he handled it quite well.

Light from the hall spilled into the bedroom so Allison didn't bother turning on the lamp, just went over to the basket and fished out the baby. Laying her on the bed, Allison changed her and noticed that she already needed a bigger size of diapers. They grew so fast at this stage. She wasn't going to fit in that basket for much longer, Allison thought. They might have to get a second crib and they definitely needed a baby monitor.

As she scooped up the small bundle, Allison had another flashback to the day she'd left. They'd been happening with increasing frequency, and no small amount of paranoia. Nobody had accused her of anything outright—they couldn't—but the blame was there, implicit.

I didn't abandon the baby. Diana was here. I was sure of it.

But she hadn't checked, had she?

Joe and the police had asked her more than once why she hadn't opened the door. Why hadn't she gone in to tell Diana that she was leaving? She would have seen that Diana was gone and that the baby was by herself. Why hadn't she gone in to check? Allison's answer was that she simply didn't think she needed to. They'd all been up late the night before. She let them sleep. She assumed that Joe would be back momentarily. She left. That was all.

Zoë whimpered, turning her head toward Allison's body, her mouth searching for the bottle. "Okay, okay, sshh," Allison crooned, rocking her. "We'll get you fed. Hush, sweetie, we'll get you taken care of." As if she knew the bottle was coming, Zoë quieted a little, her cries turning into little yelps. Another scene flitted across Allison's mind: Diana half-dressed and out of it, struggling to nurse her baby. *I can't do this.* That was what Diana had said—Allison could hear the echo of the words in her memory. It was true, Allison hadn't been a big help to Diana. Hadn't been any help at all. But Allison wondered now if it would have made a difference even if she'd been the second coming of Mother Theresa. Diana was too young and maybe she was just unsuited for motherhood. She couldn't do it. Being female and able to bear a child didn't make you automatically capable of raising one. That writing had always been on the wall with Diana. Joe, Yvonne, Sam, and anyone else could pass all kinds of silent judgment on Allison for her attitude toward Diana, but they couldn't change that truth. In the end, it was Allison who had spent the most time with Diana these past few months, even if it wasn't exactly *quality* time, and Allison who had seen most clearly that Diana wanted out. But that didn't make any of this Allison's fault.

She walked with Zoë to the kitchen where a series of sterilized, formula-filled bottles were ready and waiting. Allison had taken control of this too. She knew how much to have on hand and when to take them out of the fridge to warm. She never used the microwave to heat them. She knew how much formula Zoë should be consuming and what temperature was ideal. You didn't run an elementary-school classroom for as long as she had and not know how to be organized. It was easy to hold the baby now—to feed her. Allison didn't understand why she hadn't been able to do this before Diana had gone missing, or why it now felt almost like second nature. There was the drinking, of course, but that didn't account for all of it—maybe not even for any of it. There was something else that had broken the barrier for Allison, something that now allowed her to take charge of this infant as if . . . but no, she wasn't Zoë's mother. She looked down at the little face as she positioned the bottle just so in Zoë's mouth. You could see Diana there, of course, and maybe as she got older, Zoë would come to resemble her more. But the person this baby really looked like was Joe. It was a startling resemblance.

"Do you need some help? I can take her—finish feeding her."

Joe was standing in the kitchen doorway, freshly showered and shaved and smelling vaguely of something citrusy. Limes, Allison thought.

"I'm okay for now," she said. "Everything's ready to go. Except the cups. I just need to put some cups on the table. People should be getting here soon. If you want to take her . . ."

"It's okay. You go sit down. I'll get the cups."

Allison nodded, carried Zoë out to the living room, and sat down on the couch. Something had happened to her husband in the time she'd been holed up in her mother's house that had made him subtly but fundamentally different. She had sensed it the moment she arrived back home, but Allison, who was still wrestling with her emotions, didn't yet understand the exact nature of the change. Outwardly, there was little that was unusual about him, but the small things that were different seemed significant to Allison. He had lost weight for one thing, and even though she knew he hadn't been going to the gym or dieting, he looked leaner. He also looked tired, which could be explained by the long days and sleepless nights he'd been having, but there was something beyond just fatigue or even exhaustion in his eyes. When he thought nobody was looking—as had happened several times over the last few days—Joe had taken to staring at some fixed point in space that only he could see. In those moments, Allison thought, he looked haunted. There were other times, when he was rocking or feeding the baby, when Allison saw the corners of his mouth turn down as if he were about to cry.

She had never seen Joe cry.

Even though he never showed any trace of tears, the suggestion of them alone was enough to shock her. But he didn't always seem sad. At times his jaw clenched and his eyes flashed, and Allison could swear he was waging an inward battle against his own thoughts. He seemed, Allison thought, like a man who was undergoing a seismic shift within his own belief system—as if something in his brain had been permanently rearranged.

It was impossible for Allison to tell how any of this affected how Joe felt about *her*. Over the last few months, their marriage had become an unrecognizable form of what they'd built over the last eight years—a Jackson Pollock reinterpretation of a Renoir—so she hardly knew whether Joe was reacting to the old Allison, the Allison she'd become when Diana came into their lives, or the Allison he wanted her to be. Nor did she know which one of those iterations she most closely resembled now anyway. He was careful with her and often solicitous. Yet there was also resentment just under the surface—a sort of simmering anger that he sometimes had to work to keep at bay. And under all of that—buried in a place she was sure he didn't want her to see, Allison sensed that Joe was hurt.

They were in some sort of slow crisis mode now, juggling Zoë's care and trying to help the police find Diana with Joe's work schedule and bills that had grown out of control, too absorbed in the immediacy of these needs to talk about anything deeper than what needed to be done in the next twenty-four hours. Allison knew that eventually—probably sooner than later—something would give way and they would have to talk. Not a quiet compartmentalized conversation but a big, messy, painful extraction of the truth.

Zoë had finished more than half her bottle so Allison put the baby against her shoulder and rubbed her back in gentle circles until she heard the burp. Allison repositioned her for the rest of her meal, but she could tell that Zoë wasn't going to get through it. She was milk-drunk and sleepy, eyes closed and mouth tugging weakly at the nipple. Within a couple of minutes, she was out cold. Allison looked at her finely veined, almost translucent eyelids and wondered what she was seeing behind them—if it was all fuzzy shapes and shades of gray or whether there were vivid colors and detail. What did this tiny thing dream of? Allison stood up slowly so as not to wake her. Looking up, she saw that Joe was standing at the table, three mismatched brightly colored mugs in his hand, staring at her. She didn't know how to read the look in his eyes. There was so much emotion there it was almost fierce. But not angry. Was there love in it? Hate? Allison couldn't tell, but for a moment it froze her, weak-kneed, where she stood.

"Do you think these are okay?" he said, finally, holding out the mugs. But Allison could tell that was not at all the question he wanted to ask.

"Fine, sure," she said. "We have some paper cups too. But those are fine." Allison willed herself to move. "She's asleep. I'll go put her down."

"Okay," Joe said.

"I think I'll put her upstairs," Allison said. "In the crib. It might get loud down here. We'll just . . . We can go check on her."

"That's probably a good idea," he said. He was still holding the cups. Still staring at her.

"You know, we should get a baby monitor. We really need one."

"You're right," he said. "I can pick one up tomorrow."

"Or I can."

"Okay."

Allison climbed the stairs softly, careful not to jostle. The crib was between the bed and the closet, necessitating a sideways turn to get around. Allison lay the baby down on her back and adjusted her blankets so that she was all wrapped up burrito-style. She let her hand linger on Zoë for a moment, feeling the rise and fall of her chest, making sure that her breathing felt regular. She thought about the notion that the number of breaths you were meant to draw in your lifetime was predetermined when you were born and wondered how many had been allotted to this child.

Downstairs, the doorbell rang. She heard Joe open the door and then the muffled sound of voices, male and female. She couldn't tell who it was. She lingered a moment longer with the baby. She wasn't in a hurry to see the people downstairs—to talk to them and ingratiate herself while they regarded her with suspicion and derision. It was almost funny, Allison thought, of all the people in this neighborhood—on this block—*she* was the one who everyone now looked down on. Not Dorothy or Dick, who had done a pathetic job raising their only child; not Sam and Gloria, who had *lost* custody of their children; not even Jessalyn Martin, the neighborhood slut. Of course, Allison had no proof of her neighbors' opinion of her because nobody had said anything to her face, but she knew. She could tell. In her absence, Joe, with his missing daughter and AWOL wife, had become the object of everyone's sympathy while she'd become the villain. Well, not everyone's—Dick Werner was still as big an asshole as ever, even if he no longer seemed as if he wanted to do Joe bodily harm. But the others . . .

Allison left the bedroom door open and walked out to the landing. She hesitated at the top of the stairs, that urge for a drink pressing into her consciousness again, and took one deep breath, then another. After the third, Allison reminded herself that the whole focused breathing thing was nonsense. All it did was make her dizzy. And it wasn't going to make a single minute of the next couple of hours any easier.

When she got downstairs, Joe was standing at the dining room table with Sam and Gloria, although none of them were eating or drinking or even looking as if they might. Sam and Gloria were both dressed entirely in black: a button-down shirt and slacks for Sam and a fitted T-shirt and yoga pants for Gloria. They looked as if they'd come to a wake, albeit a casual one, and Allison found it distasteful. Beyond that, Allison, who hadn't seen the two of them together in some time, was startled by the change in their appearances. Sam, who had been pretty thin to begin with, had lost too much weight and looked gaunt and brittle. There were hollows under her sharp cheekbones and dark half moons under her eyes. Gloria had gone in the other direction. She'd been in great shape and really well toned the last time Allison had noticed but now looked big and chunky. The tight T-shirt she was wearing only served to highlight a new roll of flesh at the top of her hips, and her too-short, unstylish haircut emphasized the puffiness in her face. In inches, she wasn't that much taller than Sam, but she appeared so much larger that it almost seemed as if she were casting a shadow over the other woman. The only place they matched, Allison thought, was in their expressions. Both of them looked completely miserable.

"Hi, Sam, Gloria," Allison said. "Thanks for coming. Can I get you some coffee or tea?"

Sam smiled and said she was fine, but Gloria asked for coffee. "I'll get it, Allison," Joe said and disappeared into the kitchen.

Sam regarded Allison warily as one might a pit bull. Allison did a quick search of her memory to figure out specifically what she might have done or said to Sam to warrant that look, but came up empty. "How's the baby?" Sam asked. "Everything okay? Do you need anything?"

Allison struggled to keep from frowning. Joe had told her how helpful Sam had been while she was gone—how often she'd taken care of Zoë. How she had *rescued* Zoë for that matter after Allison had *abandoned* her to an empty house in the middle of a natural disaster. He hadn't said that last part out loud of course, but the subtext was always there and it was deafening. Allison could imagine what Joe might have said to Sam about her or about their marriage in her absence, but she would never really know for sure. She wouldn't have thought Joe capable of gossip, but then she'd never have predicted his illegitimate daughter showing up either.

"She's doing fine," Allison said. "I just fed her. She's asleep upstairs."

"Is she eating well and everything?"

"Seems to be." Allison heard irritation creeping into her voice and worked to remove it. "And she's sleeping well."

"That's good. She's probably due for her shots, isn't she? Do you have a pediatrician for her? I can recommend one. You know, it's so important that they get the shots on time. So many parents—"

"Sam?" Gloria sidled up to Sam and cut her off, her hand on Sam's shoulder. Allison noticed that she was squeezing it just a little, even though her face remained impassive. Sam sighed and moved out from under her hand. It was a call and response with no words at all—the kind couples were so good at. The kind she and Joe hadn't done for so long.

Joe appeared with the coffeepot and filled a mug for Gloria. "Sam?" he said. "Allison?"

Sam and Allison both shook their heads. Joe filled a mug with coffee for himself and set the pot down on the table. Gloria took a noisy gulp and reached across the table for a cookie. There followed a period of seconds—it couldn't have been a whole minute, Allison thought—that defined the phrase *awkward silence.* It was the type of moment that made one wish for a distraction on the order of gunfire. Or an earthquake.

"So what have you heard new, Joe?" Sam asked, finally. "Anything from Garcia or Williams? Have they had any response to that piece on the news?"

Allison felt her entire body tense up. It made her uncomfortable that Sam referred by name to the detectives who were handling Diana's case. It signified a familiarity beyond what was necessary, Allison thought. Of course, as the person who had found Zoë alone and alerted everyone to Diana's absence, Sam was de facto involved up to her eyeballs. It had been Sam's idea to push for the "missing girl" news story, even though the detectives that Sam was so chummy with had suggested it first. Sam had come up with the sympathetic angle—Diana was not just another wayward teenager but a new mom with a precious little baby who had disappeared from a nice neighborhood during one of the worst disasters in county history. Here was her father, grave and composed, general manager of an extremely popular local restaurant and a familiar figure in the community. And here was her attractive mother, distressed and pleading with anyone who had any information to please share it. And here was the neighborhood: quiet, decent, a lovely place with caring, supportive neighbors like Sam and Dorothy. It was altogether a stunning piece of fiction, Allison thought. The only thing accurate about it was that Diana was missing. Allison had been left out of that entire spot. Not that she wanted any part of it, but her exclusion seemed to highlight the negative if not accusatory attitude of everyone around her. And why the hell *was* Sam so friendly with Detectives Garcia and Williams? Paranoid fear crawled through Allison and she longed again for the blur of alcohol.

"There's nothing really new," Joe said. "It's harder, I guess, because she didn't really know anyone here. Her 'known acquaintances' were pretty limited. But they are still working on it. Detective Garcia assured me that they won't give up on it. On *her*."

"He seems like a good guy," Sam said.

Allison looked up as Sam was finishing this sentence and caught Gloria's eyes. She looked as rattled by this conversation as Allison did.

"But I was going to wait for everyone else to get here," Joe said, "and then I'll go over everything. What they're doing."

"Who else is coming?" Gloria asked.

"I asked everyone," Allison said, clearing the sudden frog in her throat. "Sorry, I mean, I asked *Dorothy* to ask everyone. She's got the good contacts, so I figured she'd be able to get people rounded up." That sounded wrong, Allison thought, like it was some kind of rodeo. She hadn't meant it to sound like that. She avoided eye contact with Sam.

"How's Yvonne doing?" Sam asked. Gloria rolled her eyes—Allison saw it plainly—and reached for a crescent roll. There was something really off about these two, Allison thought. Something beyond just a quarrel or a bad day.

"I'm going to make myself some tea," Allison said, avoiding the Yvonne question completely. "I'll be right back. Maybe you all want to go sit down in the living room? It might be a little more comfortable." Let Joe take over for a minute, she thought. Let him fill Sam in on Yvonne's well being. Why she even wanted to know was an irritation to Allison. Was there any part of her life Sam *hadn't* crawled into?

In the kitchen, while she took extra time locating the precise tea she was looking for (the one with valerian root for relaxation) and preparing it,

Allison wondered when Sam had had time to get to know Yvonne well enough to ask after her now that she was gone. Joe had waited too long to tell her that she was here at all, but Yvonne hadn't been in San Diego that long before Allison came home—not really all that much time to get to know the neighbors with any level of intimacy. And Yvonne, like her daughter, wasn't the easiest person in the world to talk to or get to know—even allowing for the odd and uncomfortable circumstances of their meeting.

Allison had expected all kinds of emotions upon meeting Yvonne—the woman whom Joe had loved, the woman who'd had his child—most of which had been roiling around in her brain since Diana had arrived. She expected to be angry at Yvonne, however irrational that was, for shredding her life by foisting Diana on them without any warning. Allison had spent many nights silently condemning Yvonne for sending her pregnant teenager to live with a father she didn't know, and thought that these feelings too would surface when she saw Yvonne. And she expected to feel some kind of rivalry with this woman from Joe's past. But beyond all of that, and perhaps what frightened Allison the most, was that she expected to feel jealousy—corrosive, soul-destroying jealousy.

Bits and pieces of all these feelings surfaced throughout the time they spent together, but none of them were present when she met Yvonne for the first time. What struck Allison at that moment and what lingered still was how fundamentally different they were. Allison was stunned to think that they could ever have coexisted in the same man's universe.

There were the obvious physical differences, of course, striking in and of themselves. Allison was blond and petite, a classic WASP with a conservative, good-quality wardrobe and a nice figure, but there was nothing overtly sensual about her body. She looked younger than she was. She was pretty. At the right angle and with good makeup, she was very pretty.

Yvonne was tall with lush curves, high cheekbones, and large liquid eyes that reflected a gorgeously tragic expression. Her skin, darker and richer than Diana's, was smooth and completely unlined. She moved as if she were walking through water, languorous and weightless. She could have been arrestingly beautiful had she not been doing her best to hide it. The only makeup she wore was an orange lipstick completely unsuited to her coloring, and she kept her hair pulled back and fastened in a severe knot at the back of her head. Her clothes were cheap and designed for women much older and heavier than she was. It was as if she was embarrassed about her own looks, as if she were purposely aging herself. Allison didn't understand it.

From the moment Joe had introduced the two of them—his own expression a tangle of apprehension and pleading—Allison felt as if just standing next to Yvonne diminished her, made her seem two-dimensional. When they began talking, planning, organizing the mundane details of their days and then discussing Diana and slowly exchanging more personal information, Allison began to feel less like a cardboard cutout around Yvonne. But she never shook the sense that Yvonne was as unlike her as another woman could be. They weren't even opposites because opposites would have implied a yin and yang, something complementary, something in common. It was beyond Allison's ken how Joe could have chosen both of them to love, no matter how many years had passed between his leaving Yvonne and meeting her. It didn't make sense to Allison. But they were polite to each other. Once or twice they even came close to having a real conversation. That was as much as Allison could ask for—and more, it seemed, than Joe had expected.

"I appreciate it," he'd told her one night, apropos of nothing and quickly as if he might live to regret his words.

"Appreciate?"

"You—with Yvonne. I appreciate it. You, I mean. I know this isn't easy."

"No, it isn't."

"She doesn't show it, but this is hell for her." He looked at Allison, saw that he was overselling his point. "So, thanks," he finished. Allison didn't ask him what it was he thought she was doing for Yvonne or if he thought that they were becoming friends. If he even wanted them to become friends.

Now Allison wondered if Yvonne had managed to forge some kind of connection with Sam, something deeper than she might ever expect to have with Allison. But where would she have found the time?

When she reentered the living room with her tea, Allison saw that Dorothy had arrived with Kevin. Dick was conspicuously absent. There was a hum in the room now, several people talking at once, and it seemed crowded. Joe was at the table cutting a Bundt cake and putting the slices on paper plates. Dorothy had brought a cake. Of course she had.

"I'm so sorry, but Dick couldn't be here," Dorothy was saying as Allison walked in. "He wanted to, but he's totally tied up with work right now. He did say he would come by later if he was able." Her hands were clasped in front of her as if she were about to pray and her expression begged for forgiveness. The words *no need to apologize* were on the tip of Allison's tongue but never managed to fall off. She was thinking about the day of the fires, how she'd opened her door and saw Dick standing in the middle of the road staring right at her, and she felt the same tingling in her spine as she had that day. Why the hell *wasn't* he here? The drunken Allison might have asked Dorothy that question. But this fearful sober Allison was careful not to violate any social boundaries like, for example, asking why Kevin *had* shown up and his father hadn't.

The last time she'd seen Kevin here was when he'd made the ridiculous announcement that he was going to marry Diana and adopt Zoë, causing the tension between Dick and Joe to boil over into that ugly scene. That had been his big stand—his attempt to assert his manhood—and it had come crashing down on him. Kevin was one of those kids who would always be stuck in the cracks that others fell through. He had privilege and access and wanted for nothing materially. He came from an unbroken home and had the attention of his parents, if not always the right kind of attention or the best quality of parent. But there was something missing in the love he got—or maybe the love itself was missing. Combined with a central weakness in his character, this lack just set him on a course for failure. Allison had seen it before—seen it coming with the kids she taught. They weren't gifted, weren't easy, weren't . . . likable. Kids like that—like Kevin—needed more, needed extra, but they didn't know how to ask for it and they never seemed to get it. Then they got into trouble or slid into depression and self-destructiveness or just ended up making other people's lives miserable.

Joe had told Allison about what had happened to Kevin—the overdose and hospitalization. Judging from what she'd seen, Allison thought that having his stomach pumped (or whatever it was that they did for him) was probably no worse than the punishment he got from Dick afterward. She wouldn't put it past the man to hit his own kid because she'd seen how close to the edge he was with Joe. When she'd seen him that day that she'd left and found him so menacing, she thought she was overreacting, but now she wasn't so sure, even though physically, Kevin didn't look any worse for the wear. He was slightly taller and slightly thinner, but still slouchy, black-clad, and ungainly; he was the same disaffected youth he'd been before. But there was a sadness about him now that was much more adult than he was. It was deep and desolate and enveloped him like a cloak. Allison wondered if he was still taking the drugs that almost killed him. His eyes seemed fairly clear and he didn't seem stoned, but you never knew anymore. It was true; she'd never liked Kevin even though she understood he was one of those kids who only became *less* likable the more he was disliked. But as she looked at him now, hovering near his mother, torment darkening his light blue eyes, Allison felt a pang of genuine sympathy for him. He was suffering—that much was plain—and Allison could relate.

"Hi, Kevin," she said, "glad you could come."

"Hey." He cast his eyes down to the floor as if he wanted to fall through it into another reality.

"Thanks for the cake, Dorothy. That was very thoughtful of you."

"It's an orange Bundt," Dorothy said in a high, thin voice, "with just a light glaze. I've used that recipe for years. It never fails, you know. Always good. And very easy."

Yes, Allison thought, it was always easy when it came from a prepackaged mix or directly from the store. But she shouldn't complain—she wouldn't. "Great," Allison said. "I think Joe's cutting it up right now."

Dorothy gave her a small, not-quite-smile, which Allison returned. She looked pretty stressed-out too, Allison thought. There was gray hair coming in at her roots, something she'd never seen on Dorothy before. Her skin looked dry and tired, and her eyes were slightly bloodshot. And she didn't seem to have nearly as superior an attitude as she usually did. Although she had never said anything about it, Allison sensed that Dorothy felt betrayed by her during those months that Diana had been living with them. Allison never would have considered them to be friends—those power walks to church hardly counted, but Dorothy seemed to think they'd bonded. When Allison lost herself inside her own house during those long hot months, Dorothy seemed to take it personally. She could feel Dorothy's disapproval snaking down the street and seeping through the walls at first, but by the time Zoë was born, Allison had stopped caring about anything, least of all what Dorothy thought of her. Somewhere in there Dorothy had changed too. There was an edgy nervousness about her now and an air of anxiety. Allison supposed having your child overdose on drugs could do that to you.

"Is Zoë here?" Kevin asked suddenly. Allison and Dorothy both turned to him, questioning. "I mean, not in the house, but down here?" He gestured toward Diana's room. For the first time it occurred to Allison that he might have spent quite a bit of time in that room when nobody was looking.

"She's upstairs," Allison said. "She's asleep."

"Can I see her?" he asked. There was something desperate in his voice. "Please?"

"Okay," Allison said. "I'll take you up there." Kevin nodded, looking at her out of the corner of his eye. Surely he didn't expect her to send him upstairs by himself? "We'll be right back then," she told Dorothy, who looked like she didn't know what to do with her hands or where to direct her gaze.

"Have to be quiet," Allison murmured as they climbed the stairs. "Don't want to wake her up." Kevin followed, treading more softly than she would have expected. They entered the darkened bedroom without a sound and Allison led him over to the crib. Zoë hadn't moved, still lying on her back wrapped up in her pink and white cotton blankets, breathing easily. Kevin lifted his hand, and for a moment Allison thought he was going to reach in and touch her, but he didn't, he just rested it lightly on the top of the crib and stared in. She was close enough to him that she could sense him trembling just a little.

"She's so little," he whispered.

Allison didn't know what to say. It felt strange to have this boy in her bedroom staring so intently at this baby who wasn't his. Who wasn't hers. Kevin drew in a torn breath and Allison realized he was fighting back tears. Allison didn't want him to start crying. She was afraid of the enormity of his emotion and what it might set off in her.

"Kevin?" she whispered.

He turned to her and even in the half dark she could see the tears shining in his eyes and all the pain behind it. He swallowed hard. "I miss her so much," he whispered.

It took Allison a second to realize that he was talking about Diana. "I know it must . . ." she began and lowered her voice. "It must be very hard, Kevin."

He nodded, wiped his eyes roughly with the heel of his hand, and took his hand from the crib.

"Kevin," Allison whispered, "do you know where Diana is?"

He backed up a little and looked away from her. "No," he said after a moment.

"I'm not . . ." Allison ran a hand through her hair. He knew *something*, she could sense it, and she searched for the right words to offer him. She didn't want to scare or threaten him. "Listen, Kevin, I'm not out to get you. I don't care if—" She caught herself, forced the desperate edge from her voice. "If you know where she might have gone, please tell me." His head was still turned away from her. "If you know *anything*—even if you don't think it's important. Even if it's just a feeling, Kevin." He looked like he might bolt. "It can stay between me and you," Allison said. "I can promise you that."

"I don't know where she is," Kevin said. "I wish I did."

She waited a second, then two, to see if he would change his mind. He wiped his eyes again, harder this time, as if he wanted to rub them out of their sockets. "Okay," she said. "I'm sorry, Kevin. I didn't mean—"

"I think she might have got into trouble," Kevin said.

Allison held her breath, let it out slowly. "How?"

"She might have . . ." Even without the benefit of full light, Allison could see the muscles working in his jaw. "I think she might have gone looking for something, you know, to . . ." He cleared his throat and then stayed silent for so long she thought he was finished, that he'd said everything he was going to. "I never *told* her where to go to get it," he whispered. "But she *knew*."

"Get what, Kevin?" She waited a beat, then two. She could hear the sound of the doorbell coming from downstairs. "I promise you," she said, "you're safe with me. This conversation never happened."

Allison could see that he was struggling. He looked at her pleadingly. *Don't make me.* Allison turned to the crib, reached over, and gently stroked the sleeping baby.

"I only gave her a little weed," he whispered. "That's all. . . ."

"Kevin—"

"But she knew . . . She knew where to get . . ."

"Kevin, please tell me—"

Kevin leaned toward Allison, his movement so sudden she twitched with the urge to back away. "I can't," he said, his voice choking in on itself. "I don't know. I don't know anything." Then, as if regretting saying even that much, he turned and walked out of the room.

As Allison followed him down the stairs, she wondered if she should touch him, pat him on the shoulder, offer some comforting words, but none of it felt right. She didn't know what he wanted to hear or what she could tell him that would make him feel any better. *He loved her,* she thought. And look where love had led him. She thought she should tell him that he could come and see Zoë again if he wanted, and although she wasn't sure that was a wise thing to do, she was going to say it anyway, but by then they were on the landing. Allison caught sight of Joe ushering Jessalyn Martin into the living room and anything she wanted to say flew right out of her head.

Since she certainly hadn't invited the woman here this evening, Allison's first thought was that Jessalyn was crashing what she must have thought was a party, although that didn't explain why she was dressed in a too-tight, too-small business suit. No, not really a business suit, Allison thought, more like a costume, something a B actress playing the part of a naughty secretary might wear. Words formed in Allison's head, something to the effect of *Why are you here?* but then, almost too late to stop them from tumbling out of her mouth, she realized that she had given over the task of rounding up the neighbors to Dorothy. It was Dorothy who had asked Jessalyn to come, not Allison.

"Allison," Jessalyn said by way of greeting, "how are you doing?"

Allison mumbled a greeting that she hoped sounded appropriate, but she could barely hear her own voice for all the loud thoughts echoing in her head. She'd never exchanged any but the most basic civilities with Jessalyn, so why was her tone so familiar and so gratingly solicitous?

"How's the baby?" Jessalyn added. "Must be a lot for you—for both of you to handle."

"She's fine," Allison said, sure that she could now hear a subtle note of accusation in Jessalyn's voice. The smell of Jessalyn's perfume, heavy and cloying, hung in the air.

"Well, that's good," Jessalyn said and gave Allison one of the least sincere smiles she'd ever seen.

Joe, who seemed to be trying to get Jessalyn away from the foyer and into the living room, looked as if he'd swallowed something sharp that was puncturing his insides. Allison had the sudden feeling that she'd interrupted a private conversation between the two of them, which she knew was impossible since she'd seen Jessalyn come in only seconds before and there had been no time for them to have exchanged any words at all. Allison felt a cold knot form in her stomach. It was possible, she thought, that she would never again desire a drink with such intensity as she did at that moment.

"Do you want to get that, Allie?"

Allison stared at Joe, completely lost, her head buzzing. "The door," he said, his eyes pleading with her, "Can you get it?" and then Allison realized that, again, the doorbell was ringing. She moved across the foyer like a sleepwalker. The door stuck, swollen with unseasonable heat, and Allison had to pull hard to get it open. The Sun kid and his mother stood in the entrance, both looking as if they'd rather be somewhere else. Allison was momentarily stunned. She couldn't remember ever seeing the woman outside the doorway of her own home and the kid only in passing as he shot baskets in his driveway. Mrs. Sun was smaller and older than she'd thought, and her son was taller. They were both dressed nicely, as if they were each going to a job interview—she in a dress and low-heeled pumps and he in a dress shirt and pressed pants. Allison was so mystified as to why they were standing there looking at her that she remained mute, one hand on the doorjamb, waiting for a clue.

"Hello," Mrs. Sun said, carefully enunciating the two syllables.

"My mother doesn't speak English very well," Sun said. "I came with her . . . to help."

Allison got nothing from his expression. He seemed uncomfortable, maybe even annoyed with his task. Allison could tell it wasn't the first time he'd had to interpret and translate for his mother, and was on the verge of asking him what it was she could do for them when it finally dawned on her that Dorothy had asked them to come as well as all the other people who were sitting in her living room. Including Jessalyn.

"Oh, yes," she said and backed away from the door. "Thank you for coming. Please come in."

Mrs. Sun looked at her son, who gestured for her to go inside. The three of them walked into the living room where the hum of voices stopped as they entered.

"You all know . . ." Allison began and couldn't finish. Her eyes wandered the room, looking for help, but everyone seemed equally baffled by the Suns' presence. Except perhaps Dorothy, who was suddenly grinning, ridiculously happy to see them. And Kevin, who was exchanging a highly charged glance with Sun. Kevin had grabbed a handful of his own T-shirt, Allison noticed, and was squeezing it in his fist. His eyes had gone wide and he looked almost frightened. He turned slightly and looked at Allison and his expression flickered. Allison couldn't tell if it was guilt or remorse she saw there.

"Please," she told the Suns, "have a seat. Would you like something to drink? Coffee or . . ."

Mrs. Sun smiled at her and looked at her son, who mumbled something in Chinese. She shook her head. "No, please," she said.

Joe cleared his throat and everyone turned to hear what he had to say. "I really appreciate you all coming over," he began. Allison recognized his take-charge tone—he used it in the restaurant to make everyone feel welcome and important, to soothe customers with both real and imagined complaints. "And I want you to know that I'm thankful for how helpful you've all been since . . . especially helping out with Zoë and—" He stopped, looked over at Allison, his expression apologetic.

"We're happy to help, Joe." That was Sam. She was holding a plate with an untouched slice of Dorothy's cake. Everyone, Allison now noticed, had a slice of Dorothy's cake and nobody was eating.

"Diana's been missing for more than a month," Joe went on. "And the longer she's gone, the harder it is to find her. I know you've all spoken to the detectives and told them everything, but I thought maybe if we all got together here there's something we could come up with together that we might have missed." He looked around the room, his eyes darting as if he didn't want to rest them anywhere. "Look, I know some of us have had our differences," he said and looked at Dorothy, who stared fixedly at the cake on her plate, "and I know I could have been a better . . ." He wouldn't say it, Allison thought. He couldn't say it. "I could have done a better job taking care of things, but you never expect this to happen. You never think you'll wind up on the news."

"It isn't your fault, Joe." Everyone, including Joe, turned to Jessalyn, who blushed deeply. Joe was responding, brushing off her comment, and moving on with his monologue, but Allison could no longer hear anything. She was transfixed by the look that passed between her husband and Jessalyn: complicity, intimacy, awkwardness, guilt—all of it there in a flash of heat and electricity running the distance from her to him and looping back around. It was there for a second and gone, nobody but Allison still looking at Jessalyn as she adjusted her skirt and primly tucked a lock of hair behind her ear, but it was enough for Allison to see and understand. The ton-of-bricks realization came crashing through Allison's painfully sober consciousness. When had it started? Had it ended? Looking at Jessalyn's buried embarrassment and watching Joe's reserved body language she was almost sure the affair was over, but when it had stopped was a mystery. It could have been six months ago or yesterday, Allison couldn't know. Her head felt thick and heavy, her thoughts suddenly sluggish. She could sense herself drifting out of the conversational loop. Someone was going to ask her something and she would be lost. She couldn't afford to seem as if she didn't care, as if she were checked out. Allison struggled to regain her equilibrium. Joe was summarizing the police investigation, telling the group something about Diana's cell phone, her clothes, that Yvonne had contacted everyone she'd ever known in Las Vegas. People were responding. Sam said something about who might have stayed in the neighborhood during the evacuation. There was always someone who didn't leave. . . . Then Dorothy's voice, adding something. . . .

But Allison's eyes and attention kept wandering back to Jessalyn. She fixated on small details—the carmine-colored nail polish, a scuff at the heel of her alligator pumps, the glint of her gold fleur-de-lis earrings. Everything about Jessalyn seemed magnified, outsize, and Allison couldn't look away. She didn't know what she was supposed to do with her sudden knowledge and she didn't know how to identify the stirring she felt in the deepest recesses of her emotions.

" . . . nice that it's a family moving in, but of course we will be very sorry to see you go."

Allison forced herself to focus. Sam, Gloria, and Jessalyn were looking at Dorothy and Kevin, who had folded himself into a small black knot and was staring down at his hands. "Family?" Allison asked, hoping she could guide her way back into the conversation with that one word.

"The new family moving in across from us," Dorothy said, "who bought the Suns' house. They have children. How old did you say they were?" Dorothy turned back to Mrs. Sun and Kevin to Allison, his eyes darkened and flashing. What was it he wanted from her? She couldn't read the signals—couldn't hear or see anything other than the huge looming presence of Jessalyn Martin in her living room.

Allison had to stand up, had to leave the room, if only for five minutes. She couldn't breathe. "I think I hear the baby," she said. "I'll be right back. I'm just going to check on her." She was gone—up the stairs and out of sight—before anyone could offer to help her.

chapter 20

"Anyway, I just want to tell you again how much I—how much *we* appreciate everything you've done, Sam. You've really been such a huge help."

Joe had been standing at his front door saying good-bye to Sam for at least ten minutes but couldn't seem to let her leave. He'd already thanked her twice and knew that if he did it again it was going to start sounding insincere, but she was the last person to leave and once she did he'd be alone with Allison. Joe wasn't ready, nor did he think he'd ever be ready to have the conversation with his wife that he knew was coming.

"It's nothing, Joe," Sam said. "I only wish I could do more." She could sense his anxiety, Joe thought, and maybe she felt it too. Gloria had already gone home almost an hour ago, apologizing and claiming a migraine. Sam said nothing at the time, but Joe could see the disapproval and tension in the look that passed between them. He'd been on the receiving end of those looks himself. It didn't require any great sensitivity to know that their relationship was in trouble. Sam probably didn't want to go home either. It was a pity for both of them that he couldn't just keep her here until daybreak.

"Is there anything you need for Zoë?" Sam added. "You know if you need me to take her—I mean, watch her . . . I mean . . . Sorry, Joe, this isn't coming out right. You know what I mean. If you and Allison need any help at all with the baby . . ."

"I know, Sam." Reflexively, Joe looked toward the kitchen, where his wife was cleaning up. Allison had taken charge of Zoë's care since Yvonne left and she appeared to like it that way. Joe didn't want to rock that boat, especially since it seemed so tenuously moored.

"We're doing okay," he told Sam. "Allison's really good with her." It came out sounding apologetic and he didn't know why.

"I know," Sam said, "I didn't mean . . . Anyway, whatever you need, just ask, okay?"

"I will, thanks, Sam."

There was nothing else to say then and they both knew it. "All right, Joe. Please keep me posted, all right?" She leaned forward and gave him a quick hug, tight and unexpected. She was gone, closing the door behind her, before Joe had a chance to say anything else. He slid the dead bolt on the door and stood there in the void for a moment, trying to figure out what face to put on. He could hear water running in the kitchen. There ought to be a rule book, he thought, a plan for what to do next.

But Joe had no idea what the new rules were between him and Allison, and he didn't think she did either. He'd seen how Allison looked at Jessalyn earlier and he was sure she knew about their affair. It was over of course, but that wouldn't matter. It wouldn't make a difference to Allison that he now thought Jessalyn was the most pathetic woman he'd ever known and he realized it was a mistake of epic proportions to get involved with her, that the only reason he *had* in the first place was because Allison had made herself completely unavailable in every way. Nor could he tell Allison that he'd been with Jessalyn the day she'd left and gone to her mother's, that he'd been unable to be reached while the area was evacuated and Sam tried frantically to find him because he was holed up in a hotel fucking the neighborhood whore. Yes, he'd found that out too. She wasn't just your average party-girl slut; Jessalyn was a bona fide pro. Not that Jessalyn would ever admit that and not that it could ever be proven, really, in a court of law, but Joe knew it. The main question—the only question, really—was why it had taken him so long to figure it out in the first place.

So, no, he couldn't tell Allison that before she'd even come back home he'd gone over to Jessalyn's house to call it off officially because he'd realized the extent of his temporary insanity and found her there, bidding good-bye to a john—or whatever she called the men that she serviced. The funny thing of course was that before that moment he'd felt doubly bad—first for cheating on his wife and second for leading on this girl who was twenty years younger than he—and was worried about hurting Jessalyn's feelings. He'd convinced himself by that point that her sudden coolness toward him after he'd left Zoë with her that one night was caused by confusion over his feelings for her. Joe hated to think about it even now, how he'd really believed the girl was in love with him and that he would have to be careful with her emotions. He had it all planned out. He was going to tell her that even though he had feelings for her he loved his wife and owed it to Allison to try to work things out; all the usual bullshit that anyone over the age of sixteen had either heard or said. And he meant it, which might have been the saddest thing of all. Then he saw her—saw *him*—and all those words strangled and died in his throat.

Jessalyn had started to explain, said, "It's not what you think" or something that was equally clichéd, but Joe stopped her before she could get too far.

"It doesn't matter," he told her. "I shouldn't have come here. And I'm going to pretend I never did." As he turned to leave, he added, "And I hope you'll do the same."

He didn't understand what Jessalyn had been hoping to prove by coming to his house that night or in which alternate reality she thought that she could be helpful in any way. He thought he'd kept it cool despite all of that—he'd let her in, hadn't he?—but Allison wasn't an idiot. He walked into the living room, picked up a mug and a paper plate that somebody had left on the coffee table, and headed into the kitchen with the frightened resolve of a man on his way to the gallows.

Allison was wrapping the remainder of Dorothy's cake in plastic wrap. She turned to him as he walked in, her face a puzzle. Joe caught his breath, waiting for it.

"Sam go home?" she asked.

"Yes, she . . . Yes." His voice sounded so strained. He wondered what Allison was waiting for. Why didn't she just come out with it?

"I don't think they're going to make it," Allison said.

"What?"

"Sam and Gloria. It looks to me like they're going to break up. It's too bad."

"You're right," Joe said. He wondered if Allison was really talking about Sam and Gloria or making some kind of obtuse reference to the two of them.

"This cake," Allison said, switching topics, "I'm pretty sure it came from a mix." Joe looked from her to the remainder of the cake in her hands and was speechless. "Because it's not bad, I tried it. Dorothy doesn't know how to make cake this edible."

"Allison—"

"But it was nice of her to bring it. I think she feels bad about everything, I really do. They all do." Allison sighed. "They all want to help now." She put the carefully wrapped cake in the fridge and turned to the countertop, wiping it clean even though there was no dirt on it that Joe could see. It was a futile gesture but still oddly hopeful, and it suddenly seemed to Joe to represent their entire lives.

"Do you think it's going to help?" he asked Allison.

"What do you mean, Joe?"

"Are we going to find her? Do you think she's . . . ?" He felt the fear gathering, paralyzing the base of his spine.

"We're doing everything we can. Joe, we're doing everything we're supposed to do."

He wanted so badly to touch her, to take her in his arms, but the strength and charge of all that was unspoken between them might as well have been an electrical force field.

"I'm going to go to bed," she said. "Will you bring Zoë's bottle when you come up?"

"Of course."

"You'll lock up?"

"I'll lock up," he said, silently begging her for more as he watched her walk away and head upstairs. It was several minutes before he could move himself to start turning off the lights and checking all the doors. He was trying to work out whether or not he'd just been given a stay of execution because while Allison had said nothing about Jessalyn, he felt implicated just the same. It was that reversal of rules again. Before Diana had come to live with them, Joe had always left the heavy lifting to Allison when it came to their disagreements. He'd always waited for her to bring up the problems and then let her take the lead in trying to fix them. Yes, it was lazy but no different from any other married man he knew. But Allison had turned all of that around since she'd come home, her behavior a cipher that Joe had been trying to work out since then.

She'd come right back to their bed for one thing and hadn't asked him to sleep on the couch. Whether that was to display some sort of united front for Yvonne or because she didn't mind still sharing the same bed with him, although she hadn't so much as kissed him since she'd come home, was beyond what he could figure out on his own and he was afraid to ask her. And then there was the way she fussed over Zoë—as if she'd always felt maternal toward this baby, as if she'd never had any doubts, as if she hadn't spent the first several weeks of Zoë's life in a bitter drunken stupor. And maybe that was it, Joe thought. Maybe Allison had come out of that alcohol haze for long enough to feel guilty about neglecting Diana and Zoë. Because she could have helped out Diana. Allison could have made it easier for her. It might have made a difference. Although Allison had seemed so wounded from the start, never seeming to get over the mere fact of Diana's existence, perhaps something had happened to her while she was at her mother's that had made her rethink it all. She hadn't had anything to drink since she'd been back, and even though she said nothing about that either, Joe sensed that she'd made some kind of pact with herself to stay sober.

And if he'd expected some kind of big blow-up about Yvonne staying with them, Allison's decent if not warm attitude toward her convinced him otherwise. They'd never be buddies, but to both of their credit, they were polite to each other and neither one of them started throwing around accusations about the other's faults and behavior. Of course, Joe thought, they both had plenty to feel guilty about and maybe that was why neither one of them wanted to throw stones, but guilt didn't always stop people from lashing out and trying to assign blame elsewhere.

But despite all of this, despite Allison's even keel, she had become more of a Stepford wife than his own. As he gathered extra diapers and a bottle for Zoë's next feeding, he wondered if Allison was going to ambush him. If not now, then at some moment that seemed right to her. He didn't know if he'd be able to wait that long.

Joe lay in bed, breathing quietly. Allison lay on her right side next to him, unmoving but awake. The room had been stuffy earlier and he'd opened the window when he got up to feed and change Zoë. Cool air hit his exposed shoulders and face. It was the first time he could remember feeling a comfortable temperature since last winter. He tried to guess what time it was, but it was impossible to tell. Allison was already under the covers with her eyes closed when he'd come upstairs earlier. The baby woke a couple of hours later and Joe got out of bed before Allison could even make a move. When he came back to bed, she shifted, changed her position, and plumped the pillow under her head.

"We'll get that baby monitor tomorrow," he said.

That was hours ago—had to have been. Joe felt like he hadn't slept at all, although he must have drifted off at some point. Allison turned onto her left side so that she was facing Joe. Moonlight came in through the open window and spilled on the bed, broke across her face, and glinted off her eyes.

"Allison?"

She sighed in assent. He turned to her slowly, looked right into her. "I miss you," he said.

"You can't say that, Joe. It isn't fair."

"But it's true. I've been missing you since the day Diana got here. You just went away, Allison. You left me."

"Is that your excuse, Joe?"

"My excuse?"

She didn't answer him and Joe could feel her body tensing up beside him. They were teetering on the edge of a knife. He wished he could ask her what she wanted him to do—whether she wanted him to lie about his affair with Jessalyn even though he knew she'd guessed at it, or whether to admit it, try to explain why he'd done it and in doing so probably end their marriage. Because there wasn't really another way, was there? Maybe she'd stay with him until they found Diana because *they had to find Diana* but after that . . . After that, it wouldn't be possible to recover. *Help me,* he wanted to tell her. *Tell me what you want.* But Allison lay still and quiet beside him. The decision was going to be his. She'd let him know if it was the right one.

"I can't change anything I've done in the past," he said, finally. "If I had it to do over again, don't you think I would have told you about Yvonne and Diana? God, Allison, if I'd even thought—"

"You've told me that already, Joe."

"But you don't believe me, Allison. You never have." He could feel his voice rising and he worked to bring it down. He didn't want to wake Zoë. "Why do you think I would *hide* it from you?"

"Because you—" Allison cut herself off with a violent sob. Joe hadn't even realized that she was crying. He leaned over to her, and then as if moving through water, he reached across and touched her face, wiping the tears from her cheeks. "Allison, Allie, please, what . . . please tell me. . . ."

Allison's whole body seemed to clench and she struggled to speak through her tears. "If-if y-you'd told me," she said, her chest heaving, "it w-would have been harder."

"What?" he said. "What would have been harder?"

"I wanted it," she said and exhaled. "I wanted to have that baby, Joe."

He stared down at her face in the dark, at the moonlight shining on her tears. He couldn't believe what he was hearing. Was it possible that everything Allison had done since Diana had come—everything she had *not* done—was caused by this one thing? He remembered the last time she'd brought it up, the day Diana had arrived. They'd talked about it and he'd assumed she'd moved on. Joe knew Allison had never felt right about the abortion, but he would never have imagined that it had poisoned her to this extent.

"I'm sorry," he said. "I *am*, Allison. I'm sorry for . . ."—he fought with himself, but only for a split second—". . . everything I've ever done to hurt you. I've never meant to. Never."

"All that time, Joe. It's been so hard, you don't know. You can't imagine how I feel and you've never tried."

"I didn't know," he said. He stroked the hair off her face and she let him. It felt so good to be touching her again. He hadn't realized how desperately he needed it. "I've done so many things wrong, Allison. I know that now. I've fucked up horribly. With you and . . . with Diana. I wish I could go back in time. I can't. I'm sorry, Allison. I'm so sorry. But all I can do is go forward. Allison, you have to forgive me. Please forgive me."

She didn't say anything for so long Joe was sure she was forming a way to tell him that she could never forgive him his sins—especially the ones he hadn't admitted to—and wanted a divorce. Which was why he was so surprised when she finally spoke.

"I didn't leave her by herself," she said. "I wouldn't have done that. It wouldn't have mattered how much I'd had to drink. I was sure Diana was in there with her."

"I know," he said, but truthfully he didn't. He'd never been sure about that but his own guilt had prevented him from exploiting hers.

"No you don't," she said, reading his mind. "But I am telling you, Joe, and you have to believe me."

"I do," he said. "But Allison . . ." He sighed, moved a little closer to her. Their bodies were touching now. The heat of her skin made his heart beat faster. "Can we . . . are we going to make it through this?" It wasn't what he had wanted to ask her and he cursed the words as soon as they left his mouth.

"Do we have to decide that right now?" she said. "Joe, I . . ."

But Joe didn't let her finish. He had stopped thinking. He drew her to him and kissed her on the mouth, softly at first then hard with need. She let him, yielding and then clutching at him, pulling him in. He leaned into her, his hands finding all the places on her body that he knew so well and had gone so long without, his desire so quick and intense he was almost choking on it. Just before he gave in to it, before he lost himself in her, a sliver of thought stung him. She was saving it up—her resentment, her knowledge of his affair, all of it to use later. It was there for a sharp flashing second and then it was gone. He thought, *Maybe she loves me again,* and after that there was only sensation and release.

When he woke up it was still dark. He and Allison were still locked together. It could have been two hours later or ten minutes, he couldn't tell. Zoë was asleep and there was no dawn in the sky. He stroked Allison's arm and she sighed; she was also awake.

"Allison," he said so softly he could barely hear it himself, "do you think she's still alive?"

She found his hand and took it in her own. It felt like an absolution, but not an answer. "There's something I should tell you," she said. "Something you should know."

february 2008

chapter 21

Joe stood in the jewelry department of Macy's staring at rings and bracelets but not really seeing any of them. Choosing something—anything—seemed suddenly an insurmountable task even though he'd felt fine on the drive over and even as he'd traversed the length of the mall, passing the dolphin fountain and the Russian woman hawking cell phone and iPod covers. In fact he'd made it all the way to these glass cases before he came to a crashing halt and felt himself glaze over. He didn't know why he'd chosen to come to this corner of the store anyway. He needed to be in the men's department looking for a black suit. But when he'd gotten there he'd walked right through the shirt racks and tie tables and past the colognes and toward the pink and red heart displays of the jewelry department as if propelled. And now that he was here it was like he was trapped in amber.

"Can I help you find something, sir?" A middle-age woman in an unflattering red suit and tortoiseshell glasses smiled at him, tilting forward a little so that her midsection grazed the edge of the case. "Are you looking for something for Valentine's Day?" She flicked her eyes toward his left hand, looking for a wedding ring and finding it. "Something for your wife?"

Something for my wife for Valentine's Day, Joe thought, *and something for me to wear to my daughter's funeral.* He wondered what kind of reaction he'd get from this woman—Jennifer was her name, it was there on her brass-effect name tag—if he repeated that to her. And then he felt bad for even entertaining the notion of speaking his thoughts out loud. It wasn't her fault after all. Why fuck up someone else's day just because yours was terminal.

"Yes," he managed to get out and hoped that his voice didn't sound as strained as it felt. "My wife."

"Are you looking for something formal or maybe a little more playful?"

Playful? For a moment, as he struggled to understand what might constitute a "playful" piece of jewelry, Joe thought he'd lost his ability to interpret social nuances. He decided her question must be a new way of asking him how much he wanted to spend and so gave her what he thought was the safest answer.

"How about something in between?" he said.

"We have some beautiful heart pendants right over here," she said. "We have them in white or yellow gold and these have diamonds as well. You can't go wrong with diamonds, can you?"

"No," Joe said, "you can't." He didn't want to look at pendants with Jennifer, he didn't want to have to talk about whether Allison preferred yellow or white gold, and he certainly didn't have money to buy anything with diamonds, but Joe needed the distraction. It was obviously why he was here at this counter to begin with and not trying on pants and jackets. So he allowed himself to be directed to another case where Jennifer pointed obligingly to a number of sparkling necklaces laid out for maximum effect on black velvet.

He couldn't stop the thoughts of Diana that followed.

They wouldn't see Diana laid out like that in a velvet box. What was left of her body was better left unseen by everyone who had known her and especially those who had loved her. There had been a debate, albeit a short and painful one, about whether or not to have her remains cremated. Joe had thought that would be best for many reasons, most of which he didn't choose to share with Yvonne. But Yvonne was adamant from the start. After all that had happened to her daughter, Yvonne felt she deserved the respect of a proper burial and a place to rest.

Joe couldn't argue with that, nor did he want to.

So they'd picked plots and caskets, arranged for services. But no, he thought, that wasn't exactly right because *they* hadn't done it; Allison had taken over together with Yvonne. Suggesting cremation had been Joe's main contribution, and after that he'd just gone along. Because since they'd found her, he'd been mostly in this state—hazy and swimming through the details of his life as if he were underwater. He kept finding himself in the middle of tasks that he didn't remember starting or conversations in which he'd lost the thread. Focusing was a struggle. His reactions and words seemed to be on some kind of time delay, even though internally his mind was whirring. Like right now. These necklaces lying still on their velvet beds were killing him. He had to look away, had to move, but it took a supreme effort.

"I don't know," he said finally. "These aren't really her style, you know?"

"Well," Jennifer answered, "we have some others without hearts. Or would you rather look at rings? Or maybe earrings?"

There were too many choices, too many decisions Joe had to make. She was looking at him now with something like concern on her face. Or was that just polite anticipation? There were so many things Joe couldn't read anymore. Those horrible thoughts just kept intruding, flooding him with waves of guilt and sadness.

"Yes," he said, "maybe earrings."

She guided him away from the dead necklaces and over to another display. Joe watched helplessly as she pointed at this pair and that, babbling on about hearts and birthstones and specials that were going on for a limited time only. What season was his wife, she wanted to know.

"Season?"

"You know, is she a fall or a winter or a . . ."

It was a mistake coming here, but now it was too late to undo it so Joe channeled all his energy into trying to remember what kind of jewelry he had bought Allison in their previous life together so that he could find something now to match it. From some recess in his memory he managed to pull out a ghost of Valentine's Day past and recall that long ago he'd given Allison a charm bracelet and promised to add charms to it every time there was a special occasion to be commemorated. He hadn't gotten very far; there was a golden apple for when she started one school year and a tiny house when they'd moved into their place and there was probably one other that he couldn't remember. He hadn't seen that bracelet in forever, but she had to still have it somewhere.

"Do you have any charms?" he said. "Like, for a bracelet?"

"Well . . . we don't really have that many. If you wanted something custom, you'd have to look—"

"Just a heart or something," he said. "Make it easy."

Again, they walked the same half square between displays but this time the box she brought out was lined with white satin. Joe was starting to feel light-headed and nauseated. Inside, there was a brushed gold heart, a key, a palm tree, and a crown. And there, in the corner, was a tiny gold cell phone. In a flash, Diana was in his head again. They'd never have found her without that cell phone. They'd have spent the rest of their lives wondering. Everyone said that not knowing was worse even than finding her dead the way they had. It had happened to other missing girls, other families who never found out what had happened to their daughters and who had their lives slowly corroded by false hope. It was better to have closure, they said, even this way, with this outcome. And they wouldn't have had it, their lives forever caught in the what-if, but for the cell phone, abandoned and half-buried just like Diana, that their new neighbors had found in their garage.

Joe pointed to the heart and said, "I think that one will do. Since it's Valentine's Day."

"Okay," she said. "And would you like me to gift wrap that for you?"

"If you have a box," Joe said, "that would be great."

"Would you like to look at anything else?"

"No, but . . ." Joe reached into the box and pulled the cell phone charm free. "I'd like to take this as well."

Happy for the addition to a sale that was below what she'd hoped for, Jennifer opted not to push for any more. She ran his credit card and Joe was relieved that it went through without a problem. He'd been piling on the debt and not really paying attention to his balances, and even though Allison was back at work, he was getting pretty deep in the hole. There was Zoë and everything she needed and then, of course, Diana. Burying her. The funeral. Death was expensive. You had to balance it out, Joe thought. All the sorrow and misery that went along with it was free after all. And there were endless amounts of it to go around.

Jennifer was finished with him by then and had to be asked twice to leave the cell phone charm out of the gift box. "I'm just going to take this one," Joe said and slipped it into his pocket. Finally, Joe managed to escape the jewelry department, clutching his small bag. He headed in the direction of men's suits only to find himself drifting again, this time to the escalators, and going up. He got off on the second floor, not even knowing where he was headed but finding it anyway—the children's department. He wandered through girls' and boys' sections and came at last to the infants'. Fluffy blankets and bibs, hooded towels and tiny socks. He wanted to reach out and touch all of it, run his fingers over the softness and feel soothed, but the last thing he needed was to draw the attention of another aggressive salesperson, who in any case would probably take such behavior the wrong way. So he milled through the baby items with purpose as if he knew exactly where to find what he was looking for. But he didn't think they even made what he was looking for. Were there black clothes for babies as small as Zoë? It seemed he was going to do everything in his power to avoid buying himself a funeral suit, even if that meant looking for one for Zoë. But she should have something to wear to her mother's funeral even if she'd never know that mother. Joe and Allison had started the process to formally adopt Zoë, but none of them—Yvonne included—had caught their breaths enough to discuss what they would tell Zoë about Diana. She wasn't even five months old, Joe thought. Not even a year. Not even a half. How would they ever be able to tell her—to make her understand?

He saw a rack of miniature dresses and he rifled through them, searching. So many shades of pink and red. Valentine's Day again, he thought. You were supposed to deck out your girl babies in these predetermined colors of the season so they could learn early the need for fake romance and store-bought sentiment. He felt in his pocket for the cell phone charm and pressed it tightly between his thumb and forefinger. He wanted to punch something. He wanted to see something break. There was nothing black on the rack. It was too late for those black-velvet-and-white-lace Christmas dresses he was sure he'd seen before, and besides, most of the garments here were marked 12 months or 2T, which he knew were too big for little Zoë.

She was small for her age, the pediatrician said, but she didn't have any problems feeding, and she was healthy, according to the doctor, so it wasn't cause for concern. She was in the bottom fifth percentile for length and weight, but she wasn't *off* the chart. You never knew at this stage anyway, the doctor said; they could catch up in a heartbeat. But Allison had taken it very seriously. She'd started looking into all kinds of organic "starter" foods for Zoë, throwing herself into the task with one-pointed dedication. He gave way here to Allison, who had done her research, but he had his own theories about Zoë. Unlike her mother and despite her delicate appearance, Joe knew that Zoë was and would always be a survivor. Look what she'd overcome already—before she'd even been born.

It seemed certain now that Diana had taken at least some drugs before she'd given birth to Zoë, even though if Kevin was to be believed Diana only smoked a little pot and even that not regularly when she was pregnant. But Kevin had made himself very difficult to believe. Joe reminded himself constantly that he was just a kid—and a scared one at that—but if he'd spent just a little less time worrying about his own ass and a little more about Diana . . . Joe still didn't know how much of the truth he'd ever really know. He remembered the day Diana gave birth to Zoë, how he'd had to tell her to go change her clothes and wash off the smell of clinging pot smoke.

He hadn't thought . . . hadn't really believed she was into anything more serious.

That was another thing that concerned Allison, although, to Joe's great relief, she shared it with only him and not Yvonne. Even a limited exposure to drugs in utero could negatively affect a baby, Allison told him. Even a small amount could lead to developmental delays and motor skill problems. And if you didn't catch these things early, it was too late to change the course. They'd have to keep a very careful eye on Zoë, make sure that if she needed early intervention to address any problems, they could get it for her. If Diana was a regular user . . .

"I think she's fine," Joe had told Allison more than once. It was true, he had no experience dealing with babies or young children, but you didn't have to be a specialist to see that Zoë was a remarkably calm and alert baby. She did everything she was supposed to do—recognized people, smiled, gurgled, ate, and slept. And although again he couldn't be sure, Joe sensed that she was also watching them all and forming her own opinions about the people around her. There was a light in Zoë's eyes that had nothing to do with her being brain damaged from drugs her mother had taken. He allowed, even appreciated, Allison's concern, but was convinced that they would never have to consider early intervention or neurologists or any other specialists for Zoë.

But then, Joe thought, his opinion plus a dollar would get you a cup of coffee. Somewhere. Diana had been living with him—he'd seen her every day—and he hadn't known what was going on with her. He would never have guessed that she was so strung out that she would leave her newborn alone and run off in search of a fix. And maybe it hadn't happened exactly like that. They would probably never know exactly what had

happened and maybe that was a small blessing in the midst of all this horror. But the coroner had enough of Diana left to determine that there *had*
been a lethal amount of narcotics in her system. Drugs had killed her, according to the ME's report, not the kid who had given them to her. Not
the kid who had then panicked when she overdosed, wrapped her in garbage bags, driven her out to the edge of the burn area, and buried her body
in a shallow grave. Was it better to know this—to accept it as the truth? It
was a question of who you were going to blame the most, how the guilt was
to be apportioned, where you were going to find room for the anger and
grief.

"Can I help you find something?"

Another needy salesperson stood in front of Joe demanding his attention. This one appeared to be in her seventies and seemed to have materialized from nowhere. He wondered why he was getting such personal
attention today when he wanted it least. It went beyond the scope of daily
ironies and into something else. Perhaps he was the only shopper in the
store or perhaps it was so unusual to see a man in the jewelry or infants'
departments that the salespeople just couldn't resist. But he'd had enough
of trying to explain himself or what he was looking for. It wasn't really fair
that he burden this grandmother, but he'd resisted once already and now it
was like the urge to throw up after food poisoning—he couldn't stop himself.

"I need a funeral dress for a baby," he said. "Can you help me with
that?"

The woman's face blanched and she looked so alarmed that Joe wanted
to bite back his words. She started to stammer and he realized that she
thought the baby in question was deceased.

"She's almost five months old," he said. "About this big." He held his
hands apart the approximate distance of Zoë's length. "It's not for *her*
funeral," he added.

"Ohhh." The saleswoman sighed. Her relief was so intense it was pal-
pable. The air between them seemed to warm up and ripple.

"It's for her mother's funeral," Joe said. "She's my granddaughter. Her mother was my daughter. That's who died." He watched as the woman struggled to keep herself composed, tried to rein in the naked dismay contorting her face, and failed. Joe couldn't understand why he was being such a prick—or even why he was sharing any of these personal details. It wasn't making him feel any better. And yet. "So I need something nice for the baby to wear."

"I'm so . . . We have . . ." She lifted her hands as if she were going to wring them. "I'm so very sorry for your loss," she said. "It must be just . . ."

"It is," he said. "Yes."

"I don't know whether . . . what I mean is, we have some spring dresses for babies, but I don't think that would be right, and I don't know if . . . we do have some other, christening-type of dresses that might—"

"Fine," Joe said. It was his own fault. He could have said nothing. He could have let it be. He let the saleswoman guide him over to the dresses she described—white satin monstrosities that he would never put Zoë in—but he bought one anyway because he felt so bad about what he'd said or the way he'd said it or for just being who he was. And then he added a white satin headband decorated with tiny pink roses to go with it and why not throw in one of those terry-cloth one-piece outfits as well. Yes, the one with the ducks on it, sure. She wrapped everything in tissue paper with great care, taking so much longer than Joe wanted her to, but he was afraid now to say anything at all. When she finally handed him the shopping bag he was almost vibrating with the need to get out of there.

"I am so sorry," she whispered, touching his hand lightly with hers. There were tears shining in her eyes.

"Thank you," he said.

She blinked and the tears fell and that, finally, was Joe's undoing. He turned and half-ran to the escalator and then pushed past people to jog his way down, out through the men's department without so much as looking at a suit, raced past the storefronts and food court and open-air vendors to his car, threw his shopping bags inside, and peeled out of the parking lot. He drove north, avoiding the freeway, taking Torrey Pines Road instead, passing the hospital where Zoë was born, the greenery and biotech firms lining the road, and breaking through at last to the ocean.

There were plenty of empty parking spaces at the beach on this mild February morning, so Joe took the first one he could after turning off the road. He got out of the car in such a hurry, he almost tripped and fell on the rocks that he had to scramble down to get to the sand. Once at the bottom he slowed his step a little, walking the short distance to the water's edge. He stood there for a moment, the marine air stinging his eyes, his body trembling or shivering, he couldn't tell, and then he bent down and took off his shoes and socks. He walked in a little farther, let the water wash his feet. The sound of white crashing waves filled his head with welcome noise. He hadn't been here on the beach for what seemed a lifetime. He lived three miles from the shoreline and saw the Pacific sparkling from the big Luna Piena patio every day, and yet he managed to avoid the beach most of the time. Every time he realized that and found his way to the surf he wondered why that was.

At first, when he'd suggested cremation, he'd thought that he'd like to scatter Diana's ashes here. In the short time he'd known her, Diana hadn't shown very much interest in the ocean, but he had some kind of poetic notion about her being born near the sea, then moving to the desert, and coming back to rest in the water. He wanted to think that Diana would have appreciated the sentiment—maybe even agreed with it—but the truth was that he didn't know what Diana had thought or felt about anything. And now he never would, no matter what anyone said about her. They all had their thoughts about who Diana was—Kevin did, and Sam and even Yvonne, who should have known her better than anyone. In a way, they all had greater claims to her than he did, but they hadn't understood her any better than he. And what tortured Joe even more was that if he had known, if he had even *suspected* . . . maybe he could have saved her.

Why? The question sliced at his brain again.

Why hadn't the kid gone for help? He was scared, yes, of course, and guilty for supplying her with drugs—supplying half the fucking neighborhood, it turned out—and in a panic, but that didn't explain the rest of it; it didn't explain how he'd *disposed* of her or that he'd kept his mouth shut for almost three months, saying nothing—*nothing*—until they found that phone and he was forced to come out with it. The kid had sat in Joe's house as calm as a summer day, kindly translating for his mother, the picture of respect, all the while knowing exactly what had happened to Diana. What kind of ice-blooded freak could do that? When he thought of Diana scared and slipping into unconsciousness—*dying*—and having that person be the last face she ever saw, Joe wanted to tear him apart with his bare hands.

His brain raging, Joe suddenly remembered something Diana had said. The memory came at him clear and complete like a video clip embedded in his brain. She was sitting at the dining room table with a glass of iced tea, balancing it on her giant belly beneath which Zoë squirmed. It was the hottest part of the day, midafternoon, and she was holding her hair away from her neck. Joe was getting ready to leave for work, already counting covers and assigning waiter stations in his head.

"Doesn't that noise bother you?" Diana asked him.

"I don't hear anything," Joe said.

"Really? That piano? You can't hear it?"

Joe strained and then as if trying to pick out one color from a mosaic, like the tests they gave you at the DMV, he managed to separate out the sound of a piano from all the other ambient noise coming in from the open windows. "I guess," he said. "It's not very loud."

"I can't believe you don't hear that," she said and lifted the glass to her forehead, pressed it there. "It's so awful."

"Doesn't sound so bad."

"He can play, it's not that," Diana said. "It's just there's so much anger in it. He sounds like he *hates* the piano and the music and everything. And he does it *every day*. It drives me crazy. I mean it."

"Well I don't know why it bothers you so much, it's not that loud. It's not like you're right next door or anything."

"You shouldn't touch an instrument if you hate it like that," she said. "It's bad juju."

Had he laughed when she'd said that? Joe couldn't remember because that was the place where the video clip ended. He hit rewind in his mind, watched her again, that face so young, so much like his. *Bad juju.*

Did she already know him by then? Had they spoken? Was he already a connection?

The tide swirled around his ankles and pulled back out, taking sand and seaweed with it. Joe's hands had tightened into fists. He unclenched them, backed up, and sat down heavily on a dry patch. The sun hit him straight on and warm. It was noon. There were no shadows. He stared into the surf, hypnotized by the rhythm of the breaking waves. He didn't move when the tide reached him, didn't care if he got wet. It didn't matter if he got soaked. It was only saltwater and sand. Nothing that could kill you.

Sometimes Joe tried to rationalize his own ignorance by reminding himself that the police had questioned the kid and his parents and had found nothing suspicious. And who would have? Nobody interacted with that family at all. Even Dorothy, who made it her business to know everything about everybody on their block, was a blank when it came to the Suns. When they moved out in December, it was as if they'd never existed.

Except that wasn't quite right. Kevin knew all about that kid. And he'd said nothing either. Joe picked up a chipped sand dollar and ran his thumb over the surface, pressing harder and harder until eventually he broke through the shell, the sharp edges scraping him. Allison had told him many times that it was pointless to get angry at Kevin, who *was* scared and trying to protect himself. He really did love Diana in his way and didn't know that she had gone over to see Sun that day. He'd been too busy obliterating *himself.* There was a cruel Romeo and Juliet irony there, Joe supposed, but he couldn't find it in himself to appreciate it.

Joe managed to stay rational. He understood that Kevin wasn't to blame. Still, he didn't feel bad for Kevin when the boy had to recount his story with more detail about how Diana had rejected him in the end. Nor did Joe care how scared Kevin was when he finally admitted that his major drug supplier lived right across the street and that Diana knew that. Joe was not disturbed that Kevin would have to live for the rest of his life with the guilt of his part in Diana's death, however unknowing that part might have been. Because Kevin did have some responsibility. He hadn't come clean about where he'd gotten his drugs—or let on that Diana even knew the Sun kid well enough to get them from him herself—until it was too late for any kind of evidence to be found.

By then the new owners had moved into the Suns' house and the place had been thoroughly cleaned. Not that there was any cause to search it. There were no witnesses, nobody who had ever seen Diana interact with the kid. At least Kevin's story about the drug dealing got support from others. It seemed that a good number of his neighbors knew the kid was dealing out of his nice little house with its nice basketball hoop and its nice piano. Joe made a decision then to make the neighbors his business. There was no chance of him becoming a vigilante—he simply didn't have it in him—but he was going to be *around*. He was going to be watching.

And he started by getting to know the family who'd bought the Suns' house. The Mitchells—Tom, Susan, and their eleven-year-old twin boys, Boston and Benjamin—were an unremarkable group. She seemed a typical soccer mom (and indeed the boys played soccer—*excelled*, to hear her tell it) with her comfortable jeans and state school sweatshirt, and he was an engineer who planned one day to open his own brewery. When he first met them, Joe thought they seemed perfect for the neighborhood—beige, pre-designed, and socially acceptable. But then Joe remembered how little he'd really known about his neighbors until recently and how so many of them turned out to be the opposite of that mold, so he started dropping by the Mitchells' just to say hello, to share a beer with Tom, to ask how they were settling in.

Inevitably, Joe found himself talking about Diana, and though he didn't want to implicate anyone, he couldn't stop himself from talking about how he wished he'd paid better attention to what was happening on his own street and how it seemed like a cliché but appearances really were deceiving. The Mitchells were sympathetic. Susan said she couldn't imagine what it must be like. One day, Joe brought Zoë around to "introduce" her. He thought he saw twin wrinkles of surprise crease Tom's and Susan's foreheads when they saw her and vanish quickly in an impressive matching display of propriety.

"Her grandmother actually lives across the street," Joe said. "Have you met her yet? Yvonne?"

"Oh, Yvonne. No, I don't think we have, have we, Tom?"

By then, right after Christmas, Yvonne had made her move from Las Vegas permanent. She'd been coming back and forth and, after the first time, staying with Joe and Allison was uncomfortable for everyone. It was convenient, though probably not for Sam, that Gloria ended up moving out just as Yvonne decided to stay in San Diego for good.

"Yes," Joe said. "She just moved in with Sam. Sam has a boy about the same age as yours. They might know each other from school."

He'd probably made a nuisance of himself at the Mitchells', Joe thought, but if he hadn't—if he hadn't made it a point to let them know who he was, they might not have given the cell phone a second thought when Boston or Benjamin discovered it hidden behind boxes and a stack of two-by-fours in the garage. And they would not have known how significant it was, and they would not have rushed over to Joe's house in person, breathlessly presenting the phone as if it were a live grenade with a look of hope and dread in their eyes: Could this be something? Could it be hers?

Without realizing it, Joe had dug his hands into the wet sand and was crushing it in his fists as if to make cement. He wasn't the one who took the call in the end. It was Allison who answered the phone that time, but he'd been home. He heard her in the kitchen talking but couldn't make out any of her words. He remembered now that he had been thinking it was the first cool day he could remember. It had been so hot for so long and even Christmas felt tropical. But that day all the windows were closed and the house was still chilly inside. They might even have to turn on the heat at some point, Joe had thought. And then Allison was standing there in front of him, holding the phone to her heart. As soon as he saw her face, he knew what was coming.

"It's Detective Garcia," she said and handed him the phone. "They found her, Joe."

Mr. and Mrs. Sun denied any and all knowledge that their son was selling drugs or that they'd ever seen Diana anywhere near their property. They went as far as to claim that the kid was covering for someone else, that somehow he'd been framed. In the end, though, it was the kid who'd led the detectives to the body. To *Diana*. It was tragic, the detectives told Joe, but the kid's version of what had happened matched the evidence and the coroner's report. Finally, that was the only truth remaining.

Joe was sobbing now, his dirty hands held to his eyes and his whole body shaking. He couldn't stop it or control it, couldn't rein in the wails that were coming out of him or the tears flooding his face, so he just put his head down and gave in to it. He didn't know how long it went on and he didn't look up to see if anyone else had witnessed his breakdown. At the end of it, he felt raw and shredded and somehow interminably worse, as if admitting his grief had somehow increased his culpability. So many things he had left undone. So many things he couldn't make up for.

Joe stood and brushed as much sand off his pants as he could. He didn't bother to put his shoes and socks back on. He was going to need a long shower and maybe even a nap before he went to work tonight. He worked evenings almost exclusively now that Allison was back at work during the day so that they could take turns with Zoë and not have to farm her out to a sitter. Yvonne and Sam took her sometimes too, but Zoë lived with them and soon she would legally be their daughter and that was where she belonged. But the late nights were starting to take a toll on him. It used to be easier, he thought. Like almost everything.

He drove shoeless through Carmel Valley, his naked foot feeling overly sensitive and itchy against the gas pedal. The neighborhood was quiet and looked clean. It had rained the other day—a major event these days—and now the eucalyptus and agapanthus looked freshly scrubbed. It had taken months for all the soot and ash to clear out, but it was finally gone. At least in all the places you could see.

Allison had an in-service day from school, so she was at home with Zoë. He took the small box containing her heart charm and pushed it deep inside his pocket so that she wouldn't see it. He'd have to remember to hide it somewhere so it would be a surprise for Valentine's Day. He'd have to remember to get a card. He had to do these things because even though they felt like pretending, he sensed they were necessary. He would never be able to feel normal again if he didn't go through the motions of life in a normal way.

Allison was sitting with Zoë at the dining room table when he came in. The baby was in a little chair that fastened onto the edge of the table. She would need a proper highchair soon, Joe thought. There was an empty bottle and the smallest bowl Joe had ever seen sitting in front of Allison. Zoë turned to him as soon as he walked in, her eyes wide and oddly serious, and Allison looked up. Both of them seemed to be covered with flecks of beige cereal.

"I thought I'd try her on some rice," Allison said, smiling, "but she's clearly not ready. Hey, what happened to you? You're all sandy."

"I took a little detour after the mall," he said, "and went to the beach. I really needed a minute."

Allison nodded. Zoë opened her little mouth and closed it. He reached over and ran his hand over her curly head, then remembered it was all sandy and dirty and felt stupid for not thinking about that before he touched her. "I really needed to get a suit," he said. "I don't have anything that's right for the funeral."

"And what happened?" Allison said.

"I couldn't face it," he said. "I don't know why. It was silly, I guess."

"But Joe," Allison started, and then checked herself, bit her lip.

"What?" he said.

"You have a black suit. It's not new, but it's a good suit. You don't want to wear that one?"

"I don't remember it," he said.

"You put it in the storage closet. It was years ago. It's still there. You said—"

"Right," he said. "That double-breasted one." He remembered now why he'd put it away and what he'd said when he did. *It's too somber. I'll leave it here for the next time I need something to wear to a funeral.*

"I did get this," he said abruptly, putting the Macy's shopping bag on the table. "For Zoë." Allison peered inside and slowly pulled out the dress, the headband, the duck-covered one-piece. "I didn't know what she should wear," he said. "What do you think?"

He sat down on a chair next to Allison and stared at Zoë, who obliged him by picking up a small stuffed orca and tossing it in his direction. Allison put her hand over Joe's and squeezed gently. It felt warm and dry. "We'll work that out," she said. "It'll be fine, Joe. I'll take care of it."

"Okay," he said. "Just want to make sure she looks, you know . . ."

"Yes. She will."

Zoë made a cooing noise and slapped her small hand against the table. Allison toyed with the headband, twirling it in her free hand. A lock of hair had worked free of her loose ponytail and fell across her face, but she didn't look messy. Nor did the hooded shirt and workout pants she was wearing or the lack of makeup on her face give her the neglected look she'd had all summer. Instead, she looked younger than she was, Joe thought, and somehow more vital. There was something else in it too, and as she reached over to wipe cereal off Zoë's face, her hand caressing the chubby little cheek and her mouth turning up into a small smile, Joe realized what it was. She looked like a mother.

All of a sudden he felt the full weight of his past selfishness pressing against his chest. Had he ever been fair to Allison? He'd never really given her a chance back then, so many years ago now, to make up her own mind. That night of the neighborhood meeting when they'd finally had it out about everything, he'd been sincere in his apology. But he hadn't put himself inside her heart. Joe hadn't thought it was possible to truly feel another person's pain, only to come to some sort of intellectual acknowledgment of it, but now he understood how he'd manipulated her, even if he hadn't meant to. He felt, crushingly now, how much he'd denied her. For the second time that day his eyes stung with tears he couldn't stop. He held his breath, not wanting to cry out loud, not wanting her to hear and feel the need to comfort him. He didn't deserve to be comforted. But she turned anyway, the ghost of a smile still hovering at her mouth, until she saw his wet face. Her eyes grew wide and bright.

"Joe?" She reached over, took his hand in hers. He clung to it like a life raft.

"I . . ." His voice was thick and broken with emotion. He tried to clear his throat, but a sob escaped instead. He struggled, squeezed her hand. "Allison, I am . . . I can't change anything. I wish I could."

"Joe, it's . . ."

"I just . . . I'm sorry, Allison. I'm so sorry."

Allison pulled her hand free and for a horrible moment Joe thought she was retreating, rejecting him. But she'd moved only so she could have her arms free to wrap around him, encase him in a protective embrace. "It's going to be okay, Joe," she said, her mouth very close to his ear. "We're going to be okay."

"I love you, Allison."

"I know," she whispered. "I know you do."

Joe closed his eyes and bent his head, his lips pressing into the soft skin of her neck. He could hear Zoë calling out behind them, sweet little sounds like the notes of a song.

chapter 22

Sam knocked lightly on Yvonne's bedroom door and called her name.

"You can come in, Sam."

Yvonne was lying on her bed, propped up on pillows, hands folded and resting on her chest as if she'd been praying. It had been a rough morning for her, Sam knew, but her eyes were dry and she didn't seem like she'd been crying. She looked tired but peaceful, and Sam felt bad that she'd disturbed her.

"Sorry, Yvonne, I didn't mean to bother you."

"I'm all right, Sam."

"I wanted to ask you if you want some tea. Dorothy's coming over and I'm wondering if you want to join us."

A look of distaste flitted across Yvonne's face and quickly disappeared. She didn't like Dorothy, Sam knew, but she was always polite to her. For her part, Dorothy had been tireless in her efforts to ingratiate herself to Yvonne. It was almost as if Dorothy took personal responsibility for what had happened to Diana, which was totally irrational, but you couldn't tell someone else how to feel, especially not someone as walled off from her emotions as Dorothy. After that first torrent of information that Dorothy had shared with Sam, she'd tried her best to avoid talking about her past again, even though Sam tried to suggest that she look into therapy or counseling for herself and for Kevin. No, it wasn't necessary, Dorothy said, that was all behind her, although she appreciated Sam listening and, please, you won't say anything, will you?—please tell me you won't. No, Sam assured her, she wouldn't breathe a word and she hadn't—not to anyone.

When the truth came out about Kevin and the Sun kid, Sam could tell that Dorothy was even more afraid that Sam would spill her secret. Sam could only guess at how hellish life was for Dorothy now, but she knew it had to be agonizing. Yvonne might have had more compassion for Dorothy had she known her secrets, but Sam wasn't sure. Yvonne was far less judgmental than Sam would have been if their roles were reversed, but it would take a saint not to blame Dorothy at least a little for what had happened to Diana. Diana had spent so much time at Dorothy's house—so much time with Kevin. How could she have been so clueless about what was going on in the next room? Yvonne never said so, but Sam knew that in some small way, she did hold Dorothy accountable. Nor was Dorothy an easy person to like.

If she were being honest, Sam couldn't say that she *enjoyed* the time she spent with Dorothy, but she never refused her offers of cake, flowers from her garden, or, today, conversation. She'd asked if Sam minded if she came over for a bit—she had something she wanted to tell her and anyway she had some cookies she'd just made. . . . Of course, Sam had said.

"Dorothy . . ." Yvonne sighed.

"I know it's probably something you don't want to do," Sam said, "but I thought I'd check with you anyway."

"It's okay, I'll join you," Yvonne said, sitting up and swinging her legs off the bed. "Be down in a minute."

In most ways Yvonne was the opposite of Dorothy, Sam thought as she went back downstairs, but in their minimalist conversational styles they were very much alike. Yvonne was slow to speak and careful with her words. It took time to earn her trust. She opened up slowly, deliberately, and without filling the time in between with small talk. Dorothy's talk, such as it was, was entirely small and punctuated with silences. With both women,

Sam found herself prompting and chattering to fill the conversational pauses. But with Yvonne her patience paid off. The more Yvonne revealed of herself the more Sam liked her and the deeper and more genuine their friendship became.

Sam filled the kettle with water and put it on the stove to boil. She hadn't yet gotten around to replacing her treasured electric kettle, which was actually Gloria's electric kettle and had departed with her when she'd moved out. Gloria had taken other things with her too, although not many and nothing that Sam cared much about. But the business with the electric kettle hurt her more than anything that had happened between the two of them—more than the arguing, the cruel words, even the betrayal of Gloria going back to Frank. It was a disproportionate reaction, Sam knew, but also symbolic of their entire relationship. Sam was the tea drinker and connoisseur. Gloria loved her coffee and had only started drinking tea regularly after they moved in together. Now that they were no longer together, she'd probably give it up entirely in favor of her mochas and lattes. So it was a pointed move on Gloria's part to insist on taking the electric kettle. It was designed to sting and it did. Sam hadn't wanted it to end that way—hadn't wanted it to *end,* period—but after Gloria told her that she was moving back in with her ex-husband there wasn't really any other option.

She hadn't spoken to Gloria—hadn't had any communication with her at all—in weeks. Four weeks to be exact, and Sam dearly hoped that she'd soon be able to stop counting them. The last time, a terse phone conversation, had involved whether or not Gloria had paid her share of their last gas bill.

"I'll get you the money," Gloria had snapped. "Whatever it is."

Sure, Sam thought, she had plenty of access to money now that she'd moved back in with Frank. It seemed impossible—worse than whorish—and she'd told Gloria that before they'd finally called it quits. It was a conversation Sam wished had never happened, but one that had an air of inevitability about it. It was as if their entire relationship had been leading toward that day in December. It was right before Christmas and Sam was hand-stringing beads to decorate the tree they hadn't yet bought for their boys who might not even get a chance to see it. Gloria was sitting on the couch, a mug of something steaming between her hands.

"I can't do this anymore, Sam," she said.

"What can't you do?" Sam answered, even though she knew. She'd known all along.

"I thought it would be okay," Gloria said. "I really thought we could make it work. But I can't live without my boy anymore. It's killing me." Sam waited, her breath held, waiting for the rest of it. It didn't take long. "I'm not going to be *with* him, Sam. I want you to know that. We're not going to be together as a couple. I told him."

"Right," Sam said, unable to hold back any longer. "You told him. Big talker you are, Gloria. But when it comes to doing . . ."

"I know you're hurt, but we don't . . . we don't have to break up. We can still see each other, Sam. We just won't be living together."

"Now you're just insulting me," Sam said. "But you know what I really don't understand, Gloria—how can you live with *yourself* if you go back to Frank? Did our whole relationship mean so little to you that you can pretend it never happened? Or are you just planning to be someone other than who you are for the sake of being comfortable?"

"That's not fair, Sam. It's not about being comfortable; it's about being with Justin."

"But it isn't and you know it."

"You can't say that, Sam, you just can't."

"What kind of example do you think you're going to set for your son by selling yourself out to his father? Huh, Gloria? If it were really about Justin, you'd never even think of doing this."

It was the last sentence that made Gloria cry and Sam knew she had wounded her deeply. But not, Sam thought, nearly as deeply as Gloria had wounded her.

The one bright if ironic silver lining in all of this was that since her breakup with Gloria, Noah had magically become a rational human being again and they were beginning the legal process to share custody of Connor. Although she resented what he'd put her through, Sam wouldn't get drawn into an argument about it all over again. And she refused to discuss Gloria with Noah at all. She didn't want to know anything about Frank or how the two of them were working out their "arrangement." It made Sam almost physically ill to think about what kind of manipulations Gloria was subjecting herself to at Frank's hand. But then, Gloria wasn't her responsibility anymore. Caring about Gloria, advising her, supporting her, *loving* her had brought nothing but misery to both of them. Sam knew what drove Gloria and could even understand why she'd done some of the things she had. But she was a long way from forgiveness.

Sam folded her arms, leaned back against her countertop, and watched the kettle, daring it to boil. They'd both lied to her, she thought—Gloria *and* Diana—and Sam had been taken in by them all the way. But then, Sam corrected herself, maybe the deception wasn't all theirs. Sam had imposed on both of them her notions of who she thought they were. This was especially true in Diana's case. It had never even occurred to Sam that Diana hadn't told the truth about herself, her mother, or her pregnancy. Sam could still feel the cold waves of shock that had crashed through her as Diana sat right there at her table drinking lemonade and telling her that her unborn baby was the result of a date rape.

Yvonne would have none of that.

"Nobody ever took advantage of Diana," she said. "She was a strong, strong girl. She was going through a phase. They do that, they all do. She made that baby on purpose."

It was one of Yvonne's more hopeful moments, before they'd found Diana, when there still existed the possibility that she had disappeared on purpose too. Bits and pieces about Diana fell from Yvonne like a broken jigsaw puzzle. There were physical artifacts: photos of her as a chubby toddler eating ice cream naked in the tub, the art projects she'd done for school complete with scattered glitter and rainbows, composition books, stories she'd written, childish poems, a sixth-grade essay on equality that had won her a hundred-dollar prize. Then, later, there were Yvonne's quiet and ashamed recollections of their last three years, which Yvonne told in short, impressionistic bursts. "Fourteen was the year," Yvonne said. "I couldn't do anything right after that. I was the wicked witch on my wicked broom."

Sam would open a bottle of red wine and they'd sit on the small back patio together in the dark, each of them having one cigarette and one glass, and Yvonne would remember. "Maybe she blamed me for her lack of a father," Yvonne said. "For a while she was even angry at me because Joe was white. It didn't matter, though. She needed me to be the villain."

"I never believed you were as bad as all that," Sam said, although she had been as guilty as anyone of prejudging Yvonne based on Diana's descriptions of her.

"I wasn't bad in the way she thought I was," Yvonne said. Sam saw the pain on her face, working its way into every pore of her being and taking up permanent residence in her eyes. "But I failed her," Yvonne said. "I did what I thought was right, but that is not enough. Mothers don't get a free pass for not knowing."

Sam started to make a soothing noise, trying to offer a word of comfort. She knew about being a mother, knew the standard you were held to and knew how impossible it was to attain. But Yvonne didn't even let Sam open her mouth. "There is no absolution," she said. "And I won't ask for any."

The day Allison came over, she'd been sitting with Yvonne, keeping her company while she prepared a packet of reference letters and résumés so she could get on with her new life in California. They had been waiting for news, anything, any sign at all, every day. But within those days there were always moments, five minutes, a half hour, when waiting was temporarily suspended and everyday activities took over. Sam and Yvonne had been in the middle of one of those moments when Allison rang the doorbell.

Allison was holding Zoë on her hip and when Sam saw her face she knew exactly why she'd come.

"Allison?"

"Is she here, Sam?"

Sam wanted to tell her to stop, that this wasn't the way, that they should get together and figure out a way to do it, but she just nodded and held the door open. Allison walked straight over to Yvonne and didn't even say hello. She just put the baby in Yvonne's lap. *No, not like that,* Sam thought, but by then it wasn't Allison or Yvonne she was thinking about but Diana. Yvonne knew it too. She lifted Zoë, so quiet, not a murmur from her, and started stroking her head. She didn't cry, not then. The baby, so much like her mother in miniature, was all that kept Yvonne from breaking apart. Sam would never have imagined Allison capable of knowing that, would never have given her credit for possessing the insight or sensitivity.

Sometimes it was still possible to be surprised by the goodness in people. Sometimes there were still moments of grace.

The kettle was whistling, blurry steam filling the air. Sam wiped her eyes and turned off the heat. Zoë, at least, was going to have something that Diana didn't—a community. There was hardly a person left on the street who wasn't invested somehow in that baby's well-being. Even the Mitchells, whose boys and whose toys Connor had taken to immediately, felt connected and a part of Zoë's life. If only that could make up for what had happened to Diana.

Sam got as far as preparing the teapot with several spoonfuls of Assam when the doorbell rang and there was Dorothy holding a plate of perfectly round oatmeal-raisin cookies, a sheaf of papers, and a box of store-brand English Breakfast teabags.

"You said something about tea," Dorothy said, "but I didn't know what kind you wanted so I just brought these. I hope that's okay."

"I have plenty of tea, Dorothy, not to worry. The cookies look great, though."

"I'll just leave these here, then," Dorothy went on. "I don't really drink much tea. I mean, today of course, I'd love some tea, but usually, you know . . ."

Sam let her carry on, familiar by now with Dorothy's need for patter. She even managed to hold up her end of the conversation while not really listening to it, laying out cups and saucers, putting sugar cubes on a plate. It was starting to look like a tea party, she thought, the kind that little girls had with their dolls. The baby was fine, yes, getting so big. Sam took the cups to the table. Kevin was doing much better, thank you. He really seemed to be getting himself together and had even started talking about college, although his grades were a problem at this point. It wasn't easy. Not that he had anything coming to him. He knew that. They all knew that. They all felt so bad about what happened. Sam poured hot water into the teapot, let it steep. Yvonne was doing okay. It was difficult, of course. She'd be down to join them in a moment.

"Oh?" Dorothy looked alarmed.

"Something wrong?" Sam asked, snapped into full attention.

"No," Dorothy said too quickly. "No, of course not."

They sat down at the table and Dorothy carefully placed her folder of papers off to the side where it wouldn't be spilled on.

"What's that?" Sam asked, pointing to it.

"Oh, I—"

Yvonne came down the stairs and Dorothy cut herself off. The two women exchanged greetings and Yvonne sat down at the table. Sam noticed again that she looked tired. But then so did she and Dorothy.

As soon as Yvonne sat down, Dorothy's chatter petered out. She sipped her tea and smiled at them both, but Sam could see her fingers trembling and feel her anxiety increasing. Whatever it was that she needed to say was trying to get out, but Dorothy didn't know how to let it.

"I wanted to ask you," Dorothy said finally, fixing Sam with an unusually intense look, "if you would . . . I mean, I thought you would be the right person . . ." Sam waited, perplexed. "I don't know what's the matter with me, sorry," Dorothy said. "All I wanted to know, Sam, is if you would take over the Neighborhood Watch list. Keeping up with it, I mean, and getting all the information from everyone. Making sure everyone's on board."

"But—"

"These are the street charts and the contact lists and everything." Dorothy handed Sam the papers as if she were handing over something precious and rare. "I haven't updated them since . . . Not since last year, so a lot of it isn't that current and it really should be."

"But, Dorothy—"

"You know, the Mitchells have moved in and Jessalyn has moved out and of course there's you, Yvonne. You're here."

"But why, Dorothy?" Sam managed to ask when Dorothy finally took a breath. "You've always been, I mean, you've always done a great job with this."

Dorothy lowered her gaze all the way into her teacup and stared at it as if she were trying to divine her fortune from the leaves. Her shoulders slumped and the air seemed to leave her body. When she looked up again there was a fierce battle of emotions in her face—fear, sadness, but also something that looked like relief.

"I'm going to be . . . I'm going away for a while," she said. "There are some things I have to take care of and I've been putting it off too long."

"By yourself?" Sam asked. Thoughts raced through her head. Dorothy was staring at her like she should know. Was it rehab? Sam was sure Dorothy said that her problem was long behind her. Had she relapsed? All the stress with Kevin. Her horrible husband. And Diana . . . But no, maybe she was planning, at last, to reconnect with the family she'd left behind so long ago?

"By myself, yes," Dorothy said. "I hate to leave Kevin, but . . ." She looked at Yvonne, who drew back ever so slightly. "I think in the long run it's better for him that I do this now."

"Dorothy, where are you going?"

"I'm not . . ." She ran her hand through her hair and sighed. "I can't really say yet. I'll tell you. Soon. But Sam, I'm really hoping you'll do this. Will you? I'd ask Dick, but . . ." In her eyes, a brief flash. Sam couldn't tell if it was anger or fear. "He wouldn't be good for it. You know. He'll have a lot . . . He'll have enough to do with the house and Kevin and everything. You know how men are, right?" Dorothy looked at Sam and bit her lip. "I mean, you'd be the best, Sam." She flushed deeply, all the way to the roots of her hair.

"Okay," Sam said. "I can do it while you're gone. Sure."

"That's great. I knew I could count on you." The color slowly drained from Dorothy's face as she poured herself a half cup of tea and drank it down with one swallow. "I'm so appreciative, Sam. Thank you."

"So when are you leaving?" Yvonne asked.

Dorothy grew flustered. "Oh, I'm not really sure. I have a few things to take care of. But soon. Quite soon." She stood up, weaving a little as if drunk, and had to steady herself against the table. "Thanks, Sam, thank you so much. I have to get back now. But if you need anything . . ." She waved at Yvonne. "I'll let myself out. Thanks, Sam."

So many thanks for such a mundane task. Sam waited until she heard the front door close and then she turned to Yvonne.

"What was all that about?"

"Gloria used to call her Dotty Dot," Sam said, and almost smiled before the inevitable creep of regret set in.

"That was weird," Yvonne said. "Even for her."

"I don't know," Sam said. "She's . . . I think she's changed since—since I moved in here. No, for sure she has because, you know, she wouldn't give me the time of day when we first got here. I wish you could've seen the look on her face when she realized that Gloria and I were a couple. I mean, it would have been hilarious if it wasn't so sad. Now she wants me to take over her famous List." Sam opened the folder and leafed through Dorothy's carefully color-coded charts. "She wants me to take over the neighborhood."

Yvonne traced her finger around the rim of her teacup. Sam could see her eyes filling again. The grief was recurrent, as ceaseless as the tide.

"What do you think about that?" Yvonne asked and Sam knew she could be talking about anything at all.

She touched Yvonne lightly on the shoulder, her version of gravity, a way of letting her friend know where she could turn and what she could count on.

"I think people can change," Sam said.

epilogue

SanDiegoNewsBlog.com

North County Mom Turns Self In

Woman had concealed crime for 30 years
By Maria Luz Martinez

SAN DIEGO NEWS STAFF WRITER

March 3, 2008
NORTH COUNTY—Local police were stunned when Dorothy Werner,
48, a married mother of one living in an affluent community, walked
into their station last week and turned herself in for crimes she committed 30 years ago. A native of Amarillo, Texas, whose real name is
Christine Kelly, the stay-at-home mom who regularly volunteered her
time for local charity drives and organized neighborhood potlucks has
a dark past that involves drugs, fraud, and prostitution. While shocked,
Werner's neighbors on her quiet, tree-lined street are sympathetic and
supportive.

"She was a teenager who fell in with a bad crowd," said Samara
Jacobs, Werner's friend and neighbor. "It could happen to anyone."

Most teenagers, however, do not skip bail after being charged with grand theft, solicitation, and drug possession. These were all charges leveled at the young Christine Kelly, a wild child who stole her elderly neighbor's social security checks and cashed them for drug money and solicited sex to support her heroin addiction.

While freed on bond, Christine Kelly literally disappeared. She changed her name, her appearance, and, by all accounts her personality. Some years later, she emerged as Dorothy Werner, community-minded wife of an insurance executive. The real mystery in Werner's story, however, may not be how she managed to elude arrest and prosecution for three decades, but why she now surrendered herself to police. If her family or neighbors know the answer to that question, they are keeping the information to themselves. Richard Werner has refused to comment on his wife's arrest other than to say, "This is a devastating blow for our family and we request the privacy to which we are entitled." A neighbor who requested not to be identified informed *San Diego News* that Werner's husband and son had no knowledge of her criminal past. Werner is being held at Las Colinas Detention Facility pending extradition to Texas.

The revelation of Werner's criminal past is the second shock in as many months for her usually calm neighborhood. In January, the partially decomposed body of Diana Jones, 17, was discovered near the Rancho Bernardo burn area. Jones, who lived a few houses away from the Werners, had been missing since October. A third resident, a juvenile whose name has not been made public by law enforcement, is currently being charged in connection with that case. Police say there is no link between the Jones case and Dorothy Werner.

acknowledgments

My sincere and grateful thanks to Detective Rena Hernandez of the San Diego Police Department, Northwestern Divison, and Lieutenant Joe Young of the Oceanside Police Department for taking the time both in person and on the phone to offer thoughtful and extremely helpful answers to my many questions.

Many thanks as well, to Kate Kennedy, Linda Loewenthal, Shaye Areheart, Wade Lucas, the wonderful Sarah Breivogel, the booksellers who continue to support me, especially the intrepid, eclectic, and altogether wonderful group in Southern California, my parents, my sisters, my brother, my son, my dedicated Facebook friends, and Gabe.

And for throwing me that line and pulling me out before I drowned in a river of doubt—thank you, Mom. So much.

Reader's Guide

1. *The Neighbors Are Watching* is told from the multiple points of view of several neighbors who all have very different perspectives on the same series of events. Is there one neighbor who seems to have a more objective view than the rest? Why or why not?

2. Pregnant teenager Diana shows up on the doorstep of a father who has never met her and settles into a neighborhood that is not quite accepting of her. Who bears the most responsibility for what happens to her? Is it Joe? Allison? The entire neighborhood? Or perhaps just Diana herself?

3. Everybody on Fuller Court has a secret or something he or she is hiding. Whose secret is ultimately the most corrosive or does the most damage? Why?

4. Did Yvonne do the right thing by letting Diana go live at her father's house? What would you have done in that situation?

5. In their quest to either help or hinder, several of the Fuller Court residents poke their noses into the business of their neighbors. On the other hand, just as many turn a blind eye to behavior or events they'd

rather not think about. Where is the line between meddling and concern when it comes to our neighbors? When would it be necessary to interfere?

6. Who is the best mother in the novel? Who is the worst? Why?

7. Compare Joe and Dick as fathers. Which one is a better dad? Which one is a better husband?

8. Which character is the most honest with his or her neighbors? Which one is the most honest with him- or herself?

9. Throughout the novel, Diana is seen and judged through many different pairs of eyes. Likewise, the stories she tells about herself are interpreted differently depending on who is listening. Who is the real Diana? Which of her stories are true?

10. For most of the novel, Joe's main complaint—and justification for never acknowledging his daughter—is that he did not have a choice in whether or not to have a child, therefore he shouldn't bear the responsibility of raising her. Do you agree with him? Why or why not?

11. Is the Fuller Court of the beginning of the novel a place where you would want to live? How about at the end? Why or why not?

12. Is Fuller Court a place you recognize? Do you know any of these neighbors? Do you know what your neighbors are up to?

about the author

Debra Ginsberg is the author of the memoirs, *Waiting: The True Confessions of a Waitress*; *Raising Blaze*; and *About My Sisters*; and the novels *Blind Submission* and *The Grift*, a *New York Times* Notable Book of 2008. She lives in Southern California. Visit her at www.debraginsberg.com.

Also by Debra Ginsberg

"*The Grift* is a gift with no strings attached . . . a satisfyingly voyeuristic vision of a mysterious stranger's supernaturally charged fortunes."

—*NEW YORK TIMES*

THE GRIFT • A Novel
$14.00 paper (Canada: $17.99)
978-0-307-38273-3

"Wicked fun and suspense from a talented new writer with an original, clever voice."

—LISA SCOTTOLINE

BLIND SUBMISSION • A Novel
$14.00 paper (Canada: $18.00)
978-0-307-34638-4